Dear Reader,

Here's something I've learned over the years as a writer: the good guys and the bad guys come out best when they're written first as *people*. The good guys might rescue kids from a burning building... but also kick puppies. The bad guys might rob banks... but call their grannies every night. The best and most relatable characters are the ones that seem most human, with all the flaws and virtues that involves. That's what makes them come alive in our minds.

When I first read Kylie Schachte's *You're Next,* I found that this intriguing murder mystery was elevated to a remarkable level by her unflinchingly honest protagonist, Flora Calhoun. Flora's past and present are littered with bad decisions, and there are times when you want to scream at her to *not* do what she's about to do. Though you believe deeply in her search for justice, there are enough faults in Flora—her lies, her secrets, her refusal to open up—to make her feel extraordinarily real.

To me, it's this kind of true-to-life writing that makes me a reader. I hope you feel the same.

James Patterson
Founder
JIMMY Patterson Books

JIMMY Patterson Books for Young Adult Readers

JAMES PATTERSON PRESENTS

Stalking Jack the Ripper by Kerri Maniscalco

Hunting Prince Dracula by Kerri Maniscalco

Escaping from Houdini by Kerri Maniscalco

Capturing the Devil by Kerri Maniscalco

Becoming the Dark Prince by Kerri Maniscalco

Gunslinger Girl by Lyndsay Ely

Twelve Steps to Normal by Farrah Penn

Campfire by Shawn Sarles

When We Were Lost by Kevin Wignall

Swipe Right for Murder by Derek Milman

Once & Future by Amy Rose Capetta and Cori McCarthy

Sword in the Stars by Amy Rose Capetta and Cori McCarthy

Girls of Paper and Fire by Natasha Ngan

Girls of Storm and Shadow by Natasha Ngan

THE MAXIMUM RIDE SERIES BY JAMES PATTERSON

The Angel Experiment

School's Out—Forever

Saving the World and Other Extreme Sports

The Final Warning

MAX

FANG

ANGEL

Nevermore

Maximum Ride Forever

For exclusives, trailers, and other information, visit jimmypatterson.org.

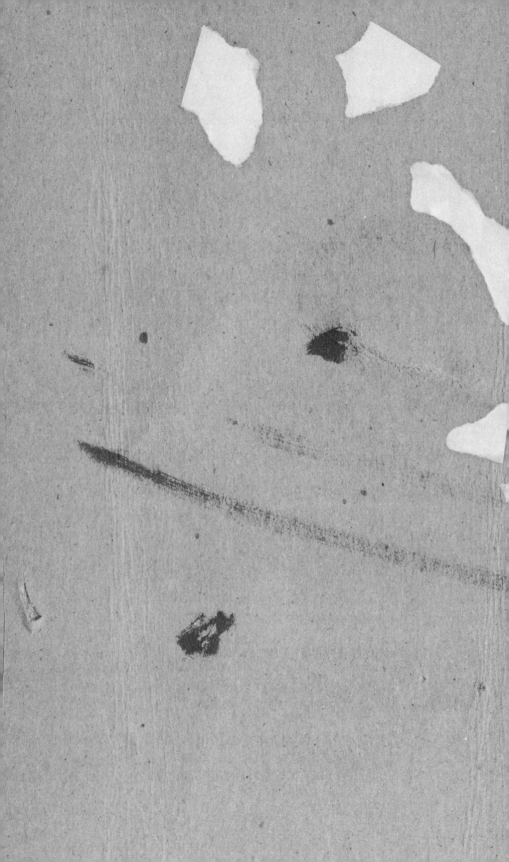

YOU'RE NEXT

Kylie Schachte

Foreword by
James Patterson

JIMMY Patterson Books
Little, Brown and Company
NEW YORK BOSTON LONDON

Copyright © 2020 by Kylie Schachte

Hachette Book Group supports the right to free expression and the value of copyright. The purpose of copyright is to encourage writers and artists to produce the creative works that enrich our culture.

The scanning, uploading, and distribution of this book without permission is a theft of the author's intellectual property. If you would like permission to use material from the book (other than for review purposes), please contact permissions@hbgusa.com. Thank you for your support of the author's rights.

JIMMY Patterson Books / Little, Brown and Company
Hachette Book Group
1290 Avenue of the Americas, New York, NY 10104
JimmyPatterson.org
First Edition: July 2020

JIMMY Patterson Books is an imprint of Little, Brown and Company, a division of Hachette Book Group, Inc. The Little, Brown name and logo are trademarks of Hachette Book Group, Inc. The JIMMY Patterson Books® name and logo are trademarks of JBP Business, LLC.

The publisher is not responsible for websites (or their content) that are not owned by the publisher.

The Hachette Speakers Bureau provides a wide range of authors for speaking events. To find out more, go to hachettespeakersbureau.com or call (866) 376-6591.

ISBN 9780316493772

Library of Congress Cataloging-in-Publication Data

Names: Schachte, Kylie, author.
Title: You're next / Kylie Schachte.
Other titles: You are next
Description: First edition. | New York : JIMMY Patterson Books /Little, Brown, 2020. | Audience: Ages 14-18. | Audience: Grades 10-12. | Summary: Flora Calhoun, haunted by a history of finding dead bodies and the murder of her ex, Ava McQueen, uncovers a conspiracy, putting herself and all her loved ones in peril.
Identifiers: LCCN 2020004787 | ISBN 9780316493772 (hardcover) | ISBN 9780316493765 (ebook)
Subjects: CYAC: Murder–Fiction. | Conspiracies—Fiction. | Grandfathers–Fiction. | Mystery and detective stories.
Classification: LCC PZ7.1.S3352 You 2020 | DDC [Fic]—dc23
LC record available at https://lccn.loc.gov/2020004787

10 9 8 7 6 5 4 3 2

LSC-C

Printed in the United States of America

For Grace, Izzy, Kashish, Devon, and all the badass students who have inspired me. Flora would not exist without you.

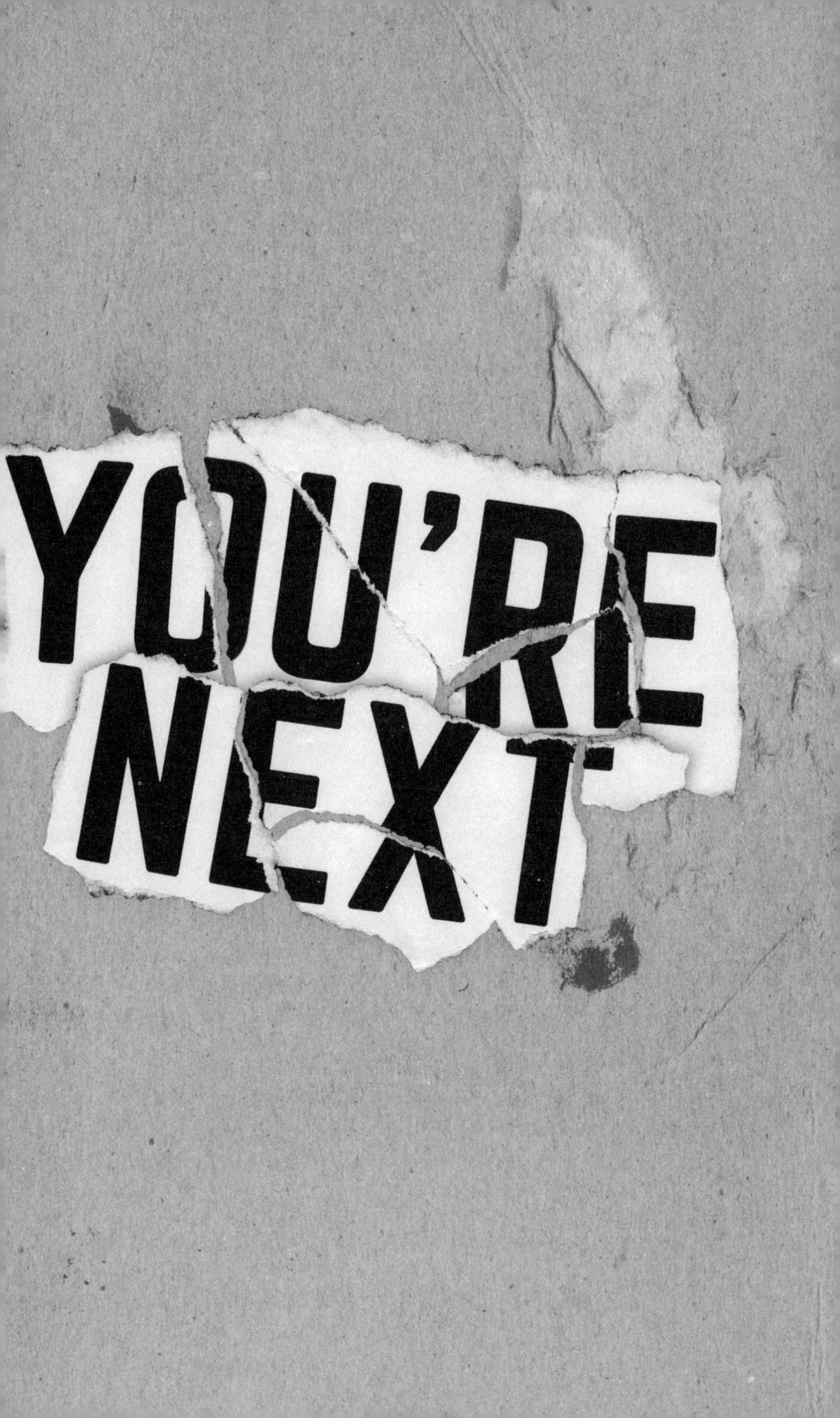
YOU'RE
NEXT

CHAPTER 1

Greg Garcy leers at me from his mug shot: bastard doesn't know I've nailed him yet. I clutch his Wanted flyer in my hand and race down the hall, but I can't look away from his crushed, sneering nose and bleary eyes.

You can't run from me.

The bell rings. Damn. I'm *so* going to be late for chem.

I spent my free period in the parking lot listening to the police scanner on my phone and lost track of time. It was worth it. Garcy is wanted for a string of serial rapes upstate. He's attacked dozens of women, and he was allowed to get away with it for years. Until now. The hot pulse of adrenaline zips through me as I dash through the halls. I got him. I really got him. I need to run a plate, but—

I slam into someone. The Garcy flyer, my bag, pens, and various notebooks scatter across the hallway. There's a brief tangle of sharp elbows, and I yelp when the corner of my chem textbook lands on my toe. Of course this is the day I *didn't* wear my steel-toed boots.

"Balls! Fuck! Ow! Shit!" I yell.

"Flora Calhoun, you kiss your mother with that mouth?"

I squint through the red haze of stubbed-toe agony.

Ava McQueen gathers up my papers, pens, and the lone tampon I dropped. One corner of her plum-painted mouth tugs up in a troublemaker's smile, and a fizzy feeling climbs the back of my neck. It's been seven months and four days since the last time I kissed her, but I still remember exactly how her lips felt against mine.

"H-hey, Ava." I drop down to help her.

"How you been? Haven't seen you around much."

Yeah. We haven't talked a whole lot since *you started avoiding me.* "Um, good. You know, same old bullshit."

She picks Garcy's WANTED flyer up off the ground and stands. "Clearly."

I blush, which is basically the most annoying thing in the world when you're a redhead. Ava always makes me feel like I've just missed the last step in the staircase.

Ava is a year older than me, but we took the same elective on the history of political activism during my freshman year. One day, she *shut down* this Young Conservatives idiot who called the Black Panthers a terrorist organization. Everyone

2

clapped, Mr. Young Con crapped his khakis, and I fell in love. Of course, it doesn't hurt that she plays bass guitar, or that she's bananas hot. I mean, with her curls done up in adorable space buns, and the lipstick, and that funny little smile she's still giving me?

Which is super confusing, since she hasn't smiled at me like that in a long time.

Seven months and four days.

Can't be thinking about that. I focus on shoving my stuff back into my bag. "Oh, uh. You know me. Can't keep myself out of trouble."

She *does* know. I've always suspected that's why she stopped talking to me—stopped kissing me—in the first place.

Ava stares at the flyer in her hand. When she glances up at me, the teasing smile has vanished, and something dark flickers in her expression. She looks down again, trying to hide it.

If there's one thing I know, it's what fear looks like.

I take a half step forward, any weirdness between us forgotten. "Ava? Are you okay?"

She fingers the edge of the paper. "You ever do something stupid? I mean, like, really, really stupid? Can't-take-it-back stupid?"

"Almost every day." My face heats again. Why did I say that?

"You know"—Ava's eyes flick from Garcy's face to mine—"I believe that."

That stings, but I ignore it. "Ava, if you're in trouble, I can help you."

She opens her mouth, but her eyes catch on something over my shoulder. She stills.

I glance behind me. Nothing but the usual throng of people trying to get to their lockers. No one looks this way.

Ava folds the Garcy flyer in half, then quarters. "No worries. I have it under control."

I take another step toward her. "Seriously, I do this kind of stuff all the time. I know we haven't, um, talked much lately, but I can—"

Ava's smile is cold, nothing like before. Shit. I shouldn't have brought up the her-and-me stuff.

"I got it. Just being dumb, right? Nothing I can't handle. You take care of yourself, Flora." She tucks the flyer back into my bag. For a second, she's close enough that I smell her warm, woodsy perfume, but she walks away before I can get another word out.

I'm being dumb, right? She just remembered that she doesn't want to talk to me, that's all.

So why is my chest suddenly tight with dread?

I shake off my confusion and chase after her, but by the time I round the corner, she's already gone.

I tap my pen on the worksheet in front of me.

Balance the equation: $C_5H_8O_2$ + NaH + HCl → $C_5H_{12}O_2$ + $NaCl$

I usually like the tidiness of balancing equations, but today I can't focus.

Was Ava worried, or am I manufacturing an excuse to talk to her? Or maybe she *was* scared, but she didn't want to talk to me about it?

"Dude, please. You have to listen." Two tables away, Damian Rivera scribbles on a slip of paper and slides it across the desk to his best friend, Penn Williams. My pen pauses halfway through rewriting the equation.

Penn knocks the note to the floor without looking up. The space beneath his desk is littered with scraps of paper. I lean forward in my seat. Is that a bruise on his cheek? It's a faint yellowy-purple, like he tried to cover it with makeup.

That's not sketchy at all.

"Please," Damian hisses. "Let me explain."

Penn's chair scrapes against the linoleum as he stands. He grabs the bathroom pass off its hook and stalks out of the room. Is it me, or is he limping a little?

Mrs. Varner calls out, "Ten more minutes, people, then we'll discuss."

I'm only on question two. Between Garcy and Ava, I have

enough intrigue in my life for one day. I drag my attention back to the double displacement reaction on my paper.

Balance the equation...

Penn never returns to class.

When the bell finally rings, Damian races out the door. Rushing to hunt down his friend, maybe?

Those abandoned scraps of paper are still on the floor.

I shouldn't. The last thing I need is to get sucked into the breakup of Penn and Damian's bromance.

I bend down and scoop the notes up. The first one says: *I'm sorry, I had to do it. Please talk to me.* The second: *You have to understand.* And the third: *You don't know what she'll do to me.*

Huh. I pocket the scraps of paper and leave the classroom.

"I have so much to tell you." Cassidy Yang, my best and only friend, waits for me in the hall. She's kind of impossible to miss in her oversize safety-orange sweater. Straw-like blond hair peeks out from under her gray beanie. She bleached her hair months ago, and now the black is making a comeback. When I try stuff like that, I look like an idiot. When Cass does, she looks like she's in some magazine spread on street style.

"What's up?" I ask, my mind still half stuck on Ava's terrified face.

Cass and I make our way down the hall. She's practically

vibrating with enthusiasm. One kid winces as he passes, like he's blinded by her sweater.

"They did it!" she says. "They finally approved the funds for rock ensemble."

"Seriously? That's awesome." For the first time this afternoon, my anxiety about Ava fades a little.

"I know!" Cass does a gleeful little shimmy. "There are only seven spots in the class, though, so I have to do some intense practice this weekend. Auditions are Monday."

"You should bring some of your original songs."

Cass stops dancing. "Maybe."

I roll my eyes. I was a little surprised a year ago when Cass bought a guitar and started teaching herself to play from YouTube videos. She'd never expressed any kind of interest in it before, but she's already really good. She still gets shy about her own songwriting, though.

I don't push it. "Hey, you're in history with Penn Williams, right? Have you noticed anything weird lately?"

Cass considers it. "Not really, but that's normal. Penn's so quiet."

I tell her what I saw in chem class.

"You think he's in trouble?" she asks.

"Maybe. Or maybe I'm sticking my nose in where it doesn't belong."

"Well, you wouldn't be you if you didn't," she says dryly. "Should we try some good old-fashioned internet stalking? If Penn's got issues, bet you it's all over Instagram."

We spend the rest of the walk to her car discussing post frequency, content, and filter choices as possible clues of distress. A few times, I almost tell Cass about the strange, tense conversation I had with Ava, but then I don't. Maybe I was imagining it. Maybe it was just the same old awkwardness between Ava and me, left over from last summer. If I bring her up now, Cass will want to *talk* about it. It might have been seven months and four days, but I'd still rather launch myself into the blazing sun than deal with all those feelings.

Cass drops me off, and I promise to call later to help her prep for the audition.

"I'm home!" I call out, dumping my stuff in the doorway.

"Yes, I was able to deduce that from the sound of the door opening at precisely the same time you come home every day." My grandfather appears in the doorway. I'm about 99 percent certain he's ex-CIA from the golden years when they had free rein to deal with those pesky Russians. William Calhoun has been retired for years, but he still wears a custom-tailored suit every day.

"You know, most parental guardians open with a 'Hello, honey, how was your day?' when their progeny return from the battlefield of high school education."

"How quaint." He retrieves my bag from the floor and throws me a pointed look as he hangs it neatly on its hook.

The scents of butter and cinnamon draw me into the kitchen. "Did you make cookies?"

"Yes, I thought you might appreciate a post-battle snicker-doodle."

"Forget those other loser grandfathers, you're the best," I call back. I've always wondered if he learned to bake when he was undercover. He's a little *too* good at it.

Gramps hums to himself as he dons oven mitts and pulls out a fresh batch of cookies. He's downright cheerful today.

I guess it's as good a time as any to ask. "So, I need a favor."

He ignores me and grabs a spatula. Maybe some buttering up is in order.

"I have a new theory about you," I tell him. "You were attempting to unveil a Soviet spy stationed within the French government. You went undercover as a baker's apprentice at the patisserie where the pinko went every morning for his *petit déjeuner,* and that's where you learned this delicious sorcery." I brandish my cookie in the air for emphasis.

"Inventive." He scrapes dried batter off the tray.

"So, this favor..."

No one sighs like William Calhoun. So soft, and yet weighted with such vexation.

He begins transferring cookies from the baking sheet to

the cooling rack. "In case I have not mentioned it yet today, I must tell you that your tenacity is a rather ugly character flaw. What can I do for you this time? Plant listening devices in the home of a Venezuelan dignitary? Order the assassination of your physical education teacher?"

"Nah, I'm saving that one for a graduation present. I was hoping one of your old buddies could run a plate for me?"

"I thought we had finally realized that potential love interests seldom appreciate stalking as a precursor to courtship."

"Yeah, well, if I never have a serious relationship, we'll know who's to blame. No crush. It's Greg Garcy." I pull the WANTED flyer from my bag. "The case has been cold for months, but I heard on the tip line he's been spotted a few times in the area. I've got a lead on the car."

"Flora, we've discussed this." He scoops fresh cookie dough onto the baking sheet. "I do not mind you illegally tapping into the police phone system; I simply don't wish to hear about it."

"Yeah, yeah, I get it. You'll call some of your friends in Virginia?"

He blinks. "I have no idea what you mean. I was nothing but a humble midlevel diplomat."

"Is that why there's a framed photo of you and William J. Donovan, founder of the CIA, on your desk?" I ask through a mouthful of cookie.

"Has anyone mentioned how off-putting it is for young ladies to be so observant?"

"Yes. You. Frequently."

"Well, all right, then. I will call up some of the old boys for you."

"I love you, and not because you're my affable and genteel grandfather, but because of the goods and services I can extort from you."

"I would expect no less."

Olive walks into the kitchen. She's dressed for ballet class, every strand of her hair pulled up tight in a perfect bun. I finger the ends of my own sloppy braid. Olive is only thirteen, but she has her shit way more together than me.

"Mom called." She grabs a banana from the fruit bowl to put in her bag. "You just missed her."

Yeah, I bet.

My mother has lived in Germany for the last two and a half years. She's a painter at this artist-in-residence thing in Berlin. She was only supposed to be gone for six months, but here we are.

She knows my school schedule, and yet somehow she always calls about fifteen minutes before I get home. It's a convenient way for her to pretend to be my mother without having to, you know, mother me.

"Hmm," is all I can think to say. Gramps watches me, but I avoid his eyes.

"She's good, if you were wondering. Her gallery show is next weekend." Olive's spine has gone very straight. She does that when she's annoyed—practices her dance posture.

"That's great." I try to sound sincere, but it mostly comes out exhausted. I don't even know how I'm supposed to feel about my mom anymore. Olive rolls her eyes. My attempts to appease her only piss her off.

Olive and I get along about as well as any sisters would, for the most part, but it's no secret she blames me for Mom leaving.

She's not wrong.

Olive turns to my grandfather. "Can we go?"

"Of course." He wipes the flour from his hands with a dish towel. As they're about to leave, he turns to me with pretend sternness. "Allow those cookies to cool before gorging, please."

I give him a salute. "Yes, sir."

"I'll get that license plate for you this evening." The look in his eyes is gentle, and a little sad. He doesn't really know how to feel about the Mom stuff, either.

"Thanks."

Later, after my grandfather has plied me with more tacos

than I should reasonably be able to fit inside me, I call in the Garcy tip. The cops aren't particularly thrilled to hear from me—we don't have the best working relationship—but Gramps cashed in a favor with the Department of Transportation and got me the tollbooth photos of Garcy entering the area, his face and license plate number clear as day. Hard for the police to ignore me when I hand them a perp on that kind of silver platter.

In the state of New York, you must be at least twenty-five years of age and have a minimum of three years' relevant experience to apply for a private investigator's license. Needless to say, I fall short on both of the requirements.

The cops pretend that I'm some dumb kid who barely stays out of their way. I play along because it protects their delicate egos and keeps them occupied while I do my job.

Because it is a job. Garcy was a special case—I found him in an article about how the NYPD finally tested thousands of rape kits they'd held in storage for years—but most of the time I work for hire, and I get paid. All under the table, of course, and if the IRS ever calls, Cass and I are simply running a very lucrative babysitting business.

I pull up all of Penn's and Damian's social media accounts and start combing through them. The two of them are part of that crowd that hangs out in the art studio during their free periods, so most of their pictures are of their work. Half of Damian's feed is taken up by progress shots of a giant white snake sculpture. There are no obvious signs of distress, but one thing sticks out to me right away: up until about three weeks ago, both Penn and Damian commented on every single one of each other's posts. And then nothing.

I hesitate, then pull up Ava's profile. I haven't let myself look at this in a long time, but I can't shake the feeling that something is wrong and Ava was too afraid to talk.

Not much has changed on her feed. Lots of pictures of her and her friends, laughing and goofing off. A screenshot of a bell hooks quote. A dark, grainy video of her playing her bass in her bedroom.

I scroll down farther. I shouldn't, but I can't help myself.

There: last July. One picture, the only proof that the two of us were ever anything. A selfie she insisted we take. We're lying on our backs, our cheeks pressed together. I'm flushed with giddy embarrassment. Ava's smile is as dopey and glittering as mine. No hint that a month later she would refuse to speak to me, let alone be in the same room. If you look closely, you can see the floral print of my pillowcase under her head.

My phone vibrates. Ava McQueen's name lights up my screen.

There's a flutter of fear and pleasure in the no-man's-land

below my belly button. Does she know I was looking at her, somehow? Does she want to talk to me?

But she had that look on her face earlier. That dark look.

"Hello?"

"Flora?" Ava whispers. "I need your help."

CHAPTER 2

I haul myself off the bed. "What's wrong?"

There's a hitch in Ava's breathing, like she's running. I close my eyes and press the phone against my ear. I can't make out any background noise. Rustling. Maybe the wind?

"Ava, are you there?" My voice comes out too loud.

"Come. Okay? I'll text you the address." Her voice is ragged with terror.

"Okay. I'll come. I promise. But—"

The call disconnects.

Each of my heartbeats comes faster than the last. My room is too warm, too small. I push my hair behind my ears and count to five. I need control.

I grab my coat and backpack off the hook on my door. Should I call Cass? Her parents probably won't notice or care if she takes her car out in the middle of the night. Plus, Ava and I haven't really been alone together, not since...Well, the coward part of me wouldn't mind a buffer.

The phone vibrates again in my hand. A text from Ava:

Intersection of Fourth and Mason in Whitley. Come fast.

I can't be thinking about my failed love life when Ava obviously needs help. I have to face this one on my own.

I open my window and pop off the screen. March air rushes in, cold on my clammy cheeks. I climb out the window and into the night.

I ride my bike to meet Ava. I can drive, and Gramps is cool about letting me take the car as long as I explain where I'm going, but I don't have time for that right now.

There's a nasty crunch in my stomach, like my gut is eating itself with nerves.

Maybe it's fine. Maybe it's nothing.

I pedal harder. It's like those dreams where you move your legs faster and faster, but they're just rubbery noodles that get you nowhere.

The night is too cold for clouds. The wind claws my face, and my fingers are numb on the handlebars, but sweat trickles down my back from all the pedaling.

It's about a thirty-minute bike ride from my house in Hartsdale—one of those cookie-cutter suburbs where everyone knows each other's secrets—to Whitley, the city next door. This late at night, the streets are mostly deserted. I ride by warehouses

17

and run-down storefronts. Past cars that have been parked in the same spot for decades, their tires sagged with defeat, no longer waiting for their owners to come back.

I try to concentrate on the movement of my body pushing me forward, but my mind keeps drifting to other stuff. Stuff I shouldn't be thinking about.

Ava and I almost dated. Or maybe we did, but it fell apart so quickly I didn't even have time to realize we *were* dating. I had liked her for ages, since I met her in that class freshman year, and we even kissed once, but all my crap baggage kept us from actually getting together. And then last year, right before school let out for the summer, I helped Ava's friend on a case. Ava and I started talking again, and before I knew it we were making out in the photo lab darkroom.

All through last summer, Ava would come over to my house, and we'd curl up on my bed and kiss and kiss until both of us were about ready to burst into flames. But I didn't know if she was officially my girlfriend, and I was too awkward to know how to ask. Then I went to visit my mom in Germany for three weeks. When I got back, Ava wouldn't answer any of my texts. She's been avoiding me ever since.

Gunshots crack through the night—three of them—and I nearly fall off my bike. I grip the handlebars tighter, but they're slick with sweat.

18

A few blocks away from Ava's intersection, I hop off my bike and prop it against a wall. I don't want to screw around with a bike lock if I need to make a run for it.

I go the rest of the way on foot. Where Hartsdale is all trees and fancy Colonial houses, Whitley is nothing but high-rise apartments, metal, and pavement. The smell of exhaust, trash left out on the street, and old coins. My footsteps are multiplied as they echo off all the concrete. I keep turning around like there's someone behind me, but I'm alone. I'm trying to watch every direction at once. The voice in my head says I'm that girl, the one at the beginning of the horror movie.

That voice can go fuck itself.

One block away. Everything's gone quiet. No gunshots, no footsteps. Nothing but the wind.

I arrive at Fourth and Mason. No Ava. No one at all.

"Ava?" I whisper. No answer.

"Ava?" I try again. I don't want to shout. Icy wind rakes through the damp, sweaty hairs on the back of my neck.

Across the street, there's a rustle of blinds in one window, but when I turn, they go still. The light turns off.

Maybe she was messing with me. She'll leap out—*Boo!*— and laugh while I try to act pissed off. We'll hold hands and get hot chocolate. We'll pick up where we left off last summer, before everything got weird.

Given my track record, this seems unlikely.

I search for signs of life up and down the street. There's not a sound, not a flash of movement anywhere. No cars driving past. No people. My throat closes up with panic.

My eyes snag on a narrow gap between two buildings. An alleyway. As I creep closer, I reach into my backpack and pull out my Taser. The slick plastic is soothing against my sweaty palm. I grip it tighter.

I am *not* the girl in the horror movie. I'm not.

I grab my flashlight, too, but don't turn it on yet.

I'm at the mouth of the alley when I hear the faintest wheeze, like a sigh of relief.

"Ava?" I pop the button on the flashlight and flood the alleyway in harsh white LED light.

Ava McQueen is sprawled on the ground. Blood trickles lazily from three bullet holes in her chest and abdomen.

I drop my flashlight. The night has become a vacuum, sucking all the air from my lungs. I scream and scream, but I can't hear it.

This isn't happening. *Not again.*

The world around me turns to jagged flashes. My vision goes black, then flares bright like a lightning strike. Each time it snags on a new, horrifying image.

Three bullet holes smolder in her shearling coat.

A blackish pool grows wider and wider beneath her.

Her eyes dart left and right.

She's still alive.

My heart slams against the front wall of my rib cage. Everything zooms back into focus all at once, and my mouth fills with warm, syrupy saliva.

I pick up the flashlight and scramble to kneel at Ava's side. The pool of her blood seeps into the knees of my jeans.

"Ava? Ava!" I turn her face toward me. Her eyes are open, but her pupils are deep, dark holes with no bottom. She can't see me. I feel for a pulse. It's there, but there's a long pause after each beat, like the next one might not come.

"W-w-wh," she wheezes. *"Wess."*

I don't know if she's trying to talk, or if this is the sound of life leaving her body. Her lips part again, but nothing comes out this time. My fingers are meaty and useless as I fumble with my phone.

"911. What's your emergency?" The operator's voice is cool and crisp. So alien to me, kneeling on the grimy pavement slick with Ava's blood.

"Hi, yes." My tongue can't get out of its own way. "I'm in the alley on the southeast side of Fourth Street between Mason and Deloit. A girl. A girl has been shot. There's a lot of blood. She still has a pulse, but there's a lot of blood." I gasp for breath, and the smell of it rolls over me in a wave. It's a smell I know. Like iron, and something else. Something rotten.

"Okay." The woman's tone is still calm. "An ambulance is on its way. What's your name?"

"Flora Calhoun." I try to balance the phone on my shoulder while I claw off my coat and sweatshirt. I lift Ava up—her heavy body lolls in my arms—and slide my sweatshirt around her waist, pulling it tight around her middle. Ava lets out a wet gurgle that makes my stomach roll. "I'm trying. I'm trying to stop the blood, but someone has to come." I tie the sweatshirt's sleeves as tight as I can around Ava's chest. It won't be enough.

"An ambulance is on its way, okay, Flora?" the operator reminds me. "Now, I need you to look around and give me some more information. Are you safe where you are?"

"I don't know." I press both hands to the highest bullet hole, the one above Ava's heart, where my sweatshirt tourniquet won't reach. The alley stretches along the backs of the buildings until it reaches Fifth Street on the other side. I see a couple of trash cans, but nothing else.

"I don't see anyone, but I don't know." Ava's blood wells up between my knuckles. I put more pressure on the wound, but the phone slips from my shoulder and clatters to the ground.

I don't pick it up.

"Flora? Flora, are you still with me?" The operator's faint voice calls to me from the phone speaker, but I can't take my hands away from Ava's chest.

Someone is on their way. An ambulance is coming.

My flashlight is still on the ground next to me. Half of Ava's face is cast in light, and the other half in darkness. Her brown skin is gray and ashen.

"Wess," Ava slurs again. "G-grays." Her eyes close. They take several seconds to open again.

"Keep talking." My voice comes out tattered and desperate. "Talk to me, please. Ava. They're coming. They're on their way. Please, keep talking to me."

Her eyes lock on mine. For the first time, she can see me. She knows I'm here.

"Wes Grays." Her voice is stronger now.

"Wes Grays," I repeat back to her, even though I have no idea what that means. "I'm right here."

Ava's eyes stay fixed on mine, like she's using all her energy to tell me how serious this is. Wes Grays. I have no idea who that is. Is it the shooter?

Ava sucks in a rattling, high-pitched breath. Her eyes widen with a look of pure terror, but they've lost their focus. She can't see me anymore.

"I've got you," I choke out. "I'm trying, Ava, but you have to hang on a little longer. They're coming. I promise."

For once, the universe listens to me. An ambulance shrills plaintively in the distance.

"Hear that?" There's something wet on my face. Tears. "They're going to be right here, and you'll be okay. I promise. Stay with me."

Ava doesn't say anything else.

I check her pulse again. I can't find it. My fingers leave bloody smears on her neck.

Blue and red lights create a sickening strobe on the walls of the alleyway.

"Ava, they're here." I paw at her neck for that drumbeat. "They made it. They'll take care of you. Please."

Her lips are parted. She's still wearing the same eggplant lipstick from earlier. It's a little faded and peeling, like lipstick always gets at the end of the day. The sheer humanness of that detail blurs my vision with fresh tears.

Footsteps behind me, but I don't look away from Ava's face. It is so still. Stiller than any living thing should be. The wild terror is gone from her eyes, replaced by a vacant, staring nothingness that is somehow more horrible.

The EMTs shunt me out of the way, and the world is quiet again. I still see, and hear, and feel, but it's all muted as the

EMTs crowd around Ava, as they shout instructions and questions. As they poke and prod at her body, trying to figure out what I already know.

That's all she is now: a body.

One medic asks me a question over her shoulder. I don't understand the words. I blink in response, and she gives up on me.

Another one of the medics grabs me, tries to ask me something. My tongue is too thick and dumb. He shines his flashlight in my eyes, then says something to the others before hustling me away, one arm around my shoulders.

I look back. Ava's face is blocked from my view as the EMTs work, but I can see her foot. Her olive-green pants have ridden up, exposing a sliver of bare ankle above those chunky black boots. The hem of her coat is visible, the shearling lining gone sticky red.

My sweatshirt is still tied around her waist.

Out on the street, the EMT sits me on the curb while he rummages around in the ambulance. He reappears with a package, ripping it open to pull out a shiny space blanket. The strange fabric rustles against itself as he hands it to me. I stare at it. The whole world is like a jigsaw puzzle knocked to the floor. I can't figure out where the pieces are supposed to go.

"You're shivering," he explains, and I realize that I am.

My sweatshirt is still tied around her waist.

I take the blanket and unfold it around my shoulders. My blood-soaked clothes are sticky and cold where they brush against my skin.

"Are you injured?" The EMT crouches down and examines my eyes, my skull, my arms. He pulls my limp body this way and that.

"No." My voice comes out hoarse. "I'm fine. I..." I don't have any more words.

"Do your parents know where you are?" he asks gently.

It's 7 a.m. in Berlin right now. Mom is waking up without a single thought about where I am.

I shake my head.

More wailing sirens. Squealing breaks. Two police cars pull up on the street.

"You hang tight." My EMT stands and jogs over to meet the cops, leaving me alone on the curb.

The other medics come flying out of the alleyway, rolling a stretcher between them. Through the whirl of activity, I catch a glimpse of Ava's face: slack and gray and horrifying all over again. And then she's blocked from my view, and the doors are slamming shut, and the medics are shouting instructions to each other the whole time, urgent and fast like they can still save her, but it's all for nothing.

I already know. They're too late.

CHAPTER 3

I keep leaving my body, then smashing back into it. My mind is blank. Empty. Except for one thing: Ava is dead.

Ava is dead.

Her bloody shearling coat.

Ava is dead.

The look of horror as the last bit of life left her.

Ava is dead.

The smear of blood I left on her neck.

Heels click on the pavement as someone approaches.

"Flora." Detective Jennifer Richmond appears in front of me. I know her. She looks tired, and not surprised to see me.

Richmond takes in my bloody clothes, the tears still streaming down my cheeks, the way my shaking hands clutch the space blanket to my chest.

She sighs. "Are you okay?"

I don't answer, and she nods like she didn't really expect it. I am very obviously not okay.

"Wait here, please. I'll be back in a few minutes to talk to you." Richmond turns and joins the other cops at the mouth of the alleyway. Two patrol officers and Richmond's partner, Detective Roy Clemens. I know him, too. They disappear out of sight, and I'm alone again.

Ava is dead.

My clothes dry stiff and itchy in the freezing air. My space blanket crinkles every time I move. A car alarm goes off a few blocks away. It keeps going and going, ignored, until it gives up out of neglect.

Ava is dead.

The slushy gurgle as she tried to force out her last words. But they were pointless. Meaningless. No final good-byes or messages for her mom.

I tilt my head up to the sky and take a deep breath of icy air. The light pollution in Whitley has turned the sky to a sickly bruise, and the lack of stars makes me claustrophobic.

Ava is dead.

Richmond returns. "Okay, Flora, I'm going to need you to tell me what happened here tonight."

I don't know what to say. Yesterday, Ava was a girl from my school. I passed her in the halls. I thought about kissing her sometimes. A lot. We talked for the first time in ages. Now Ava is dead.

I open my mouth, but still nothing comes out.

Richmond's radio crackles at her hip. "Two-two-one, this is Dispatch."

Richmond speaks into the radio. "Go ahead."

"Two-two-one, be advised victim died."

Ava is dead.

I knew. But now it's real.

I blink once. Twice. I turn and throw up on the pavement, less than two feet from Richmond's shoes.

In the corner of my vision, she shuffles her feet. Embarrassed for me. I keep my eyes trained on the dark orange splatter of my vomit. What did I even eat for dinner tonight? Sweat breaks out all over my body. I'm freezing. The shaking starts up again, and I rattle so hard my tender, adrenaline-soaked joints ache.

Distantly, I hear Richmond respond to Dispatch. Her eyes averted, she takes her time silencing her radio and returning it to her belt.

I don't want to be here anymore.

"Have you called my grandfather?" I ask.

"He's on his way. Flora, I'm very sorry for what you've been through." Her voice is full of an awful, careful gentleness, like she's reading from a training script. "I know this must be traumatic, but I need you to tell me what happened tonight."

My words won't come. I found my first dead body at age fourteen, and I was never the same again. Lucy MacDonald.

Another girl like Ava. Like me. I found Lucy broken, bloody, discarded. The person who did that to her walked away untouched and unpunished.

I learned something then that most people don't know: no one is safe. We all think we are, but at any moment someone can erase you without a second thought. The world will go on, unchanged, like you were never there at all.

Yesterday, Ava was alive. She had a normal day, just like mine. Math homework. Texting her friends. Dinner. Her eyeliner was never exactly the same on both eyes.

Today, Ava is dead.

But why? Who would kill her? What was she so scared of when she called me?

Richmond watches me through my long silence. "If you need to take a minute before you feel ready, that's okay. I do need to search your backpack, though."

The bag is next to me on the curb. I pull it closer. "Why?"

Richmond clenches her jaw. A crack in her mask of professional sympathy. "Calhoun, you were standing over a dead body when the EMTs got here, covered in blood, and the murder weapon is missing. You know what probable cause is. Hand me the backpack."

I give it to her.

"Thank you." Richmond sets the bag on the hood of the

patrol car behind her. I watch wordlessly as she opens it and pulls out item after item. The Taser. My tactical pen, which writes in three colors and can shatter an eye socket. Lockpicks. Leather gloves.

"What the hell is this?" She holds up a vial of fine grayish powder.

"Dust." I read about it in a book about the FBI. They use it when they want to break in somewhere and make it look like they haven't touched anything. I don't tell her that part.

Richmond looks at me a long time, then places the vial on the hood along with everything else. When the bag is empty, she pulls out her phone and takes a picture of everything laid out on the car hood.

"Now"—Richmond turns back to me—"do you feel ready to tell me what happened?"

No, but I nod anyway.

"I'm going to record you," she warns, pulling out a digital recorder from a pouch on her belt and setting it on the hood of her car. I know I could kick up a fuss about a lawyer right now, but I don't have the energy.

I take a long breath. "Ava asked me to meet her here."

Richmond crosses her arms over her chest and stares at the ground, her brow furrowed in concentration as I tell the story. The phone call, the gunshots, the alley. Wes Grays, or whatever Ava tried to say. Each horrifying image flashes through my mind again, but I don't let myself really see any of them. My voice is flat and even.

When I finish, Richmond stops recording. She busies herself shoving all of my stuff back into my bag.

"Thank you for your statement," she says, holding my backpack out to me. "I am very sorry about your friend."

That unbearable practiced sympathy is back. Part of me wants to lose it. Scream and sob. See how she reacts to that, how well she could stick to her script.

I swallow. "Do you guys have anything yet?" The question is more a reflex than anything. The familiar urge is there to get up, look around, ask questions, but the feeling is distant, like an echo from the depths of a dark pit. I'm trying to climb out of it, but I'm weak, and my arms hurt, and Ava is dead.

"That's none of your concern." Richmond won't meet my eyes. She's trying to treat me like any other bystander, following protocol to the letter.

I sit up straight, some of the numb fog gone. "It *is* my concern. I found her."

She snaps, "Flora, do you realize what's happening right now? *You* were found at the scene of the murder. The killer has mysteriously vanished. This is the second time you've conveniently been the first one to find a dead body, and you knew both girls personally. You get how that looks, right?"

"You know I didn't do this. You *know* who killed Lucy." Tears prick at my eyes again, but I grit my teeth against them. Guilt flashes across Richmond's face, and it only makes me feel smaller, more childish. I hate her for it.

She tries to regain her professional demeanor. "This is a sad thing that happened, Flora. I'm sorry that you have to go through it again, but I need you to understand that I'm not going to tolerate any interference this time around."

I know what Richmond thinks of me. I'm just some privileged, unbalanced kid without enough discipline in her life, inserting herself into places she doesn't belong.

I look away. My eyes land on the puddle of vomit again.

Richmond isn't done. "You have an arrest record. Now, your grandfather might be powerful enough to have that expunged when you turn eighteen, but get in my way this time and not even he'll be able to help you. Do you understand me?"

I nod. I can make out a kernel of corn in the puddle. Tacos. We had tacos for dinner tonight.

Richmond inhales, collecting herself. She takes a long, pitying look at me huddled on the sidewalk, space blanket still clutched around my shoulders.

"By the way." She hesitates, as if deciding whether or not she wants to say it. "Patrol officers picked up Greg Garcy a few hours ago. He's going to jail."

Garcy. The tip I called in earlier. The flyer. Ava running a finger along its edge. Already that feels like years ago. I open my mouth to respond, but nothing comes out.

Richmond shrugs awkwardly. "Thought you'd want to know. Your grandfather will be here soon." She departs.

The patrol officers walk back toward their car. They're not needed anymore. They don't bother trying to keep their voices down as they load back up.

"The Calhoun girl found her? Gotta be the unluckiest kid in the world."

I swallow. My tongue is still sour with vomit.

"I don't know, man. Have you met that girl? I could see her going all psycho killer, easy."

"Maybe. Or maybe she's just cursed."

The doors of the patrol car slam behind them.

I *am* cursed, only not like they think. First Lucy, now Ava. Twice I've seen up close what the world is capable of. What it can do to people. Trouble is, no one else has seen the same thing. I get to walk around knowing it all by myself.

A car pulls up. My car. My grandfather gets out. His eyes find mine, and the fear and then relief in his expression are so powerful that shame slices through me. He woke up to a call from the police, and I wasn't in my bed. Again.

Two and a half years ago, I was arrested in the middle of the night. When they led me out of the holding cell, he was the one waiting for me. I was surprised. I had thought Mom would come. That was the last time I was ever surprised when she didn't show up.

But Gramps always comes for me.

He talks to Richmond at the mouth of the alley, and she looks increasingly pissed. Their conversation ends, and he approaches. Red and blue lights play across his face. He's wearing a suit, even though it's the middle of the night. No one but me would notice that the knot in his tie is slightly looser than normal.

"Flora, I thought—" His voice shakes. I blink and look away. He places a hand on my cheek, like he's checking to make sure I'm really here. His palm is warm and dry.

His arm falls to his side. "You're free to leave. They will follow up with more questions if necessary."

"Thank you." I suck the tears back in. "For coming. For..." I lose my words.

My grandfather nods with grave understanding. "Let's go home."

I leave a streak of blood on the car door when I close it

behind me. So much blood all over me. Under my fingernails. These clothes will have to be thrown out—there's no saving them. I feel a smear of it drying on my cheek, left over from when I tried to wipe away the tears.

Inside the car, the sounds, feelings, and smells of the outside world are deadened. The smooth, chiming click of the turn signal is surreal after the horror and violence of the alleyway.

The silence between us stretches on. We say nothing as we retrieve my bike from where I left it a few blocks over. We're quiet as the streetlights and buildings give way to the dark, wooded streets of Hartsdale.

We're nearly home before he speaks. "I know that on occasion you leave the house without my knowledge."

I pick at the dried blood under my nails.

When I was three, my heroin addict dad left my mom. She was pregnant with Olive, and so depressed that she could barely get out of bed for months. Then she was busy with the new baby.

My grandfather raised me. He fed me and tucked me in and took me to the park on weekends to people watch. He taught me how to look at a person and read all their secrets. Olive was always Mom's kid. I belonged to Gramps.

She applied for an artist residency in Berlin the same week

I was arrested. The same week she didn't come to the police station in the middle of the night.

"I didn't mean to scare you," I tell my window. "I didn't think—"

"I know," he stops me. "I know. You do not need—" He pauses to collect himself. Finally: "All I ask is that next time you leave a note."

I look at him now. His eyes leave the road and find my face.

He's the one who stayed. Who chose me.

"I will," I say. "I'll do better."

His eyes are back on the road. "I believe you."

Silence fills the car again. Gramps and I have never needed to say much to understand each other. But sometimes, I wonder if it's really that we just don't know what to say.

He doesn't speak again until we're pulling onto our street. "I called Cassidy on my way to meet you. She should be here shortly."

Is it even possible to love someone this much?

Olive is waiting for us in the front hall. She takes in the blood that's drenched my clothes, my skin, even my hair. She's fresh and clean in her fluffy robe.

I shift my weight on my feet, but my soles stick to the wooden floors. I'll have to scrub the bloody footprints away tomorrow. I'm always tracking filth and tragedy into my family's clean, normal existence.

An old image comes back to me. My mom, standing at the kitchen sink. The line of her shoulders tight as she scrubs Lucy MacDonald's blood off my running shoes.

Gramps walks past us into the kitchen. Water pings against the bottom of the kettle as he makes tea.

Olive is still watching me. I start pulling off my shoes.

"The phone woke me up," Olive says finally. "When the police called."

I nod. Ava's blood has wicked up my laces, gluing the knot together.

Mom never said a word about those shoes with Lucy's blood on them. Later, I found them lined up neatly in the front hall, mostly clean except for a few ambiguous brown stains. I never wore them again. Mom left three months later.

"Do you want help?" Olive asks. I shake my head. She steps closer, like she might touch me, and I tense. She stops.

"I'll just…be upstairs if you need me, then." Seconds pass. Olive turns and walks up the stairs. I continue picking at my laces.

The front door slams open. Cass is here. She's wearing sneakers and a sweatshirt over her pajamas. She throws her arms around me, all elbows and bleached hair.

For a second, I sag against her with relief. Cass holds me together. Her hair is in my face, and the smell of her shampoo is so unbearably ordinary.

I push at her shoulder. "Get off, I'm disgusting."

She squeezes me until it hurts.

"All right." She pulls back. "Time for a shower, and then I'm putting you to bed."

Cass doesn't let go of my hand as she leads me upstairs. She hustles me into the bathroom and helps peel off my sticky, crusty clothes. Her nose is red, and the corners of her eyes are damp, but she's quiet except for soft commands to raise my arms or move my hair.

I stand in my underwear and look at my stained skin in the mirror.

Cass leaves. I lose track of time standing in the hot blast of the shower with my hands braced against the wall. The water swirls around the drain, at first a rusty pink, then finally clear, but I still don't move.

Today, I saw a dead body for the second time in my life. It wasn't any less horrifying. I saw the exact moment Ava went from alive to dead. The first girl I ever kissed. The girl who put on that purple lipstick yesterday morning. Gone.

This life I've reconstructed for myself over the last two and a half years is a lie. Other people might be able to fool themselves, but I know: none of us are ever safe. No amount of hot water can burn that knowledge out of me.

I emerge from the shower flushed and tender, as frail as one of those blind, hairless baby mice.

When I enter my room, Cass turns her face away and sniffs. She was crying. Her sweatshirt is draped over my desk chair. It's stained with Ava's blood from when she hugged me.

I focus on getting dressed. I don't know what I'd say that could possibly make it better.

My pajamas are so normal against my skin. Another reminder that the world has stayed exactly the same, even as a seismic shift has occurred inside me.

We get in bed and turn off the lights. Under the covers, Cass grabs my hand. We used to sleep this way all the time when we were kids. Cass's parents travel a lot for work, and she's spent at least a couple nights a week at my place since elementary school. Back then, it was always my job to cheer Cass up, distract her, anything to make her less sad that her parents had left without her again. It had been years at that point since my dad left, and I already knew how to pretend until it didn't hurt anymore. Later, when Mom disappeared, too, I was prepared. Cass and I both learned how to not need them, how to be each other's family.

It's been a long time since I've taken care of her like that, though.

She whispers, "I can't believe Ava's just *gone.*" Through our clasped hands, I can feel her shake and shake as the sobs break free. I squeeze her hand tighter, putting all of my own pain into that fierce grip. I *want* to cry, want to let it all out, but I swallowed my tears one too many times earlier, and now they refuse to come.

After a long time, her shivering eases. "You went without me."

"I know," I say. "I'm sorry."

More seconds pass before Cass says, "I'm scared."

My grandfather wouldn't say it in the car, but it's what he was thinking. Scared it's all starting again.

I am, too. But my throat is too tight to speak. I squeeze her hand again and hope she knows what it means.

She trembles against the pillow as fresh tears start. "We'll be okay. We're going to do this together." She doesn't say it like a question, but I hear it anyway.

"Always," I answer. "You and me."

My last murder investigation ended with my mom leaving. That hurt, but it was a hurt I was ready for. Who am I going to lose this time?

"Promise you won't go without me again?" she asks.

"Promise."

A sick part of me wishes that she *had* been there. Saw what

I saw. Maybe I wouldn't feel so alone. But then Cass would be just as broken as me, and I can't stand the thought of that.

Eventually, Cass's breathing slows. She sleeps. I try to do the same, but every time I close my eyes, the haunting rattle of Ava's last breath jolts me awake.

CHAPTER 4

"I heard she found the body," someone says.

I clutch my notebooks closer to my chest. *Ignore it. Ignore it.*

"Yeah, over in Whitley. Middle of the night."

The whispering gauntlet of the school hallway stretches in front of me. It's Monday. The first day back in school since Ava...since the alleyway.

Cass and Gramps wanted me to stay home. The two of them tracked me around the kitchen this morning like bloodhounds with separation anxiety. I swore I could handle it.

"Didn't she find that other girl, too? Lucy MacDonald?"

Cass's locker is on the other side of the building. Now I'm alone and exposed.

Heads turn as I pass. Up ahead, there's a poster on the health-class door naming every kind of STI. I keep my eyes trained on that list.

Syphilis.

Gonorrhea.

"Why was she even there?"

I don't really want to be here, but I couldn't stand another day at home. I spent the weekend in a kind of numb delirium, staring at my bedroom wall with hollow, aching eyes. Occasionally, Cass or Gramps brought me mugs of tea. Plates of food. I took bites, but didn't taste. And then there were the nightmares.

I needed out of there.

Besides, Cass has her audition today. If I had stayed home, she would have insisted on staying with me.

"Weren't she and Ava, like, a thing? Maybe *she* did it."

Chlamydia.

"So weird that she came to school today."

Human papillomavirus.

"I'd be way too upset."

This morning, I made the mistake of turning on the news. Ava's face was everywhere. Someone chose to use her yearbook picture. She's cute, like always, but even Ava couldn't take a school photo without looking awkward. There must be a million better pictures of her on social media. In her yearbook picture, she looks like any other high school girl, instead of *Ava*.

According to the news, the police think it's a mugging. When they searched her belongings, her wallet was missing. Someone tried to rob her, then panicked.

That doesn't explain why she sounded so scared when she called me. Why she was nervous in school on Friday. People don't usually get advance notice before a robbery. But, just like everyone else, the police love easy explanations.

This was how it all started with Lucy. The cops made a show of looking into it, but weeks passed, and the only suspect was someone rich enough to be beyond consequences. The media moved on. The police shifted their attention to other cases. But I couldn't forget the way Lucy looked when I found her. She was barely recognizable as a person, let alone a girl I knew from school. If no one else was going to get justice for her, I would.

But in the end, I failed her, too.

I don't know if I have it in me this time. The numbness I've felt the last couple days is a shield, but I can feel it starting to slip. Watching the news made my hands shake with anger. I spilled hot coffee on my wrist. Still, that was only the barest flicker of the rage that usually powers me.

"What was Ava even doing?"

"Yeah, who goes wandering down some dark alleyway in Whitley at night? I mean, do you *want* to get shot?"

Herpes. Hepatitis.

I remember this part, too. Everyone was sad and shocked when Lucy's murder first broke. But under that thin layer of horror was *Where did she go wrong?* The second the media figured out that Lucy hadn't been some precious baby angel, everyone was ready to blame her for her own death. Because we're all safer if it was Lucy's fault, right? It could never happen to us.

A locker slams with a bang like a gun, and I jump.

Snickers. More whispers. They make my skin itch.

"Flora?" Mr. Kelly appears in the doorway to my English class. "Come on in. You don't want to be late."

A wave of weakness washes over me, and my legs nearly give out. What I want, more than anything, is total darkness and silence. A pause on the world.

Instead, I go to English class.

Cass is already in her seat. I take mine next to her as the bell rings.

The PA crackles to life, and Principal Adams says, "Good morning, students and faculty." Long pause. "As you may have heard, we lost one of our own last week. Ava McQueen was a pillar of this community, and I'd like to take a moment of silence to honor our beloved student and peer." She goes quiet. Uncomfortable fidgeting. What is it about a moment of silence that makes everyone suddenly want to dance and scream?

Adams continues. "I know this is a troubling time for us all. There are grief counselors available in the guidance office, if anyone needs support. A memorial service will be held Wednesday during sixth period, and all students and family members are welcome to attend. Take care of each other, please."

That's it. One moment of silence. Today will be weird. Every teacher will mention it in class. We'll have the memorial, and then everything will go back to normal. It's all so unbearably familiar.

"All right, folks," Mr. Kelly says. "I know we were supposed to have a quiz on the first three chapters of *Slaughterhouse-Five*, but I'll postpone that until tomorrow."

Someone in the back hisses, "Yes!" It's met with awkward giggles.

Mr. Kelly ignores it. "I thought it might be best if we took the day to remember our friend Ava." He leans against the whiteboard. "You're all young. You haven't had much experience with death. I've found that it really helps to share stories about those who have passed."

It's a nice thought, but it annoys me for a reason I can't name. Mr. Kelly is that teacher who wears band shirts under his button-downs. All the artsy girls have crushes on him. They eat lunch in his classroom and titter over stories about his Burning Man days.

He's still talking. "Does anyone have a story they'd like to tell?"

Everyone shifts in their seats, avoiding eye contact.

"It doesn't have to be anything monumental," Mr. Kelly says. "Even a fleeting moment can be profound."

Silence. The old-fashioned clock hands tick away, counting our breaths.

"I'll go," Maggie Quinn says. Everyone turns toward her. Maggie blushes and picks at her sweater. "Ava was in my drama class freshman year. She started this game. Whenever Mrs. Duneski wasn't looking, you'd point a finger gun at someone, and they had to fall to the ground. Like, even if they were holding coffee or something. We never told anyone about it. It was like a code? Mrs. Duneski thought there was some kind of fainting spell going around."

A nervous laugh rustles through the room.

"Good, that's good," Mr. Kelly encourages. He's got that artificially soft voice that's supposed to be comforting.

More people chime in. Ava argued with someone about reparations for slavery at a Diversity Club meeting. Ava sang about mitosis to the tune of a Beyoncé song for a presentation in bio. Ava's band played an awesome Prince cover at Devon Miller's house party.

I squeeze my eyes shut. These stories are so particular, each one a distinct image of the girl I knew: Ava bold. Ava generous. Ava funny. But they're all so peripheral. Ava's stuck in the shadows at the edges of all our lives. That's all she'll ever get to be now.

I have a lot of the same kinds of memories. Ava dressed up as the Bride of Frankenstein one Halloween. Freshman year, in that intense, often heated class about activism we took together, she'd throw out a one-liner that was so smart, so sharp, that the entire class and Mrs. Bennett would burst out laughing. I remember the Ava the outside world saw and loved.

But I also remember other things. Like the warmth of her mouth. Like the warmth of her blood on my hands.

The softest touch on my forearm forces my eyes open. Cass looks at me in a way that is both a question and an assurance: *Are you all right? You are all right.*

I nod, but who knows if I'm reassuring her or myself?

The classroom door opens, and a sophomore walks in with a yellow slip in his hand. He hands it to Mr. Kelly and leaves.

Mr. Kelly reads the paper, then looks at me with those gentle English teacher eyes. "Flora? They want to see you in the guidance office."

I should have expected it. No way they'd let me get through this day without some counselor wanting to poke and prod inside my head.

Out in the hall, my feet carry me in the wrong direction,

away from the front office. I should go see the counselor. If I don't, they'll call my house and it'll be a whole thing.

After Lucy, Mom sent me to therapy a few times. A nice middle-aged lady with frizzy blond hair and a thick gold wedding band that she twisted around and around while she waited for me to talk. The first time, the silence wasn't so bad. The second time, it was uncomfortable and kind of boring. The third time, I waited until Mom pulled out of the parking lot and then wandered the neighborhood for an hour. Mom looked so disappointed when I finally came home, but I was used to that by then. There was no fourth time.

I pass a display of student artwork. I lean in to examine a still life of a breakfast spread: coffee, toast, eggs.

Those three gunshots ring in my ears.

I shouldn't be here today. I could text Cass. She'd leave with me in a heartbeat. She'd understand. Reschedule her audition or something.

I sag against the wall. I have no idea what I want or need right now. The least I can do is let Cass have her day. I'm not so screwed up that I need to ruin that for her, right?

Footsteps down the hall. A whirl of blue-green hair disappears through a door.

I recognize that hair. I follow it into the photo lab.

"Hey, Lainie." I ease the darkroom door shut behind me.

Lainie Andrews, Ava's best friend and the photo editor for the school paper. She looks up from her trays of chemicals. Tears track down her cheeks, glittering in the hazy red light.

"What do you want?"

I flinch. Lainie and I aren't friends, but we usually get along.

Last spring, she was accused of plagiarizing a bunch of essay assignments. One of the other reporters on the school paper was also the lead in the spring musical, and he didn't like Lainie's review of his performance. He stole a bunch of her papers from her backpack and uploaded them to the school's anti-plagiarism software under a different name, so it would look like she copied someone else's work. Ava, Lainie, and I set up a sting operation involving a fake essay left lying on Lainie's newsroom desk as bait, and we caught the guy in the act.

On the day we closed out the case, I stood around talking with the two of them until Lainie left, and then it was just Ava and me. At the time, we hadn't spoken since freshman year. We kept filling the space with chitchat, neither one of us wanting to leave, until finally I couldn't take it anymore. I pulled her into the darkroom and kissed her against the door.

This very darkroom.

Lainie's still watching me warily.

"People were talking about Ava in my English class," I tell her.

Lainie turns back to the negatives in front of her. "Yeah, me, too."

On a normal day, I would ask her some questions. She knew Ava better than anyone. I lean back against the door. The same door that I once pressed Ava against. Twisted my fingers in the hem of her shirt.

Lainie sniffles, dragging me out of my memories again. "Was"—she chokes on her words—"was she scared?"

The question catches me off guard, and suddenly I'm ripped open all over again.

The blind terror in Ava's darting eyes. The air thick with the smell of her blood.

How do I tell her best friend any of that?

"I don't understand how she can just be *gone.*" Lainie grips the edge of the table. "I saw her Friday afternoon, and now she's dead?"

She curls her chin to her chest and tries to hold back the sob, but a tiny cry escapes her.

I'm paralyzed. Do I hug her? Console her? Cass would know.

"You were there with her," Lainie says, and a note of accusation cuts through her suffering. "*Why* were you there?"

Her blood under my hands, flowing and flowing no matter how much I tried to stop it.

I force the words out. "Ava called me. She asked me to meet her, but when I got there..."

"Why?" Her voice cracks, and she swipes angrily at a fresh wave of tears. "Why did she call you? Why did *you* get to be the one with her, when sh-she—" Lainie can't hold it back anymore. Her body goes rigid with pain as she sobs and gasps, beyond words.

Hesitantly, I lay my hand on her arm. She tenses but doesn't move away.

"I tried to help her," I say. Lainie squeezes her eyes shut. I ache with the kind of hurt you feel when you look at a wounded animal, but I keep going. "I didn't get there fast enough, but I stayed with her. She wasn't alone, at the end." I don't know if that matters at all, but it's the best I can offer.

Lainie takes wet gulps of air. "Why would someone hurt her? The cops are saying some guy took her wallet and then shot her anyway. How does that make any sense?"

I don't know. The police's theory sounds even weaker in the face of Lainie's overwhelming loss. Again, I feel the urge to untangle the knot. If I could get answers, maybe this wouldn't hurt so much—for all of us.

But I've been here before, with Lucy, and I only made

things worse for everyone. There are a lot of people who could get hurt if I fuck up another murder investigation. Not just my people, like Gramps and Cass, but people like Lainie, or Ava's family. Do I trust myself to get things right this time?

Lainie hugs her arms to her chest, her shoulders hunched and shaking. In the tiny, close space of the darkroom, her every whimper is magnified until it rings in my ears.

"I don't know why," I tell her, then hesitate before asking, "Does 'Wes Grays' mean anything to you?" Ava's last words, if that's even what they were, have been playing on a loop in my head for days. I tried googling it this morning while I was waiting for Cass to finish getting ready. There are more than a thousand Facebook profiles for people with some variation on Wes Grays, but only twenty within a thirty-mile radius of here, and zero with an obvious connection to Ava. Oh, and there's an architecture firm in California.

Lainie wipes her damp face. "No. I don't think so. What does it mean?"

"I don't know. It's something Ava said to me that night. She didn't know anyone with that name?"

"No. I mean, not that I know."

"Had she been acting strange at all lately?" I ask.

Lainie looks at her shoes. "Yeah. She'd been weird for a while now. I was gone last summer, doing this photography program at Yale. When I got back, Ava was different. She was never around."

Her words make the hairs on my arms prickle.

Lainie's voice is still thick with tears, but it steadies as she speaks. "She said she got a job as a messenger for her dad's office. He works for the *Whitley Gazette*. I thought that was kind of weird, because she didn't tell me until after she'd started, but I didn't ask a lot of questions." She makes an ashamed grimace at the floor. "I was jealous. I've always been into journalism stuff, and Ava never really cared about it."

I thought it was me. For months, I thought Ava was avoiding me because I'm such a disaster. But maybe there was something else going on the whole time. From the sound of it, the changes began right around the same time she ditched me. New, mysterious job. Pulling away from friends. It all started last summer.

"You couldn't have known," I say. "It might not even be related."

Am I comforting her, or myself? How did I not realize Ava was in trouble?

Those are messier thoughts than I have time for now. "What about more recently? Anything else?"

"A few days after Thanksgiving she showed up at my house crying. She kept apologizing. Said she knew she'd been a crappy friend. After that, things got better. She was around more often, but she still seemed distracted all the time." Quiet tears start up again. "It's senior year. I thought we were drifting apart. Normal stuff. I thought we'd work it out, eventually." Lainie looks at me with wide, glassy eyes. "She used to talk about you, you know."

Everything inside me goes cold. I don't want to hear this. I want to hear it so much.

Lainie goes on, "She thought you were a badass. When Lucy died? She thought you were right. She was mad when he got away with it."

I can't speak. I bite down on my tongue to keep myself here. Now.

Lainie asks, "You think she called you because she needed help?"

I nod.

Lainie's mouth quivers, but she holds it together. "Will you still do it? Help Ava, I mean. You could find out who did this to her."

I'm quiet a long time.

I don't know if I'll find any answers, but it doesn't sound like the police are going to, either. To them, Ava is just one girl. At best, she's one name on a long list of victims. And then there's the undeniable fact that it's all too easy for the cops to shrug their shoulders and move on when a black girl is shot to death in an alleyway.

But Lainie will never move on. *I* will never move on.

So who's going to fight for Ava?

"I will," I tell Lainie. "I promise."

I ask her to find me if she thinks of anything else, then slip out of the darkroom, leaving Ava's best friend alone in her grief.

I make it three steps down the hall before I have to stop and catch my breath.

Cass and Gramps were right. I shouldn't have come to school today. Gramps would come get me if I asked, but Cass would be furious if I left without telling her.

I text her: Can't do this anymore. I need to go home, but you stay for your audition. I'll be fine I promise

She writes back within seconds: Meet me out front in 5. Don't argue

Outside, I perch on the stone wall to wait for Cass. I tilt my face to the sky to catch some of the weak winter sunlight. Barely five seconds out of the building, and I already feel a little better.

The distinctive *pong!* of a bouncing tennis ball makes me look around. Elle Dorsey is waiting by the curb, scrolling through her phone with one hand and bouncing a tennis ball with the other.

Elle is the dark queen of Hartsdale High. She's one of those perfectly coiffed, perfectly tweezed girls who could (and would) slit your throat with one of her manicured nails.

She knows everything that goes on at this school.

I hop off the wall and sidle over.

Elle continues playing catch and release with her ball. "What do you want?" Her eyes never leave her phone.

"Tell me everything you know about Ava McQueen."

She shrugs one dainty shoulder. "Hardly knew her. We didn't exactly run in the same circles. I guess I wasn't her type." Elle bounces the tennis ball again. It hits the ground less than an inch from my foot. I don't blink.

With Elle, there's no appealing to her better nature or trying to find common ground.

"Come on," I coax. "You know everyone's secrets. Do you expect me to believe that you had nothing on Ava?"

"I don't know why you even bother. I watch the news: she got mugged, the guy freaked out and shot her." Elle turns her full attention to me now, not bothering to catch the ball on the next bounce. It rolls away off the curb. Her eyes sweep over me in calculation, and she smiles. I swear her teeth have been filed to points. "I'm sure you're devastated, God knows we've all watched you make puppy eyes at Ava for long enough, but it's hardly a mystery what happened. Go find another hobby."

Don't react. Don't slap her. She likes it too much.

I ask, "What was Ava doing wandering around Whitley in the middle of the night, then?"

Elle twirls a strand of hair around her finger. "Who knows? Maybe Little Miss Power to the People was slumming around the inner city, communing with the unwashed masses. Or maybe she had a secret fuckbuddy." She shrugs and turns her attention back to her phone. "I wouldn't waste your time, though. Whatever her secret was, it'll be disappointing and boring, like everyone else's. She was just in the wrong place at the wrong time."

"What are you even doing out here?" I switch tracks. Elle has French this period. Her classroom is across from my locker, and it's good to keep tabs on apex predators.

"Campaign event." She says it lightly, but there's an undercurrent of annoyance. "Without his perfect trophy daughter at his side, how will voters know my father's a family man?" Elle's dad is a congressman, but he's running for a promotion to the Senate this year.

"I thought he was all about education reform. Surprised his own daughter is cutting class," I throw back.

She tucks her hair behind her ears. "Apparently, we all have to make sacrifices for the public good, also known as his political career. Besides, the last time he ran for the Senate he lost. Pretty sure he'd offer me up as a blood sacrifice if voters demanded it."

She looks away, but not before I glimpse a strange vulnerability in her eyes. Still, Elle's daddy issues are so not my problem right now.

The soft *whirr* of an expensive car makes me turn. A black town car with tinted windows rolls to a stop at the curb.

The driver steps out and opens the back-seat door. "Miss Dorsey."

"Nice talking with you, Flora." Elle tosses her coat and bag into the driver's hands and slides into the back seat with a final swish of her dark hair.

CHAPTER 5

Cass circles the block where Ava's family lives. There's a squad car parked out front to keep an eye on things, but the house is still and dark.

On our way over here, I called the HR department at the *Whitley Gazette,* pretending to be an assistant in Detective Richmond's office. Despite what Lainie told me, the paper has no record of Ava ever working there. Elle might think Ava was just in the wrong place at the wrong time, but she was right about one thing—Ava obviously had secrets, and I want to know what she was hiding.

Cass parks the car a couple blocks away. She peers out the window, checks all of her mirrors. Watching our backs. Guilt ripples through my gut again.

I made her miss her audition. I know that's not what good friends are supposed to do, no matter how many times she says it's okay.

"Cut it out." Cass gives me an all-knowing eyebrow. "I'm fine. You're fine. We're fine. I can do the audition tomorrow. Literally everything isn't life-and-death, okay?"

My guilt only deepens. "I can't worry about *you* sometimes?"

She gives me a sad smile. "Today's my turn."

My throat is suddenly thick and cottony. I nod.

"You sure you want to do this today?" she asks for the billionth time. "It's okay if you want to take, like, a minute. We can go home and order pizza or something."

I know that's the healthy thing to do, but every time I sit still for more than a few seconds, I see Ava's pale, lifeless face in my mind.

"I need this. I need something to focus on, or I'll lose it."

Cass hesitates but doesn't push any further. If this is where I am today, she's with me. "It's going to be a lot. Being in Ava's house, with all her stuff. Go slow, okay?"

I nod.

The officers on watch are probably eating potato chips and grumbling about their crappy assignment, but I don't want to waltz through the back door if they're in the middle of a secondary sweep. I open the police scanner app on my phone. The radio crackles about traffic stops and an injured deer blocking the northbound side of Elm. Not a whole lot happens in Hartsdale, usually.

62

I check the many pockets in my lavender backpack. It's my work bag, where I keep my flashlight, stash of dog treats, and other assorted accessories for the resourceful girl treading on the wrong side of the law. The familiar task is soothing.

Finally, "Car 43 checking in. All clear at 27 Southwest Twelfth."

That's Ava's address.

I turn to Cass. "What do you think?"

She considers the clock on her dash. "It's twelve-ish now. They're either ready to switch shifts, or they've ordered food. Either way, they're distracted. Go in through the back, be quiet, and stay away from windows."

"Okay." I take a deep breath. "You'll keep watch?"

"Make sure your phone's on Vibrate. I'll call if they move."

I reach for the door.

Cass sighs. "Wait."

If it were anyone else, I'd be out the door already, but Cass has earned her best-friend rights the hard way. The least I can do is listen, even if all I want to do is *go*. I turn back but keep my hand on the door.

She runs her hands over the stitching on the steering wheel. "We're, like, an hour into this investigation. I'm not going to tell you not to do this, but just don't be reckless, okay? You can't afford to get caught. Not again." Her eyes are shiny and dark with worry.

I remember my grandfather's disappointed face as he watched the police lead me out of a holding cell two and a half years ago. "I know. Believe me, I know."

"I know you do. But for real, text me if you need backup. Or diversionary measures."

"I will." I pop the door handle.

"Oh, wait! One more thing!"

I'm going to throttle her. "Stop stalling."

"This is helpful," Cass promises as she roots around in her back seat. She pulls free a pink flat-brim hat with GRRL stitched on the front in white block letters.

I look at the hat. I look at Cass. I look back at the hat. I blink a few times.

Cass huffs, "It's for your hair, you idiot. Put it in a bun and tuck it under the hat. If you have to run and someone sees you, it won't be hard to figure out who the fleeing redhead is."

"Fine." I snatch the hat from her and do as she says. "How do I look?"

"You don't want me to answer that."

"Right. I'm leaving. Pull up closer as soon as I'm clear." I open the car door and climb out.

"Don't get arrested," Cass calls after me. Our version of "Good luck."

I walk down the road, scanning the houses for a good mark.

One has all its lights out. I sneak along the side into their yard and cut across the backs of houses in the direction of Ava's place.

It's noon, but the clouds are already dark and heavy. We're going to get one of those bitter winter rainstorms tonight. It'll be miserable later, but for now it's exactly what I need. I stick to the shadows. If I get caught, Richmond will make sure I can't get within a million yards of this case again, and that'll be the end of the story. No answers. No justice.

One yard has those little white flags that mark the boundary of an electric fence. I reach into my backpack to arm myself. Sure enough, a golden retriever trots over a moment later, but he's easily bribed by my fistful of treats. Rover licks my palm clean, and I continue on my way.

I always wanted a dog. I asked once, but Gramps gave me this look and said maybe, if I were home to walk it more often. I didn't ask again. He had a point.

I reach Ava's backyard and pull my gloves out of my bag. Soft, supple black leather, specially fitted to my hands for maximum dexterity. They were a gift from my grandfather last Christmas.

This morning, he gave me a knowing look and said, "Chilly weather forecasted today. Make sure you've packed your gloves." I read the subtext loud and clear. No matter how scared he is of where this case could go, I might as well be careful.

There's a police sticker across the seam of the McQueens' back door. If anyone enters the scene, the sticker will break and the police will know. I pull out a razor blade and set to work peeling up the edges, then try the doorknob. Locked, but that's okay. It's a basic knob lock. I have a set of picks in my bag, but these locks are so easy it's not even worth unpacking them. I always keep an emergency bobby pin in my back pocket, and with a few shimmies and twists, the door pops right open.

Inside, I take careful steps, peering around corners as I go. As I move through the darkened house, my brain is blissfully silent for the first time all day.

I haven't been here since last summer, but my feet follow the familiar path up the stairs to Ava's bedroom. It looks pretty much the same as I remember it. String lights crisscross the ceiling. Her bass guitar, with its sparkly butterfly sticker on the body, is propped in one corner. One wall is a collage of concert tickets, sketches, and Polaroids of Ava and her friends. There's a new poster over her bed: young Angela Davis, walking into a courtroom with her fist raised in the air.

I step through the doorway, and the lingering smell of Ava's woodsy perfume makes my pupils dilate.

I stop. Close my eyes. Count to five. I don't know how long I have in here. I can't get hung up on emotional stuff right now.

I stand in the center of the room and turn in a slow circle. There's a ruffled look to the place—the cops have already conducted their search. Still, a bunch of middle-aged men searching a girl's bedroom? There's no way they got everything.

In Ava's closet, I search through pockets and up all the sleeves. I fight to keep my head blank. Clinical. Don't think about Ava wearing that flannel shirt, or the dress with the cutouts.

An egg-yolk-yellow halter top makes me pause. I remember the feel of it underneath my hands, the way the warmth of her back radiated through the silk.

Ava was my first kiss. From a girl, I mean. This was in ninth grade, way before our almost relationship last summer. Lucy was killed that September. I was arrested in October, and murmurs of "freak" and "psycho" had started to follow me through the halls at school. Cass convinced me to go to some stupid party, where Elle Dorsey called me an attention-seeking creep. I went outside for fresh air, and Ava followed.

I was surprised. Ava was a year older than me, beyond intimidating, and cute as hell. She flashed me one quick, unsteady smile, like maybe she was as nervous as I was. It was such a bewildering thought that at first I didn't react when she kissed me.

I already knew I was bi at that point. The kiss didn't bring on some kind of divine revelation or anything. But it was the first time I kissed someone I truly, desperately wanted.

She pulled me close by the belt loop of my jeans. Her mouth was cold with the tang of stolen vodka, and the skin behind her ear was warm with the scent of her perfume, like trees and campfires. I had kissed two boys before that, but this was different, or better, or scarier. I felt like I was all chin and teeth, but then Ava sighed a little into my mouth and suddenly I figured out how to really kiss.

Ava pulled back first. All of my blood had pooled in my face, in my lips.

She curled one strand of my hair around her finger and said, "Don't let the assholes get you down." She went inside, looking back once before she slipped through the glass doors.

I let out a slow breath and slide the yellow silk halter to the right. The rest of her closet doesn't yield much besides a lipstick and a crumpled five in one coat pocket.

After the kiss, Ava waited for me to come to her. She kept looking at me in class with that little secret smile. I wanted to talk to her. I wanted it so much. But every day my life fell apart a little more.

Mom left for Germany a week after the party. I hated that it hurt, but it did. Olive stopped speaking to me, at least for a while. My court date got scheduled. With Mom gone, Cass was the one who helped me figure out what to wear. Gramps baked cake after cake and couldn't meet my eyes. I didn't say anything to Ava.

Kids in school thought I was weird. Scary. I'd never had a ton of friends, but there had been the usual crowd I ate lunch with and sat next to in class. Suddenly they didn't want to talk to me, didn't want to hear me go over my obsessive conspiracy theories yet again. But some people started bringing me cases to solve. They heard what I did for Lucy, and even though Matt Caine never got arrested, never paid for what he did, they all knew that I was right. I threw myself into the work, glad to tackle cheating boyfriends and stolen laptops if it meant I could ignore the dumpster fire of my life.

And then one day I came out of a bathroom stall after fifth period, and Ava was leaning against the sink.

"Look, are we ever going to talk about it?" She picked at her black nail polish like she didn't much care about my answer. All I wanted to do was wash my hands.

"You're avoiding me," she said. "And I don't do well with being ignored." She slanted me one of those smiles that always made my belly button feel too tight.

I could have moved closer. I could have pressed her up against the sink. I could have told her I'd been wanting to kiss her again ever since she pulled away that night at the party.

Instead I stepped to the side and used the other sink. "I don't have time for that stuff right now." I kept my eyes fixed on the lukewarm water running over my hands. After a moment, she brushed past me out the door.

I need to get it together.

I try the dresser. If you have something to hide, a false bottom is easy enough to rig up. I rummage through Ava's clothes and feel along the base of each drawer, but there are no telltale lumps or loose contact paper.

The incident in the bathroom was the last time I really spoke to Ava for a year and a half. It was Lainie's plagiarism case that broke the dam. After our kiss in the darkroom, we spent half the summer curled up in my bed or hers, laughing and making out and not talking about anything too difficult. I thought maybe I would finally get it right with her, but I couldn't quite figure out if she was my girlfriend or just someone I made out with a lot. I came home from my trip to visit Mom determined to settle the question once and for all. I must have sent Ava a million texts after I got back, every one of them unanswered.

The first week back at school, I found her outside the chem lab. Her eyes darted to the left, like she was thinking about walking around me but then decided against it.

"So, are we taking turns avoiding each other?" I joked awkwardly.

She didn't laugh. Didn't give me that slanted smile. "I can't, Flora. I'm really busy. I don't have the time right now."

I don't think she turned my words back on me to be cruel, but it hurt anyway. She did look at me then. A sad look, desperate to get out of an uncomfortable encounter. I stepped aside and let her go.

It made sense. It had always seemed a little too weird that someone as cool, as beautiful, as *together* as Ava could want me. After all, no one else did. Ava was my first kiss from a girl, but she was also my last kiss from anyone ever, if you want to get real particular about it. Being a sixteen-year-old detective is a highly effective mode of contraception. Not as many people have Nancy Drew kinks as one would think.

I thought I scared Ava off, just like everyone else, but maybe there was something bigger going on. According to Lainie, Ava believed in the work I do. I can't let her down. And that means I need to put all these stupid, useless memories in a box and seal it shut.

I close the last drawer in her dresser and rock back on my heels. My gaze lands on the desk. I open the first drawer and find a big stack of papers; the sheet on top is a history quiz, dated last October. The papers are creased, like someone already shuffled through them and decided there was nothing worthwhile.

Maybe the cops missed something? I'm about to flip through the stack when my phone buzzes in my coat pocket.

Shit.

I pull it out. Cass's name flashes on the screen.

Shit. Shit. Shit.

Someone's coming.

What are my options? It's too risky to run. I could end up halfway out the back door right as the cops walk into the kitchen.

Downstairs, the front door creaks open.

Heavy footsteps on the stairs, then male voices. "What did they say on the phone?"

"Richmond says there was a page missing from a diary. She wants us to check the girl's room."

Don't panic. Don't panic. My eyes land on Ava's bathroom door.

No time to shut it behind me. I step right into the bathtub, yank the curtain in place, and lie down. I've got Ava's papers clutched to my chest and one hand over my mouth to muffle my frantic breathing. This is a ridiculous situation, but I'm too terrified to find it funny yet. My pulse rabbits away in my chest, loud enough that I swear it echoes off all the hard surfaces of the bathroom.

The voices are at the landing. "Richmond thinks an awful lot of herself, making us do her grunt work," one of them says.

"Wouldn't mind her doing a little grunting for me," the other replies. His partner laughs.

Ick.

"What are we looking for?"

"She said to double-check all the drawers and books. It's a page from one of those Moleskines."

"What?"

"You know, black leather notebook? You see all those hipster kids carting them around."

"You keep a diary, Berger?"

"Yeah, you know me. *I don't know why Detective Richmond hasn't asked me to the prom yet.*"

Drawers open and slam. I just have to wait until they leave. There's no reason for them to come in here. If only my racing heart would believe that.

My phone buzzes again. Shit. I stab at the Ignore button, trying not to rustle the papers in my arms. The noises in Ava's room pause.

"You hear something?"

Fuckfuckfuckfuck. I bite down on my gloved hand to vent some frustration.

"You spooking on me?" the other officer asks. "Let's just find what Richmond wants and get out of here."

Once the search sounds resume, I pull my phone out and silence the volume. The call was from Mom. That can't be good.

Moments later, a text: Heard what happened. So sorry for that poor girl. R u ok? I'll come home if u need me.

The words punch the air out of me, but I clench my teeth and shove my phone back in my pocket. I'll deal with her later.

"I've got nothing. You?" one of the cops says.

"Same. Why are we even bothering with this? Kid was mugged, she got shot. Over and done."

"I'm starving. Let's go back to the car. Cho and Eckman should be here any minute to take over."

I relax an inch, but then the other guy says, "Go ahead, I'll be right there. Gotta take a leak."

Oh, no.

I stop breathing as he stumps into the bathroom. He stands about thirty inches from me, a shadowy silhouette against the shower curtain. Zipper unzips, grunt of relief, and then the sound of urine hitting toilet water.

I do not know what kinds of liquids this man consumed, but new universes are born and die while he pees. Finally, the waterfall turns to a piddling stream and dribbles out. The zipper *schwicks* up. The cop's shadow looms closer for a second, and all my internal organs freeze. He exits, slamming the bathroom door behind him. He does not wash his hands.

The tension runs out of me. I'm an exhausted puddle of

goo in my dead almost-girlfriend's shower. I text Cass: About to head out. All clear?

A couple seconds later: You're good

I clamber out of the tub and catch sight of myself in the mirror. I look ridiculous in Cass's GRRL hat, but there's a brittle, haunted expression on my face. I haven't seen it in a while, but I know that look well.

I book it out of the house.

CHAPTER 6

Outside, the pre-storm wind freezes the smell of Ava's perfume out of me, and my legs nearly buckle with relief. I shove the papers in my backpack and reseal the police sticker over the door.

Cass starts the car as soon as I'm in. I pull her stupid hat off. There's a cold slick of sweat across the back of my neck. All the fine little hairs stick to my skin.

Cass keeps glancing in the rearview mirror. "Are we being followed?"

I shake my head. It gets the whole rest of me shaking, too. I slump against the window and shut my eyes. The glass is cool against my warm, damp forehead.

"You get anything?" Cass asks.

I keep my eyes closed. "Not sure yet. Some papers. Cops interrupted me and I had to hide."

"What did you hear?"

"Some casual sexism and a very full bladder."

"Not even going to ask."

For a second, I consider telling her about the text from my mom.

I'll come home if u need me.

A stupid, little-girl kind of hope twists in my chest. An automatic reaction: I want my mommy. That part only lasts a second.

Another two-year-old memory resurfaces. I was standing in my kitchen. My mother, still wearing her bathrobe, sipped her coffee at the kitchen table, her chin slumped in one hand.

"Oh, come on, are you really this lazy?" I asked. "Is this the example you want to set for your daughter?" I bounced on the balls of my feet, testing my laces. I had been running every morning that summer, and my legs felt strong and ready to go.

"You're going to have to do it without me today, kid. Too early. Too hot."

Annoyance flared in me, but I kept my tone light and teasing. "Sloth is a sin, you know. A deadly sin. We're talking about the fate of your soul here."

She snorted, and it turned into a yawn. "How's this? We both skip the run and get ice cream instead. Gluttony and sloth—the perfect combo."

I felt it again: the fight instinct rising inside me. "I can't. Track tryouts. Four days away. Remember?" She knew how important those tryouts were to me.

She waved that off. "Oh, please. You've been working so hard. One day off won't kill you."

"Come on," I nudged. "Getting out the door is the hardest part, right?" I smiled, but it was too shiny. My face muscles twitched and pulled, trying to figure out what the right friendly-daughter expression was. Not too sullen. Not too fake.

Running was the last thing we had left that was ours. No Olive, no Gramps. Mom and me.

And she was going to bail.

She gave an apologetic smile, but it was only for show. "You go. Ice cream after, okay? And I'll run with you tomorrow, I promise."

I found Lucy's body on that run. Mom and I didn't go running the next day. I didn't try out for track. I never went running again.

I stare at the screen, my fingers hovering over the keypad. I have to say *something*.

I can't picture Mom in the house anymore. What would having her home even mean? There's about seven landfills filled with emotional bullshit that we need to work through, but neither one of us is really capable of that.

And then there's the real truth: it took her three days to bother to contact me after I found *another* dead body. She only offered to come home because she knew I'd say no.

I text her back:

It's very sad, but I'm okay. You don't need to come home

Back at my house, I pull the crumpled stack of papers out of my pack. Cass sucks in a little breath of anticipation.

"The diary page?" she asks. I'd told her all about the cops' conversation on the rest of the ride home.

I flick through the pile, but nothing sticks out. "Let's go through all of it. Maybe it'll turn up."

We sit on the floor and each take a stack to sort.

A perfume ad.

A boarding pass to Miami.

An outline for a paper about *The Scarlet Letter.*

Ava's room looked like she had only stepped out for a minute. Her scent was everywhere. The same nail polish stain I remember from last summer was still there on her comforter. My dumb heart had raced every time I glanced toward the doorway, waiting for her to come back.

This kind of work is more manageable. For the first time today, my head is almost quiet. Nothing but the mindless *swish-flick* of paper sliding against paper and Cass's even breathing.

A set of history notes on the Franco-Prussian War, dated two years ago.

A couple leftover flyers from a "Dorsey for Senate" campaign event back in October.

Cass breaks the silence. "Are we going to talk about the other night?"

My hand stills on a minutes sheet from the Human Rights Club.

I close my eyes, but all I see are those three bloody holes in Ava's chest and abdomen.

I flip to the next page in my pile: a French test on the subjunctive. Ava got a 93.

Cass chooses her words carefully. "I can't even imagine what it was like, seeing her die. I don't know what to say. 'I'm sorry' sounds stupid, but I didn't know what to say after Lucy, either, and we kept not talking about it, and...I don't want us to do that this time. I *need* to talk about it. Ava is dead, and I know I didn't know her as well as you, but I'm so sad for her, and I can't stop thinking about it, and—" She breaks off, sucking in a shuddering breath.

I'm holding an events calendar for a coffee shop. I smooth a wrinkle in the corner of the page. My hands shake, and the crinkle of paper fills the entire room.

I could tell Cass about how I can't stop hearing Ava's last, wheezing breaths, or even something as basic as the stuff with my mom.

"Flora." This time it sounds like a plea.

I look up. "I can't." After the intimate stillness of Ava's room, the only thing that's keeping me together is the task at hand. The pile of paper in front of me. If I start talking, I might fall apart.

Cass's eyes search mine, and I force myself not to turn away, even though a swarm of ants is marching up my spine.

"Okay," she says finally. "If you're not ready, that's okay. Just...how can I help?"

When we were little, I was Cass's protector. I was the first kid to talk to her when she was the new girl in second grade. In middle school, I made Sarah Neumann cry because she made fun of Cass's poem in English.

But then a girl named Lucy MacDonald was murdered when we were fourteen.

I wasn't surprised when, one by one, I lost all my friends. We'd never been that close anyway. Everyone else wanted to think nice things about Lucy for a little while and then forget, but I couldn't. I couldn't forget the way Lucy looked when I found her. When she stopped being a person and became a body.

I *was* surprised that Cass was the one to snap first. Some

older guys had taken to harassing the creepy, obsessive fresh-man (me) in the hallway. One of them had me backed up against a locker, and he was saying he knew just what freaky girls like me wanted when Cass tapped him on the shoulder. He turned around, and she hauled off and punched him in the face.

When high school started, Cass had wanted to join French Club and band and maybe field hockey. People liked her. She never would have ditched me, but part of the reason I wanted to try out for track in the first place was so that I'd have some-thing of my own.

The thing is, Cass is the one who really lost all her friends, back then. Even when I had other people to sit with at lunch, they all basically belonged to her. But in the end, she chose me.

"I'm sorry." I keep my eyes glued to the piece of paper in my hands.

"For what?" Cass sounds genuinely surprised.

"Being such a crap friend." I smooth my thumb over the wrinkled edge of the page again and again. "I know it sucks."

"Flora, cut that shit out," she says.

I open my mouth, but she holds her hand up. "No. Listen. Do you think I do these investigations with you for the money, or out of loyalty to you?" She pulls her bleached hair into a sloppy ponytail. "You're my family. If you're going through hell, I'm coming with you. But that's not the only reason I'm here. What happened to Ava is wrong, and I want to help. If you think I'd rather be hanging out with Megan Prince or Shelby Tang doing my nails, and I'm only here *doing something meaningful* out of some twisted sense of obligation, then you are even dumber than I thought."

"I know that," I insist, and it's true. She could have walked away when everyone else did.

As always, she sees right through me. "Flora, all your baggage? It's not too much for me. I can take it. Just don't shut me out, okay? That's all I'm asking."

I don't want to, but there's that dark door inside me. If I open it, all the nightmares I've kept hidden will come pouring out. Cass might be here because it's the right thing to do, but I do this because I will never, ever forget the endless warm fountain of Ava's blood beneath my hands. The way Lucy's body looked, beaten beyond recognition. How can I let *anyone* in there, even Cass?

She's still staring me right in the eye, her expression fierce.

"I won't shut you out," I tell her. "I promise."

She nods slowly. "Good." Cass shifts her attention back to the pile of papers in her lap, flipping to the next page. "I know it's hard for you to talk about right now. But when you're ready—" She freezes.

I sit up straight. "What is it?"

Her eyes skim the page in front of her. "I found something." She hands me the paper. It's a typed letter with "New York University" emblazoned in purple across the top.

"'Dear Ms. McQueen,'" I read under my breath. "'We are pleased to inform you...' *Oh*."

It's an acceptance letter. It hits me, again. All the things Ava will never get to do.

I swallow. "Well, Ava was a senior. She probably got a few of these."

"It's early decision." Cass looks at me like I'm supposed to know what that means. "Oh, honestly. You're aware we're juniors in high school, right? College is imminent! You need to know all of this stuff, like, tomorrow. Early decision is binding. If you get in, you have to go."

Huh.

She adds, "NYU is really expensive. One of the top ten priciest schools in the country."

"Okay, what's with the college obsession?" Cass is smart. She's a good student. But she's never been Miss 4.0 GPA, Look at My Volunteer Work and National Honor Society Merit Badge.

She looks at me like I'm nuts. "College is the way *out*. Haven't you thought about this stuff?"

I shrug. "Not really." And it's true, I haven't. Kind of been a bit preoccupied.

Her eyebrows climb even higher. "We hate this town. We've been going to school with the same people since second grade, and now we have the chance to go anywhere. We could live in California, or some huge, totally anonymous city. We could study abroad. Don't you want any of that?"

I do. I really do. She's right, I have been wanting to get out of Hartsdale for as long as I can remember, but college has always seemed so distant. Meanwhile, Cass has been plotting her escape without me.

I look back at Ava's acceptance letter in my hands. It feels impossible to think about that future life, beyond this place and everything that's happened to me here. Especially right now.

I read the letter again. Ava's mom is a librarian. Her dad is an accountant at a small paper in Whitley. Neither one of those jobs is getting anyone rich.

I look back at Cass. "Okay, so NYU is expensive. You think she needed money?"

"It's at least a possibility. She could have gotten a loan, or a scholarship or something, but it's worth looking into."

There's an old saying that there are only three reasons to kill: passion, power, or money.

My eyes catch on something at the bottom of the page. Log-in credentials for the NYU student portal.

I grab my laptop. Cass crowds close to read over my shoulder. Her hair brushes my cheek as I pull up the website and type in the username and password.

The page loads.

Welcome, Ava McQueen!

Cass and I breathe in.

Along the right side of the page, there are tabs for Courses, Grades, Student Life.

Tuition.

I click.

The page loads. My eyes try to take everything in at once, and then it all fits together.

Fall term tuition: Paid in full. Spring term tuition: Paid in full.

Cass and I breathe out.

"Well, that rules out a loan," she says.

"How come?"

"You wouldn't pay for the whole year up front with loans. What if she had to drop out? She'd still be on the hook to pay the money back. Same for a scholarship. I guess she could have had a rich aunt who coughed up the whole amount all at once?"

It seems like reaching for an explanation. Then again, the alternatives are just as weird.

I don't know what to think. Even with all the confusing stuff between us, I thought I knew Ava. The picture of her is so distinct in my head.

But how did she get her hands on so much cash? What was she into?

"Ava needed money," I say finally. "She obviously got it. Now she's dead. That's a pretty clear sequence of events." It's a heavy thought, and neither one of us has anything else to say for a moment.

The sudden, angry buzz of Cass's phone makes both of us jump.

Her mouth goes small when she reads the text. "My mom wants me to come home for dinner."

"Why?" Cass's mom never cares about normal stuff like that.

Cass tosses her phone aside. "God knows. I guess it's finally sunk in that a girl I knew was murdered, and she feels like she needs to be 'there for me.' As long as nothing urgent comes up at the office, of course."

Cass's mom is the managing editor at *Maison* magazine. She's always off ordering people around on a photo shoot or traveling to some artisan furniture maker's studio in Provence. Cass's dad is a hedge fund manager who once contemplated purchasing a sleeper couch for his office in the city. Most nights, Cass has dinner either with us or with Netflix.

She chews the inside of her cheek. It's there on her face, too. That reflexive flutter of pleasure that her mom cares, followed by anger that her mom thinks she can just jump in and play parent for a minute, then flutter away as soon as something more interesting comes along. It's a look I've seen on Cass's face a thousand times, and it always makes my heart twist.

"Use me," I offer. "Tell her I'm having a nervous breakdown. She'll believe it."

She gives me a rueful smile. "Nah. Gotta save that one for when it inevitably happens."

We laugh, but there's an edge to it.

Cass closes her eyes like she has a headache. "It's easier if I go. Let her do the Mom thing, so she can go back to leaving me alone. Besides, I should practice a little more tonight."

Her phone buzzes again. She glares at it like it's personally offended her.

"'When will you be here?'" she reads, doing a high-pitched impersonation of her mom. "'Need help in the kitchen. Found a new recipe for vegan buffalo wings. Yay!'"

"That sounds positively horrifying," I say.

Cass looks miserable. "I better go. Who knows what kind of unholy creation she'll concoct if I leave her alone in the kitchen? You'll be okay here?"

Who the hell knows? But Cass has her own shit to deal with. She can't worry about me all the time.

I gesture to the papers scattered across my floor. "Got this stuff to keep me busy."

"You'll call me if you find anything?" Her eyebrows are drawn together with anxiety, and I remember the slightly hurt note in her voice the other night.

You went without me.

Don't shut me out.

"I will," I promise.

I walk Cass to the front door. "Don't choke on a vegan buffalo wing, okay?"

"I won't." She starts to leave, then pauses and pulls me into a hug. For a moment, I'm overwhelmed by the temptation to collapse and burst into tears, but it passes. Cass squeezes me tighter, like she knows.

CHAPTER 7

My fork scrapes against my plate, and I wince. Olive looks at me, then away. She's been doing that a lot.

The bloody, wet gurgle as Ava gasped for her last breaths.

When I'm with Cass, and we're going, moving, doing, I can almost keep it together. In the quiet of dinnertime, the screams and gasps of the alleyway return.

Dinner is ratatouille. Gramps is a great cook, but it's hard to eat when the smell of Ava's blood is so strong in my mind.

He's watching me again. "How was your afternoon? The school called. You left after first period."

I draw figure eights on my plate with a piece of eggplant. "I'm okay. You were right. School was too much."

Three gunshots crack through the night.

I know my grandfather doesn't miss my flinch.

"Understandable. And where did you go?" His face is calm, patient. Sweat beads on the back of my neck.

What's safe to tell? Mom used to get angry when I lied, but when I told the truth she'd get this heavy, defeated look on her face that made me feel unbearably guilty. We got in fight after fight about it, and then she wasn't there to fight with anymore.

Gramps has never been like that, but this is my first murder investigation since Lucy. Since Mom left. Until now, nothing has been this serious.

I twirl the eggplant round and round on my plate. His gaze weighs on me while I work through this stuff, but he doesn't push.

He's the one who stayed. I can't forget that.

"I looked through some of Ava's personal effects," I finally say, tiptoeing around the great big woolly mammoth of how exactly I got my hands on her stuff. "I found out she was accepted into NYU. Early decision."

"So what?" Olive leans forward in her chair. I hesitate, but her expression isn't resentful or guarded, like usual. Only curious.

"Cass thinks she needed money. She paid her tuition for the entire year already." I turn to Gramps again. "Weird, right?"

He tilts his head. "It does seem an odd thing to do. Of course, there *are* plausible explanations." He pauses. "I believe I have a contact in the Global Affairs department at the university. I don't know what they would be able to find, but I could inquire."

"Yes. Please," I say quickly. It's relief enough that he takes me seriously, that he didn't press me on how I got those papers, even though he must know. Now he's offering to help.

He chose me. I don't know why I always have to remind myself of that.

"Have..." Gramps sounds strangely hesitant, and I pause with my fork hovering over my plate. "Have you heard from your mother?"

I don't look at her, but I can still *feel* Olive going completely still, 100 percent of her attention on me.

Why did he have to bring up Mom? He should know better.

I spear a piece of squash with my fork, still ignoring Olive. "She texted me. She said she'd come home. If I wanted."

The clatter of Olive's fork makes me look up.

"What did you say?" she asks. That open, curious look is gone. She's staring at me so hard her eyeballs might vibrate out of their sockets.

I have to rip the Band-Aid off. "I told her to stay in Berlin."

"Why?" She stands.

"Olive." Gramps gives a low warning.

"No." Ugly red blotches appear on Olive's creamy, freckled skin. "Tell me why! Why did you say that to her?"

What am I supposed to tell her? It's one thing for Mom to hurt me. I can take it. I look at Gramps, lost.

He does his best. "Olive, you know she has her gallery show next week. Even if—"

Olive doesn't want to hear it. "She would have come back. All you had to do"—she points an accusatory finger at me—"was ask her, and she would have come back. Everyone comes running for you."

She's so loud. How is someone that small so loud? The other sounds are creeping in. Gunshots. Screaming. Sirens. Last gasps for air.

I raise my voice, too, trying to block it all out. "What do you want me to say? Sorry I didn't use emotional blackmail to get Mom to come home?"

"It's your fault she left in the first place!" Tears glint in Olive's eyes. "She couldn't stand being around you! This is what you do. You ruin everything, and I have to deal with it."

Gramps stands. "Olive! That's enough. Apologize to your sister."

We ignore him.

It's all stuff I've said myself. Still, those words from my little sister's mouth unleash something hot and vicious inside me.

I stare right into Olive's eyes. "Mom left because she's a crappy mother. She'd rather run away from her kids than deal with their problems. Why do you even want her back?"

Gramps turns on me. "Flora, you're not helping. Both of

you need to calm down. Your mother has made choices I don't agree with, but—"

Olive steamrolls right over him. "Of course I want her back!" Her words come out gulpy and wet. "She's *Mom*. And it's only *your* problems she couldn't deal with. I never have problems because everyone's so busy worrying about you. Meanwhile, you don't care about anyone but yourself."

My last bit of control snaps. "If you want her back so badly, why don't *you* ask her? Guess it's easier to blame me, instead of admitting that Mom didn't love us enough to stay. A girl is dead. Someone I knew. I'm not going to sit around crying for my mommy when I could help."

"What are you going to do about it?" She sniffles, such a childish sound, but the look on her face is pure, black-eyed malice. "You act like you're helping people, but it's just an excuse so you can avoid actually dealing with anything. You only ever make things worse."

I open my mouth, but the fight has left me. She's right. That's the thing about sisters: they're living embodiments of the awful, whispering voice in the back of your head.

Olive turns and walks away. Her back stays rigid until she's out of sight, but her footsteps pound up the stairs like she's trying to make it to her room before the tears start falling for real. It doesn't make me feel any better.

My grandfather watches me, but I can't look at him. He won't say anything, but it will all be there in his eyes. The pity. The sorrow. His own confusion about how to parent two very damaged kids who are not his own. I don't want to see it.

I knew two other girls, once. Two girls like me, or Olive, or Cass, more or less. With homework, summer jobs, family dinners. Two girls who turned into bloody, ruined bodies right in front of my eyes. That's when I learned something Cass and Olive can never really understand: none of us are safe.

Whatever Olive thinks, I do care. I care about both of them, all of us, so much. But it only leaves me raw and aching and terrified.

Each breath comes sharper, more panicked. No matter what Cass says, I'm going to lose them. All of them. No matter how hard I try, I will push everyone I love away from me.

"Flora," my grandfather says, but he doesn't go anywhere with it. Maybe, like me, he doesn't know how.

I bolt from the room.

I take the stairs two at a time. The desperate stench of my own fear has me more and more furious with each step. By the time I slam into my bedroom, rage rolls off me in shimmering waves like heat rising from asphalt in July. My skin itches, pulled too tight around my bones. My vision pulses black and red. I am glass about to shatter into a thousand million cutting shards.

I press the heels of my hands into my eyes, trying to hold myself in before I sob, or scream until my throat bleeds raw, or smash my fist through my window, or light a match and burn my bed to ash, or laugh and laugh until I make everyone scared I might never stop, until stinging tears roll down my cheeks, until I'm sick with the stomach-cramping absurdity of it all.

It builds in me, higher and higher, and if I don't do something it'll come booming out of me, blacking out my whole existence.

I can't lose it. I'll only prove Olive right.

I pull the rest of Ava's papers from my floorboard safe. There's still a bunch I haven't sorted through. I sift through page after page. The cool, flat feeling of paper on my overheated hands calms my breathing.

I turn over the next page on the pile—a half-filled-out job application for counselor at Rock 'n' Roll Camp for Girls—and a small, folded-up piece of paper falls out of the stack. The paper is cream-colored, like it came from a Moleskine notebook.

The lost diary page.

All of the pain and screaming inside my head goes instantly, mercifully silent.

The page is folded up so small, it must have gotten stuck behind another sheet. My hands shake as I try to unfold it.

I hold it close to my face. Too close. I lean back, trying to focus my eyes and also not hyperventilate.

My eyes track back and forth across the page. Mostly doodles. Eyes. Lips. A few flowers. Saturn. An egg in a frying pan. There are bullet points squished into the empty space between drawings: a note about buying extra cups for the Human Rights Club, a date circled in purple pen (November 30). Lainie said Ava came to her house crying right after Thanksgiving—maybe that's related?

And then my eyes land on the top right corner, where Ava wrote *4044 West Grace St.*

My heart flatlines.

West Grace. *Wes Grays.*

In fast-forward, I relive Friday night. Ava's limp, heavy body. My pathetic sweatshirt tourniquet around her waist. Blood on the knees of my jeans. The cool, efficient voice of the 911 operator. The wild dread of death in Ava's eyes.

Wes Grays. West Grace. Wes Grays. West Grace. My heart picks up again, each pump keeping time with the syllables.

It's an address: 4044 West Grace Street.

My hands are shaking so hard I drop my phone. A quick search reveals the address is in Whitley, about two miles from where I found Ava's body. That's it. No business website or apartment photos. Street View shows a desolate city road and a huge gray building, but there are no obvious signs. It has

97

a large parking lot, bigger than a typical office building, but hardly any cars.

I'm off my bed with my boots in hand before I've even consciously decided I'm leaving.

Olive's blotchy red fury snares in my mind. The worried crease between Cass's brows.

I promised. Different this time. Better.

Cass answers after one ring. Her mom chatters away in the background, apparently not caring that Cass is on the phone.

"I found something," I tell her.

"Hold on." Her mom's voice recedes. "Okay, what do you have?" Cass's cool practicality eases my ragged breathing.

I tell her about the diary page. "I want to scope it out," I finish.

"Yeah, definitely." She hesitates. "Tomorrow, though, okay? My audition's at lunch, so we can go first thing after school."

The gaping maw of my panic opens wide again. "Cass—"

"Listen, I can't get away tonight. She's being all intense about this bonding stuff. Wants to do a *Gilmore Girls* marathon. Please wait for me?" Her voice goes up higher than usual on the question.

Don't shut me out.

I hate myself a little for the frustrated, desperate tears that scratch at my throat. The idea of sitting still in my room all night makes me want to scream, but that doesn't make Cass's problems with her mom any less real. And it's not like it makes an actual difference to the case if we check the place out now or tomorrow afternoon.

"Yeah, okay. Tomorrow. I promise," I say.

"Thank you." She exhales, and I can practically see her shoulders unclench.

"How were the buffalo wings?" I ask, glad for even a tiny distraction.

"We haven't eaten yet," she groans. "Mom forgot, like, half the ingredients, so we ordered Indian food. I'm officially starving."

I force a laugh. There's a muffled clatter on the other end.

"Cassidy!" Constance Yang singsongs in the background. "Baby, can you come back in here?"

"I have to go," Cass says. "Tomorrow, right? We'll scope out the address?"

It physically hurts, but I say it anyway. "You got it. Good luck."

"Thanks for telling me."

A fresh wave of guilt crashes over me. "Of course."

After we hang up, I go through all of Ava's papers twice, but there's nothing else there. I shower. I brush my hair. I make tea. I get into bed early. Maybe tonight I'll actually get some sleep.

I want to keep my promise to Cass.

Midnight rolls around. I doze, but then Olive's voice drifts through my head.

This is what you do. You ruin everything.

Too hot. I kick the covers off my legs.

I close my eyes, but Ava waits for me in the dark.

The frantic look in her eyes as I held her bleeding body. No moment of peace. No acceptance. She died scared.

I pull the covers back up to my chin. I stare at the ceiling.

Don't shut me out.

I could call Cass again, but I can't expect her to fix me every time I have a panic attack. Stuff with her mom is complicated enough without me screwing things up tonight. And it's late. She already put off her audition once for me.

I roll over and watch the shadows of tree branches bend and sway against my window.

Phone in hand, I watch as 12:16 rolls, slow as sap, into 12:17. 12:18.

At 12:19, I get out of bed. By 12:27, I'm lacing up my combat boots in the dark.

I leave a scribbled note for Gramps on my pillow. The one promise I won't break tonight.

At 12:31, I climb out my window.

CHAPTER 8

4044 West Grace Street looks the same in person as it did in the Street View photos. The building is nondescript. Rows and rows of identical windows, but not a single one illuminated. It's like the building the city forgot.

But it was important enough that Ava used her last words to tell me about it.

The rain from earlier has stopped, and the whole world is icy fresh. I chain up my bike in the mostly empty parking lot and prowl around. The only sound is the dull rush of the highway to the west. The bitter light of a half-moon glints on broken glass, and the slap of my footsteps echoes off the wet pavement. My brain is almost quiet.

Except seventy-two hours ago I was out in the free night air, too. That night ended with Ava dead.

I pull my jacket tighter around me. On the north side of the building, there's a large set of double doors. Faded letters above the doorway read CEDAR GROVE HOSPITAL. The sign was taken down who knows how long ago, leaving only a shadow of the words behind.

I continue my perimeter search. On the back side of the building, farthest from the street, a swath of light cuts across the parking lot. It's coming from a propped-open door. I slow, easing closer on cautious feet. A stairwell, leading down to a basement. I crane my neck, trying to see where it leads. There's a tunnel down there, but from this angle I can't see more than a few feet past the bottom of the stairs.

It's like a taunt: *Come and see...*

My pulse kicks up again. Fear, or exhilaration? I can't always tell the difference.

I rock on my heels. Moment of truth. I could go home. I could get back in bed. I could tell Cass I came, I saw, I decided to come back tomorrow with her. Even *I* don't love the thought of wandering around a creepy-ass murder tunnel by myself at night.

A streetlight pops and gutters, and the sudden sound makes every muscle in my body pull tight.

Olive's face flashes through my mind. That look of disgust, the corona of blazing hair flying free around her face. A thirteen-year-old Valkyrie of rage.

You ruin everything.

I keep my steps light as I descend the stairs. In the tunnel below, industrial emergency lights are mounted at intervals along the walls, but there are long stretches of dark shadow in between.

I take a closer look at one of the lights. They're battery-powered LEDs. Newish. Someone took the time to light this place so that they wouldn't need to run on the building's electricity, if it even has any.

The tunnel stretches back into the shadows. There's a steady dripping sound from some unidentifiable source. Every wet *plink* makes my heart jump. I take a step forward, then another.

My pulse pounds in my ears, seeming to echo against all the concrete. It sounds almost like footsteps, but no matter how many times I look, there's no one behind me.

The tunnel branches. The left path is completely dark. To the right, more lights on the walls. I go right.

Follow the bread-crumb trail of lights. Right. Left. Right. Right.

And with every step, I wait for the crack of a gunshot. For a rough hand to reach out and grab me by the shoulder, drag me into the shadows.

Left. Left. Right.

The harsh glare of the lights distorts my vision. Dark corners swell and bulge at the edges. My throat closes up tight and dry.

My foot snags on something, and for a moment, I am weightless, suspended in the air. I scream before I can stop myself.

The scream goes on and on, echoing through the tunnels like the screams of a thousand girls.

I catch myself against the wall and go completely still. If there's anyone in this tunnel, they for sure know I'm here now. My ears throb from listening, but there are no footsteps. No one's coming for me.

But there is *something*. A dull, droning roar. I take a step forward, more mindful of my feet now, and then another. The sound gets louder. It's like...cheering? Like people. A lot of them. A crowd.

I turn left, then right. The sound sharpens. Bloodthirsty shrieks. The thunder of applause.

I take another turn and stop short. At the end of a long stretch of tunnel, there's an open door. Inside, lights flash and pop, illuminating a crowd of people. A behemoth of a man guards the entrance. He doesn't look surprised to see me. Doesn't say a word.

Beyond the doorway, the crowd cheers. It's the kind of sound I imagine you heard a lot at the Roman Colosseum, back in the day. Gleeful but vicious.

All of my fear evaporates in fast-forward. I want in there.

"Twenty," the man grunts as I approach.

I stand on tiptoes while I count the money, hardly paying attention to the bills as I strain to see over his shoulder. He takes my cash and jerks his head inside.

I step through the door and into a nightmare of flesh, screams, and smoke. I blink, trying to adjust to the sudden change in light—it's much darker in here than in the tunnel. The air is thick and humid with the smell of sweat and spilled beer. Pulsating, bass-heavy music throbs inside my brain. From what I can see, we're standing in some kind of massive underground storage space, long since left empty. Just like the tunnels, the walls and floors are concrete. The ceiling is low and close.

And there are people everywhere. Hundreds of them. Yelling to be heard over the music, jostling each other for space.

What is this place? There's music, but no one's dancing. It's not a club. A bar?

Nearby, a girl in teetering heels laughs with her friends, liquid sloshing from the red cup in her hand. To my right, two guys start shoving each other. Their friends grab them by the arms, pulling them apart. The whole room has the electric feel of a mob teetering on the brink of a riot.

I'm caught up in that current. My skin hums with pure aliveness.

The space is hazy and dim, but for a cluster of blazing bright lights grouped in a circle at the center of the room. The crowd reacts as one sinuous blob, jeering, gasping, shouting at something in that circle of light, but I can't see over the wall of bodies.

I push forward. People press and jam against me on all sides. Someone stomps on my foot. An elbow to my ribs. I don't feel a thing.

I break free at the edge of an elevated platform with netting along the sides. A ring. Inside, two girls are beating the shit out of each other. A referee in traditional black-and-white stripes watches from the corner. The audience shrieks and howls.

Holy fuck.

One of the girls lands a kick to her opponent's jaw. Her long brown braid whips out behind her as she spins. The other girl crumples backward, and the crowd swells around me. The ref counts the girl out on the floor. She doesn't get up. Her sports bra is a jarring hot pink under the glare of the ring lights. The ref gives two short blasts on his whistle.

"And that's the Butterfly, down for the count!" An announcer appears with a microphone. He's got Elvis hair and a ridiculous salmon-colored suit. "This signals the end of the Butterfly's winning streak. I know there will be some unhappy folks in the audience tonight!"

He's not kidding. People around me are still yelling, although it's unclear who's celebrating and who's furious. A man turns and screams right in my face. The stale stench of his breath washes over my cheeks. The humming electricity inside me skitters and jumps between thrill and terror and back again.

"The Butterfly" fell on my side of the ring. Up close, her face is very young. My heart lurches. She's my age, maybe younger. A man carries her off. Her neck flops lifelessly in his arms.

There are kids here. Kids my age. Fighting.

That feeling from earlier creeps over me again. Ava was the girl who taught me how to kiss. Who was always picking at her nail polish. Who ran the voter registration booth at the homecoming fair. I can't make her fit in *here,* whatever this screaming hellhole is.

I'm trying to look everywhere at once. There's a makeshift bar on the other side of the ring. Two bartenders work side by side, one filling plastic cups from a keg, the other mixing drinks from giant bottles of liquor and soda. It's hard to make her out in the low light, but I'm pretty sure that girl in the silver dress is Penelope Simmons—the lead in the school play—laughing with another girl as they hand over cash to the bartender. A man passes in front of them, and then they're gone.

I scan the rest of the crowd. There are some of your basic underbelly types: shifty-eyed dudes and low-rent crime lords, along with assorted bimbos and hangers-on. But there's also a lot of teenagers.

I spot a tall kid in a green shirt I could swear is a sophomore at my school. He turns and walks away, the crowd reabsorbing the empty space he left behind like he was never there at all. I spot another guy, not from Hartsdale, but I feel like I've seen him at a party before, back when I still got invited to parties. I think he goes to one of our neighboring schools. Maybe Garfield?

The announcer gets on the mic again. "And now, for our third match of the evening, a true clash of titans!"

I turn my attention back to the ring.

Announcer dude struts around, his slick showmanship an absurd contrast to the grimy, makeshift feeling of this place. "In one corner, we have the Destructinator!"

Yikes. That name has to be a joke, right? The first contender lumbers into the ring and raises a meaty fist in the air. He's older than the last contestants, probably in his twenties. The crowd cheers. I wrinkle my nose. People root for this guy?

"And in the other corner, his opponent! Coming off a twelve-round undefeated streak! Can he maintain it? It'ssss...VT!"

This guy gets a much louder response. A group of girls shoulders up next to me at the edge of the ring. They press against the platform, tossing their hair and adjusting their sparkly dresses.

A second later, I get it. VT—whatever that stands for—lopes into view. I am not above noticing he is far and away the prettiest boy I have ever seen. He's young, got to be close to my age, and his face is almost girlish, with a delicately angled jaw and long lashes. Soft little-boy curls are pulled back in a stubby ponytail. He's wearing an old-fashioned mauve silk boxing robe, like he thinks he's in *Pulp Fiction* or something, and nothing but tight black shorts underneath.

VT is much, much smaller than Destructo-whatever, but he doesn't seem worried. He feints back and forth, hamming it up for the crowd. Blows kisses to the girls next to me, who shriek and fall against each other, giggling. His massive opponent tracks VT's movement with his eyes, like the ugliest house cat watching a fly.

The bell dings.

VT is whip fast. He darts in and lands three lightning punches, then dances back out of range before the giant can grab him. Destructinator lunges and VT dodges the wrong way. One monstrous fist comes down hard on top of VT's head, leveling him to the ground, but before I finish my gasp, he rolls out of the way and lands a kick to his opponent's knee-cap. A gruesome crack echoes through the room.

I've seen Ultimate Fighting Championship–type stuff on TV before, but this is brutal. There are clearly no rules.

VT gets in a few more good hits to the other guy's legs and face, avoiding Destructinator's torso altogether. Smart. The guy's built like a rhino. He wouldn't even feel a chest hit through that thick hide.

I don't know much about fighting, but VT is weirdly... graceful? He throws a few leaping kicks to his opponent's head, and his body jackknifes so elegantly, I have the crazy thought that he must have been a dancer who fell on hard times.

The giant almost goes down after a ruthless blow to his face, but then he reels forward and swings an almighty arm out, grabbing for that fly.

The shattering force of his fist connects with VT's face, and he's sent spinning toward me.

For half a second, everything slows. VT is suspended in air, caught midway through his fall. His eyes meet mine. A bead of sweat slides from his temple down one cheekbone to collect in the bow curve of his mouth. He blinks once in slow motion. I can count his eyelashes.

The animal frenzy of the crowd returns.

VT whips himself around to attack his opponent with a wild savagery that makes something squirm in my stomach. I force myself not to look away. The predatory grace is gone.

He's feral now, mauling the other guy's face like he wants to kill. Destructinator, poor dude, doesn't stand a chance. He's down and out within a minute.

"And VT, our reigning champion, brings down the Destructinator!" the announcer screams. People yell. VT wipes some blood from his forearm and preens for the crowd. He doesn't look my way again.

His back is to his fallen enemy. He doesn't notice the guy heft himself up. I yell some kind of warning, but it gets lost in the din. Destructinator bellows, cocks his fist back, and lands a mean sucker punch to VT's kidneys.

Ouch.

VT goes down hard and doesn't get up. A bunch of guys swarm the ring and haul the Destructinator away, but my eyes are locked on VT, still out cold on the ground. A man in a gray suit bends over him and jostles his shoulder. With a little help, VT staggers to his feet and exits through a pair of doors at the back. I lean forward on the balls of my feet and watch him go.

Green flashes in my peripheral vision. It's the green-shirt kid! I squint across the ring at him. I'm almost positive that guy goes to my school. His eyes catch on my face, and even in the dark I swear there's a shiver of fear.

He knows me.

The guy immediately turns and shoves past the people

behind him, but I've got him in my sights now. His head sticks up above the crowd enough for me to track him. Being tall must suck sometimes.

Still, it's like the people around me have merged into one many-limbed creature. Hands and legs drag at me as I fight my way through a spiderweb of human flesh. I finally burst out the door I entered through, but Green Shirt is gone.

"Which way did he go?" I ask the bouncer. "The guy in the green shirt? Tall string-bean dude? Which way?"

The tiniest movement of his shoulders. I guess it could charitably be called a shrug.

Fan-fucking-tastic.

I take off down the hall, following the lights out the way I came. Left. Right. Right. I have a stitch like a tiny Swiss Army knife in my side, but I push harder. I don't want to wait until school tomorrow for answers. That guy is going to explain what so many people I know are doing in this place.

Last turn. Up the stairs. Out the doors.

The parking lot is empty. I gasp for air, and the icy specter of my breath shimmers in the moonlight. A cold tendril of sweaty hair sticks to my forehead. There's the coyote howl of a siren in the distance.

The guy is gone.

A scream of frustration wells up inside me, then pops just

as fast, like a balloon. All the exhaustion of the last few days barrels into me at once. My ears ring in the absence of the crowd. That shivering bloodlust ecstasy has left me wrung out, my nerves shredded. I'm sticky and cold, and my guy has vanished.

A new lead is like a drug—euphoria, adrenaline—but it disappears so quickly, leaving nothing but more questions behind.

It's time to call it a night.

I trudge across the parking lot and kneel down to unlock my bike. My bones creak under the weight of my fatigue.

"And she rode her bike here. Isn't that darling?"

It's like something out of a comic book: the flash of flame in a dark corner, the glowing red ember of a freshly lit cigarette. A person slouches out of the shadows. I stand up. His face passes into the light, and I'm stock-still like a deer in the road. He's bruised and bloody, but still strangely beautiful.

"Been waiting for you, Red."

CHAPTER 9

The soles of my feet itch with the flight instinct, but I don't run. Yet.

"What do you want?" I ask.

"Thought we might get a chance to chat." VT's showered—his hair is out of its ponytail, hanging to his shoulders in damp curls. His hands have been bandaged, and a black eye swells across his cheek.

"Yeah?" I tighten my grip on my bike. "About what?"

"Got some things worth knowing." He takes a drag on his cigarette.

"What makes you think I'm here looking for information?" Convenient as it is, informants don't usually waltz up and offer me their life stories.

He sneers. "Oh, I can tell, Cherry. You'd love to hear all my nasty secrets."

"Hard pass." I throw my leg over the bike seat. I do want

info, but I'm not going to let this greasy little rat jerk me around.

"Know a thing or two about this establishment, for one." He takes a sideways step closer. "Insider's knowledge, yeah? Be happy to pass it on if you'll let me buy you a soda pop."

His eyes are hard, almost resentful. Not sure what I've done to piss this guy off already. That usually takes at least five minutes, and after all, *he* approached me.

I toggle my bike pedal with my foot, deliberating.

I'm tempted to make a break for it—I have indeed heard about the dangers of accepting candy, or in this case soft drinks, from strangers—but I have so many questions, and this guy might have answers. The humming buzz of adrenaline starts up again.

Sensing my hesitation, VT continues. "There's a diner not far from here. Twenty-four-hour place. We can talk in public."

That girl. The Butterfly. Crumpled on the floor of the ring, she looked nearly dead. The address of this place, scrawled in Ava's handwriting across the top of her diary page. The hollow stillness of my bedroom.

Do I want to go home? Stare at my ceiling and try not to think about Ava, or Cass, or Olive, or any of the other people I've let down today?

"Okay." I hop off my bike. "But I have a Taser and three

knives on me. Get any creepier, and I promise you'll find out where I'm hiding them."

Something like delight flares in his eyes. "Deal."

We don't talk for the first few blocks. I keep glancing at him, but he's looking straight ahead. I'm still a little winded from the emotional roller coaster of today, plus the dystopian hellscape acid trip of the fight club, and now there are little flutters of hope that this guy might have actual information. But in all likelihood he's luring me back to his place, where he can cut me up into little pieces and tuck into some Flora fajitas.

"Why do they call you VT?" I ask eventually. It's a pretty bland stage name, compared to the Butterfly or... Destructinator.

"It's my name."

I frown. "Your mother named you VT?"

"In a way."

"Does it stand for Vermont?" I guess.

He snorts. "No."

"Victor Theodore?"

"No."

I throw out a wild card. "Vanya Telemachus?"

"My girl's well-read, huh? Still no. This bothers you, doesn't it? Not knowing."

"I'm Flora. I know things. And I'm not your girl."

He rolls his eyes and flicks his cigarette away. "My apologies, didn't mean to offend your delicate sensibilities."

We turn onto a street lit with the fish-tank glow of a 24/7 diner. Inside, a bored waitress seats us in a back corner booth. Under the diner's fluorescents, VT looks a lot more beat up than he did on the dark streets.

"You look awful," I tell him.

He drapes an arm over the back of the booth. "Not so charming yourself, Cherry. Could do with a shower and a good night's sleep, I bet."

I hold back a snarl and resist the urge to smooth my hair.

He gestures to his battered face. "And you should see the other guy."

"I did."

He tilts his head to one side with a look of sly calculation. "That's right. So what's a girl like you doing in my club?"

I cross my arms. "What's with the questions? I thought you were supposed to be the one with the information."

"Gotta give a little to get a little, Pippi."

"Do you just sit around all day thinking up nicknames in case you meet a redhead?"

"Oh, absolutely."

Our waitress appears. VT and I realize at the same

moment that we're leaning across the table toward each other. We both sit back. She dumps menus in front of us and departs without a word.

I'm suddenly starving. Recon always makes me hungry.

I hold the menu up in front of me, pretending to study it so I can examine his face. He takes a sip of his water. His bruises are sort of sexy in a way that makes me have all kinds of weird guilty thoughts about The Patriarchy and the sexualization of violence.

"See something you want?" he taunts.

"Yeah." I fold up my menu. "French fries. And a milkshake. Possibly pancakes down the line, but we'll see. You're buying, right?"

"Sure, Ginger. I'll buy you dinner."

Once we've ordered, he says, "Back to my original question. What brought Anne of Green Gables to the club tonight?"

"Why should I tell you?" I ask. It's making me nervous, how interested he is. Why did he seek me out?

"Come on, you spill a couple secrets, and I'll tell you my whole story," he coaxes.

I want it, but I don't want him to know how bad I want it. "Whatever. I could guess, anyway."

He raises his eyebrows. "Oh, yeah?"

"Yeah. I'm good at that sort of thing. Could read you right now, not so hard."

"That is a tempting offer. Not exactly unreadable yourself, sweetheart."

"You think?" I'm well aware he's manipulating me, but I can't help it. I'm charged with the same ferocious voltage from earlier, and I'm ready for a brawl.

"Oh, yeah." He looks away like he couldn't care less, but he's sitting on the very edge of the bench, too. "It's written all over you."

"Well, let's have it."

He tilts his head as he considers me—a long, sweeping evaluation—then says, "Sure, a little game, then? I'll show you yours if you show me mine? If you're as good as you say, I'll tell you what I know. Gotta warn you, though. Might not like what you hear."

No way I'm backing down now. "You first."

He looks me dead in the eyes, hardly blinking. My mouth goes dry, but I meet his stare head-on.

He begins, "Well, there's the absent-father-figure thing practically radiating off you, but I won't bore you with cheap thrills. I'll start with this: you weren't there as a spectator tonight. Didn't even know what you were walking into, I'm thinking. It's the clothes. Jeans. Leather jacket. The other girls, they come dressed for a party. Tottering around in their heels." He leans over the side of the table and looks at my feet. "You, on the other hand, chose combat boots. Now, lots of people imagine themselves punks these days, but your treads are all worn down on the sides, like sometimes you get caught places you shouldn't be, and you gotta make a break for it."

Elbows on the table, he leans in closer, voice low. "You didn't flinch once watching me fight, not until that bastard sucker punched me after the bell. Before that, I cracked his face open real good, blood all over, but it was that last punch that made you look away. You're no stranger to violence, but you like things fair. No cheating. People have two good reasons to sneak around a place like that: crook, or cop. What with the whole honor code, I'm going to go with cop.

"Course, you're no older than seventeen, so not a real cop. Cheerleader assassin? Girl detective? Avenging angel?"

I force myself not to twitch. He gets a look in his eyes like a jaguar with the scent of blood.

"But then," he drawls, "pretty little redheaded schoolgirls don't go sneaking around playing detective because they're well-adjusted. There's some dark tale of woe in your past. Unsolved mystery? If you could just figure it out, you'd be done?"

I focus all of my energy on remaining still.

He traces a finger around the edge of his water glass. "I'll bet you have help. Family connection? Ex-cop? FBI? Yeah, something slick like that. Quantico, criminal profiling. All about reading people, getting into their heads. 'Cause you're young, and you're small, but you are always, always smarter than everyone else. And if you're that smart, you can *almost* forget that a bad guy like me could reach across the table and break your little wrist before you had the time to move away."

I scoot back, bringing both wrists under the table.

He laughs. "Almost. But not quite. So, how'd I do?"

Scary well, but I'm not telling him that. "No Quantico." VT raises his eyebrows, a challenge, and I relent. "My grandfather. CIA."

He grins. "And the rest?"

"The rest was right enough. Got a little Psych 101 for my taste, but trueish."

"All right, then, Cherry, let's hear what you've got."

My awareness sharpens. I'm ready to rip a hole in that smile.

I lean back and tilt my head, mimicking him, then begin. "It's an act, obviously. The tough-guy thing. That's always the case with you *Rebel Without a Cause* types in some way or another, but this is something more. You're smart, but it's not Artful Dodger street smarts. You recognized Vanya and

Telemachus as literary characters, so you like to read everything from classics of Russian drama to *Pippi Longstocking.*"

VT is eerily still. No reaction yet.

I continue. "*Pippi* and *Anne of Green Gables* are what stupid people call 'girl' books, but you read them anyway. You were one of those kids. Up late, flashlight under the covers, reading anything you got your hands on. You're not huge now, more like wiry. You were probably small as a kid, and a small boy who reads girl books means bullied.

"But you grew up to fight in illegal underground clubs, so at some point you came home crying and your father told you to handle it like a man. A dad like that wouldn't buy *Pippi* for his son. You had an older sister."

VT blinks. He wets his lower lip. His expression is still blank, but I swear his breathing has gone shallow.

I see you. You can't hide.

"You read her books. You obviously looked up to her, worshipped her, even, and she protected you." I keep my voice soft. "But nerdy little boys don't grow up to be street fighters because they're well-adjusted. Something horrible happened."

His jawline is as hard and straight as an arrow. One bandaged hand grips the tabletop. His cuticles are white and bloodless.

"If I were a betting girl, I'd say it was the sister. If she were around, she'd hardly approve. Her darling, sensitive baby brother getting his face beaten in every night? She'd be so disappointed. She's gone, isn't she? And you've never been the same.

"So you turned into this." I gesture in his general direction. The black eye. The bloody knuckles. "This ridiculous caricature of a *bad boy*. I mean, who even smokes anymore? And the way you talk? It's like you've read *The Outsiders* too many times. No way that's real."

I go quiet for a second. "Here's the thing, though: this is who you are now. Maybe it started out fake. An identity you made for yourself because something awful happened, and you needed to be a new person. But now you've been *this* for so long, you don't know what's real anymore."

For a moment, the world is soundless except for our breathing. Neither one of us blinks.

This time, I'm the first one to look away.

I pick at the peeling edge of the linoleum tabletop. "Oh, and I've also got this theory you're a down-on-your-luck dancer, but I'm waiting on more evidence before I commit." I take a sip of water and risk another look at him. "How'd I do?"

The spell is shattered, and his mask slips back into place.

He smirks. "Not half bad, Red. Won't say what's true and what's not—too fun watching you squirm—but not half bad."

I resist the urge to jump over the table and hyena maul his stupid, pretty face. "You're scum."

"Bet that took all your detecting skills, Nancy Drew."

The waitress returns with our food.

I take a minute to bask in the glory of French fries and chocolate shake, but something bothers me. "What you said before, about me flinching?"

He gives me a wary look. "Yeah?"

"You were watching me from the ring?" My voice wavers, and I already regret asking. I just want to know why he followed me, but now he's going to get all kinds of ideas.

He surprises me with the tiniest, softest smile. "Your hair, Cherry. Catches the light." The smile disappears, like he didn't mean for it to slip out.

We both look down.

Time to get back on stable ground. "Are you going to give me anything useful? I thought you had intel."

"Be easier if I knew what you were looking for."

I chew a fry. "Tell me about the club. Who runs it?" I don't want to ask about Ava, not yet. He might spook if he figures out I'm investigating a murder, and then I really will go home with nothing.

He drums his fingers against the tabletop. "The big boss? Don't know for sure. We don't see any trouble from the police, though. My hunch is it's all connected up top with local business or politics."

"Why?"

"I see them sometimes, in the VIP section. Nice suits and American flag pins. They go there to make deals. It's too loud for a wire, or for anyone to overhear. The profits must be a decent chunk of change. Could add some nice padding to a campaign slush fund, or maybe they've got a mistress to pay off. Who knows?"

What he's saying lines up with what I've been thinking, but it's also exactly what I've been afraid of. If Ava had anything to do with that place, it sounds like she might have gotten tangled up with some shadowy and corrupt people. The kind who can make things dangerous for those who get in their way.

I set that aside for now. "So what's the setup? For the club, I mean."

"Schedule changes every week. Some weeks, there's nothing. Others, might be a fight every other night. You have to know someone who knows someone to get the schedule for that week. Then it's twenty at the door, plus betting and booze inside."

"You get paid?"

"I get a cut of the night's take, nothing much, plus a purse when I win. Usually works out to around five hundred a night, give or take."

I take a slurp of my milkshake, remembering those words on Ava's NYU student page: *Paid in full*. What VT's talking about is decent money, but Ava would have had to fight multiple nights a week for eight months, at least, to make tuition. How did she not get caught? And that's not even factoring in all the bruises and injuries she would have had to cover up.

"The girl," I say. "The Butterfly. You know her?"

He twirls the saltshaker between his fingers. "A bit."

"She was pretty young." The milkshake sits heavy in my stomach as I remember her round cheek smushed against the dirty floor.

He looks up at me, surprised. "Yeah." He squints, like he's reassessing me. "Most of the fighters are kids. High school, college students needing a little cash. Figured a girl like you..." He trails off with a flash of that shark's smile.

"A girl like me what?" It's infuriating, but it's safer to be back at each other's throats like this.

He laughs. "You live around here, yeah?"

"And?"

"There's got to be at least a dozen kids from every high school in a fifteen-mile radius fighting in that ring. Bet you know more than one person who's in on it. You pass these people in the halls, trade notes in math class, and you didn't notice?" He shrugs. "Thought a smart girl like you wouldn't be so clueless to what's going on around her."

I look down at my lap. I don't want him to see that he got me, but my skin is too hot. Too tight.

What's wrong with me? The kinds of fights I watched tonight, they leave scars. Fractures. Bruises. Penn's limp in chem class the other day, his bruised cheek, come back to me in a rush.

What other injuries have I written off as nothing? Matt Sharma got to type our history midterm because his arm was in a sling. I think he said he fell on a ski trip? Tara Jacobson was absent from Spanish for like a week with a concussion, but she's a really intense soccer player so it's not like that's the first time it's happened.

Have I been oblivious all this time? Were all of these little things, each one barely a blip on my radar, actually connected to something much darker?

He says, "Bet you're having one hell of an identity crisis right about now. Not as observant as you thought, huh, Cherry?"

Enough. I want what I came here for, so I can get this guy out from under my skin.

I pull up a picture of Ava on my phone and turn it to face him. "You know this girl?"

He stares at her photo for a long time. "This is the girl who got murdered." He slides my phone back. "Seen her around. And you're, what? Going to find who killed her?"

I nod.

VT's eyes travel all over my face, like he's picking out every detail, every clue. "Why? She a friend of yours?"

"It's the right thing to do." I'm not going to get into the situation with me and Ava. Not giving him that ammunition. He gives me a shrewd look, like he sees through me.

But all he says is, "Cops think it's a mugging. Senseless act of violence, that whole deal."

"The police like convenient explanations as much as anyone."

"And you don't?"

"I don't."

A second passes, then two. He's still watching me. There's a sharp, quick curiosity in his eyes, like I can see his brain whirring too fast. It's uncomfortably familiar.

He breaks the moment. "Like I said, saw her around. Don't know much more than that."

"Did she fight?" I ask.

"Not that I ever saw." He shrugs. "Could find out, though. Call you if I learn anything."

I stir my straw in my melted shake. "Why?"

He props his chin in his hand and bats his eyelashes. "It'd give me a chance to see you again, wouldn't it?"

I know he's not telling the truth. He's hiding something.

I'm not going to push, though. Not when he has something I want.

He pulls out his phone and takes my number. A second later, I get a text:

Hello, Cherry.

For some idiotic reason, the words on the screen make my pulse stammer.

I hate myself for it. Three nights ago, I was kneeling in an alleyway, covered in Ava's blood. I'm here investigating the murder of the one person I ever had real feelings for. And now I'm flirting with informants?

"Why are you helping me?" I ask again, hating how desperate I sound.

He gives me a strangely earnest look. Maybe I'll get a real answer.

He shakes it off. "What can I say? I've always been a sucker for redheads."

We don't say much on the walk back to my bike. I expect VT to disappear right away, but he lingers while I put on my helmet.

"Well, good night, then. Sort of okay to meet you, I guess." I flip up the kickstand with my toe.

VT starts to say something, then stops. He looks down and takes a deep breath, as though bracing himself. "It's Valentine."

My foot hovers over the pedal. "What?"

"My name. VT. Stands for Valentine."

"Oh. Thanks." The mood between us has changed, gone serious somehow, when neither of us was paying attention.

"Yeah, well. My girl knows me so well, should probably know my name." The bravado is back, but his eyes keep twitching from the ground to my face, like he can't help it.

I don't know what to think about him at all.

"Not your girl. But thanks."

CHAPTER 10

Olive is sitting on my bed when I get home.

She watches me with wide eyes as I climb through my window. "Where were you?"

The day hits me like a pillowcase full of bricks. God, I'm tired. I ignore Olive and hunt for pajamas.

"I came in here to apologize, but you were gone." Her voice is soft.

I concentrate on unbuttoning my jeans. This is exactly why I snuck out, so I didn't have to think about this stuff anymore.

Olive says, "I am sorry, you know. I didn't mean it." I look at her, and she wilts. "Okay, I did mean it. But I was dumb."

A smile tugs at the corner of my mouth. "It's okay. I'm dumb all the time. You had to catch up eventually."

She laughs, a little too loud in the late-night hush of the house.

I finish changing and climb onto the bed next to her. We face the same direction, staring straight ahead.

"I called Mom," she says eventually.

My chest aches. "You did?"

Olive picks at a thread on my comforter. "I told her she should come home."

"And?" I already know the answer.

Olive's mouth tightens. "She said everything's confusing enough right now. She doesn't want to shake things up."

Another time, Olive might have believed that excuse, pitiful as it is, but I can see from the sad, worn look on her face that she's too old for it now.

"I'm sorry," I tell her.

"I know." Her breath catches. "I just wish she was, too."

There's that familiar swell of rage toward my mom. I've felt it a million times before. Only now, I don't need her. It still hurts that she left, but I'm used to the pain.

Fuck her for doing this to Olive, though.

I reach over and grip her hand so tight, it must hurt.

She turns to me with serious eyes. "I want to help. With the case, I mean. I can be helpful."

She's thirteen. A kid, really, but so was I when this all started. Do I want Olive to be like me, though?

I'm too exhausted to get into that now. "We'll see."

A long silence, then Olive says, "I'm sorry about Ava. I know you guys dated, or something."

I've never talked to her about Ava before, so who knows how she figured that one out. Then again, Olive is observant, and Ava came over almost every day last summer. My heart constricts, remembering Ava giggling and kissing me in this very bed.

I know you guys dated. I don't correct her, because what would I even say? It feels wrong, though. Like I have a claim to Ava, or something. Like she's mine to grieve. I don't know how to feel about that, not after tonight, with all my confusing thoughts about this girl I thought I knew.

We sit together in the silence for another moment, then Olive lifts herself off my bed.

She pauses in my doorway. "If we're going to survive this, you and me and Grandpa, we can't be so scared of each other."

I nod, staring at the wall. "I'm trying."

I wake up sore the next morning. My spine crackles like *I* got the crap beaten out of me last night.

I can't stop seeing the Butterfly, crumpled and limp on the ground. I've been turning the same question over and over in my head since I saw her in the ring.

How did I miss something this huge?

I need coffee.

Gramps is sitting at the kitchen table, and I pause in the doorway. I don't want to talk about Mom or Olive. Even though she and I made up, I'm still covered in a thousand little cuts from the things we said.

He takes in the sight of me—motionless, half in the kitchen and half out—with the same blank, patient attitude as always. When I don't move or speak, he takes a sip of coffee and turns the page of his newspaper.

I make my coffee. Mug. Milk. Two sugars. Stir. Don't look at him.

He speaks. "Thank you for the note."

The knot between my shoulder blades releases a bit.

I sip my coffee and turn to face him. "Sometimes I listen."

"Indeed." He turns the page. "Well then, what did you find?"

Images from last night flash through my head. The spray of blood and sweat under the ring lights. The shoves and screams of the crowd.

One ankle rests on his other knee, the pant leg of his suit pulled up to reveal a sliver of his periwinkle argyle socks. His posture is meant to show he's relaxed, but I know him better than that. He's waiting.

Olive's words from last night come back to me. *We can't be so scared of each other.*

"I followed up on an address Ava wrote down in her journal. I don't even know how to describe it. Like a fight club?" I check his expression, but he doesn't appear to be freaking out. Relieved, I run through the rest of the details, only leaving out the parts with VT. No need for Gramps to know that I went off alone with an informant.

"Have you heard of anything like that?" I ask once I've finished.

He thinks it over. "I don't believe so, although that sort of petty local crime would hardly have been on my radar."

I hesitate. I don't want Gramps to think I'm jumping to conclusions, but what VT said last night made sense. I keep my tone casual. "This place was pretty well organized. Someone must be covering it up, right? Like the police, or a politician maybe?"

"Possible," Gramps says, watching me carefully. "But why? It seems like a needlessly extravagant enterprise. Those types tend to be more discreet."

"Yeah, but they're also raging narcissists. Maybe they didn't think anyone would ever be smart enough to catch them."

Gramps doesn't answer right away. I know what he's thinking. The last time I went head-to-head with the rich and powerful, I didn't come out looking too good.

This would have been the moment where Mom lost it. Where she threatened and begged me not to go any further.

"I'll look into it," he says eventually.

He's the one who stays.

"By the way," he adds, "I called in a favor with that old colleague of mine at NYU. Apparently, she's good friends with someone in the bursar's office. She asked a few delicate questions about the tuition money, and it appears that Ava paid for both semesters in cash several weeks ago."

Cash. I didn't even know you could pay school tuition in cash. That definitely rules out a scholarship or a loan. Where the hell did she get that kind of money?

A breath rushes out of me. "Thank you."

"Yes, well. Have a nice day in school." My grandfather can make his expression perfectly neutral and at ease whenever he wants. The worry in his eyes is there because he wants me to see it. To know that he is scared.

Unease tightens in my gut, but I force it aside. He's scared, but he's helping me anyway. Trusting me not to let him down this time.

"You look like hell," is the first thing Cass says when I get in her car. "Did you sleep at all?"

"At all? Sure. You'll never believe what I found." My questions about the fight club have been hammering my brain all night, and I want to share them with someone who will get it.

Cass pulls out of my street, her eyes flicking from the road to me and back again.

"Well?" She sounds a little on edge. She did spend all of last night with her mother, which always puts her in a bad mood. Maybe I should let her rant first? Do the best-friend thing?

She wouldn't want me to sit on something this huge, though. It all spills out of me, the fight with Olive, the hospital, the fight club, VT. Unlike with Gramps, I don't hold anything back.

There's a long silence, punctuated by the clicking of the turn signal.

I wait, but Cass is freaking me out. "What do you think? I mean, I'm more observant than your average bear, right? Kids from school have been fighting for cash in an abandoned hospital. How did this slip past us?"

Cass doesn't respond. She's very focused on looking up and down the road to make a turn.

I get that unsettled feeling again, the same one I felt with Gramps in the kitchen.

We arrive at school. Cass focuses on parking the car so intently, it's like she's landing the Mars rover.

I stare at her the whole time, but she ignores me. "Are you mad at me?"

Cass finally turns the car off. "You said you'd wait."

I shift in my seat. My winter coat is stifling and bulky in the confines of the car.

"I know, I'm sorry. But I had to—"

"No, you always do this!" she explodes, and it's like stepping on a land mine—I thought we were on safe ground, until the earth blew apart under my feet. "You are *always* a disaster, Flora. That doesn't mean you get to just treat me however you want and expect me not to say anything."

Cass bites her lip like she's trying not to cry, and that makes my own throat close up with tears. She's one of the few people in the world I absolutely could not survive losing, and I'm fucking it up.

I grab her hand. "I'm sorry. Okay? Really, I am." The words come jumbling out of me. "Please. I was a mess last night, and I know that's not an excuse, but I kept hearing those gunshots, and I couldn't take it anymore, and I know I broke my promise, and that's not okay, and I *won't* shut you out, or at least I'll try, but—"

She squeezes my hand. "Stop."

"Cass—"

"No, shit, I'm sorry. It was a really long night with my

mom, and I'm nervous for the audition. I shouldn't have unloaded on you like that." She gives me a tentative smile. "We don't need to be in a fight right now."

I frown. "*You're* sorry? I think you have it backward."

"Come on. Let's go to class." She starts to get out of the car. Something feels off, though. It shouldn't be that easy.

"Cass, seriously—"

She grabs her stuff out of the back seat. "We're good. Swear." She gives me an earnest look. "I wouldn't lie to you. I promise we're okay."

But all that stuff she said didn't sound like it was only about last night. It sounded like it's been brewing for a while.

"C'mon," she calls over her shoulder as she walks across the parking lot. "We'll be late."

It doesn't feel right. But I grab my stuff and run to catch up with her.

In history class, I squint at Ruby Eaton's neck. There's a splotch of mismatched skin, like she didn't fully blend her makeup. Covering a bruise? Or maybe a hickey.

In Spanish, Jack Kimora keeps stretching his knee under his desk like it's sore. Did he fight yesterday?

I scan the hallways between classes, but the tall green-shirt sophomore is nowhere to be seen. I'm questioning everything, unsure of what's real or normal anymore.

My phone vibrates in my bag during math. I pull my eyes away from a scratch on Grace Kirkland's arm.

It's a text from Olive: In the computer lab. Found the address of the fight club in your room and looked it up. Want to know what came up?

My eyebrows shoot up. I type: I thought I said MAYBE you could help. I pause, then add: But yeah. Send me what you have

It takes a few minutes for Olive to respond: The hospital was closed six years ago when they built a nicer one across town, but they couldn't sell the land because of some zoning thing. I also checked out crime in the area. There's been a 30% increase in crimes like robbery and assault since this summer, but all of the incidents are at least three blocks away from the hospital

You'd think some of the club's violent energy would spill into the streets, but crime records only document police activity. If what VT said is true, if the police have been told to look the other way, there wouldn't be a record.

So who would have the kind of clout that could persuade the police to ignore something like that?

I write: Thanks. Email me the links? Then stop digging through my stuff. And texting in class

Her reply: Hypocrite! Links sent

I chew my lip. I don't want Olive to turn out like me, but the fight with Cass this morning still has me on edge. I text her again.

Thank you. Really.

At lunch, Cass picks at her sandwich. Her guitar is propped against the table next to her. She's supposed to eat quickly, then go to the music room for her audition, but she's chewing on her lip more than her food.

"You nervous?" I ask. Hopefully it's performance anxiety and not lingering weirdness from earlier.

She sighs. "Wanting something sucks. I can't even remember the last time I really tried to go for anything."

She doesn't mean it as a slight, but it stings anyway. There's a reason Cass isn't in any clubs. Doesn't play on any teams. It's because I suck up all her time.

Cass doesn't notice my flinch. "Distract me. Tell me more about this club."

I hesitate.

She drops the hunk of bread she's been shredding onto her plate. "Stop. I know you want to talk about what you found last night, but you're feeling all guilty that you're not paying enough attention to me. I'm really nervous, and I want something else to focus on. Might as well be our classmates beating the ever-loving crap out of each other for cash."

I cave. "I just can't get my head around how I missed something this big. Am I that self-absorbed?"

Cass gives me a pitying look. "I don't think that's what this is. For one thing, I didn't notice, either, and I'm not half as self-centered as you are."

"So how do you explain it? How did this many people keep a secret? And from us?"

Cass looks around the crowded cafeteria. "If I was fighting in some illegal club on the weekends for cash, you and me would basically be the last two people I'd want to find out about it."

"True. Olive dug up some more information on the hospital." At Cass's raised eyebrows I add, "I swear I didn't ask. She found the address in my room and went rogue. I have no control over her."

"Wow, that must be annoying," Cass deadpans.

I ignore her and explain what Olive found. "This guy, VT, he thinks it's got to be someone with serious power running the place. Maybe Ava got on their bad side?"

Cass doesn't look convinced. "Maybe." She casts another troubled glance around the room. "What makes you so sure it's not someone we know? A bunch of teenagers beating each other up for money? A fight could have gone wrong, or someone had a grudge. It was bound to get out of control at some point. Maybe Ava was just the one who paid the price."

"It was a pretty sophisticated operation I saw last night. You really think one of the idiots at our school is capable of something like that?"

Cass gives me a look. "I don't know, do you really think a sixteen-year-old girl can solve a murder?"

Right.

Cass's expression turns more serious. "Have you considered telling Detective Richmond?"

"No. Why bother? She wouldn't believe me anyway."

"Maybe." She hesitates over her next words. "But she did send those officers back to search Ava's room. Why would she do that if she was totally sold on the mugging thing? And if what we really want is for Ava's killer to pay, isn't it better if everyone has all the information?"

Cass has a point, but if someone *is* paying off the police, then what could Richmond really do anyway? Richmond's not incompetent or corrupt, I don't think, but she follows orders.

I'm about to respond when I notice Penn crossing the room.

I nod in his direction. "Do you see that? Tell me Penn isn't totally limping."

Cass follows my eyes. Penn finds a seat at a table by himself.

"Let's go talk to him." Cass stands.

I don't move. "Um, audition?"

Cass slings her guitar over her shoulder. "I have time. Come on, you want me there for this. You need my people skills, on account of you have none of your own."

She's not wrong. "If I find out you blew off your audition for this, you and me are going to be the feature showdown in the ring next week, because I will have to kick your ass."

Cass is already walking away. "If you think I couldn't take you, you're seriously deluded."

I grab my stuff and follow her.

Cass sits down at Penn's table. "Hey, Penn, how's it going?"

Penn's lunch is set to one side, and he's sketching on a pad of paper. His face is drawn tight with concentration, hovering bare inches above the paper as he draws.

He doesn't look up. "You know. Weird week."

Penn tends to fade into the background. He's that quiet kid who's been in all your classes since you were four, but no one ever seems to remember him.

"What are you drawing?" Cass asks. I keep my mouth shut. Cass has this way of striking up a conversation about something totally random and innocent, and before the person knows it they've spilled their whole story.

But Penn's not taking the bait. "Nothing." He tilts his face closer to the page.

Cass cranes her head to look at the sketch. It's a close-up of someone's hands. They're slender and manicured, like a woman's, with a dainty ring on the right hand.

Cass's voice is gentle. "Penn, that's beautiful. Who is it?"

No answer.

I try a more straightforward approach. "Is something going on with you and Damian?"

His pencil pauses for a second. "Why are you asking?" Under the table, Cass's foot presses down gently on mine. A warning.

I keep my tone casual. "I saw you fighting in chem. How come?"

Penn resumes sketching. "We weren't fighting, and you should pay better attention in class." He smiles like he's teasing, but it's forced.

"Yeah, you and Mrs. Varner should have lunch sometime to discuss my issues. It looked like fighting to me."

He turns his fake smile to Cass. "She always this way?"

"Pretty much," Cass commiserates. "Hey, how's Victoria doing these days? I haven't had a chance to talk to her since our global lit class ended. Is that her?" She nods toward the drawing.

I don't know what Cass is talking about, but Penn's smile vanishes. He slams the sketch pad closed.

Good cop obviously isn't working. I reach into my bag and pull out one of the notes I snagged off the floor that day: *I'm sorry, I had to do it. Please talk to me.* "What about this? What did Damian do?" Cass's pressure on my foot isn't gentle anymore.

Penn stares at the note for several seconds, then looks between Cass and me with cold eyes. "You know, people at this school really suck. I try not to listen, because they have dumb shit to say about me, too, but now I'm thinking maybe they weren't wrong about you two. You have nothing better to do than pick up some stupid note I dropped?"

I'm done being nice. "How come you're limping?"

"Fuck off." He grabs his things and shoves them in his backpack.

I stand, too. "I know about the fights, Penn. I'm going to find out more. Tell me."

"I have no idea what you're talking about. I'm going to class." He swings his backpack over his shoulder. "And you"— he turns to Cass—"you might want to reconsider your friends. Safer to stay away from her." He sneers at me.

Cass grabs my hand before I can jump across the table and attack him.

Penn limps away.

"That went well." Cass is still holding my hand. She gives

it a little squeeze. "Next time give me a little longer to build the bridge before you blow it up, 'kay?"

She's right. I'm wound up, and it's making me sloppy. I flop back into my seat and bang my forehead against the table.

"What was that about Victoria?" I ask eventually, face still pressed to the table. It smells like a hundred years of spilled school lunches.

"Victoria Ramirez," Cass answers. "She and Penn just started going out. I figure two friends fighting, there's at least a chance it has something to do with the new girlfriend."

I lift my head. "You're brilliant." She preens.

"Cass? You ready? Hi, Flora." Elliot Graham approaches our table. He has some kind of instrument case slung over his shoulder, and he keeps twisting the strap around his hand.

Elliot is our resident musical prodigy. I think he can play something like twelve instruments. It's in his blood: his dad, Dennis Graham, is a semifamous blues guitarist who owns a record store in downtown Whitley. Elliot works there after school sometimes, picking out vintage new wave and Motown records for customers with those long pianist fingers.

He's staring at Cass with the sweetest, most earnest smile on his face.

Well, this is interesting. Frustration with Penn momentarily forgotten, I look at Cass. She's very determinedly *not* looking at me as she gathers up her stuff, but the back of her neck is bright red. Perhaps her excitement about rock ensemble isn't purely extracurricular.

"Did you have to reschedule your audition, too, Elliot?" I ask innocently.

A flush to match Cass's creeps across his cheeks, making his light brown skin glow.

"Um, no." He rubs the back of his neck. "I went yesterday, but I'm the student coordinator for rock ensemble, and, um"—he clears his throat—"I thought I should oversee Cass's audition, for, um, leadership. And moral support."

"Uh-huh." Very convincing.

Cass is somehow even redder. "Are you okay by yourself?"

I shoo her off with promises to behave. "Good luck!" I call after them.

As I watch Elliot and Cass walk away, their arms very close but not touching, the dull ache in my chest eases for the first time in days.

CHAPTER 11

My good mood lasts about three seconds. With Cass gone, the other people in the cafeteria don't even bother to whisper.

"My dad's friend's cousin is a cop. He says she's a person of interest."

"Yeah, they interrogated her for like six hours."

I don't turn my head. Don't indulge them.

"Megan told me she totally lost it when Lucy was murdered, and she got obsessed with that Matt Caine guy. Like, fell in love with him and stalked him or something."

I grab my stuff and stand up. I don't have anywhere to be, but I'm not going to sit in the fishbowl and let them stare at me.

I try not to look at anyone as I walk out of the cafeteria, but my eyes land on Elle Dorsey. She's watching me. She doesn't look away.

I approach her table.

Without taking her eyes off me, she says to the table, "Could we have a minute? I'll see you guys in class." As one, her minions depart.

I get right to it. "Tell me about the fight club."

She blinks. "I have literally no idea what you're talking about."

"I know kids from this school fight in the basement of an abandoned hospital. I know money changes hands. Now I want to know what you know."

She gives me a demure, pouty smile. "How fascinating. You need something from me." Elle pretends to look over my shoulder. "Where's the trusty sidekick?"

"Cass isn't my sidekick." I can't stop the twitching in my eye, and she notices it.

"No, she isn't, is she? We all know who's the brains of the operation. Did you chase her off, too? I guess it was only a matter of time before you actually made it to zero friends."

I clench my fist to stop myself from reaching across the table and ripping her glossy brown hair out at the roots. My nails dig into my palm. I haven't cut them in a while. They're sharp.

"I'm not here to talk about Cass. Tell me what you know."

Her smile widens. Her teeth are so white. So straight. "Honestly, I'm surprised *you* don't know. If anyone loves to insert themselves into other people's business more than I do, it's you."

She's not going to distract me. "Yes, we're all amazed by my ignorance. Now tell me about the fights."

She lets out a dramatic sigh, like I'm ruining her fun. "I know that only the most desperate losers in this school have anything to do with that place. They're trash doing trashy things for money. If Ava was involved, I guess she really did hit rock bottom."

The tight leash I've kept on my temper snaps. I slam my palms down on the table loud enough that Elle jumps, as do a few people at nearby tables. The whispering resumes, louder, but I'm not listening.

"What is the matter with you?" I lean across the table. "A girl died. A girl you knew. Have you surgically removed all the humanity from your body? You can't spare five seconds of decency for a goddamn murder victim?"

Elle blinks at me several times. I'm a wreck, and I'm never going to get anyone in this school to talk to me if I can't get my stupid emotions under control. This is why I let Cass do the talking, if that wasn't already clear enough today.

"They call it the Basement," Elle says.

Wait, what?

She looks down at the table. "I'm not a monster. I get that

it's fucked up Ava died." She shakes her hair out of her face, looking away.

I sink into the chair opposite her. Elle twists the cap on her water bottle. We're both silent for a moment.

Finally, I ask, "Why the Basement?"

"Because it doesn't sound super sketchy, I guess. If your parents read your texts and find out you're going to the Death Dungeon or whatever every week, that's something of a red flag."

I nod, thinking it over. The Basement. It could sound totally innocent. This is the suburbs. Hanging out in someone's basement is one of approximately four things to do in this town.

"When did you first hear about it?" I ask.

"When school started up. I thought it was a rumor at first, but then there were so many people talking about it."

That would make sense. Last summer was when Ava stopped hanging out with Lainie. When she started ignoring me.

Elle adds, "It must pay well, because a lot of people do it. People you wouldn't expect."

I think of what Cass said before, about grudges. "Has it caused any problems? Rifts?"

"There have been some shifting alliances lately."

"What do you mean?"

"Fights at team practices, people storming out of rehearsals, friends not speaking to each other." She slides the diamond pendant on her necklace left and right, considering me. "Here's the thing: money at this school? People never used to notice it, but everyone's finally starting to realize who's a have and who's a have-not. The proletariat is restless, and now they know how to fight."

It's a ridiculous way to put it, but I see her point. Our school sits on the border between Hartsdale and Whitley. Half the kids get brand-new cars the day they turn sixteen. The other half make minimum wage working at the grocery store.

"Okay, so what about Ava?" It still doesn't seem like her to be involved in something like this, but then I feel weird and judgmental for thinking that.

Elle says, "If she was fighting, I never heard about it."

"So who have you heard about?"

Elle looks around the room. "Jack Teller?" She nods to where Jack sits with the gamers and amateur coders, a few tables away. "Processors aren't cheap. Everyone else at that table? Their parents buy them new computers, new graphics cards. Jack wants to go to MIT. Hard to keep up with the latest technology when your single mom is a part-time paralegal.

"And Georgia Felton?" Elle's head swivels toward her new victim, like a snake with the scent of prey on its tongue. "Her father was sentenced to five years in prison for insider trading. All their accounts have been frozen, she's sharing a bedroom with her mom and little brother in some sad apartment, and yet Georgia shows up to school with a new bag from the Gucci fall/winter line?"

Elle turns her attention back to me. A pretty flush has risen in her cheeks, and there's the mad glint of delight in her eyes. For Elle, secrets equal power.

"What about Penn Williams?"

"Well, he did finally score a date with Victoria Ramirez. Her father co-owns a football team. Girl like that, I can see why he might not want to take her out to Sal's for pizza." So Cass was right. She really is a genius.

I consider Elle again. Everything she's said makes sense, but can I really trust Elle Dorsey?

"You could be making all of this up."

"True." She takes a dainty sip of her Diet Coke. "But it's all right there if you bother to look."

"Why are you helping me?"

She folds her hands in front of her on the table. "This fight club thing is upsetting the natural social order of the school. I don't want that, for obvious reasons. But I wasn't lying to you yesterday. If you're after Ava's killer, I think you're going the wrong way."

I lean back. "And why's that?"

Her eyes are sharp and sincere on mine. "Maybe Ava was involved with the fights, maybe she wasn't. But my father has

154

friends on the police force. I've heard the evidence. I know it's all pointing toward a mugging. And I know you, Flora. You'd rather believe in some conspiracy than the sad truth that Ava was in the wrong place at the wrong time. You're trying to play the hero, but it's too late. Ava is already dead."

I flinch, and I know she sees it.

She says, "Whatever you might think, you're one of the few people at this school I don't actively despise. But you walk around broadcasting your inner trauma to the entire world. You obviously care. You should stop that." The pity in Elle's eyes has me ready to scalp her again.

My chair shrieks against the linoleum as I push back from the table. "Thanks for the advice."

I spend the rest of lunch period attempting to corner some of the people Elle pointed out, but no dice.

Jack Teller sees me and immediately walks in the other direction. When I catch up, he seems to have lost the power of speech. I mention what Elle told me, and he darts away into the post-lunch throng before I can stop him.

And Georgia? Yeah, that doesn't go well.

"You're pathetic!" she screams when I ask about her father's legal troubles. "Don't you dare talk about my family." Everyone stares as she spins on her heel and walks away, clutching the Gucci bag tight to her body.

As I walk away, the whispers follow.

"Crazy bitch."

"What a freak—"

"—completely making it up."

Nothing I'm not used to. Besides, the voices in my head are much louder. Cass, telling me to go to the police. Elle, saying I'm trying to be a hero, with that infuriatingly sympathetic tone. Ava wheezing, *Wes Grays*.

I walk faster, plowing into a few people along the way. English is my next class. Cass will be there. I can hear about her audition, let her distract me. Tell her what I heard from Elle.

My locker comes into view, and I freeze. The rest of the people in the hall don't stop. They carry on laughing and chatting and pushing each other around, but I am motionless.

There's a message for me. Scrawled on my locker door with thick black marker pen.

STOP ASKING QUESTIONS.

I look up and down the hall. People stare at me. A few of them smirk and laugh.

Cass's theory isn't totally crazy. Someone in this school could be Ava's killer. If that's true, they might have been standing here just a few moments earlier.

Someone knows I know, and they want me to back off.

The whispers press in close around me.

Or someone knows I'm paranoid as hell, and wants to fuck with me.

I touch the black ink. My fingertip comes away stained purple-gray. It's still fresh.

In the bathroom, I pull out my phone. My hand shakes, and I have to redial the number.

I've been doing this too long to let these people get to me.

I hesitate before hitting the Call button. I know this isn't going to help. If anything, it's going to cause more problems. But Cass had a point. Elle even had a fucking point. It's worth a try.

Don't shut me out.

You're trying to play the hero, but it's too late.

Ava is already dead.

The detective picks up after two rings. "Homicide, this is Richmond."

"Detective, it's Flora Calhoun. I think I have something for you."

"Shouldn't you be in class?"

"Yeah, and the longer I'm on the phone with you, the longer we delay my education. Do you want what I have or not?"

She's quiet for a moment. "I thought we agreed you were staying far away from this case."

"I am," I lie. "I haven't gotten in your way, right?"

She doesn't respond.

I push forward. "Fine, take it or leave it. But you need to go to 4044 West Grace Street. It's this abandoned hospital, but there's illegal fights being held in the basement. I'm not sure if it's happening tonight, but there's gambling, underage drinking, the whole deal."

"And you're telling me this because?"

"I think Ava McQueen might have been involved. Her last words were *Wes Grays*. I think she was trying to tell me the address."

There's a sharp little exhale of frustration. "Flora, I'm not playing this game with you. We are not partners. We are not collaborators on this case. You're a kid, and I'm a cop. You need to stay out of my case, or I *will* make good on those consequences I mentioned."

I knew I would regret this. "All right, I heard you. But will you go check it out? Please?"

Another long pause, then she drops her voice and says,

"I'm busy right now, but I'll see what I can do. Get to class."
Richmond hangs up.

I do want Ava's killer found. I know I come across as some adrenaline-junkie freak, but I want justice. I just wish I believed the cops were capable of that.

CHAPTER 12

I splash some water on my face. The skin under my eyes is paper-thin.

I will make it through the rest of this day.

I leave the bathroom, but the sight of my locker makes me stop dead in my tracks again. This time, it's for a different reason. Static crackles across the top of my scalp. How did he even get into the school?

VT is slouching against the locker next to mine—hands in his pockets, bored eyes at half-mast.

"Figured this one was yours." He tilts his head toward the angry black threat smeared on my locker door.

I tighten my grip on the strap of my bag and march up to him.

"VT."

"Red." The black eye has already faded to a plum-colored stain over his left cheek.

"What do you want?" The low, simmering anger I felt around him last night starts up again. It feels good.

He shrugs one shoulder. "Caught a lead. Wanna play hooky?"

The droning buzz of whispers builds behind me, like a swarm of bored wasps. I glance over my shoulder. Several people are watching. Did one of them write the words on my locker?

"Freak," someone hisses, and a low chuckle ripples up and down the hall.

They've called me much worse before. I don't want them to think anything they say can touch me.

"Where?" I ask VT.

He watches me with keen eyes, not missing a thing. "Where does every good investigation start? The scene of the crime."

All the breath whooshes out of me.

Ava, on the ground. The smell of blood on asphalt. My fingers plugging the hole in her chest.

I grit my teeth and blink the memories away. "Okay. I'm in."

I make sure to text Cass before I leave to see how her audition went and if she wants to come with. She promises to fill me in later but has to stay behind for a French test.

Guess it's just me and this idiot, then.

The second I walk out the front doors of the school, my shoulders relax an inch.

The radio comes alive when he starts the car. Classical. Something by Tchaikovsky. Huh. And it's a CD, not the radio. Every new piece of information I get about this guy only makes him harder to figure out.

We park down the block from our destination, but I don't get out of the car. By the entrance to the alley, a tattered strip of crime scene tape flutters half-heartedly on the ground. I can't make myself move.

"All right, Cherry?" VT asks. "This too much for you?"

I know he's trying to piss me off, and it works. I get out of the car.

The alley looks so ordinary in the light of day. A couple of garbage cans tucked against one wall. The tacky smears of old gum on the ground. The smell of urine, road dust, and fast food.

But there, in the back left corner: a brown stain, about two feet wide. It looks almost innocent in the bright gray March light, like it could be oil or rust. But I know better.

Every hair on my body stands straight up. I close my eyes and breathe through my nose.

"Sure you're okay?"

I open my eyes to glare at him, but the mocking challenge from before has been replaced by real concern.

VT. Valentine. I can't help but think of them as the two sides of him. The sly drawl. That soft look in his eyes. I can't figure out where one ends and the other begins.

Honestly, that's more confusing than I can deal with right now.

"Fine," I mumble. "Just getting my bearings."

I walk the length of the alley twice. Open both trash cans, but they must have collected the garbage earlier today. Nothing inside but a few soda cans and what looks like a bag of dog poop.

Brick buildings loom tall on either side. The only windows are the long, narrow kind with frosted glass, like each apartment was built with its bathroom facing this way. Convenient place to murder someone. Witnesses are unlikely.

VT leans against the wall, spinning a cigarette between his fingers. The feel of his eyes on me is more than a little bit distracting.

I trace my finger over a chip in the brick wall. At its center is an almost perfectly round hole, surrounded by a crater of brittle, crumbling edges. Another hole comes to mind, this one in soft, delicate skin. Blood oozes out of it, slower and slower as Ava's heartbeat falters. I swallow down the sticky, warm thing that climbs up my throat.

I force my gaze to the bloodstain again. It's rippled and faded, like someone tried to wash it away. I'm probably imagining it, but I swear there are two lighter patches where my knees would have been.

"What're you thinking, Red?" I jump when his warm breath scrapes against the back of my neck.

Maybe this was a mistake. Coming here has my brain all scrambled.

"I don't know," I force myself to answer. "Nothing stands out. Why did you bring me here?"

He shrugs and lights his cigarette. "Figured you should get another look at the crime scene. Fresh eyes, light of day, that sort of thing."

"But you said you had a lead," I insist.

He takes a long drag. "A lead? Well, I don't know. I looked into this place, though. This block alone has had six counts of armed robbery within the last four months, plus a dozen car thefts and a sprinkling of larceny for flavor."

"What are you saying?" He told me he had something, and now he's backpedaling.

He squints at me. "You so sure it's *not* a mugging?"

I stare at that bullet hole in the wall again, but now I notice others, scattered across the length of the alley. Too many to all have been from Ava's killer.

Maybe he's right. Maybe everyone's right. It could be a coincidence, I guess, that Ava had a connection to this super-dangerous fight club and now she's dead. Other kids from school are involved, and none of them got shot in an alleyway.

VT watches me as the doubt creeps in. I watch him right back, trying to pick apart his unreadable expression. I can't shake the sense that he's trying to push me away from my investigation.

"Why?" I ask.

"Why what?" He fidgets under my gaze, reaching for his pack of cigarettes before remembering he already has one lit.

"Why bring me here?" I step closer. "Don't lie. What are you really after?"

He rolls his eyes. "What, you're so determined for there to be some conspiracy, now I'm part of it?"

I won't let him shake me off. "Why do you want me to believe that Ava's death was an accident? What do you know?" I move closer still.

He doesn't back down. We're nearly nose to nose. "A girl wanders down a dark alleyway at night, gets shot, wallet missing. I was never much for math, but I can do my two-plus-two with the best of 'em."

My arm coils tight with the urge to slap him.

I step back, away from the mad, violent impulse. "We might as well go if you're not going to be helpful."

"Look at this place." He gestures back into the alley. "See that?" He points to an opening on the right side, about halfway between the two street entrances. "They're all interconnected, these little alleys. This one feeds into the next and the next. Prime real estate for pickpockets. People think they're shortcuts, or they come out here to empty their trash, and some kid in a hoodie can snag their wallet and run off without ever getting spotted on the road. A perfect getaway path, made for criminals."

I stare at the opening. I didn't think much of it before. I take a few steps forward to see where it leads. It's another alley, nearly identical to the first.

I keep walking. Down the next alley there's another turn, and another. They all feed into each other, just like he said.

Jogging footsteps behind me. "What is it?" VT asks. I ignore him.

My pace picks up, excitement itching in the soles of my feet, until I'm practically running.

He's right. It's the perfect getaway route.

I turn left and come up short at a dead end. VT is a few paces behind me, but he keeps his mouth shut.

The other end of the alley feeds into the street, where cars and taxis blur past. I look out onto the road. We're fewer than ten blocks from the crime scene, but this is already a more populated part of town. A woman with tall boots and big headphones barely glances my way as she walks by.

The killer must have come through here. I have no way to know that for sure without a witness, but they'd want to stay off the streets for as long as possible. Which means that just a few nights ago, Ava's murderer might have been standing in this exact spot.

There's a dumpster pushed against one wall. I finger the plastic lid, testing it. It's not chained.

VT can't keep quiet any longer. "Oh, what now?"

I flip the top up, brace my hands on either side, and jump into the dumpster.

VT blinks at me. "You know, you are not who I thought you would be."

I survey the garbage. I don't know what I'm looking for, but I'm pissed, and I have to do *something*. The bags shift beneath my feet, hissing out putrid clouds of trash gas. I teeter on the unsteady surface.

I start to open one bag, then pause to pull on the black leather gloves I keep in my backpack. It's unlikely that there's anything in here, but I don't want to contaminate any evidence with my prints.

"Come on, Cherry, get out of there. You're being ridiculous." VT extends his hand to help me down. I ignore him.

Inside the first bag is what looks like the contents of a kitchen trash can, all moldy food and takeout containers. The smell is delightful. I tie the knot off and set it to the side. The next one is more of the same.

VT keeps up the running commentary as I sort, but the whole world has fallen away now that I have a job. Some unidentifiable orange fluid leaks out of one bag, staining the sleeve of my coat, but I don't care. I must look like a manic demon, tossing garbage this way and that. My scalp is sweaty and my hair sticks to my face. I am high on trash fumes.

I open another bag. This one holds a bunch of papers. I reach inside and pull a few out. Xeroxes, all kind of faded and wobbly. The rejects. I flip through. They're flyers, all the same: DORSEY FOR SENATE.

My vision sharpens.

I interrupt VT. "Look out on the street for me. What kinds of businesses are on either side of us?"

"Why?"

"Do it!" There's a serrated edge to my voice that makes him fall quiet. VT walks out to the sidewalk and looks around. There's a flicker of recognition in his eyes, like he spotted something familiar, but then it's gone.

He comes back. "On our right"—he points with his thumb—"we have FedEx and Thai food. And left"—he points in the other direction, toward the wall that the dumpster is pushed up against—"a laundromat and the Dorsey for Senate campaign headquarters."

I suck in a breath. Congressman James Dorsey. Elle Dorsey's dad. He's the congressional representative for Hartsdale and part of Whitley, but he's running for a Senate seat this year. I am standing in his dumpster.

"What is it?" VT steps closer.

I hand him the stack of flyers without a word.

He glances through them, and there's that flicker of familiarity again, but then he tosses the papers back into the dumpster.

"So what? Some local politician has a campaign office a few blocks from the site of a murder? Yeah, too strange to be a coincidence."

He's right, of course. There's nothing inherently suspicious about any of this. But didn't Ava have one of his flyers in her papers? Then again, she used to do that kind of thing all the time—canvass, volunteer at campaign events.

I look down. There's garbage juice leaking on my sneakers. What the hell am I doing? It's a dumpster in the middle of the city. Even assuming the killer did come through here, they what? Paused for a sec to throw out their Big Gulp? I need to get it together.

I'm ready to not be standing in garbage anymore. I kick the bag under my feet out of the way so I can jump out.

That's when I see it: a wallet, tucked underneath all the garbage bags. It's the long, skinny kind, made of mint-green leather.

VT peers over the edge. His eyebrows shoot up when he spots the wallet. Standing on my mountain of trash, I tower over him a little, and when we make eye contact there's something curious in his expression.

I pick up the wallet. Its gold zipper is tarnished with something purple and sticky. Inside, everything is shoved in haphazardly, wherever it will fit.

There's a thick wad of cash. I count it out: nearly a thousand dollars. Who would throw out this much money?

Frowning, I look through the other contents. A punch card from a local coffee shop. A bus pass.

A driver's license.

I nearly drop everything.

Ava's face smiles up at me from her ID photo. It's a pretty good shot, not sullen and angsty like my own. She clearly dressed up to have her picture taken, red lipstick and all.

My heart pounds. This is it. My proof that I'm not some crazy, paranoid freak.

VT's waiting for answers. I turn the ID so he can see it.

"That's the girl," he says slowly.

When I can breathe again, I say, "So how come her mugger didn't care about all this cash?"

The world is incredibly bright, like the sun came out. I'm standing in a literal dumpster, leftover Thai food pooling around my feet, but I have one of those rare feelings where you know you're exactly where you're supposed to be. It's not happiness, but rightness.

VT looks up at me again. There's a deep crease between his eyebrows. He nods once to himself like he's made a decision, only I don't know what about.

"How do you feel about meatball subs?" he asks.

Not where I thought this was going. "Um, good?"

"Let's eat. We have some stuff to talk about."

CHAPTER 13

This time, I take VT's offered hand and hop out of the dumpster. My balance wobbles a bit on the landing, and for a second we're startlingly close.

He doesn't let go of my hand. My eyes fall on the perfect Cupid's bow of his mouth. I am holding my dead ex-almost-girlfriend's wallet in my other hand. Still, he doesn't let go.

Then: "You smell delightful, Cherry."

I jerk my hand away. "Well, one of us had to get our hands dirty. If it were up to you, we'd be nowhere with nothing right now."

VT leads the way to some sandwich shop he knows. I keep at least a foot of distance between us as we walk.

I was really starting to doubt myself, thinking maybe the police had it right after all and I was seeing ghosts. Finding Ava's wallet confirms what I've thought all along: someone murdered her, then set it up to look like she was mugged. So what's the real reason they killed her?

Valentine bumps me with his shoulder. "Stop thinking about it. You need food, time to think. It's not going to make sense yet."

It's like he's a totally different guy from the one who got in a screaming match with me in the alley.

"What are you doing?" I ask. "Why are you being all *nice* now?"

He slips a chummy arm around my shoulder. "Are you always this suspicious of everyone? Can't a guy take his girl out for lunch?"

I poke him in the side hard enough that he's forced to let go. "Let's be perfectly clear: this is not a date. You need my permission for this to be a date." He holds his hands up in defense but backs off. I straighten the collar of my coat where he rumpled it.

After collecting our sandwiches from some greasy hole-in-the-wall, VT leads me to a park a few blocks over. It's one of those sunny, early spring afternoons where you can almost convince yourself the warmth is here to stay, even though you know it could snow again tomorrow.

We sit on the grass near a big tree. As usual, finding a big lead like the wallet has me ravenous, and for a few minutes I can ignore the intense way VT is still *staring* at me while I scarf down the most delicious meatball parm of my life.

Until he sets his sandwich down and leans back on his hands. "Tell me why."

"Why what?" I ask, but my appetite has disappeared. I put my sandwich down, too.

"You know what."

I pick at a clump of grass. "I thought you knew me so well. 'Some dark tale of woe,' remember?"

He narrows his eyes. "That's it, then? A friend of yours got hurt? Killed?"

The leftover taste of marinara sauce turns sour on my tongue. I haven't talked about Lucy, not really, in about two years. Cass used to try, but I developed this nasty habit of breaking whatever I was holding, and eventually she stopped.

With everything going on right now, I'm not sure how much longer I can outrun my past. And there's something about VT. I don't really know him at all, but I have this weird feeling our demons are a matching set.

I'm not sure if that makes me trust him more, or less.

I chew my lip. "I'll show you mine if you show me yours?"

He takes his time to think it over, like it's a big decision for him, too. He nods once.

Okay, then. I guess we're doing this. It's a bit like skydiving, not that I've ever been. You close your eyes and jump.

I keep my eyes on the ground. It's easier if I don't look at him, but it still takes me a while to make the words come out.

"I used to be a runner. Around two years ago, there was this heat wave. I was doing my runs early, before it got too hot. The sun was barely up, but it must have been ninety degrees that morning."

Something dark swirls in my gut, and I swallow a few times. "It was the smell I noticed first. Blood. I came around a bend in the trail, and there was this red *thing* in the middle of the path." I close my eyes. I was soaked with sweat, my heart pounding from the run, then from terror. "It took me a minute to realize it was a person. A girl, maybe, but what he'd done to her face..." I breathe through my nose and look at the sky. "I didn't find out until later, when the police arrived: I knew her. Her name was Lucy MacDonald."

Valentine inhales. He remembers the name. Lucy was all over the news for a time.

I pluck a blade of grass from the ground and tie it into a knot. "You were wrong about one thing—she wasn't a friend. Lucy was a bully. Everyone hated her. She didn't deserve what happened to her, though." My voice cracks.

I toss my blade of grass aside. "Anyway, maybe you know the rest, but the press turned on Lucy. She'd been dating this rich older guy in New York City. Matt Caine." I hate that even now, more than two years later, I still tremble saying his name.

"Her parents thought she was working as a junior leader at a summer youth program, but she was actually clubbing and taking a bunch of Molly with this guy.

"Caine's lawyers painted this picture of Lucy as some unhinged stalker. They leaked these horrible photos of her high and hooking up with him and his friends. It became this whole slut-shaming, 'Where were the parents?,' 'She should have been more careful' victim-blaming situation. It made me so angry."

I never lost it, that rage. I don't know if I ever will. Even talking about it now, I feel like my bones could shake apart with fury.

That was the thing about Lucy. The sight of her body changed me forever, but that's not what broke me. It was the way everyone turned their backs, how easily they could convince themselves that Lucy deserved it, that *they* would never make such bad decisions.

I glance up. Valentine's looking at me like he knows that kind of anger, too.

My voice is a bit stronger now. "I couldn't drop it. The more I looked, the more I was convinced about Caine, but then I turned on the news one day and he was walking out of the Whitley police precinct. Smiling." A nerve pulses in my jaw. "That was when I knew: it didn't matter that he'd bashed her face in. It didn't matter that the police had smelled all that blood, too. Nobody was going to do anything about it."

I pick at a hangnail until it bleeds. "I didn't really know what I was doing, though. I got arrested breaking into his apartment."

"You *what?*" Valentine interrupts for the first time.

"He was supposed to be on vacation. It was stupid. *I* was stupid." I keep peeling the strip of skin from my cuticle. The tiny pain is terrible, but it's not as bad as my memories. "He opened the door right as I was digging through his desk." I bite down on the inside of my cheek. "He didn't even seem surprised. I couldn't move. He was blocking the door, and I kept thinking: *Run. Run. Run!* But I froze."

I feel at once tuned in to the world around me and very far away. I can hear Valentine's breathing and a truck passing on the road. I can smell Matt Caine's aftershave.

I still remember every heartbeat of that moment. Matt Caine walked closer, and I didn't move. His eyes ran up and down my body. He talked about Lucy. He never came right out and said it, but he wanted me to know that he'd been the one to crush her face like that. He reached out, and I still didn't move. He patted me on the shoulder. I was wearing a tank top. He touched my bare skin, soft like a caress, and the spell broke. I ran.

"I got around him," I tell Valentine. "He didn't chase me. I could hear him laughing as I ran out the door. I was halfway across the city before I'd even blinked. The cops picked me up somewhere on the Lower East Side. Matt Caine had reported a break-in."

Valentine leans toward me, his eyes dark.

I'm drained. It's an effort to get the rest out. "It all kind of blew up at that point. I had to go to court. Caine took out a restraining order. All that stuff is going on my college application one day." I try a laugh, but it comes out flat. "My mom left. It was supposedly a work thing, but we all knew the truth—she just couldn't handle me anymore. And my grandfather made me drop Lucy's case. Once I got arrested, he said that was it. If I wanted to do this sort of thing, I couldn't afford to be a child about it, and it was childish to think I was going to get Caine at that point.

"But people at school had heard what I did, and they started coming to me with cases." I pluck another piece of grass from the earth and curl it around my fingertip. "Nothing like this, though. Not since Lucy."

I tie my blade of grass in a pretty little bow and toss it aside. Any second now, he'll tell me I'm crazy, that I need to move on with my life. Learn to deal. That's what everyone else thinks, after all. That's what the fear in my grandfather's eyes was about this morning. Why Cass has been skeptical about my theories. I know they both think I'm reliving Lucy.

He takes a deep breath and says, "All right, then. What story do you want? The big one?"

Thank you, weird boy I just met.

I shrug. "I gave you mine—seems fair."

He looks away. Sighs. Rolls his shoulders back. Clenches and unclenches his jaw. All the classics.

He lets out a short, bitter laugh. "You know, I really couldn't believe it when you guessed. I mean, I knew you were good right off the bat. You did your whole Sherlock bit, guessing at my life, half right here, half wrong there, and then you threw it in at the end, like a joke. I almost bit off my own tongue."

I have no idea what he's talking about. I wait.

He looks straight at me with defiant eyes. "Little over a year ago, I was a freshman at Juilliard. Dance program."

I'm stunned. The dancer thing *was* a joke.

He leans back on his palms and scowls at the sky. "You were close enough about dear old Dad. I'll spare you the details. Mean to me, to my sister. Absolutely vicious to my mother. And who was I to defend them? A weakling, like you said."

I didn't say that, not exactly, but my heart aches with guilt anyway.

He sniffs and picks at a hole in the knee of his jeans.

"Annabelle protected me, like a good sister should. She baby-sat to pay for my dance lessons so he'd never have to know. 'Course he found out and beat us both, but she wouldn't let me quit. He'd find out and fly into one of his rages. Drink, forget, find out all over again, whale on us.

"But the look on Annabelle's face when I got the letter from Juilliard. It was like nothing I'd ever felt, seeing her smile like that. Almost made it worth it. All the bruises. All the broken bones.

"So I left, and for about a second, I was happy. I was out. Dancing wasn't this dark, shameful thing anymore. I remember the feeling of leaping onstage. Straight up in the air. It's joy, you know? To throw yourself into the sky like that. Exultation. People yelling for you. Clapping." With closed eyes, he tilts his face into the sun, and I can almost see what he must have looked like airborne. Free.

He opens his eyes. "Didn't go home much, not even for Annie. He was half dead at that point, but it didn't matter. Couldn't bear to go back to that rotting hole. Didn't think about how hard it was for *her*. After all he'd done to them, they had to change his sheets, spoon his food, wipe his ass. How that must have killed her. How angry she must have been. I never thought about any of that.

"They came to visit me that spring, Mom and Annabelle.

It was my big show. The only first-year student with a solo. I was so arrogant. They loved me at school. I was the youngest in my class, only seventeen. Graduated high school early to go. Teachers couldn't stop talking about how talented I was. Other kids asked for tutorials. I was high on it."

There's a long pause, and I know we've arrived. The terrible part. The part that broke him.

Unlike me, he doesn't look away. He lets me see it. The fury, the hatred, the anguish. I don't avert my eyes.

"They came to see me. We lived around here, it wasn't far, but things at home made it hard for them to come into the city much. Only, they never quite made it. Nasty accident on I-95. A truck. An explosion. Fire." A violent tremor overtakes him, but he fights it off with gritted teeth. "They burned alive in the car."

He pulls out a cigarette. I wait.

When he speaks again, his voice is flat and controlled. "So that was it for me. No more dancing. I dropped out of school. Joined the circus, of all things."

I can't help myself. "Shut the fuck up."

He snorts. "I was such a romantic. A fool. Run away with the circus. Find myself." He rolls his eyes. "But I could dance, and I learned the tightrope and acrobatics quick enough. On our off nights, we'd get hammered and fight, so I learned that, too. I traveled around the country, leaping from the trapeze on the weekends and falling out of my bed drunk on the week-nights." He pauses. Opens his mouth to say something else, then snaps it shut. Finally: "I lasted six months before I got bored. Friend of mine knew a guy in Whitley running underground fights, said it was decent money, I could choose when I worked. So I came back home."

We stare at each other, both spent.

I didn't think he'd be honest with me. That he'd tell me this much. I didn't think I'd be that honest with him, either. I didn't mean to be.

Can't take it back now.

CHAPTER 14

Valentine drops me off at home. With him gone, I feel scooped out. Empty, but painfully so.

Talking about all that old stuff didn't make me feel better. Not like people always say it will. It feels like someone took a bread knife to my insides, and now my guts are raw and ragged.

I drag myself up the stairs. Low murmuring voices are coming from Olive's room. One of them sounds like Mom. Must be time for her weekly check-in with Olive.

In my room, I drop my stuff and flop facedown on the bed. Eyes closed, I see again that look on Valentine's face. Tilted to the sun. Remembering what it felt like to fly through the air.

I can see him so much more clearly now, and to be honest, it doesn't look good. This awful, ugly thing happened to him, and now he's like the halogen group on the periodic table. We learned about this in chem last week—one electron shy of eight, so they can't help but react with everything. Always combusting, or whatever. The thing is, I'm pretty combustible myself.

Okay, so my metaphors need work. I'm exhausted.

A knock on my door. I roll over to see Olive standing in my room.

"Mom wants to talk to you." She holds her phone out to me.

I search Olive's face, watching for any signs of resentment. Here I am, stealing her spotlight again. Cutting into her mommy-daughter time. But there's nothing there except maybe awkward sympathy.

"Hi, honey!" Mom's overchipper voice, tinny and wobbly, comes through the speaker.

Olive gives me a look, asking silently if I want her to stay and be my emotional buffer.

I shake my head. I have to face this alone. She hands me the phone and leaves.

"Hey, Mom." I perch on the edge of my bed, muster a weak smile, and hold the phone out so I'm within the camera frame.

My mom is sitting at her kitchen table, a mug of tea in one hand. Her eyes trace over my face, taking me in, looking for clues. Signs of how fucked up I am today. She does it every time we have one of these calls, even when there's no murder investigation going on.

I do my own examination. She looks happy. Her cheeks are rosy, her hair is tied up in a sloppy bun, and she has a smear of blue paint on her cheek. There's no way she doesn't know it's there, so she must have seen it and decided it looks cute. It does.

"Baby, how are you?" Her eyes go big and sad with gooey maternal concern, but it feels overexaggerated. Like she's trying to compensate for the distance.

"I'm fine."

The skin around her mouth tightens at the obvious lie, but she doesn't push it. Of course not.

"How was school?" She moves right along.

Well, I missed half of it to go dumpster diving with a violent street fighter who's as mentally unstable as I am, but...

"It was okay."

"How's that history paper going?"

I stare at her blankly. History paper? Did I forget to hand something in?

And then I pick up the thread again. Right. History paper. On the first Red Scare. I mentioned it last time we talked in an attempt to fill one of those long silent spells.

If that's any measure, I haven't spoken to Mom in at least three weeks.

Video chat was one of the cornerstones of Mom's propaganda mission before she left. *In this day and age, with modern technology, you'll hardly notice I'm gone! It'll be like I'm right there in the room with you.*

I hated her then. I don't think either one of us can remember the last time we really got along. Even before Lucy, it was always like we were speaking different dialects of the same language. Just different enough that we got the gist but never fully understood each other. But those weeks before she left for Germany, that was the first time I truly *hated* her. I hated that she could pretend nothing would be different, when of course everything had already changed.

When Lucy died, it was like I was seeing the world for the first time. The violent, horrible truth of it. All Mom wanted was to go back to Before, but I couldn't.

I hated her for the lies more than I ever hated her for leaving.

"I got a 90," is all I say.

Mom gives me an encouraging smile. "That's so great, sweetie."

Another long silence. The little thumbnail image of my face in the bottom of the screen is distracting. Even shrunk down to an inch tall, I look tired.

Two minutes into this call, and Mom hasn't mentioned Ava. It's the last thing I want to talk about, especially with her, but the dishonesty of it fills me with poisonous rage.

I swallow it down. "How's the gallery show coming?"

Her smile grows warm and genuine as she tells a probably humorous story about misplaced paintings, art world intrigue, and German hijinks. I nod and go *hmm* in all the appropriate places.

These days, she looks so young, so pretty. She was only twenty when she had me. She and Olive share the same delicate, rosy kind of beauty. They're a matched set in family photos. I always look like a scrawny goblin, eyes too big for my face, sulking at the edges of pictures.

Going to Germany was good for her. I can see that, and I hate myself for resenting her.

A long pause. Shit, I've missed one of my cues. The good humor leaves her eyes, and she's back to evaluating me with concern.

"I miss you," she says, finally. I don't think she's lying. I'm sure she does miss me, but that's because she can only like me from four thousand miles away. "I want you and Olive to come visit again this summer." She launches into a long description of her neighborhood, and her face is animated and cheerful again. She'd love so badly to bring her two girls on a summer adventure in Berlin. Laugh together in the shops. Show us the work she's making. Let us drink a glass of wine at dinner, sometimes. Hop a train to Paris or Amsterdam.

I can see it so clearly, this adventure we could all have together. Or really, I can see Olive and Mom and some other girl. Prettier. Better rested. Cracking sarcastic jokes. All the wit with none of the snarl. Her idealized version of me.

It hurts that a part of me wants it. Wants to be that Flora. The if-only girl. The could-have-been.

Mom's telling me about a museum she wants to take us to that used to be a Nazi bunker turned gay nightclub. As usual, she doesn't notice the existential crisis I'm having.

I cut her off. "Listen, Mom, I gotta run."

She stops midsentence, confusion turning to hurt. "Oh, okay—"

"Olive needs something," I lie.

That sad, burdened look settles on her face. "Okay, honey. Well, uh, I love you, and I miss you. Please be careful, okay?" She gives me a wide-eyed, meaningful *look*. That's it. All of the acknowledgment she can manage.

"Uh-huh. I will. Good luck with the gallery stuff. Send pictures. Love you, bye." I hang up before she can say another word.

I take a shuddering breath.

"You okay?"

Olive's standing in my room again.

"Who knows?" I say, which is a little more honest than I mean to be. Seems to be a theme today.

Olive smiles. "I think I have something that'll cheer you up." She hesitates. "But you have to promise not to be mad, okay?"

Well, that's not suspicious at all. "I am 100 percent not promising you that."

She stamps her foot in a way that makes her look exactly thirteen. "Flora!"

"Show me what it is, and then we can negotiate how angry I am."

She wars with herself for another second, then relents. "Fine. But I think I did pretty good, and I expect the appropriate amount of gratitude in return. Come here."

I follow her into her bedroom, and Olive pulls out her computer. She angles it toward herself so I can't see. It's almost cute, but I hold back my comments about her ridiculous cloak-and-dagger behavior.

Olive types a few things in. "Okay. I think your first impulse is going to be anger, but in the long run you'll see that this is an awesome and useful thing I've accomplished."

I won't lie, the suspense is starting to get to me, but I call upon the DNA I inherited from my grandfather and attempt to look cool and detached.

She says, "I hacked into the police evidence database."

"You did *what*?" So much for detached.

It all comes out of her in one rushed breath. "I was at Zoe's house after school, and then I remembered that Zoe's mom works for the district attorney, so I told Zoe I had to go to the bathroom but instead I went in her mom's office to see if I could find anything for you, and I got all her log-in information."

She is way too pleased with herself. Part of me is her big sister and wants to crush that smug little smile off her face, and part of me is super impressed. She can never, ever know about that part.

She must be reading my mind because she says, "Oh, come on. This is cool. You don't have to fake it."

I cross my arms. "You could get in huge trouble for this, and you know I'll be the one to take the blame."

She waves me off. "I was totally careful! I assumed they would have extra security, so I did some research before I logged in. I guess it sets off all these red flags if you sign on from somewhere besides the police precinct, so I've spent the last couple hours learning how to fake an IP address." I scowl at her, and she mutters, "It's not that hard. You can find tutorials for anything on YouTube."

I hold out for another three seconds before I sit down beside her on the bed. "Show me."

She navigates through the directory. "This has all the

evidence for the entire state of New York, so you can use it on future cases, too."

"Yeah, if the FBI doesn't bust us."

"This is totally not their jurisdiction," she says, and I grab a fistful of her comforter to stop myself from shoving her off the bed.

Olive opens Ava's file, and I scoot in closer. There are a few reports that detail the evidence from the scene, plus interviews with several people in the area, including me.

Our breathing syncs as we skim through the interview transcripts, but just as I suspected, no one saw anything that night.

"How is that possible?" Olive frowns at the screen. "There were gunshots and everything, but no one came to look?"

I shrug. "The killer chose the location well. I was there today. No windows with a line of sight onto the alley."

Olive looks at me sideways. "That sounds pretty carefully planned for a random mugging."

It feels good not to be the only conspiracy nut for once. Must be in the Calhoun blood.

Olive is only saying what I've been thinking. That Ava's death was no accident. It was planned, premeditated. And then covered up to look like a robbery gone wrong.

I try to imagine what kind of person could pull that off. It's not that I think Cass is definitely wrong; I watch the news—kids kill each other all the time. But Olive's right: it's such a well-thought-out plan. Ava's murderer has done an excellent job of convincing almost everyone that her death was nothing more than a random act of violence.

I know Matt Caine has me biased. It's easy for me to believe that a powerful older man killed Ava, that this is all tied up in some intricate web of corruption, but I have to be more careful this time. I need proof, and I don't have it yet.

Then again, if there's one thing I learned from Lucy's murder, it's that the world is a fucked up place, and the people who benefit most from that are people like Matt Caine and Congressman James Dorsey.

Olive clicks back to the main menu. There's another folder for photos. Her mouse hesitates over it.

"Are you ready?" She asks so gently, it makes me feel like *I'm* the little sister.

I already went back to the crime scene today. I talked about Lucy, really talked about her, for the first time in years. I can do this.

I nod.

Olive pulls up the first photo. I don't think either one of us is breathing.

The first few are from the scene. By the looks of the light, they were taken in the early dawn hours, after Gramps and I left. A photo of the entrance to the alley, cordoned off with yellow crime scene tape. The pool of Ava's blood, still fresh and glistening, not yet the unidentifiable brown stain I stared at this afternoon. More blood splattered around the scene, each stray droplet neatly numbered with one of those yellow placards.

I breathe through my nose. I can feel Olive watching me out of the corner of her eye. I'm okay. I was there earlier today. I've seen all of this already.

Olive clicks on the next picture, and I stop breathing.

This one was taken in the morgue. Ava is lying on her back. Someone closed her eyes. Her shoulders are bare, but there's a sheet pulled over her chest. The lighting is cold and sterile, emphasizing the gray lifelessness of her face.

Olive's voice is small. "Is that what she looked like when you found her?"

My vision goes soft around the edges. "She was still alive when I found her."

Olive hesitates, then continues clicking through the pictures. A close-up of Ava's face. She's still wearing the same winged eyeliner she had on that day at school. The left side is a little higher than the right. A shot of the bullet wounds. Two close together, one about six inches up. They wiped away the excess blood, and now all that's left are congealed red holes.

The surrounding skin is covered with a scattering of purplish brown dots, almost like freckles. It's called tattooing, from the gunpowder.

"Then again"—Olive's voice is shaky, but determined, like she's trying to prove she can do this with me—"three bullet holes, scattered all over her chest so she didn't die right away, that doesn't seem like this person knew what they were doing. Right? Isn't that, like, an amateur thing when the gunshots are all random?"

I'm underwater, and she's calling down to me from the surface. I can't move, can't blink, can't do anything but stare at the holes the killer blasted through Ava's body. They're not large. Smaller than a quarter. They still killed her, though.

Olive's shoulder brushes mine. We're on our stomachs on her bed. We could almost be a catalog spread for sparkly tween clothing or maxipads, if not for the grisly pictures on the screen.

I spring off the bed. "I can't do this."

Olive looks at me with concern. "Do you need a break? I can make us soup or something."

"No, I can't do this with you. At all."

"Did I do something wrong?"

"I can't look at pictures of murder victims with my little sister! You're getting all involved, and you shouldn't be."

"That's completely unfair." Olive stands. "You do this kind of stuff all the time. What difference does it make if I help?"

"You're going to get in trouble, or hurt, or I don't know, like, grow up too fast or something. I don't want that for you." I turn for the door.

She steps in my path. "Well, that's not really your choice, is it?"

"Yeah, it is. I'm the older sister. I make the calls for both of us, and I don't want you to turn into me. I'm enough of a disaster for the whole family, trust me."

She rolls her eyes. "Oh, my God, you are so self-centered! Look around, my life has already changed." Olive enunciates like I'm very dumb. "Mom is gone, and I get that it was her choice and it's not your fault, but you're still the reason she left. Everyone at school knows who my sister is, and not in a good way. Today I got pushed to the ground playing *touch* football in PE, all because I told Dan Maeller to shut his stupid mouth about you."

I don't know who Dan Maeller is, but he's dead. "I'll deal with him. Tell me when people say stuff, and I'll deal with them."

"That's not the point! If everything's going to change anyway, I might as well have a say in it!"

It's an uncomfortable echo of my thoughts earlier. The way Mom treated me after Lucy died, like everything could go on the same as before.

But every second, I inch a little closer to completely falling apart. I can barely take care of myself, and now I'm going to drag Olive into this?

I don't like disappointing her, but it's better this way. Safer.

"I'm sorry," I tell her. "I can't."

The coffee maker trills. Upstairs, I can hear Olive slamming around in her room. She's pissed, and she has a right to be. I know I overreacted. I should apologize, but my heart is still racing and I can't get the image of Ava's lifeless face out of my mind.

I watch fresh coffee stream into the pot below. In the front hall, our mail slot grinds open. Something drops into the house with a soft *thwack,* and I pause.

Our mail usually comes around eleven in the morning. It's almost four now.

I leave the kitchen to investigate. There's an unmarked manila envelope lying on the floor in the hall, illuminated by a square patch of sunlight. I pick it up. Nothing on the other side, either. No stamp, no address, no name.

It has to be for me. Sketchy, anonymous manila envelopes are standard accessories for the Flora Calhoun action figure.

I slip my finger along the front flap of the envelope, loosening the glue, and slide the contents out. Photos.

The first one is of me leaving school yesterday. I'm leaning against the stone wall out front, waiting for Cass. I can just make out Elle Dorsey's shoulder at the right edge of the frame.

The next was taken today. I'm standing in the mouth of the alleyway where Ava died. VT's leaning against the wall to my left, but he's slightly out of focus, like the camera lens was locked in right on me.

The last one is a shot through my bedroom window. I'm putting my hair up before I go to bed.

There's a buzzing in my ears. Something hot and tight winds around my throat.

Someone is watching me.

I throw open the door. I look up and down the street, but of course there's no one around.

I keep inhaling but I can't get any air. My chest expands and contracts but I'm drowning. I'm still standing in the open doorway. Someone could be watching me from the house across the street, or that blue car parked down the block. I step back inside, slamming the door and locking it behind me. I clutch the photos to my chest hard enough that they start to crumple.

They're just pictures. If some asshole from school can write a threat on my locker just to mess with my head, couldn't they also have taken these? This feels different, though.

Three long, slow breaths. I have to pull myself together. Olive is still moving around upstairs. She could come down at any moment. I don't want her to find me like this, wild with terror, collapsed against the front door.

I flick through the photos again, trying to see them more objectively this time.

The one from the alley is taken at a slight angle. The photographer was behind me and a little to the right. I close my eyes and try to re-create the street in my mind. I don't remember seeing any other people, but there were a few cars parked on that road. Three, maybe four. It's not like I was writing down license plates or anything, though.

I flip to the one through my bedroom window. It must have been taken last night. I'm wearing the sweatshirt I changed into after I got home from the Basement. It was nearly five in the morning. The angle is down low, like the photographer was shooting from a parked car on the street.

The doorbell rings, and my heart stops. I straighten and, slowly, every inch of me shaking, peer through the peephole.

Cass is standing on my front steps. I choke out something halfway between a laugh and a sob, my nervous system shot to shit. Her overnight bag is slung over her shoulder. She's fighting to contain a small, secret smile, like she had an impossibly good afternoon.

I reach for the doorknob, but the photos are still in my hand.

She probably came over to tell me all about her audition. If I show these photos to her, the terror I am barely holding back right now will swallow me completely, and Cass will get sucked in, too. Isn't that what she said yesterday? *If you're going through hell, I'm coming with you.*

Through the peephole, I watch as she tucks a loose strand of hair behind her ear, that giddy smile still playing at the corners of her mouth, her cheeks flushed and rosy with happiness.

She rings the doorbell again.

Olive yells down, "Are you going to get that or not?" Footsteps. She's walking out of her room and into the hall.

"It's for me!" My backpack is still lying where I dropped it under the coatrack. I grab it, shove the photos inside, take one last deep breath, and open the door.

"Hey!" It comes out a little breathless.

Cass frowns. "You okay?"

"Yeah, sorry, just woke up from a nap." I yawn for effect. Cass only looks more suspicious. "You want coffee? I just made some." I leave the door open and walk into the kitchen.

Cass follows me. I can feel the questions radiating off her, but I make myself busy grabbing two mugs out of the cabinet. I pull milk and that disgusting vanilla creamer we only keep around for Cass out of the fridge. I stir and hand her the mug. Her worried gaze is heavy on my back as we tromp up the stairs to my room.

The coffee is already working its magic, calming me down as I take the first sips. We sit on my bed, backs against the wall. Cass watches me over the rim of her mug the whole time.

She starts, "Are you—"

I cut her off. "Haven't been sleeping much." She nods, full of understanding that makes me feel sick about lying to her. But if I think about the photos again—the totally at ease, safe-in-my-own-home look on my face as I pulled my hair into a ponytail before bed—I might come apart at the seams.

And I really do want to hear about her audition. It's one of, like, two things in our lives that aren't completely terrible at the moment. Olive's right. I am self-centered, but I don't want to be.

"I'm okay," I say again, and this time it sounds more real. "Please, I've been waiting all day to hear how it went."

"I think I got it," she whispers after a second. Her voice is tight with nervous pride and excitement. It fills me with a sudden burst of warmth, and sappy tears prick my eyes.

God, my emotions are all kinds of fucked today.

I lean my head against her shoulder. "Tell me about it. I want the whole story, and if you leave out any of the parts with Elliot Graham, I'll kick you."

She squirms in her seat. "We got to play together, a little bit at the end, after I'd gone through the stuff I prepared." She sighs, long and sweet. "He's so...you know? We were playing together, and he kept looking at me, and sweet baby Jesus, Flora, have you seen how long his fingers are?"

"Now you're making me blush." I laugh, and she does, too. Already, my pulse has slowed. I can deal with those creepy photos later.

Cass hesitates. "Are you sure this is what you want to talk about right now?"

I smile at her, and it's not forced at all. "I'm sure."

CHAPTER 15

My spoon chimes against the side of the mug as I stir my morning coffee. Once again, I barely slept last night. Three separate times, I almost woke Cass up to tell her about the photos, but I never did. Still, every time I closed my eyes I saw the picture taken through my bedroom window, my face relaxed like I had no idea I was being watched.

Gramps is sitting at the kitchen table. His newspaper rustles as he turns the page. I could tell him now. He's not like Mom. He won't freak out first and ask questions later. But this investigation is only a few days old, and I'm already getting threats. Serious ones. What if this time it's too much for him?

Without looking up from his paper, he says, "You missed three classes yesterday. Your chemistry teacher called. She's concerned."

I bet. "I had a lead to follow up. It was important."

"Be that as it may, let's not make a habit out of it. I know this is important to you, but you need to apply to college next year. I don't want you to lose sight of the future." He turns the page with a shade too much deliberation.

What is it with everyone and college? When did this become the thing we have to worry about all the time, no matter what else is going on? Kind of hard to think about my future when someone's leaving death threats on my doorstep.

I try to keep my voice light and easy. "I get it. It's not like I blew off school to get high and play video games."

"Well, then, what did you find that was more important than your STEM education?"

Talking about case stuff is way less scary than worrying about college, or those photos.

I grab a mug for Cass and go back to making coffee. "Ava's wallet, filled with cash. Doesn't exactly spell mugging, does it?"

Long pause. "You found Ava McQueen's wallet?"

"In the dumpster by Congressman Dorsey's campaign office." I hesitate. I'm not even totally sold on this idea myself, at least not yet, and Gramps was less than convinced yesterday when I told him my theories about who's running the Basement. I keep my tone casual. "Might explain why the police are so eager to believe it's a robbery, if someone as powerful as Dorsey is involved."

He takes his time carefully folding his newspaper. "You took the wallet with you?"

"Yeah..." I know the Dorsey theory is still kind of a stretch, but is he really not going to react at all?

His paper now folded into a perfect square, he turns his full attention to me. "You have it here?"

Too late, I get the feeling this might be a trap. "Yes."

He nods several times. My pulse picks up again.

Gramps looks over my shoulder. "Cassidy, you should go to school. Flora will meet you there."

I look back. Cass is standing in the doorway. Her eyes dart to mine, but I have no idea what's going on, either.

"Why?" I ask him.

He runs a hand over his close-cropped beard. "You and I are going to the police station to turn over Ava's wallet."

Sweat breaks out all over my body. "What? No!"

He stands and buttons his suit jacket. "Flora, you found evidence. It belongs to the police."

I can't breathe. What is happening? I've done way sketchier shit than this, and he's turned a blind eye or even *helped* in the past.

Gramps retrieves his wallet from the kitchen island, his demeanor as cool and efficient as always, but it's like he's a totally different person right now. Like he's Mom.

"They'll never believe me." I follow him around the room as he searches for his keys. "Richmond said the cops are already suspicious of me, and it's not like they're going to do anything with the wallet anyway, not when it totally debunks their mugging theory. It's just going to—"

He turns to me abruptly. "Flora, the adult thing to do is to bring the wallet to the police. If you cannot make that choice yourself, I will have to make it for you. Now, kindly go retrieve the wallet from the safe you think I don't know about in your room, and we can all proceed with our day."

As predicted, Richmond flips her shit. She parks us in an unused conference room that smells like mildewy socks—I think if my grandfather weren't here, she would put me in an interrogation room just for fun—and yells at me for a solid fifteen minutes. There's a lot of "What were you thinking?" and "No respect for the law!" getting thrown around.

Everything she says washes right over me. I keep looking at my grandfather. I don't know how we got here.

He looks everywhere but at me. I'm on my own for this one.

"I mean seriously, Calhoun!" Richmond concludes. "I told you to stay far away from this investigation. Was I not clear about the consequences?"

"I don't see how I can stay out of it when you guys are barely even trying. Someone killed Ava to rob her, then threw all of her credit cards and a thousand bucks in a dumpster? You're right, makes perfect sense."

"Maybe they got spooked. It happens. The guy gets nervous, pulls the trigger, and then they want to throw it all away like it never happened." She catches herself. "Why am I even debating this with you? All of that's irrelevant, because I told you to stay out of it."

"Why are you so desperate to make the mugging thing work?" My voice is rising, and I fight to keep it under control. It makes me furious to hear her talk about Ava's death like it was some random accident, but I don't want to prove to Richmond, once again, that I'm nothing but an overemotional teenager.

"Flora, I'm not messing around," Richmond says. "Some of the other detectives think *you* planted the wallet. It certainly wouldn't be the first time you made something up to suit your story."

"What's that supposed to mean?" I ask at the same time that Gramps says, "Excuse me?"

Richmond addresses him like I'm not in the room. "Your granddaughter here called in a tip yesterday about some teen fight club in Whitley. I sent a bunch of patrol officers down there last night, but all they did was wander around a rat-infested basement for two hours. There was nothing there."

It takes all of my willpower not to bash my head repeatedly against the table in frustration. I can't believe I didn't take pictures the other night. So stupid.

Richmond laughs bitterly. "Should have known better than to go chasing after another wild Flora Calhoun theory. You know my sergeant nearly took me off the case? Trust me, Flora. Another detective gets assigned to this, you're going to need a lawyer."

"You're just pissed you looked bad in front of your boss," I say. "You always do this. You care more about your precious career than solving murders."

This is how Richmond was with Lucy, too. She's not a bad cop. She knew Matt Caine did it. But when she got the order to drop the case, she did as she was told.

So who would be powerful enough to keep the police from looking too closely this time around? Obviously Dorsey, but he's not the only rich white dude with the police commissioner's number, either.

For a second, Richmond looks like she's going to lose it. She reels herself in and turns sharply to look at my grandfather. "Listen, Mr. Calhoun. I could have her arrested right now for tampering with evidence or obstruction of justice, and that's just off the top of my head. But I've had my fill of dealing with your granddaughter, so I'm going to give you guys one last chance to settle this within the family. Am I clear?"

I open my mouth to defend myself, but Gramps beats me to it. "Flora found this wallet yesterday, and she brought it here within twenty-four hours. She discovered this fight club, and she shared that information with you. I don't appreciate you speaking to her as though she's hampering your efforts, when Flora is, in essence, doing your job for you."

Richmond rocks back on her heels. Her eyebrows nearly touch her hairline. Honestly, I'm a little taken aback, too. Everything he just said is what I'd expect the usual Gramps to say. So are we back to normal now?

He stands. "I need to take Flora to school. If you have any further questions, I must insist that we have legal counsel present. Come along, Flora."

I follow him out of the room. He doesn't look back at me.

Somehow my grandfather defending me after our fight has only made me feel worse. I'm so used to being able to predict exactly how he'll react. Now I don't know where we stand.

"I know you're upset," he says on the drive to school. We're nearly there. Most of the ride has passed in tense silence. "If they already consider you a person of interest, imagine what kind of trouble you would have been in had they found the wallet in your room. It was too great a risk to keep it in the house."

I keep my eyes trained out the passenger-side window. It's starting to rain.

We pull up in front of the school, but I don't move. For a moment, the only sound is the rain and the swish of windshield wipers. I count cars in the parking lot so I don't have to look at him. A green station wagon. A black sedan. A white utility van.

Gramps continues. "I want you to understand something. Flora, I am so proud of you."

That makes me turn around.

He keeps his hands on the steering wheel as he speaks. "I have the utmost respect for you and your desire to help people, even when it costs you personally. It frightens me at times, but I would rather be scared than see you become a less courageous person."

All morning, I've been remembering the way Mom and I used to fight when she would get scared. But he's *not* Mom. Mom would never say anything like this to me.

Now that I'm looking at him, though, I see all the signs. The tightness around his mouth. The corners of his eyes creased with exhaustion and fear. One of his shirt buttons has only been pushed halfway through its hole.

He chose me, but all I've ever done is make his life harder.

Gramps breathes a heavy sigh. "With your mother gone, I have to make decisions for you and Olive. Decisions you might not always agree with. Please do not take it to mean that I do not believe in you."

I look at him sideways and nod.

As I walk into school, I think again about the photos, still hidden in my backpack. It meant something to me, what he said, but I know for sure now that I can't tell him how much danger I'm in.

We're not there yet, but I can see it in the distance: the breaking point between us, where I've finally pushed him too far.

Cass is pacing in front of my locker when I arrive. The ache in my chest eases. She pulls me into a hug. Doesn't bother asking if I'm all right, and I love her for that.

Her arms still tight around me, she says, "I got you a present. Damian Rivera is ready to talk."

She fills me in as we make our way to the art room, where Damian has class now. She cornered him during morning break and leaned on him a little.

"He cracked in, like, two seconds." She matches me stride

for stride as we speed walk through the halls. I'm ready to forget everything that just happened at the police precinct, and there's nothing like intel to help with that. Cass continues. "I told him we already knew about the Basement, and he got really nervous. He claims he doesn't know much, but between the two of us I bet we can drag something out of him."

The art room is filled with the sound of gently scratching pencils and the smell of wet watercolor paper. The spring show is next month, and everyone's busy working on their projects. Mr. Danziger looks up when we walk in, but he takes a sip of tea and goes back to reading his book. He's been teaching art here for decades, and he doesn't care about anything anymore. Last year I saw him smoking a joint in the faculty parking lot.

Penn is here, too. He looks up when we walk in, scowls, and bends his head back over his work. The pencil in his hand looks ready to snap.

On the opposite side of the room, Damian's working on a large sculpture. Every few seconds, he glances at Penn.

"Hey, Damian," Cass says once we get close. "Got a minute?"

Damian glances toward Penn again, then at me. "Um, okay."

"Tell me why you and Penn are fighting," I say before I can stop myself.

"We're not." Damian crouches next to his work. The sculpture is made of white stone. It's a snake that knots and twists around itself, eating its own tail. The same one from his Instagram feed. He runs his hand over the surface, looking for flaws.

Cass purses her lips at my lack of finesse. I don't *try* to burn bridges, I'm just naturally good at it, and I'm still rattled from everything that happened this morning. I give her a look, silently telling her to take the lead.

She crouches down to inspect the sculpture. "This is really impressive. What kind of stone is it?"

He wipes away some more of the dust. "Carrara marble. Beautiful, right?"

Cass gives him an encouraging smile. "Is it for the art show?"

Damian hesitates. "Well, yeah, I'll put her in the show. But"—he looks in Penn's direction again—"she's my entry into this contest, the Prisma Project."

"Oh, I've never heard of that. What do you get if you win?" Cass leans closer to look at the snake's scales, each one carved in intricate detail. I can't help but admire for the millionth time how good she is at this.

Damian says, "There's a ten-thousand-dollar prize, and it looks amazing on art school applications. The last kid who won got offered a full ride at Parsons *and* the Rhode Island School of Design."

I consider the sculpture. "Carrara marble, you said?"

Damian nods and traces a finger over one of the snake's eyes. His palms are covered in pale white dust.

I try to copy Cass's casual we're-all-friends-here tone. "Wow, you must really want to win this thing. I guess for ten grand I wouldn't want to use plaster from the art room."

The corner of Cass's mouth twitches. She nods at me encouragingly.

Damian nods without looking up. "People go all out for this thing. I *have* to win."

There's a desperate edge to his voice that makes me pause.

Cass is still looking at the snake. "I can't get over how pretty the stone is. How did you even pay for this much marble? It must have cost a fortune."

Damian hesitates, looking nervous again. "My mom. She helped me buy it."

Cass gives me a nod. My turn.

"Is your mom the 'she' in your note?" I ask.

He grabs his chisel, refusing to meet my eye. "I don't know what you're talking about."

I push harder. "I saw you guys the other day in chem. *I'm sorry, I had to do it. You don't know what she'll do to me?*"

He runs a hand through his hair, streaking white dust through the black. "You shouldn't be reading other people's notes."

"Damian," Cass chides, "you told me you were ready to talk."

213

His eyes dart between us, then flick back over to Penn on the other side of the room.

Cass says gently, "I already told you, we know about the Basement. We know Penn has been fighting there for money. You're not ratting anyone out. Tell us what happened."

Damian casts one last, desperate glance at Penn, who's stopped drawing.

"Okay." Damian gets even quieter. "Yeah, I needed the money for the marble. My ma, she doesn't take the artist thing seriously. She wants me to go to dental school or something." He looks down at the snake again and traces a hand over its undulating body. His touch is tender. Loving. "See how the marble has these natural blue and gray tones to it? The veining? I had this dream about the snake's scales, how each one would be a slightly different color. It would almost look real. But it only works if it's big. Like, if this were the size of a shoebox, it wouldn't be so impressive, right?"

Cass and I both tilt our heads. He has a point. The thing comes up to my knees. It's huge. On this scale, it's like something out of a Greek myth.

Damian continues. "I could never afford a piece of marble this size. I work at the gas station. I make nothing per hour. One night, my mom was doing dishes in the other room, and her credit card was sitting right there."

214

Cass puts it all together. "But she found out, and you needed to pay her back."

Damian looks at us with pleading eyes. "I tried to explain it to Penn, but he wouldn't listen! She was going to sell all my art supplies, my brushes, *everything.* I tried to tell her I'd pay her back once I won the contest, but you know. Parents, right?"

Yeah. I know.

"Why's Penn so mad?" I ask.

Damian picks some of the marble dust out of his cuticles. "I bet against him."

"You bet against your best friend?"

"It's not like I made him lose!" Damian insists. "Penn pulled his shoulder that day. I told him he shouldn't fight at all, but he wouldn't listen!" He leans closer. "Penn's quiet. People overlook him. When he first started fighting, everyone thought he wouldn't last, but he turned out to be really good at it. The odds were on him to win, but I knew about his shoulder." He exhales. "I didn't sabotage him or anything. I needed money, and this was the only way I could get it, like, immediately."

"What about Ava?" I ask. "Did she fight, too?" So far, no one's been able to tell me exactly what her connection was to this place.

Damian shakes his head. "I don't think so. Besides Penn's stuff, I didn't know much about the Basement. That place freaks me out. I tried to talk him out of fighting in the first place, but he wanted to impress that stuck-up bitch Victoria."

On the other side of the studio, the pencil finally snaps.

Penn flies across the room. "You asshole! What, it's not enough to sell out your best friend, you have to mouth off to the nosiest girls in school?"

Everyone turns to watch as Damian shouts back, "I'd rather talk to you about it, but you won't listen!"

Penn looks at him with disgust. "You've been a self-absorbed dick since we were in the sixth grade. I don't know why I keep waiting for you to change."

"Gentlemen!" Mr. Danziger puts his book down. "As exhilarating as this brotherly feud is, I think we all want to simmer down. Let's make art, not war, okay, folks?"

Penn is gripping the neck of Damian's shirt. He looks like he might punch him any second.

"All right." Mr. Danziger stands and claps his hands once. "Ms. Calhoun? Ms. Yang? I think that's quite enough excitement you've stirred up for one day. Perhaps you could see yourselves to your actual classes?"

Eyes follow us out the door. Penn's words echo in my head. They sound uncomfortably similar to what Cass said to me in the car yesterday.

CHAPTER 16

Sixth-period classes are canceled, and we all file into the gym. It's a totally inappropriate place for a memorial. The smells of sweat, old shoes, and basketball rubber have soaked in over the years. The McQueens are holding a private service for Ava this weekend, but it's family only. This memorial is the one chance for the school to honor Ava—a week from now, everyone will have moved on to something else. I know. I've been here before.

Eyes trail after Cass and me as we walk up the bleachers. Heads bend closer together as we pass.

"I heard she totally started a fistfight between Penn and Damian in the art room."

Ignore it. Ignore them.

But they're not only whispering about me.

"Why is Cass even still friends with her?"

"She used to have normal friends, but she's, like, obsessed with her."

I start to turn, but Cass puts a hand on my arm.

"I don't know, Yang is pretty psycho, too. One time, she punched Chad Westfall in the face for no reason. They deserve each other."

I rip my arm out of Cass's grip and spin around.

The four gossiping senior girls abruptly fall silent. I lean right down in their faces. The one closest to me scoots back, and I smile.

"Do you know what's a really bad idea?"

The girls trade glances.

I smile wider. So sweet. "Insulting a psycho's best friend. You never know"—I lean in closer—"when she might *snap*." I pop the *p,* and one of them flinches.

I straighten. The girls all look at Cass like she might have some explanation.

Cass shrugs. "Sorry, she's rabid. I can't control her." She starts to turn, then looks back. Her smile matches mine. Twin freaks. "If you think she's scary, you don't want to see what happens when you piss me off." Cass grabs my hand and pulls me up the bleachers.

"You don't have to do that," she mutters. "It doesn't bother me."

"It bothers *me.*" She does such a good job defending me. I can do the same for her.

"You know, they're not totally wrong about Penn and Damian," Cass muses as we take our seats. "They were best friends. Now look at them."

Penn is sitting a few rows ahead of us. His posture is stiff. From the way other people keep glancing at him, those girls aren't the only ones gossiping about him and Damian.

Cass gestures around the gym. "There's got to be all kinds of resentment festering over the Basement. Friends beating up friends, people betting against each other. It's not like that stuff just gets left at the door when the fight is over."

It's not the first time she's mentioned it, but she has a point. From the moment I walked through the doors into the Basement, I've had this feeling that there had to be something big at play here, more than just a brawl gone wrong.

But after seeing the way Penn—the quiet, artsy kid in my chem class—clenched his fist like he was about to beat his best friend into the ground, I'm not so certain anymore. Maybe Cass is right.

It seems like half the student body is involved with the Basement in some way. Any one of them would have reasons to keep it a secret. The question is, would one of them kill for it?

The sight of Ava's broken, limp body curled up on the dirty ground flashes through my head. Which one of our classmates would be capable of leaving someone they knew, someone they saw every day, to bleed out in the street?

I look around the gym. People are still filing in, finding their seats. The space is filled with the low, rumbling chatter of high school kids set free from their regular classes.

I should know by now that anyone is capable of that kind of darkness.

"You might be right," I say slowly. "Maybe things just got out of hand and Ava ended up dead. But if that's the case, nothing has changed. The Basement is still up and running. It's still hurting people."

Cass looks at me with sad, serious eyes. "So how long before someone else gets killed?"

Her question hangs in the air for a moment. Someone takes the seat next to her, shaking us out of those disturbing thoughts.

It's Elliot Graham. "Hey, Cass. Flora."

Cass immediately turns to mush. It's been an extremely shitty day, but I do enjoy seeing Cass turn that particular shade of pink.

"Hey, Elliot," I respond, since Cass seems to have lost control of her verbal faculties.

"So, Cass." He leans a little closer, and her face flushes brighter. "I wanted to talk to you about band stuff." Elliot's gentleman enough not to comment on her radioactive red cheeks.

"Oh, ah, sure," she stammers. It's incredibly endearing. She looks at me with big, imploring eyes: *Save me!*

As much as I'm enjoying her self-destruction, I can't let her flail like this.

"Elliot," I jump in, "Cass barely told me anything about her audition. How did it go?"

He grins. "Oh, she was incredible! I knew she'd be good, but she totally blew everyone away. That Bowie cover?" He nudges Cass's elbow. "Brilliant."

Cass smiles weakly.

"So are you up for a rehearsal tonight?" Elliot asks her.

Cass glances at me, a different kind of nervousness in her eyes now. "Oh, um. Tonight? I thought we were meeting on Mondays?"

"Yeah, we'll get on a regular schedule eventually, but I think for the first couple weeks I want to meet as often as possible to help the group click together. That doable for you?"

Cass's eyes flick to me again, and suddenly I get it. She's worried about leaving me alone tonight.

"She'll be there," I answer for her. Elliot gives me a funny look, probably wondering why I'm micromanaging my friend's schedule, but Cass understands.

"Yeah." She blows out a shaky breath and nods. "Tonight is great. I'm there."

His smile is blinding. "Excellent." He lets out a wheezy little laugh, like he's sort of winded talking to her. The cuteness is unbearable.

Elliot rubs the back of his neck and looks around the room. His smile falters.

"You know," he says quietly, "Ava sure would have liked being the center of attention like this."

It's like a punch to the stomach. Listening to Cass and Elliot's ridiculously awkward flirting, I could almost forget for a minute. But Elliot was friends with Ava. Another person whose life is irreparably altered by her absence.

Ava would have been in rock ensemble with Cass and Elliot for sure. I would have gone to meet them after rehearsal sometimes. To see Cass, technically, but then Ava would be there, too. I would have stood in the doorway and watched Cass leaning into the mic, harmonizing with Elliot. Ava's hands gliding up and down the fretboard of her bass, her fingers fast and sure.

That possible future is gone now, for all of us.

Elliot's picking at one of his fingernails. The glow from talking to Cass has faded, and there's something worn and fragile in his face that hurts to see.

I'm seized by the impulse to say something comforting, to

reach out and pull him into a hug, but I don't really know how to do either of those things.

Microphone feedback cuts through the din. The chatter dies off.

At the center of the basketball court, Principal Adams stands behind a podium.

"Welcome, students. Hartsdale family members. I am deeply saddened to be here today. Ava McQueen was a star student, a passionate young activist, and a dear friend to this entire school. She is missed."

Someone sniffles a few rows ahead. I can't see who it is. My ears pop.

I've been to one of these memorials before. In this gym. Principal Adams said almost the exact same words.

Lucy MacDonald was a bright and special girl, a force of nature. She charmed everyone she met.

It was like she was describing a girl I didn't know. Lucy wasn't like that at all. She was a bitch. Everyone thought so, until she died. Until I found her. What was left of her, anyway. That pulpy red mess lying in the middle of the trail like forgotten medical waste. After that, everyone had nothing but nice things to say about her. At least for a little while.

Principal Adams says, "Ava's father hoped to speak with you all, but today he finds himself beyond words. Instead we will hear from one of the leaders of this community and a parent at this school, Congressman James Dorsey."

Goose bumps rise on my arms, even though they've way overheated the gym.

Dorsey pauses to shake hands with Principal Adams and Ava's parents, who are sitting in the front row. The lines of his face are drawn together in a caricature of sympathetic concern. I can see even from this distance that Ava's dad is openly weeping, endless tears streaming down his face. I met him a few times last summer. He had Ava's same sly wit. Sometimes when we were holed up in her room, we'd hear him yelling at the news while he made dinner. Ava and I would laugh against each other's mouths as we kissed.

Hot, poisonous anger roils in my stomach. I can't fault Mr. McQueen for not wanting to speak, but Ava was loved. She had friends who cared about her. Teachers who believed in her. Even setting aside my suspicions about Dorsey, at best he's just some fake politician who didn't even know Ava. They're going to let him use her death to score publicity points?

Dorsey adjusts the mic like a pro, no awkward fumbling. "Thank you, Principal Adams. It is a great honor and an even greater tragedy to speak here today, remembering the life of a remarkable young woman. Mr. and Mrs. McQueen, my heartfelt condolences are with you, of course, and with the entire Hartsdale community, for Ava's death is a loss to us all."

224

He takes the microphone off the stand and walks a little to the left and then right as though he's at some kind of folksy town hall event.

"I come here today not as your congressman, not as your hopeful senator, but as your neighbor." He dives into a litany of praises, like he's reading from Ava's résumé or, more likely, some dossier his staff put together ten minutes ago. "Top 10 percent of her class...young activist...underserved communities...organized her peers for change..."

I dig my nails into the knees of my jeans.

A flash of blue-green hair catches my eye. Lainie Andrews, Ava's best friend. She hunches over in her seat. Her shoulders shake. Another girl puts her hand on Lainie's back, but she flinches away.

To my left, Elliot's posture is rigid. His eyes are locked on Dorsey as he continues spewing generic, meaningless praise about Ava.

It's kind of like English class the other day: everyone had nice things to say, but they only made Ava sound like an idea instead of a person. Meanwhile, Lainie curls in on herself with grief, Elliot's jaw tightens, and I remember the real Ava. The one who always laughed too loud in the library. Who walked right up and kissed me at that party. Who avoided me for months with no explanation, no matter how many desperate texts I sent her.

The cavernous space of the gym is quiet except for Dorsey's speech, so I can hear the tiny whimper that escapes from Lainie's mouth, even though she's several rows ahead. It's the sound you make when you're trying your hardest not to scream. I want to scream with her.

My eyes keep flitting around the room, desperate for a distraction. Most of the crowd is calm. Half listening. It could almost be a regular old assembly on bullying, or drugs. How do they all do this? Go back to normal like nothing happened. Fill the space Ava left behind like she was never there at all.

Is her killer in this room right now? Bored and waiting for this to be over so they can go back to class? Or maybe fidgeting in their seat, afraid to confront what they did?

Dorsey proselytizes, "And we must ask ourselves: How can this happen here? In our town. In our country!" There's a slight flush to his cheeks. His eyes are dark and shining. "How can someone so brave and bright be taken from us?"

I can't take it anymore. Elliot was wrong: Ava would have hated this. Her own memorial isn't even about *her*. Dorsey's turned it into some kind of campaign event.

Something brushes against my ankle, and I barely avoid screaming. Cass and I both look down.

VT's face pokes out between our feet. The weirdness of the image is enough to jolt me out of my fury for a moment.

I lean over and whisper, "What are you doing here?"

"Need to talk to you. Come down."

I turn my attention back to Dorsey. He's moved on to some stump speech about innovative policing strategies. I need to get out of here.

I touch Cass's hand. She nods. She has my back.

I slide through the gap in the bleachers, landing light on my feet.

"What is so urgent?" I turn to Valentine and cross my arms over my chest. Light winks through the slats of the bleachers and hundreds of legs above our heads.

He's looking at me strangely. No smirks or shifty, clever eyes, but straight on and intense, like he's reading me.

I try not to fidget under his gaze. Yesterday, we shared our darkest secrets, and now I feel laid open in a way that is both beautiful and horrifying, like a butterfly pinned under glass. As excruciating as that feels, as much as I've told myself it's a bad idea to get too close to him, there's a part of me that wants it.

The thought immediately makes me feel dirty. This is Ava's memorial.

"What do you want?" I repeat.

He finally looks away. "Never figured you for a snitch, Cherry."

Not what I was expecting. "What are you talking about?"

"You tipped off the cops. I was booked for a fight last night, but when the police got there the show had already been called off. Lot of people lost out on their pay."

"So?" After everything I've learned, I'm not going to feel bad. One less night for someone to get hurt.

He takes a step forward. "Boss in charge must be pretty powerful to get a warning from the cops like that."

Out in the gym, Dorsey's voice rises to the big finish as he calls for commonsense gun legislation to keep our children safe.

Valentine jerks his head in that direction. "Takes a special kind of evil, doesn't it? To kill her and then speak at her service."

His words send a chill shuddering through me. I know there's no hard evidence pointing toward Dorsey, and a million other possible explanations for Ava's death.

But Cass and Gramps have both given me that same sympathetic, dubious look every time I've brought Dorsey up. Valentine is the first person to see what I see, to act like it's not all in my head.

The air is thick and close under the bleachers. The ceaseless vibrating charge between us reaches an almost painful intensity.

I don't want to be feeling this right now. The guilt of it is suffocating. But every time I remind myself of that, he goes and says something that cuts right through to the heart of me. I find myself stepping forward, drawing closer to him without meaning to.

Carefully, he steps back, and it's both a relief and a disappointment. "I have to tell you something. Something you won't like."

I go still. Nothing good is about to happen.

It takes him a while to work up to it. "The other night, at the Basement, I didn't follow you on a whim. I was told to check up on you, ask a few questions, get on your good side."

That ever-shifting ground between us falls out from under my feet again.

I don't know why I'm surprised. I've been suspicious of him from minute one. But yesterday at the park, I thought I saw him—really *saw* him. I certainly let him see me.

"By who?" I manage.

"Man named Boyd. He runs things at the Basement. He wanted me to point you in the right direction."

My voice is eerily calm. "And what direction would that be?"

"Ava McQueen's death was a tragic accident. The killer was a nervous, trigger-happy kid looking to score her wallet."

I knew. I knew I shouldn't trust him.

Valentine's expression is serious. "There's something else. Boyd manages the fights, but he's not the top of the pyramid. I don't know for sure who he answers to"—he hesitates, like he's deciding if he wants to tell me this next part—"but I'd bet anything it's Dorsey pulling the strings."

"You've been lying to me this whole time. Why should I listen to anything you have to say?"

"I wasn't totally straight with you yesterday." He steps forward, but this time it's me who steps back. I can't bear being any nearer to him. I *was* straight with him yesterday. I told him stuff I haven't even told Cass.

"The beginning parts, my sister, Juilliard, that's all true, but I didn't come back to town because I got bored." He rubs the back of his neck. "After about six months with the circus, I got a package in the mail. No return address. It's a bunch of documents from the Daylight Foundation. You heard of 'em?"

I shake my head. I should walk away. He knows I want answers so bad, and he's using it to get me to stay, to listen to him, to trust him. I just don't know why.

"They track dirty money. Political contributions, money laundering, that sort of thing. My sister worked for them. Then she died. I got that package in the mail, and I started to think maybe her death wasn't an accident. I don't think your girl Ava's was, either. I think someone"—he shoots a meaningful look in the direction of Dorsey's voice—"wanted something kept quiet."

It's too much information. Too many questions screaming in my head.

I go with the easiest one. "Why tell me now?"

"I've spent the last year doing one thing: searching for my sister's killer. The other night? I was following orders. I found out what you knew and gave you a push in a convenient direction, so I could get back to my own work. Then you found that wallet." There's a flicker of a smile near the corner of his mouth. "I was staring up at you, knee-deep in trash, and I thought: this girl is the real thing. I'm telling you the truth now because I think we're better off fighting together. Side by side."

"Why should I believe you?"

He looks down, struggling with the words. "I haven't told a single soul besides you about Annabelle's death, or why I'm back in this hellhole of a city. I figure you can understand a vengeance quest better than anyone." He reaches out slowly and takes my hand. His rough, calloused fingertips graze the soft skin on the underside of my wrist.

Maybe he's finally telling the truth, or maybe that open, vulnerable look he's giving me is just more bullshit. I can't make the mistake of trusting him again.

Then again, if Dorsey's really behind all this, Valentine's too valuable a source of information to give up completely.

I pull my hand away. "I have to think about it. You can't lie to me and then expect me to have your back."

A heavy moment passes. "Yeah. Guess not."

He tilts his ear toward the gym. Dorsey has finished speaking. Adams takes the microphone again, but her words are muddied and slow to me down here. A shaft of light cuts across the floor as someone crosses their legs above. "Sounds like they're wrapping up out there. Be seein' you, Cherry."

He leaves me alone in the stillness under the bleachers.

CHAPTER 17

I need air. I find the drinking fountain in the hallway and cup some of the lukewarm water in my palm. Splash it on my cheeks and neck. Wet tendrils of hair cling to my skin.

I'm shaking so hard I feel almost weak with it. Hard to say who I'm angrier at, Valentine or myself.

So stupid. I let myself think maybe I could have him on my side. I knew it was a bad idea, knew I shouldn't trust him.

I lean my head back against the wall and try to catch my breath. I text Cass and tell her that I'll meet her in class.

Voices down the hall. Voices I recognize.

"That speech was terrible."

"Enough. I don't need it from you on top of everything else on my plate."

I hug the wall and peer around the corner. My heart thumps double time: Elle Dorsey and her father are arguing in the hallway, just feet away.

Elle's hands are clenched in fists. "Could you be any more transparent? Everyone knows you're only here to boost your polling numbers with soccer moms. You couldn't care less about Ava McQueen."

It's almost exactly what I was thinking during the memorial. Elle wasn't all that broken up about Ava's death the last few times I spoke to her. Why is she suddenly acting so upset on Ava's behalf?

Congressman Dorsey scrolls through his phone. "I may not have known the poor girl well, but it's my responsibility to be a leader during times of hardship."

Elle and I both roll our eyes at the same time.

"Yeah, your concern is *super* believable," she says.

He switches subjects as though he didn't hear her. "Listen, I spoke with a friend of mine at the *Whitley Gazette*. They want you to write an op-ed about crime and Ava's death. Get a student's perspective."

"Absolutely not."

Dorsey pockets his phone and turns sharp eyes on his daughter. "Elle, don't test me. You'll do this because it's advantageous to me. When I look good, the whole family succeeds."

His tone is cold and flat, with just the edge of a threat underneath. So this is the real Dorsey, the one I suspected was hidden under the veneer of homespun, blue-collar charm.

Elle scoffs, "Funny how you don't care about the *whole family succeeding* until we're politically useful to you."

"That's enough, young lady."

She crosses her arms. "I barely knew Ava. I'm not going to take advantage of her death like that."

I can't get over how weird it is to see Elle acting like a decent human being. Sure, she gave me some information the other day, but she also said some truly horrible things about Ava. Was she just pretending not to give a shit about her death before?

"Yes, Ava's death was a tragedy." Dorsey's bored, dismissive tone is so at odds with his fervor in front of the crowd. "But it's also an *opportunity*. One that I'm not going to let you pass up." He smiles. It's the same smile I've seen him give at political rallies. Inhuman.

Hatred burns bright in me. He just called Ava an *opportunity*.

I can't deny it anymore: I think this man killed Ava.

I just have to prove it.

Elle looks at the ceiling. "You're repulsive, and you're trying to make me be repulsive, too."

Dorsey's voice has the deadly calm flatness of lake water before a storm. "No, I'm trying to show you how to wield your power and moral authority in the world. Those are important lessons. But if you can't find it within yourself to support my ambitions, I have no need to support yours. You've been awfully excited about that Future Businesswomen of America seminar at Stanford this summer. I can make that go away, like last year."

Elle sniffs and tucks her hair neatly behind her ears. "You wouldn't do that. It makes you look good if I do something impressive this summer."

He sticks his hands in his pockets and shrugs. "I'm sure we can squeeze in a photo op of you manning the phones at the campaign office. That'll serve fine. Now, get me your draft by the end of the week, okay, sweetheart? I'll see you at home." He claps her on the shoulder once before walking away. Elle stays put. She stares at the ground, blinking fast.

Holy shit, is she crying?

Elle looks up. I freeze in place. We stare at each other, and I swear there's something fragile and scared in Elle's eyes.

"Tell anyone what you heard and I will ruin you." The heels of her boots click against the linoleum as she walks away.

I head toward my locker, my mind still running over everything I just heard. All of the voices play at once in my brain, jostling for attention with an endless loop of questions I can't answer.

Do I feel bad for Elle Dorsey?

How could I let myself trust Valentine?

Did Congressman Dorsey kill Ava? It *feels* true, but at the same time I have no real clue what his motive would be. Even

236

if he's the man behind the curtain at the Basement, and even if Ava was involved in some way, that still doesn't explain how she ended up dead. Maybe he killed her to keep her quiet, like Valentine said? But what could she possibly have on Dorsey that would make her such a threat?

The questions circle each other, round and round, louder and louder in my brain. And even if I figure it all out, how am I ever going to convince someone to take me seriously?

I have a headache again. I think it might be a permanent condition at this point.

A knot of people clusters around my locker bay. How many kids does it take to write another threat? I quicken my pace. This is something I can handle. These idiots think they can scare me, and I'm not taking it anymore.

But this time, it's not my locker they're gathered around.

"You like that, you ice-queen bitch?" Austin Yi, one of those muscly square-jaw football players, looms over Paige Thomas as she tries to get into her locker.

Her shoulders are hunched around her ears. "Stop. Leave me alone." She scrambles desperately with her locker combination. Her curly black hair is pulled up in a high bun that makes her look like a tiny, delicate ballerina compared to Austin's brawn.

I get in between them. "Hey, hey! What's going on here?"

Austin doesn't back down. "You know what you did. You

better watch your back. She has a lot of friends." He leans over me to get to Paige.

"Hey!" I try to draw his attention to me. My mind is racing again. Who's Austin talking about? Who did Paige piss off?

With a bang, Paige finally gets her locker open. She barely looks at me as she swaps her books. "It's okay. I'm fine."

Jake Ellis, one of Austin's friends, pulls at his shoulder. "Stop it, man. She's not worth it."

"What the hell is the matter with you?" I demand.

Austin's furious eyes are stuck on Paige. "She knows. She knows why."

I cross my arms. "Yeah, well, maybe I'd like to know why, too."

"Go ask Molly Sawyer. I bet she'd love to tell you," Austin yells.

"Shut up." Jake finally succeeds in yanking Austin away. He shoots us an apologetic grimace. "Sorry."

Austin looks back to glare at Paige as his friend leads him down the hall.

I turn to her. "What was that all about?"

Paige slams her locker closed. "Nothing." She gives me a resentful look, which is kind of confusing, seeing as I'm on her side.

"Paige—"

"I said it's nothing. Don't worry about it." Paige walks away, and then, as if remembering her manners, tosses back a "Thanks."

Other eyes follow Paige as she departs. There's something scratched into the paint on her locker. Someone carved out the words *You know what you did.*

Someone's trying to scare Paige, too. But why? I honestly don't know much about her, even though I've probably had at least one class with her every year. I rack my brains for details. She always hands her homework in on time in our calculus class. Her family's so rich that even Hartsdale's extremely white, extremely racist country club couldn't find an excuse to reject them like they do with most black applicants. Paige plays the part perfectly—golf, pearls, the whole deal. I think I've heard her mention a horse? That's all I've got, though. Nothing that would kick up this kind of shit storm.

So who the hell is Molly Sawyer?

Add that to my never-ending list of questions.

I switch out my books and head to English. We have a big research paper coming up, so Mr. Kelly relocates us all to the library for a work period. Cass and I set ourselves up at a pair of computers and pretend to do research while she grills me about Valentine. I go over the basics of my conversation with him, but I'm not in the mood to unpack the whole thing.

I stay focused on the mission. "Molly Sawyer. That name mean anything to you?"

Cass shrugs. "Sounds familiar. So, like, how *much* older is this VT character?"

Anger and shame burn through me again at the sound of his name. "Eighteen, and enough, seriously. Unless you want to share all your squishy feelings about Elliot?"

Her mouth snaps shut.

I take the opportunity to switch us to a safer subject. "I saw Austin Yi harassing Paige Thomas in the hall. I tried to talk to him, but all he said was to go find Molly Sawyer."

That gets her attention. "Why Paige? She's so normal."

"Exactly." I have the same feeling I got when I ran into Ava in the hall the day she died. She seemed so scared, and she died before I could figure out why. Is Paige in that kind of danger now, too?

"Molly Sawyer definitely rings a bell, but no one with that name goes here. Hold on." Cass pulls up a search of Molly's name. Millions of hits pop up.

"Try 'Molly Sawyer Whitley,'" I suggest. It's a long shot, but if she's connected with the Basement in some way, she must live nearby, and we already know she doesn't go to Hartsdale.

Cass types it in. The first link: GIRL IN COMA AFTER ROBBERY

TURNS VIOLENT. There's a whole bunch of other articles with similar headlines. MOLLY SAWYER, 17, ASSAULTED IN WHITLEY. NO LEADS IN BRUTAL ATTACK ON LOCAL GIRL.

"Where?" I ask. "Where did it happen?"

Cass skims one of the articles. "She was found in an alley off Vaughn Avenue." She looks up the intersection. It's about three blocks from where Ava was killed. Cass grabs my arm, digging her nails in, but I can barely feel it. I'm right there with her.

The article was published December 1. There's a ringing in my ears. Ava's diary page had a date circled in the top corner. November 30. And Lainie said Ava came over to her house crying one night, not long after Thanksgiving.

In my mind, the puzzle pieces slide into place with a satisfying click. Two violent crimes committed against two different girls in practically the same location, only a few months apart. Both with the same explanation: mugging gone wrong.

How likely does that seem?

"Hi there, I have a flower delivery for Molly Sawyer. Any chance you could give me her room number?" Cass asks the front desk nurse at Park Memorial. She's holding the giant pink and white floral arrangement we picked out at the grocery store. This is the third hospital we've tried, and some of the roses are looking a little sad around the edges.

We entered separately, and now I'm standing a few feet away, trying to listen while pretending to read a poster about flu shots. I really want this to be the one. There are five hospitals within Whitley city limits, and eight more just over the border in the surrounding towns. It's not like any of those news articles about Molly helpfully included which one she was being treated at. Most hospitals will just give out room numbers to anyone who asks, but not all do, and Molly's the only lead we have right now. I can't risk getting stonewalled by a nurse before we can track her down. Thus, the Forgetful Florist subterfuge Cass is playing right now.

The guy behind the desk gives her a skeptical look. "Don't you have that already?"

"I *should,* but the card got smudged and I can't read it." She holds the card out so he can see the ink we smeared ourselves. "I've been calling and calling the sender, but I can't get ahold of them, and I have like twelve other arrangements to deliver before my shift ends. My boss will kill me if I get the van back late again." Her voice cracks with the stress of it all.

The nurse takes pity on her. "Let me look it up for you, hang on." He types something on the computer. "Okay, she's on the third floor. Room 317."

242

My heart leaps. She's here. Molly Sawyer, our mystery girl, is in this building.

"Thank you! Seriously, you are an angel." Cass grabs her flowers and scurries off, looking harried. I wait until the nurse turns his attention back to the computer, then follow.

Once we're on the elevator, I grin at Cass. "A breathtaking performance, truly."

"Just doing my job," she says with faux modesty.

When the elevator doors open onto the third floor, I am immediately assaulted by the cheerless sounds and smells of a hospital. The powdery scent of latex gloves. Kids crying over broken, germ-riddled toys in the waiting room. Phones ringing endlessly. Doctors paged over the intercom.

In room 317, a girl lies still in the bed. Molly Sawyer, I assume.

I freeze in the doorway. She looks dead. Her skin is gray and paper-thin. Her arms lie straight at her sides like a fairy-tale princess in her glass coffin.

The steady pulse-beep of monitors reminds me: she's alive, she's alive, she's alive. But she looks so pale, so lifeless, that for a moment I am paralyzed, reliving that moment when I turned on my flashlight and saw Ava sprawled on the concrete in a pool of her own blood.

Molly's chest rises and falls, lifting her hospital sheets ever so slightly. I unfreeze.

Molly is seventeen, a year older than me, but she looks impossibly young in her hospital bed. She has no visitors. The TV isn't on. Her heart rate is slow but regular. If there were any signs she was beat up, they've long since faded in the months she's spent here.

Cass crosses the room quietly, practically tiptoeing, as though trying not to wake Molly. She sets our flowers down on the bedside table, carefully turning the vase so that the prettiest blooms face the bed.

"Who would do this to her?" she asks quietly.

"I don't know," I murmur. A couple of hours ago, I felt in my gut that it was Dorsey. The way he called Ava an *opportunity*, like she meant nothing beyond what she could do for him. But I also saw the hatred in Austin's eyes as he loomed over Paige. I say to Cass, "Every time I think I have an idea, it all gets screwed up in my head again like a minute later."

Whoever it is, I'm not going to let them leave any more girls to die in an alleyway.

"Excuse me, who are you?" someone says behind me.

A nurse wearing purple scrubs looks Cass and me up and down.

"We're friends of Molly's," Cass explains in her best nice-young-lady voice.

The nurse is immune to Cass's charms. She grips her

clipboard tighter. "I'm very sorry, but you can't be here. This patient is no-visitors. Family only."

That's weird. I guess they might limit visitors if they thought Molly was still in danger, but everyone thinks her attack was a mugging, like Ava's. It's not like the guy would come back and finish the job.

"Please," Cass asks, "can we just stay for a few minutes?" She looks back at Molly, and I know the sickened horror in her eyes isn't an act at all. "Molly's been in here for so long. We don't want her to think she's been forgotten."

The nurse's expression softens. "I'm sorry, it's hospital policy. We'll take good care of your friend, I promise, but you girls need to leave." She pivots to the side and gestures for us to pass her.

I think about arguing, but here's the thing I know about nurses: don't fuck with them. If Cass can't get her to bend the rules, I doubt my brand of persuasion is going to be any more effective.

As we leave, I pause in the doorway and take one last look at Molly. The slightly crushed flowers we left at her bedside are the sole personal touch in the room, but they only make the whole place seem more lonely.

Halfway down the hall, Cass says, "So Molly and Paige must have something to do with the Basement, right?"

I nod. "Not that I can picture either one of them fighting, but it's the only thing that makes sense."

Molly's story is so similar to Ava's, the two incidents have to be related. So did Dorsey hurt them both? Was he trying to cover something up? Or maybe he's more like Matt Caine, and he just likes hurting girls.

"Austin and Paige obviously know something," I say, "but no one's talking." I have that leaden feeling again, the one that always seems to follow the lottery-win high of a big discovery.

"You could ask that guy. VT?" Cass says.

I feel a spiky thorn of irritation. I choose not to answer her.

Cass won't drop it. "I still haven't heard exactly what happened with him earlier."

I don't want to remember the way Valentine stood so close to me in the dim light under the bleachers. It's too much. I don't want to remember, but I can't stop.

"He's ... a question mark," is all I say.

"Uh-huh."

We walk out into the weak late-winter sunshine.

Cass can't stay quiet for long. "Look, obviously he's not a model citizen or anything, but he didn't have to come clean. Maybe he really does want to partner up, fight the good fight."

My phone vibrates in my pocket. A text. The message makes me stop walking. Chill fingers rake down my spine.

Rows and rows of cars surround me on all sides. Not a person in sight, but someone could be watching from inside any one of those cars right now. The hospital's twelve floors of windows loom overhead. Are they above us? Looking down on me right now as I panic in the middle of the parking lot? Do they have their camera lens trained on Cass right now, or worse—the barrel of a gun?

A car door slams in another aisle. I whip my head around with such force that my neck cracks.

Cass realizes I'm not following her. "What is it?"

I hesitate, then hand her the phone without a word.

She reads it and looks at me with pure horror.

Stay away from Molly Sawyer, or you and your friend will both regret it

CHAPTER 18

"Okay, who can tell me how many radians we have here?" Ms. Hernandez, our calc teacher, points to the diagram of today's challenge problem on the board. I have this class with Paige, and I was half hoping I could get another crack at questioning her, but she's absent.

After receiving that text in the parking lot, I could feel eyes on the back of my neck the entire ride home. Watching us.

Someone knew we were at the hospital.

Cass's knuckles were white on the wheel. I couldn't stop checking the rearview mirror.

A white van stayed exactly two cars behind us the whole way back to Hartsdale, but it turned off a few streets before mine. Maybe I was only being paranoid. There are millions of white vans in the world.

It's hard to pretend that text didn't scare me, especially after the photos the other day. But those pictures were only of me. Now this person is after Cass as well.

But whoever sent it is obviously scared, too. *We're* scaring them. Which means we're on the right track.

"Flora?" Ms. Hernandez calls me back to the present. She taps the problem on the board. "Any ideas?"

My notes are missing the last three steps, courtesy of my space out, and the whole problem's lost to me now.

"Sorry, I'm stuck." I shrug.

Ms. Hernandez narrows her eyes. In her class, if you don't know the answer, you're supposed to have questions prepared. I watch her take in the blue circles under my eyes, my unwashed hair. She calls on someone else.

Math is usually my best class, when I'm not wrapped up in a murder investigation.

Back at my place, Cass and I took a closer look at the text. Instead of a regular phone number, it just had a jumbled string of letters, symbols, and numbers. Neither of us had any idea what that meant, and eventually Cass had to go to rehearsal.

"I'm fine," she tried to assure me before she left. "If someone wants to scare us, they're going to have to do a little better than some cheesy threat, right? What, did they get that from an episode of *Law & Order*?"

She had a point. *You'll regret it* isn't exactly the most original. Then again, Cass doesn't know about the photos. Those felt real.

For all her assurances, Cass couldn't quite meet my eyes

as she walked out the door, and I still couldn't bring myself to tell her just how serious things actually are. Not when she had to go play music and not look like an idiot in front of her crush.

After she left, I tried to research Molly some more. Nothing new came up. Before she got hurt, she lived in Whitley and went to Roosevelt High. One article mentioned that she was on the honor roll and the dance team, but that's it for personal details. It's like she didn't exist before this terrible thing happened to her. Just like Ava, in a way. When you're alive, you get to be a three-dimensional human being, and then when you die everything about you gets erased and flattened until your memory is just a cardboard cutout of who you used to be.

Only Molly's not dead.

All the articles were published the first week of December. After that, the press lost interest. It was just a random robbery. Sad, but mundane. In a city like Whitley, who thinks twice about that kind of thing? Months have passed, and the police are no closer to figuring out who hurt Molly. So far, it doesn't look like Ava's case is going to be any different.

If the same person is behind both of these crimes, Molly would have been almost like practice for Ava's murder. The killer knew exactly where and how to dump the body so that the police would forget about it and move on, just like they did before. And have there been others? How many kids have been dumped in Whitley alleyways to be forgotten?

My math class has fallen silent around me. Everyone is staring at the doorway.

Paige Thomas has finally showed up for class. Her arm is in a sling, and her shoulders and neck are rigid with pain. But that's not what everyone is looking at.

The entire right side of Paige's face is a swollen mass of purples and reds. Her skin is stretched tight and shiny like overripe fruit. Her eye is barely more than a slit.

Looking at Paige's wrecked face, I am suddenly back on that trail in the ninth grade, staring with uncomprehending eyes at the heap of blood and bone and black flies that couldn't possibly be a human body, let alone a girl I knew.

I blink, and I'm back in math class.

Ms. Hernandez snaps out of her stunned silence. "Oh, dear. Paige, are you all right?" She realizes what an absurd question it is and collects herself. "Maybe it would be better if you went home to rest?"

Paige looks around the room, her eyes passing over every face. The accusation in her gaze is undeniable.

You did this to me.

For their part, our classmates shift in their seats. They're no longer staring—now they can't look at Paige at all.

Something must have gone horribly wrong in the Basement. Maybe Austin finally snapped, or someone is trying to send a message. Could be the same person who's been watching me.

"I'll be fine, thank you," Paige says. Her voice is slightly thick. It can't be easy to talk with her injuries. She takes the only empty seat in the room: the one next to mine.

Ms. Hernandez tries to pick up where we left off, but she's flustered. She drops the dry erase marker twice.

I watch Paige. She's close enough now that I can see sweat beading at her temple, above her lip. She must be in a ton of pain.

I lean over in my seat. "What happened to you?"

Paige keeps her eyes trained on the board. "I fell off my horse this morning. I'll be fine."

"Did your parents actually buy that?"

Paige doesn't answer.

I try again. "I went to see Molly at the hospital."

Paige turns to me slowly. Up close, her face is even more horrifying. A diffuse nebula of maroons and indigos and sickly greens. Her one slitted eye gives her a grotesque, carnival-mask look. Her hair is pulled up in another high, tight ballerina bun like yesterday. The contrast of her neat hair and nightmarish face only makes her look more grisly.

"Flora, look at me," she says. "If you like your face the way it is, I'd stop asking questions about Molly."

Paige doesn't speak to me again for the rest of class. She darts out as soon as the bell rings.

Paige's injuries weren't just a message to her, or to me. The warning has been made clear to the whole school: keep your mouth shut. No one is going to answer any of my questions now.

I have another source, though, if I could set my feelings aside for long enough to deal with him.

I duck into the closest bathroom. Valentine's phone rings for a long time before he answers.

"Wasn't sure I'd hear from you again, Cherry." He sounds genuinely pleased. I get that tight little *zip!* in my gut.

"This isn't a social call." I keep my tone flat and business-like. "Paige Thomas, Molly Sawyer. You know either of them? They've got some kind of connection to the Basement."

"Don't know many people's real names," he admits.

"Molly's white, blond, she's in a coma?" I try.

"Sorry, I got nothing. I can ask around."

"Okay, what about Paige—short black girl, kind of quiet? Looks like she got seriously beat up last night."

He inhales sharply. "Yeah, her I know. The Ice Queen. Brutal, what they did to her."

Ice Queen. That's what Austin called her. I didn't realize it was a stage name. So Paige was actually fighting in the Basement, as hard as that is to imagine.

"What happened?" I ask.

"Mismatched her fight. The girl she was up against, they call her the Viking. Must be closing in on six feet, and she wasn't holding back."

I lean against the bathroom sink. "Is that unusual?"

"'Course it's unusual," he scoffs. "Look, it's good business if the fights seem out of control, but they're not. At least not for the minors. Can't have anyone's parents finding out, right? Any kid gets an injury they can't easily hide, they get taken off the schedule for three months, minimum. There's an honor code, of sorts. You don't fuck with someone else's face unless you want payback."

I chew my thumbnail as I think that over. "Your face is always a mess, and the fight I saw wasn't very even, either. That guy must have had a hundred pounds on you."

"Took him down anyway, didn't I?" Some of his usual arrogant swagger is back, but he falters. "Besides, not like there's anyone who'd care if I got hurt."

I don't know how to respond to that.

"Anyway," he says, "that girl—the Ice Queen? She's good. Lot of money gets bet on her fights. After last night, I don't think she'll fight again. Whatever she did to piss off the boss, it was bad enough they decided she was expendable."

And she wouldn't even talk to me. How much worse would they do if she had? Would they kill her like Ava?

Before, I only wanted to find Ava's killer and make them pay. But the Basement needs to be shut down. None of us will be safe if it's allowed to continue to exist.

Valentine says, "There's another fight tonight, Cherry. Want to play recon, be my date? Can get you behind the velvet rope."

My face goes warm at the word *date*. It's a mix of anger and shameful pleasure, but as usual I don't know what the ratio is.

"I am not your date for anything, ever," I snap.

I can practically hear him roll his eyes. "Just pretend, Red. I heard Dorsey might show tonight, is all." He drops his voice. "I know I screwed up. Let me make it up to you."

The thought of being alone with him again ties my gut up in knots. But if I have a chance to eavesdrop on Dorsey, I can't pass up the opportunity.

"Fine," I mutter. "I'll meet you in the parking lot."

"It's a date." He hangs up before I can protest.

I exit the bathroom and keep walking toward my gym

class. How much can I trust what Valentine told me? He could still be holding stuff back, feeding me just enough new information to make me think he's finally on my side for real.

I turn down the hall and spot a familiar pair of broad shoulders walking ahead of me.

I hustle to catch up. "Hey, Austin."

He walks faster. So do I.

"Austin, I think you might be in danger." I didn't consider it before, when I thought he might have been the one who hurt Paige, but Austin's the one who let Molly's name slip in the first place.

He doesn't slow down. "No idea what you're talking about."

"I saw what happened to Paige. They know you're the one who told me about Molly, you're not safe—"

He stops walking and bends close to my face. A vein pulses in his temple. "Look, you crazy bitch, I don't know what you're talking about. Everyone knows you're a lying psycho who makes shit up for fun. Stop following me. I don't need anyone to see me talking to you."

He stalks off, throwing open the door to the boys' locker room and disappearing inside.

I hesitate for a moment. I could follow him into the locker room. It's not like I haven't done it before, and I don't think it even matters if he's seen talking to me at this point. Lots of people heard him yell Molly's name in the middle of the hallway. Whoever wants her kept quiet has to be gunning for him already.

But he's obviously terrified. I don't need to torture him with a public confrontation—he's not going to listen to me anyway.

I turn and head down the hall. I'm running late. The girls' locker room is basically empty. I start pulling gym clothes out of my bag.

I'm pulling my shirt on when a bone-shattering scream cuts through the air. It goes on and on.

I run back out into the hall, still pulling my arms through my sleeves. It's coming from the weight-training room. Everyone in the gym must have heard it, too, because they're all stampeding in the same direction. There's a bottleneck at the door. Several people taller than me are looking into the room with horrified expressions on their faces. I fight my way to the front.

Austin is lying on his back on one of the weight machines. His neck is crushed under the weight bar. His terrified eyes dart around the room like he's an animal with his paw caught in a trap. He struggles, but he can't lift the bar.

"That's fucked up," someone says from behind me.

"Nasty," someone else agrees.

I rush forward and pull at the weight, but it's too heavy for me to lift. "Someone help him! He's going to suffocate like that." Everyone looks at me like I'm speaking in tongues.

Coach Rieger pushes her way through the crowd. "Everyone get back! Carson, Walker? Get that bar off his neck!"

Two guys do as she asked. The weight lifted, Austin lies on his back and pants for breath.

Someone must have sabotaged his machine. I crouch beside it to look. There's a safety-lock mechanism that's supposed to click into place when you set the bar down. It's been taped over with duct tape.

Austin sits up slowly. His neck is already swelling with the beginnings of a huge purple-red bruise.

He looks right at me. "*You*. This is your fault."

The whole school knows Austin's injury wasn't an accident, especially after what happened to Paige. The whispers pick up momentum, which only makes my omnipresent headache worse.

Cass and I make a pit stop at her place to pick up supplies, then head to my house to get me ready for my mission. I sit on the edge of my bed while she applies my makeup.

Cass turns my chin from one side to the other, evaluating my face. "Okay, so this date. What kind of look are we going for?" Her tone is brisk, but she's blinking a lot.

"Not a date," I remind her.

She grabs her makeup bag. "I'm thinking Leather Sandy from the end of *Grease* meets Imperator Furiosa from *Mad Max*."

I groan, but Cass is a genius with wardrobe stuff. Whatever she says, goes. Plus, a disguise might not be so bad. I wouldn't mind being someone else for a night.

Cass grips an eye-shadow brush so hard her knuckles turn white. I know she's really rattled about what happened to Paige and Austin, and now it's harder to pretend the text we got yesterday was just an empty threat. I wish I knew how to reassure her.

"Are you okay?" I ask.

She smudges black glitter over my eyelids. "I don't know."

I try to think what she would say. "Things have seriously escalated in the last twenty-four hours. You can be scared. I am."

It strikes me as I say it—this is the first time I've admitted that out loud since the night Ava died.

Cass concentrates on removing every last clump from her mascara wand. "I *am* scared. The more we investigate, the more people will get hurt, and it could be me or you, but it could also be some totally innocent bystander. I hate thinking we could be responsible for that."

The makeup is already making my face itch. "I know. That scares me, too."

She tilts my chin back and begins coating my lashes. "I *know,* but you make it next to impossible to talk to you about any of this stuff, and it's not like I have anyone else. So I just end up freaking out on my own."

It always amazes me. How effortless it is for Cass to just say how she's feeling. I want to be more like that.

It's easier when I don't have to meet her eyes. "I know I'm a train wreck. I get all obsessive about the case so I don't have to deal, and I end up shutting you out in the process. I'm sorry."

Cass snorts. "Well, at least you're a self-aware train wreck." She switches to my other eye, pausing for a long time before she says, "But the thing is, I really think we're on to something. I want us to bring this person down, no matter how scary things get. Right?"

I lean back to meet her eyes. "Right," I promise. "You and me, together."

She caps the mascara and chews her lip. "Are you sure you don't want me to come?"

Elliot called yet another rehearsal tonight, theoretically to help the band bond, but I suspect it's at least a little bit so he can hang out with Cass again. More than anything I wish she could watch my back tonight, but I remember yesterday at the memorial. How hesitant she was to commit to extra practice, because she was afraid to leave me on my own.

I give her my best stern face. "You are going to rehearsal, young lady, and you *will* have inappropriate thoughts about your bandmate and you *will* tell me about them after."

Cass gives me an impatient look. "That's pretty rich, considering you've told me more or less nothing about your guy."

He's not my guy, I almost say. A reflex.

When I try to talk about how I feel, sometimes it's like there's something physically blocking the words from coming out of my mouth.

For Cass, though, I can try.

"I don't know. I trust him, and then I don't, and then I do, but he screws it up." I lie back on my bed while Cass rifles through her makeup bag. "Plus, it's too weird. I only met him because Ava was murdered."

Cass shoots me an exasperated look. "You're right. If you ignore your feelings entirely, they'll definitely go away."

I throw DeeDee, my stuffed monkey, at her but miss.

What she's saying sounds right, but there are actual consequences to trusting him. He's sold me out once before, and I know there's someone after me. Valentine could be dangerous if he wanted to be.

Cass holds up an electric-purple wig.

I sit up. "What the hell is that?"

"Your new Barbie dream hair." She combs her fingers through it, primping and fluffing the ends.

It must be her mom's. It's clearly expensive, not some cheap, ratty thing you buy at the mall.

"I'm not wearing that," I say.

Cass gives me a sharp look. "Don't be stupid. The last time you went there, they sent VT after you, and things have only gotten more dangerous. You can't be recognized tonight."

I scowl at her.

She's unmoved. "Now, go get me some bobby pins."

I stomp over to my desk, but my pins aren't in their usual drawer. I hunt through the chaos of papers—it's been a while since I've bothered to tidy up. My eyes snag on something that wasn't there before.

Newspaper clippings. Two of them, stapled together.

I glance over my shoulder at Cass. She's texting someone. Probably Elliot, from the smile on her face.

I pick the clippings up. The first one is Lucy MacDonald's obituary. In the accompanying photo, her eyes have been scrawled over with Sharpie, leaving nothing but black, staring voids behind. Something cold trickles down the back of my neck.

The second page is Ava's obituary. Her eyes are scratched out, too. Over her face someone wrote in thick, dark letters:

YOU'RE NEXT

They were here. In my room. The papers rustle slightly in my shaking hands.

The makeup Cass just applied feels hot and tight on my face. I can hear her behind me, tapping away on her phone. She's probably still smiling. The shaking gets worse.

"Where are those pins?" Cass asks.

Without turning around, I slide the clippings underneath the other piles on my desk.

"Olive must have borrowed them. Be right back." I walk out quickly, before she can get a good look at my face.

In the bathroom, I bite down on my knuckles to keep from crying out.

Did they do it while I was at school? Or was I here, maybe sleeping? Did they stand over me, watch me? Smile with satisfaction that they could violate me like that, stand in my private room with me curled up and vulnerable? Powerless to do anything, even if I woke up.

I stand there, teeth embedded in my own fist, eyes squeezed shut, and ride out the wave of terror and panic.

When the shivers finally stop, I'm left feeling empty again. I stare at myself in the mirror. The sparkly black raccoon makeup makes it hard to tell I just had a complete mental breakdown. In efficient, mechanical movements, I grab a fresh packet of bobby pins from Olive's stash and head back to my room.

My grandfather is passing through the hall. We both pause. We haven't talked much since our conversation in the car yesterday.

He looks me over. "Where are you off to?"

I still don't know exactly where we stand. I have no idea how he'll react if I tell him where I'm going.

He sees my hesitation, and I don't miss the flash of sadness in his eyes.

"Recon," I say. "I have a lead on Dorsey." I leave out the part about the fight club.

He knows it's not the full truth, but he only says, "Please remember to bring your Taser, and your cell phone must be on you at all times."

My heart expands in my chest. We're both struggling. But we're trying.

CHAPTER 19

Valentine's smoking next to his car in the parking lot. His eyes trace over the wig, the tight, high-waisted jeans Cass picked out for me.

"You dress up for me?" He gives me one of those wolf grins.

The sight of him has me furious all over again, especially because that aching pull hasn't gone away, either. I pull my jacket tighter. These clothes so aren't me, but they make me feel a little safer. It's like armor, pretending to be someone else.

"A boy can dream," I say tartly.

"Nah." Valentine steps into my space. He runs his fingers through the purple ends of my wig, watchful eyes waiting to see if I pull away. "In my dreams, you're never anyone but Red."

It's so tempting to listen to Cass on this one. To give in and stop worrying about it.

But people are getting hurt, and someone was in my room, and what I really need right now is answers.

I step back. "Let's do this."

Valentine leads me around the side of the building to a different entrance. Employees only, I guess. When we reach the bottom of the stairwell, he slips one arm around my back.

I tense. "What are you doing?" His hand rests underneath my jacket, and I can feel the heat of his palm through the thin cotton of my shirt.

"Playing the part." He quirks one eyebrow.

A door opens to the left, and a man in a gray suit appears. Valentine pulls me tighter to his side. I can feel the press of each of his fingertips through my shirt.

The man approaches with an easy, slouchy gait, hands casual in his suit pockets. Medium-brown hair, a little gray around the temples, average height. He looks familiar, but I can't place him. Then again, all middle-aged white dudes kind of look the same to me.

"VT. I was about to call you." The man turns his attention to me. "And who is this?"

"My new girl, Violet," Valentine drawls. "Violet, this is Mr. Boyd. He runs the place."

During our conversation under the bleachers, Valentine said it was Boyd who gave him the orders to throw me off the case. This guy knows *exactly* who Flora Calhoun is. He might even be the one following me. The one in my room.

I resist the urge to tug on my wig. Suddenly, it seems like a pretty weak disguise. It's cold in the dank tunnel, but a bead of sweat drips down my spine.

I shove my fear away. I'm here, and he's seen me. It's too late to run.

Tonight I'm Violet, and I'm not afraid of him.

I pout and offer him a limp hand. He shakes it with a tight-lipped smile.

Valentine turns on the smarm. "I want my girl to see the action from the good seats." He stage-whispers, "You know how the girls are with the blood and violence. Gets them all *agitated*."

Gross, but Violet just giggles inanely.

Like he can read my thoughts, Valentine looks back at me and winks.

Boyd's expression remains neutral. "Martin didn't show. I need you to take his slot."

Valentine's lazy smile falters. "C'mon, man. It's my day off."

The two of them maintain their casual posture, but Valentine's fingers have tightened on my hip, and Boyd picks a piece of lint from his suit jacket with too much precision.

Something's wrong here.

Boyd says, "I've done a lot of favors for you, VT, and now I'm asking you to extend me that same kindness."

The implied threat gets my hackles up.

I turn to Valentine and use my brattiest Violet voice. "It's date night. You can't just abandon me!"

Valentine gives me a tight smile, but there's a warning underneath. "It's fine," he says to Boyd. "Let me get her set up at a table, and I'll come back."

"Excellent." Boyd gives me another lukewarm smile and walks past.

I have a million questions, but I hold my tongue while Boyd is still within earshot. Valentine's unease sets my own nerves on edge.

The clamor of the crowd thunders through a set of metal doors. I step through into the throbbing darkness of the club. The air is a thick, gritty fog of smoke and body odor. We're standing on a raised platform area behind the ring. A dingy velvet rope separates this section from the commonfolk.

Valentine leads me over to a table and sits. He stares at me like he's about to say something, but nothing comes.

He's making me nervous, so I inspect the room. There are a few people seated at the other VIP tables, but Dorsey is nowhere to be seen. I peer out into the crowd. A couple faces stand out. Two girls from my math class drinking by the bar. A whole cluster of kids from the lacrosse team standing in line to place bets. And there are other people our age I don't recognize. Kids from other schools.

Valentine drums his hands on the tabletop, but every time I make eye contact he looks away.

I have to shout to be heard over the laughs and swears of the crowd. "What's wrong?"

Blue shadows pool in the hollows of his cheeks. "Don't like the thought of leaving you alone in the lion's den."

I'm getting that feeling again like he's not telling me something. And I've been horribly right every other time.

He props his elbows on the table and leans closer. "I need you to promise me something. You stay here while I'm gone. No rogue missions, okay?"

"You can't expect me to sit here and do nothing if—"

He cuts me off. "There's scary people here. What they did to that girl, Paige? They'd do worse to you in a heartbeat. I know people who can keep an eye on you, but you have to stay put. Don't go off by yourself. This is real, Flora. Promise me."

If the seriousness in his voice didn't do it, the use of my real name certainly gets my attention.

"If we're in this together," I tell him, "I have to know what this is really about."

He picks at a scab on his knuckle. "I don't like it, the fight getting switched at the last minute. Boyd's up to something."

"So why did you say yes?"

He shakes his head. "I walk out, I burn bridges. Bridges I need, yeah? For Annabelle."

Right. His sister. I can understand that. If it were Olive, or Cass, I'd do anything. Is that all this is, though?

Whatever he's hiding, he's not going to leave me alone if I don't agree to his rules, and I need to be here when Dorsey arrives.

"I'll stay here. I promise."

"Thank you." He touches my hand, the barest brush before he pulls away. "I better get back there." I watch him put that anxious part of himself away. Now he's the same guy I first met, all slick, sideways smiles. That's my cue, too.

I lean back in my chair, sprawled and relaxed as Violet. "Fight good."

He laughs once, edgy and quick, then departs.

Announcer guy enters the ring. Tonight his suit is baby blue, and he has a fedora.

"Aaand ladies and gentlemen, it's time for our first fight of the evening. Give it up for Dodging Jack and the Razor!"

Two guys dance into the ring. They're about my age, but I don't know them.

They grapple and gnaw at each other, fists against flesh, but there's none of that poetic artistry I noticed right away with Valentine. I suppose that's not surprising. They can't all be classically trained dancers turned super MMA fighting machines.

The night drags on. My eyes twitch to the door so often it turns into a permanent tic. I'm all wound up with nowhere to direct my energy.

Until the fourth fight, when the congressman arrives.

Electricity crackles over my skin. He's here. He's really here. All those doubts about whether Dorsey was really involved or it was just my own biased paranoia vanish, because he's here.

Valentine told the truth—he wasn't playing me.

Dorsey looks the same as he did at Ava's memorial, with the shiny helmet of thick, dark hair and a perfectly tailored suit. He casts a careful look around, but no one besides me notices him.

He takes an empty table near the wall. It's deep in the shadows, but I can still see my mark well enough in my peripherals.

"And now it's time for our fan favorite: the one, the only VEEETEEEEEEE!"

My idiot jogs into the ring, silk robe fluttering behind him as he shadowboxes for the crowd.

Valentine's eyes meet mine as he goes to his corner. He glances Dorsey's way, and I give him a reassuring nod. I'll behave myself. A little of the tension leaves his shoulders.

One corner of his mouth tugs up, and mine does the same of its own accord.

How is it that he elicits this completely out-of-control reaction from me?

Valentine's eyes fall closed. He rolls his neck and shoulders. Sucks in a deep breath through his nose.

His eyes open, still locked on mine, but they're darker now. Hungry.

I recross my legs.

The bell rings.

Valentine's opponent is a bit closer to his weight class than last time, but the guy still looks like 'roid rage personified. I check back in with Dorsey. The chair opposite him is still empty.

Now that Valentine's told me about his tragic career as a dancer, I can see it even more clearly in his moves. He leaps through the air, and his face is cast in the dim glow of the ring lights. His words from the park echo back to me.

That feeling of leaping onstage. Exultation.

He lands a savage one-two combo to the other guy's jaw.

Dorsey's on his phone. He has one hand pressed to his ear to drown out the violent soundtrack of the club.

The crowd hisses, and my eyes snap back to the stage. Valentine is on the ground. His opponent bashes his fist into Valentine's cheek, once, twice, three times. My stomach turns over. Blood coats the guy's knuckles. Valentine springs back to his feet. The other guy barely has time to turn his head before he's down on the ground.

The bell dings, and Valentine's eyes meet mine. His tongue darts out to swipe a trickle of blood pooling in the corner of his mouth. I grit my teeth against a racking full-body shiver.

Shouts and cheers. Valentine exits without looking my way again.

I check back in with Dorsey. He's scrolling through his phone. The light of the screen gives his face a sickly alien glow.

On the other side of the ring, movement in the crowd snares my attention. The next match hasn't started yet, but there's a cluster of people screaming and jeering like a fight is about to break out. I squint against the bright glare of the lights, and with a flash of horror I realize I'm staring at Paige Thomas.

A small but very angry mob is forming around her. One guy shoves her. Paige winces as he jostles her broken arm, but she stands her ground.

What does she think she's doing? Showing up at school to prove you're not scared is one thing, but she shouldn't have come here. She's going to get killed.

A vicious wave ripples through the crowd, gaining momentum. Paige looks so small in this ocean of seething hatred.

Someone throws their drink in her face. Little droplets trickle across her ghastly bruises, but she barely blinks.

I'm trying to keep one eye on Dorsey, but I'm half out of my seat. Could I get to her before she's torn apart? The crowd begins to part around her, and I spot a big guy dressed in all black, speaking into a walkie-talkie. Security. He wraps an arm around Paige's shoulders and attempts to escort her out, but she's had enough. She shakes the security guy off and pushes her way through the crowd on her own, back toward the exit. Another asshole tries to shove her as she passes, but she stomps on his foot.

The security guard watches her all the way out the door. Once she's gone, he shakes his head and melts back into the shadows at the perimeter. The crowd merges back together, all hostility forgotten as the next fight begins in the ring. I ease back into my seat.

In the corner of my eye, I see someone approaching Dorsey's table. This new man is also wearing a suit. An expensive one with sharp, crisp lines. He's in his thirties. Clean-shaven. He looks like your basic Wall Street type, which means he is very, very out of place here.

Wall Street unbuttons his suit jacket and sits. His expression is cordial, like they're meeting over coffee. In the ring, a new fight starts, but I barely notice.

Dorsey and his friend are deep in conversation, but I can't hear a thing. Something happens in the ring that makes the crowd screech and howl. I guess that's the point of meeting in a place like this.

Dorsey stands and adjusts his suit. Wall Street does the same.

Panic seizes me. They're leaving, and I haven't learned anything at all.

The two of them walk toward the back entrance.

I look around. Valentine is nowhere to be seen.

I promised him I would stay put.

For a second, Dorsey is illuminated in the light of the hall, and then he disappears. The door swings closed.

Valentine hasn't been totally straight with me, though. Twice now I've found out he was lying. Even tonight, I don't think he gave me the full truth. Am I really going to miss out on a lead for him?

I stand up. Conscious that Valentine has people looking out for me, I slink out the back door and shut it carefully. Dorsey and Wall Street are walking away. They don't notice me as they round the corner, out of sight. The echo of the empty tunnel distorts their words.

I edge along the wall, mindful of how I place my feet. The voices sharpen.

"—can't believe you wanted to meet here, of all places," Dorsey says.

"I didn't want us to be overheard."

"Still. The optics aren't great. If anyone recognized me—"

"Relax, no one was paying attention."

Dorsey lets out a brief chuckle. "Yes. Whoever runs this place certainly has a knack for show business."

Their voices fade again. They're on the move. I creep closer to the corner. Any farther and my shadow will be visible.

"So when can I expect deliverables?" Dorsey asks.

"Soon, now that we've removed certain *obstacles*. Very soon."

My heart kicks into high gear. I'm a child playing hide-and-seek, while two men casually discuss murder a few feet away. One of them could turn around at any moment, and I wouldn't have time to make it back inside unnoticed.

"That is excellent news," Dorsey says.

The grinding sound of a metal door opening, then a slam as it closes. The hall is silent.

I already broke my promise. Might as well go all the way.

I race down the hall after them. Up the stairs on light, quiet feet. Out the door and into the parking lot.

No one's there.

I spin around, but Dorsey and his friend have vanished.

It's that stupid promise I made. If I hadn't sat there dithering over it, I might have gotten something real from Dorsey's conversation.

"Aw, now, don't be disappointed," a voice slithers out of the shadows. "*We* can always keep you company."

CHAPTER 20

Three men approach me. If we were in a movie, these guys would be listed in the credits as Bad Dudes One, Two, and Three. Bad Dude Two cracks his knuckles. It could almost be comical, but the hairs on the back of my neck stand straight to attention.

My eyes flick from one to the next, trying to catalog details in the dim light in case I need to make a police report. Three white guys, maybe in their twenties. One of them is wearing a yellow hoodie. Another has acne scars.

I take a tiny step backward.

One of the guys takes a step to my left, blocking me in. "Where you going, sweetheart?" He looks me up and down but doesn't come any closer. For now.

My Taser is tucked in my jacket pocket. Am I fast enough to reach for it before they make a move? There are three of them. I can't keep my eyes on all three at once.

Sprinting footsteps behind me. "Cherry!" Relief floods through me.

I keep my eyes on our enemies as Valentine jogs up behind me.

"Thought I told you to stay put," he mutters.

"Got distracted."

The three men close in. Valentine and I step closer together. We're still outnumbered.

"Cherry"—Valentine's voice is low and even, as though we've stumbled upon a pack of gorillas—"get in the car."

In slow motion, he reaches over and hands me his keys. Everyone's eyes track the movement. My hands tremble as I take them.

Acne Scars takes another step closer. He and his friends exchange grins.

"Red," Valentine says again, this time more urgently. "The car."

It's parked four spaces away. I raise my chin, steel my spine, and take a step toward the car.

The world erupts.

Valentine darts in front of me, and the men fall in around him. He fights to kill—none of the showy moves from earlier. He lays one guy out flat, but another one gets his hands around Valentine's throat from behind.

Valentine wheels on him and catches sight of me. "Red, move!"

I remember myself and reach for the car door.

Someone grabs me from behind and spins me around. A metallic *shwing* sound, and then there's a knife inches from my eye. The man leans in close. His breath is warm on my skin. He traces the blade in the air over my face. Choosing where to start.

"Wanted to get you alone," he murmurs like a lover. "I know you've been a nosy girl."

I knee him in the balls as hard as I can.

He doubles over but doesn't let go. His fingers bruise my arm. "You fucking bitch. Think you're so fucking cute," he pants. Presses the knife to my cheek. "Let's just see."

The knife goes in. I cry out. Blood trickles warm down my cheek and over my lips. It tastes like panic.

The guy is ripped away from me. His knife clatters to the ground, the sound a dull, slow-motion echo. Valentine drags the man to the asphalt. He punches him in the face again, and again, and again.

"I. Said," he screams in time with his punches. "Get. In. The. Fucking. Car."

I climb in the passenger side, scrambling over the console to reach the driver's seat. My hands shake, and I drop the keys on the floor, but I finally manage to start the car.

Valentine is still busy pummeling the guy into a red slick.

"VT, come on!" I yell out the window.

"You go!" His fists don't stop.

"Not without you!" I yell back. One of the other men peels himself off the pavement. Valentine doesn't see him.

I fumble in my jacket pocket and pull out the Taser. I grip it with both hands and aim it out the car window. Two wires unspool in front of me, flying through the air and latching into the back of the man's bright yellow sweatshirt.

He goes rigid as a plank as fifty thousand volts surge through his body. He teeters and goes down hard.

The sound of the man hitting the pavement finally penetrates Valentine's bubble. He hurls himself into the car, half slumped over with one hand pressed to his side.

Blood trickles through his knuckles. "Drive!"

I slam on the gas, and the car screams out of the parking lot. I don't even make it to the driveway, just thud over the curb. The impact makes Valentine hunch over with a gasp. I have no idea how bad that wound under his hand is, but blood blooms across his white T-shirt like ink.

"You alive?" I glance sideways. He's not holding himself up too well.

"Peachy," he spits.

"Did you know those guys?"

"Seen 'em around. Never did anything to piss them off, though."

My cheek itches as the blood dries to a crust. "It's me. This is Dorsey's message."

"Smart girl." He rolls his eyes.

"Really not in the mood for sarcasm while I'm driving our getaway car."

He snipes back, "I'm pissed at myself. I left you alone. Should have known you would pull some stupid stunt like this. Turn left."

God, he knows how to make me furious. His shirt is half red by now, and it's my fault he's hurt, but it kills me to hear him say stuff like that. Like I'm some naive kid in over my head.

I take the turn a little too aggressively. Valentine slides into the side of the car and groans.

"You know who I am. What I do," I say. "How can you call me reckless when you get yourself beaten half to death every week?"

His voice is wheezy with pain, but no less vicious. "These people are dangerous, Red. You hear me? They are *criminals*. Murderers. You pulled some amateur, wannabe Nancy Drew shit, and it nearly got us both killed. If we're doing this together, no more mistakes like that. I trust you. You trust me."

"Fine!"

"Then it's been a learning experience for us all. Turn right up here." He flops back against the seat, breathing hard and watching me through half-lidded eyes. "You're bleeding."

"So are you," I bite out.

"Yeah, but I bleed all the time. It's practically my job."

I adjust my grip on the steering wheel. "I'll be okay. Just a scratch."

"That bastard nearly sliced your face off."

"But he didn't."

"Right up ahead." He takes a few more panting breaths. "You always this brave?"

"Brave. Stupid. Crazy bitch. I get called a lot of names."

"No. You're perfect," he murmurs. Two seconds ago he was yelling at me, and now he thinks he can say stuff like that?

"You're suffering from blood loss," I tell him. He laughs, but it turns into another groan.

We pull up in front of Valentine's building. He takes the four flights of stairs to his place slowly, wincing all the way, but refuses to lean on me when I offer.

With a jingle of keys, Valentine ushers me into his apartment. His kitchen table has one chair. I'm positive he found his living room couch on the street.

Valentine throws his keys on the couch. "Bathroom's this

way." He limps down the hall with one hand still pressed to his side.

I follow. There are no pictures on the walls. You'd think maybe at least one of the sister, but it's like a ghost lives here.

In the bathroom, Valentine pulls his bloody shirt over his head. My face heats, and I look at my feet. He's still bleeding, but he's also very close to me, and this bathroom is very small, and he's not wearing a lot of clothes. His tile could use a good scrub.

"Wash your face," he says.

I force myself to look in the mirror. A two-inch slash below my left eye. I am detached. Clinical. I probe the cut gingerly with one finger. It's not that deep—it just bled a lot. I'm okay.

Cass's dark, glitzy eye shadow looks particularly gruesome with all the blood. Some of it has crusted in my hair. Nothing to be done about that until I shower. I fish my lock-picking bobby pin out of my back pocket, bend it back into shape, and twist my hair up in a bun. My eyes keep dragging back to the cut. It's hard not to look at. It's not huge, but it swallows my entire face. It throbs. I can still feel that man's bruising grip on my shoulder, the tearing of my own skin as the knife sank in.

Turn on the faucet. Focus on the task. I cup water in my palms and dab it over my cheek. It stings, but the bleeding has stopped. With the dried bits cleared away, it's not so bad. All it needs is a bandage and an explanation for my grandfather. That thought makes me want to never go home again.

Behind me in the mirror, Valentine turns on the tub and grabs a washcloth. I take one last look at my face. I'm still a wreck, but I'll be okay for now.

My voice is hoarse. "Hey, let me."

He hands me the washcloth without a word.

"Sit," I tell him.

He hoists himself up on the sink, jaw clenched and forearms trembling slightly with the effort. He's in pain, a lot of it. Because of me.

He inhales sharply through his nose when I pass the washcloth over the long, deep cut. It's much worse than mine.

"What happened?" I ask.

"Knife," he says. I bite back the *duh* that's fighting to escape my mouth. He is hurt, after all. Guilt twists in my throat. I gently wipe the blood from his skin.

"You need stitches," I say eventually. "Give me back your keys. I'll drive us to the hospital."

"Under the sink," he grunts, eyes closed.

Confused, I crouch down and open the cabinet in question. Inside, there's a bottle of whiskey and a neat stack of hospital suture kits.

I rock back hard on my heels. "No. Absolutely, emphatically not."

He gives me a teasing pout, but it's undercut by the bloodlessness of his face. "Where's that brave girl from earlier?"

I don't budge.

Valentine rubs a hand over his eyes, dropping the act. "Listen. This fucking hurts. I don't have the cash to pay for a hospital visit, and you don't want doctors asking inconvenient questions or waking up your parents. Truth is, Cherry, you messed up tonight. You gonna take care of me, or leave me to bleed out in my own bathroom?"

I glare at him a moment longer, then grab one of the suture kits and slam the cabinet closed.

"Whiskey, too," he says.

"You're going to need it." I take the bottle out, too, and shove it at him. "Drink up."

He unscrews the cap and drinks deep. His Adam's apple bobs with every swallow. I busy myself with washing my hands.

"Where do you get these things?" I examine the contents of the suture kit. A curved needle. A length of surgical thread. Sterilizing wipe. Pair of scissors.

"Internet."

I stare at the wicked curve of the needle. "Okay, slugger. Talk me through this."

"Use the swab to sterilize the area. Don't want to die of sepsis or something." He takes a last swig of whiskey and sets the bottle down. Some of the tension slides out of his face.

I clean his cut and the skin around. Goose bumps rise to meet my touch. Despite the totally screwed-up nature of the situation, a tiny traitorous voice in the back of my head reminds me that this is the most I have ever touched him.

His breath stirs the air by my ear. "Now thread the needle. We're going to do an interrupted stitch, right? Means each stitch is its own thing, disconnected from the others, not like the frilly needlepoint you do."

I look up at him from under my lashes. "Do you want to make jokes, or do you want me to save your life?"

He laughs, then winces. "Look who's found herself a God complex now that she's got a needle in hand. All right, Cherry, hold the sides of the cut together with one hand. Take the needle, slip it through the skin on one side, and use the curved bit to scoop under and come out the other. You tie off the stitch with a knot and start again."

I stare at the deep cut in his side. I look at the needle in my hand. This seems like a very stupid idea. I'm not sure Valentine's drunk near enough whiskey.

"C'mon, Red. I know some part of you has always wanted to stab me."

I pinch the edges of his wound together. He hisses.

I push the needle into his skin. His knuckles grip white on the edge of the sink.

"Great," he grunts. "Now do like I said. Under and out the other side."

I pass the needle through, cut the thread, then tie the whole thing off.

"Whoa." My face is inches from his side. He twists around to see, nervous. "That was cool," I breathe.

"God help me," Valentine mutters and takes another slug of whiskey.

I slide the needle back through his skin. A tiny, choked moan escapes him. In and out. Tie off each knot. Again. Valentine takes slow breaths, like he's trying to meditate or something.

After the last stitch, I paste a clean white bandage over his side.

"Thanks." He hops off the sink and pats the counter twice. "Your turn."

"I'm fine. It doesn't need anything." I turn to leave the bathroom. Nothing good can happen with the two of us in this confined space.

He steps in front of me. "Let me take a look." He's still not wearing a shirt. My arguments dry up in my throat.

I take his place on the counter, and Valentine stands between my legs. I'm too warm, even though my jacket's in a heap by the front door, and I'm only wearing the flimsy black tank top Cass chose.

"Chin up." He wraps his pale, beaten fingers around my jaw, turning my face under the light to inspect my wound. Just like that first night, at the diner, his bruises look so much worse under the fluorescent lights.

"You ever get banged up like this before?" he asks. "On your first case. Lucy. Did he...?"

"No." The only time Matt Caine ever touched me was that hand on my shoulder. His thumb sweeping under the strap of my tank top.

My arm still aches where the guy tonight grabbed me. Pinned me to the car. Couldn't move. Couldn't run. Helpless.

I pull myself together and keep talking. "I was running from some guys last year, and I slipped in broken glass." I extend my right arm, exposing the jagged white thread of a scar that runs from my wrist to my elbow. "Seventeen stitches, but I got away. Not the same thing as a knife."

Valentine runs a finger over it. I shiver, but only slightly. Maybe he didn't notice. He swallows and pulls his hand back.

I angle my face back into the light. There's a dead wasp that's found its final resting place inside the light fixture.

Valentine wets a cotton ball with antiseptic. The smell is cold and sharp. I hiss at the sting as he swabs my face.

"Oh, don't be a baby," he says. I look down from the wasp to glare at him.

His eyes slide away from mine. "You took it pretty well. Lot of people couldn't handle a switchblade to the face."

I shift my seat on the hard counter. "You make it sound like I had an eye gouged out. It's just a cut."

But his gentle fingers on my face make the wound more real. Here, in his bathroom, no longer running for my life, all of my fear catches up to me.

I got hurt. Someone wants me dead, and tonight they nearly made it happen. I bite down until my teeth creak.

"You don't have to do that," Valentine says.

"What?"

"Pretend you're not afraid." He squints in concentration, cleaning my cut in quick, meticulous strokes, but I know he's watching my reaction out of the corner of his eye.

With inches between us, there's no room for that other side of him, the part of himself he uses like a wall between us. There's no room for that part of me, either.

"I am afraid." I'm so quiet, but he's close enough to hear. "I just don't see what good it does to admit it."

His eyes meet mine, and this time he doesn't look away.

I am painfully aware of his bare skin. So much of it, inches away. I never let myself look at him this much. There are two parallel freckles just below the outer corner of his right eye. His heartbeat flutters against the thin skin of his throat. Fragile and rabbit fast.

I could lean back now. Let those walls slide back into place.

I reach out, the pads of my fingers grazing his pulse point. He tenses, then leans into my touch. His skin is so, so warm. He closes his eyes, and a low hum of pleasure escapes him.

I lean forward to the very edge of the counter and press my lips to his.

Valentine's reaction is immediate. His arms wrap tight around me, pulling me close. He tastes warm and faintly sweet, like whiskey. I am touching him everywhere, hands on his back, his waist, the low dip of his hips. His fingers tangle in my sticky, bloody hair. My bun comes loose from its mooring.

My fear is gone. The only thing I feel now is the sharp scrape of his nails against my scalp, the desperate press of his lips to the skin behind my ear. I have held myself back from trusting him, from wanting him, since the day we met. But he was right there beside me in the fight tonight, and now all I can think is *closer* and *more*.

He stills. Exhales a ragged breath against my cheek and steps back.

I blink against the harsh lights. Valentine's not looking at me anymore. He fumbles to open a fresh bandage. His lips are swollen pink from kissing, and an electric bolt of longing zaps through me. He's still not looking at me.

"What the hell was that?" I manage.

"Turn your face back into the light."

I wait, but he keeps his eyes on the ground. I do as he asked, still waiting for a real response, but he just smooths the bandage over my cheek. His touch is light and fast, like he's trying to avoid too much contact with my skin.

He hesitates, then offers his hand to help me down from the sink. He doesn't immediately let go once my feet are on the ground.

He did this that first day, too. At the dumpster. Here we are again, back where we started. We keep spinning around in circles. It makes me want to scream.

We stand there, chest to chest, with my hand wrapped in his. His eyelids are heavy and his lips parted. I could reach out and touch him again. I can see the tension in his wrist, in his shoulders, his jaw. How much he wants me to do it.

I'm suspended in amber. Unable to move. Too confused and vulnerable to make that choice again.

After a moment, he lets go of my hand.

"Let's get you home, Cherry."

I can feel Valentine's eyes on the side of my face as I watch the road. We're about a minute away from my house.

I'm driving again. No way was I getting in the passenger seat after all the whiskey he drank, and he didn't put up much of an argument. After the kiss, I think he just wanted to get rid of me as fast as possible.

He keeps almost saying something.

He drums his fingers against his knee. I gnaw on my lip. When he does this, it usually means he's lying about something.

I park down the street from my house, but neither one of us moves.

He finally speaks. "I'm sorry."

I stare out the window. I don't want to hear him apologize for the kiss, or tell me it was a mistake. That much was already clear.

"I didn't mean what I said before," he says. "If it were me, if it were Annabelle, I'd have chased after Dorsey, too."

I look around, surprised. The lights are off. He's lit only by the thin, silvery light of the moon.

"Yeah, but you got hurt," I say slowly. "That's my fault."

He shakes his head once. "Dorsey did that, and you and I will make him pay. For all of it."

I'm suddenly aware of how small the car is, how little air there is between us. I remember again the way his skin shivered under my hands, the ruthless grip of his hands in my hair. Even in the dark, I can tell he's remembering all the same things.

He says, "I want to teach you self-defense."

The moment breaks. "Excuse me?"

He takes a breath to say something, then pauses, like he's changed his mind. "I won't always be around, you know? Can't be your muscle all the time."

My chest constricts at the thought of him gone. It's the same unsettled feeling I got in his barren apartment. Like he might vanish at any moment.

Valentine adds, "Plus, if I ever really piss you off, I want you to be able to kick my ass."

He's deflecting. Putting the walls back up. I guess it's his turn to do that.

Still, it's not a bad idea. I got cornered tonight, and it didn't feel good.

Another vision flashes through my mind. His hands on my shoulders as he shows me how to punch. Valentine, flushed and sweaty, tackling me to a gym mat. His mouth inches away.

I suck in my cheeks. Not going there.

His shifts in his seat as he waits for my response, like he's afraid I'm going to tear him apart for the suggestion.

I say, "Yeah, okay. Teach me."

He smiles. The good smile. I feel myself doing the same.

I wait for a moment. Give him one more chance. He doesn't move.

I unbuckle my seat belt. "Okay, then. Night."

He ducks his head. "Night, Cherry."

CHAPTER 21

I stand in front of my bedroom mirror in the dark. My arm is tender, and I twist to see the bruises on my biceps. Five of them. Five fingers that grabbed me. There's another sore spot on my lower back, where he pressed me into the car door.

My joints ache. That happens when adrenaline wears off.

The white bandage on my cheek looks blue in the moonlight. It's freckled with small dark spots where blood has leaked through.

The shaking starts at the tips of my fingers and spreads through my whole body. My knees go weak and give out. I am alone in my room, and there are no more distractions from my fear. My bones tremble with the force of it. A sob surges out of me so strong, it's soundless.

The lights blink on. I don't lift my face from my hands.

My grandfather's voice. "What happened?"

I want to hide my face forever. I never want him to see.

I lift my head and blink into the bright lights. He's standing over me. As he takes in the bandage on my face, his expression shifts from mild concern to a blind terror that matches my own.

He sinks to the ground beside me. "Who hurt you?"

I don't think I've ever seen him on his knees before. The shaking starts up again. There's a block in my throat. I can't speak.

He touches my face, turning my cheek to see the bandage. He's gentle, but I shrink away.

"What happened?" His voice rises with desperation. "Tell me."

"It's just a scratch." DeeDee, the stuffed monkey I threw at Cass earlier, is still lying on my floor. A point to focus on, so I don't have to look at anything else.

He says quietly, "Don't lie to me."

DeeDee blurs.

"Look at me," he says. Then louder: "Look at me!"

I tear my eyes away from the monkey. He's a tall man. It's unbearable to see him at my eye level.

I look at my knees. "I followed Dorsey, okay? Some guys didn't like that, but I'm *fine*. I got away. It's just a cut."

I screamed when the knife went in. What would Gramps do, if he'd seen me like that? Pinned up against the car. Helpless.

He doesn't need to know.

I take a deep breath. "Look, I get that it's scary for your granddaughter to come home hurt, but—"

"You understand nothing." He rises to his feet and paces the room. "You're reckless. You are reckless, and foolish, and this stops now. You will end this."

Two and a half years ago, he said something similar. We were sitting in a parked car outside the police station. His hands gripped the steering wheel.

This is over. You are a child *if you think you're going to get him now.*

He was right that time. I *was* a child. But I'm trying so hard to be different now.

My bones scream in protest as I stand. "What happened to yesterday, all that stuff you said in the car? I thought you trusted me." I don't mean to yell, but I can't help it. In the back of my mind, a voice reminds me that he's afraid, too. But I'm tired, and I'm hurt, and I just need him to decide what kind of parent he wants to be because I can't take this whiplash anymore.

His voice rises to meet mine. "I trusted you not to be reckless, and you've betrayed that trust. You're *hurt,* Flora. What will make you take that seriously?"

Noises in the hall. Olive's awake.

"I do take it seriously, but what am I supposed to do? Cry? Hide? That's not me. You're supposed to know that."

He sighs. "I thought I could trust you to learn from your past mistakes. You have disappointed me."

We've arrived. This is the moment I am finally too much for him. I knew it was coming, but the pain of it knocks the wind out of me.

"Right back at you," I choke out.

His face looks more worn than usual. I've barely slept since Ava died. Maybe he's staring at his ceiling every night, too. I want more than anything to reach out to him now, for him to reach out to me.

We stand there—both exhausted and heartbroken, neither able to cross the few feet of distance between us.

He leaves. I wait until I hear his bedroom door close, then fall face-first on my bed and weep.

This used to happen a lot, with Mom. She would scream and plead and say horrible things that made me hate myself and her. And then she'd walk away, and I'd know she could hear me sobbing, but she never, ever came back to make sure I was okay.

It hurts more with him.

Someone enters the room, but I don't lift my head. I know it's Olive. I know he didn't come back.

The mattress sinks under her weight. "He didn't mean it."

"Yeah, he did. We both did. That's the problem." The pillow muffles my voice.

"No, the problem is that you two are practically the same person. You hold in your feelings until you explode."

I lift my head. "Stop being wise. It's annoying."

"I know." She puts her hand on my back. It's something Mom used to do when we were little and couldn't sleep. The gesture is comforting and disturbing at the same time. "You're both just scared. Maybe if you admit it, we can all deal with it together instead of yelling at each other."

"I mean it. Say one more smart thing and you're out on your ass." I sit up a little, leaving mascara smears on my pillow.

"I overheard you and Cass talking earlier." Olive picks at the black smudge. "I looked into that text message."

Oh, for fuck's sake. "What, were you listening at my door with a shot glass?"

She rolls her eyes. "Your room is next to mine. Don't yell so much if you don't want to be heard. Anyway, the text was sent as a chat, like in iMessage? They created an account with a fake email—that's how they managed it. It wouldn't be hard to do at all."

I know I should be keeping her away from this stuff. Under the bandage, my cut throbs. Whatever Gramps thinks, I do understand how serious, how scary, this has gotten. I don't want to see Olive in the same kind of danger.

But Olive and I haven't really gotten along in years, not since Mom left. Things with Gramps are such a disaster, it's hard not to want my little sister right now. She's going to keep doing this stuff whether I yell at her or not. For all of our differences, Olive and I are the same like that.

"Thanks," I say.

She continues picking at the teary mascara on my pillow. "The thing is, because they set it up that way, there's no way to know for sure who sent it. I could tell that it was sent over Wi-Fi, though, which means I could trace the IP address."

Hope strains my overexhausted heart. "Yeah?"

She wipes my mascara crust off on her pajama pants. "It came from inside the high school."

My concealer isn't doing me any favors. The makeup is chalky and yellow next to the crisp white edge of my bandage. I wipe it off.

I stayed up for hours after Olive went to bed. I found an old stash of security cameras in my grandfather's office and spent the rest of the night creeping around the house, the backyard, stashing them in hidden corners. No one is getting into this house again without me knowing about it.

I went to bed at dawn.

My head pounds, my skin itches around the cut, and the bags under my eyes have their own luggage now.

Gramps and his newspaper are not at the kitchen table. Coffee has been made, but he's not there. He continues to be *not there* until Cass shows up for school.

He's avoiding me. I don't think he's ever done that before. Mom used to do it all the time.

"Holy shit, what happened to your face?" Cass says the second I open the car door.

I buckle my seat belt. Finding the words for everything that happened last night makes me feel weak and empty. Cass pulls out of my driveway, but she continues to look at me expectantly.

"Things went bad last night," I say eventually. "But I'm okay, I swear. It's just a little scratch." As if on cue, the cut pulses.

"Yeah, I'm going to need more detail than that," Cass says.

My grandfather's words play over and over in my brain.

You have disappointed me.

I can't let Cass down. Pretty soon, she might be all that I have left.

I take a deep breath and start. I don't pause, don't linger

on any details. I keep my eyes trained out the window. The March sun glitters on hunks of icy snow, left over on the side of the road from months of plowing. They're thawing. I try to keep my voice even, but Cass and I both suck in a sharp breath when I get to the part where the knife goes in.

When I finish, there's a long silence. Nothing but the slick *whirr* of our tires on the slushy road.

Finally, Cass speaks. "I know you're going to say yes, but seriously, are you okay?"

There is a part of me that wants to get it all out. I open my mouth, ready to tell her how scared I am, how much the knife hurt, how much my grandfather's words hurt.

That man's breath on my face. The glint of his teeth in the parking lot lights.

The bright slash of pain as the knife sinks into my flesh.

My wrist twisted behind my back.

Helpless.

I bite down on my tongue to bring myself back to the present.

"You can tell me," Cass says gently. "Flora, someone wants you dead. It's okay to be afraid."

"It's not *someone*," I snap. "It's Dorsey. I've been saying it for days, and none of you believe me."

She gives me a bewildered look. "I never said I didn't believe you."

I shrug. "Not exactly feeling the support here. I nearly got killed last night, not sure what else it's going to take to convince you that maybe I know what I'm talking about."

Now she's pissed, too. "Hey! It's not like your theory doesn't have all kinds of holes in it. Tell me again how Dorsey's sneaking around school, leaving notes on your locker and sabotaging weight machines without anyone noticing? Don't act like I don't have your back just because I actually give a shit about logic."

My headache batters the front of my skull. "Can we not do this? I got hurt, and I know that's not great, but I'm not dropping the case, so everyone can stop asking."

I know immediately it's 100 percent the wrong thing to say.

"I didn't say that." Her voice shakes with both anger and hurt. "Do you really think I would ask you to do that?"

I don't. But I didn't think Gramps would, either.

When I don't answer, Cass says, "You're doing the thing."

"What thing?"

She pulls into the school parking lot. "The thing where you're an asshole, and in an hour you'll realize and have to apologize."

"Then I guess I'll talk to you in an hour." I bite down on my lip, but it's too late to stop the words from coming out.

Cass parks the car. "Yeah, you know what? I could use a

break from…" She gestures vaguely in my direction. From me. She needs a break from me.

Yeah, me too.

Cass gets out of the car and walks into school without looking back. I never even asked how her rehearsal went. I didn't think I could feel any worse, but this day keeps proving me wrong.

By the time I walk into the school, Cass has vanished. I walk through the halls alone. I have history first today, but we're doing some role-playing thing about the Jazz Age and I honestly can't think of anything I'd rather do less right now. On the other hand, I can't afford many more absences.

As I pass the guidance office, a photo of Austin Yi snags in my line of sight. I stop walking.

Austin's photo is tacked to a bulletin board. Purple bubble letters across the top: RISING UP, UP, AND AWAY! The board is covered with construction-paper balloons. Each balloon has a photo of a senior, and underneath the picture is the name of the college they're going to next year. It's one of those barbaric things that guidance counselors dream up without any understanding of irony or high school social dynamics. Delilah Beecham's CORNELL balloon is pasted next to Dylan Baker's STARBUCKS BARISTA TRAINING.

Austin smiles in his picture, but his jaw is strained. SUNY PURCHASE.

Something clicks in my brain. When I leave the bulletin board behind, I walk much faster than before. In the opposite direction from my history class.

Austin has statistics this period. Last year, I stole the log-in credentials for the master attendance server. It was awful nice of Mr. Carpini, the front desk secretary, to leave all his information on a Post-it like that. Now I can find anyone in the school on my phone.

I tell Mr. Wagner that Austin is needed in the main office. I've never taken stat, so Wagner doesn't know me. He waves Austin out of the class with barely a pause in his lecture. All eyes follow Austin as he walks out into the hall with me.

He shuts the door behind him. "What do you want? Haven't you done enough?" The bruise on his neck is a hideous shifting continent of yellows, purples, and reds.

I lean against a locker and pick my nails. "You know, that's an excellent question. I *want* the truth about Paige and Molly Sawyer. But we'll get to that. For now, let's talk about what *you* want. You want to go to college. University of Michigan—they offered you a scholarship, right? That's a Division I school, very impressive. Everyone thought it was super obnoxious how much you bragged about it in gym, by the way."

I push up off the locker and stalk closer to him. "And then today I was walking past the college counselor's office. Apparently, you're going to SUNY Purchase now. Decent school, but not as good as Michigan. And D-III! Quite the fall from grace."

Austin's ears turn red.

I, on the other hand, feel much better. My headache is gone. For a moment, Cass and my grandfather's words shrink to background noise. It's petty, but making guys like Austin squirm always makes me feel more like myself.

"Here's what I think," I continue. "I think something went wrong with your Michigan scholarship. Now you're going to a cheaper school with a less promising football program. I think you started fighting because you need the money to pay tuition. What I *want* is to know why."

The thick, corded muscles in his neck are rigid. "My knee. I tore my meniscus. I missed all the final scouting opportunities, and Michigan pulled their offer." He paces away from me. "You like gloating over people losing their chance to go to college? Really nice. Funny, there's a rumor going around that you're an actual witch. That's how you know so much."

You know what? The assholes at this school have been making dumb-ass comments about me for years. I ignored it because I didn't want them to think they could hurt me.

But they *can't* hurt me.

I've been apologizing to everyone—Cass, Gramps, Olive—for days. I've been trying so hard to prove I'm not just the reckless, dangerous Flora I was before, and it's never enough. The truth is, I like doing this. I like figuring this stuff out. If that makes me a witch, then I'll stock up on eye of newt.

I smile. "I do indeed enjoy the thrill of the dark arts. Okay, so. Good job being honest for once. Second test: Paige and Molly."

He pales. "I can't."

"Austin," I coo, "don't make me hex you."

He looks around. "They'll kill me. Come on, you know the weight room wasn't an accident. That's the same machine I use every day. Somebody knew that. And did you see what they did to Paige? Anyone finds out I talked to you, I'm dead for real, and you might be, too." His eyes land on my bandage.

It itches, but I don't react. "Thanks for your concern, but I'll take my chances. If you don't talk to me, you might be alive, but you'll also be one of those sad sacks roaming the streets of Hartsdale for the rest of your life, because you won't be going to college. All it would take is one well-placed call to the dean of admissions at Purchase. Big bad football player harassing sweet, innocent Paige Thomas? They won't like that at all."

He scoffs. "You're bluffing."

"Austin, I'd like to think that you and I have gotten to

know each other over the last couple days. So here's my question: do you really want to cross the witch?"

He looks at me with pure hatred, but I'm so far past caring.

"Fine. Anybody asks, you got this somewhere else." He does one last scan up and down the halls. "There was a fight last November. Paige hit Molly in the head, and she went down hard. She didn't get up."

So Dorsey or his minions dumped her in an alley and left her there to die. All to make sure the Basement stayed a secret.

Was this his protocol? A fight goes badly, dump the body in a "bad" neighborhood, and blame it on rising crime rates? Valentine rattled off all those numbers about robberies in the area. I thought he was just trying to throw me off track, but how many of those stats were other casualties of the Basement?

Austin scuffs his shoe on the linoleum. "I would never have actually hurt Paige. I was just pissed. Molly was my friend." His anger rushes back all at once. "Paige is one of the richest girls in school. What did she have to fight for? Now Molly's in a coma for three months, and no one does anything about it? It's messed up."

"You didn't come forward, either," I point out.

He rubs the back of his neck. "I thought about it, but it's like you said, right? I have to go to college. I can't be one of those freaks who never leaves. Forget bullying, no school would take me if I got caught fighting for money. Most of the fighters, we're not doing it for fun. People need cash. No one talks because we'd all have to pay."

Something Cass said earlier rattles in my brain. The text, the note on my locker, the weight room—how could Dorsey have pulled all those things off without being noticed on campus? At the same time, I've had a hard time picturing one of my classmates sending those guys after me last night.

But the threats don't all have to come from the same place. Austin's right: there's no shortage of people with something to hide, including him.

"I've been getting threats, too. Messages." I watch Austin's reaction.

He shrugs. "Well, obviously they know you've been asking questions."

I try a more direct approach. "Did you send me a text message Wednesday afternoon? Warning me to stay away from Molly?"

He shakes his head. "Nah, not my style. I got a problem, I get in your face about it. Besides, I was in training Wednesday after school, and Coach always takes our phones during practice. Ask anyone."

"I will." Austin does have a temper. The whole reason he got hurt is because he lost his cool and blurted out Molly Sawyer's name in front of me. And setting up an iCloud account isn't exactly technical wizardry, but it's definitely more creative than I would have believed him capable.

So whoever sent that text, they're still watching me.

I try to get back on track. "What about Ava? Did she fight, too?"

Austin cocks his head. "Ava? I thought you knew. She recruited us. She was the boss. It was her show."

His words hit me like a blow to the gut, knocking the air straight from my lungs. A million puzzle pieces race to reorder themselves in my mind.

Her NYU tuition. So much money. Too much to make by fighting. Lainie said she'd been acting weird for months. Since last summer. Elle Dorsey thought that's when the Basement first got started.

And me. It had always seemed a little too wild, a little too miraculous, that Ava even looked at me. When she broke it off, it was like everything made sense again.

But maybe that wasn't it at all. Ava would have known that if I got even a glimpse of what was happening in the Basement, I would want to shut it down. It's not like I'm the kid who calls the cops because there's alcohol at a party, but I wouldn't have been able to stand by while people were getting hurt. Ava knew that.

Then again, I would have thought she'd feel the same way. But apparently, I didn't know her at all.

CHAPTER 22

My footsteps echo in the empty halls. The lockers bend and curve in funhouse distortions. Austin went back to his class. Theoretically, I'm walking to history, but I don't even know if I'm going in the right direction.

Ava was running the fight club this whole time.

I picture Molly Sawyer's bruised eyelids, the steady beep of her heart rate monitor. Paige's distended, mottled face. Austin, desperate to get out of Hartsdale for college. Valentine letting himself get beaten to hell every night for information about his sister's killer.

And Ava ruled over them all.

Stray bits of instruction trickle out of open classroom doors—a math problem, a song in French. I keep walking. One foot in front of the other. It's surreal how normal everything around me is.

I remember last summer. Ava, lying in my bed. Tucking a

strand of hair behind my ear. I slid my hand across her stomach, underneath her shirt, and she drew in a sharp breath.

"I like you, girl detective," she whispered, her smiling mouth millimeters from mine.

I thought I knew her.

I push those memories away. It's sick that I'm even thinking about this stuff. I've been so frustrated with everyone for the sanitized version of Ava they want to mourn, but maybe I've been just as guilty of putting her on a pedestal.

Whatever she was wrapped up in, Ava didn't deserve to be killed. I have no right to judge her.

My mind conjures up another image. Ava, standing in the shadows at the edge of the ring. Watching with cold, emotionless eyes as Molly's head cracks against the hard ground. Long moments pass, and the girl doesn't stir.

My stomach flops like a fish on dry land. I might be sick, right here in the hallway.

A hand grabs my shoulder. I spin around so fast I nearly jerk my arm out of its socket.

Elle Dorsey holds her hands up in mock surrender. "Sorry!" Her brow furrows when she sees the giant bandage on my face. "What happened to you?"

The fingerprint bruises on my arm pulse.

His breath on my face. My back against the car door.

Sweat breaks out on my upper lip.

"What do you want?" It comes out breathy and weak. I swallow.

Elle slowly lowers her hands. "I want to help you."

"What?" It's such an odd combination of words coming out of Elle's mouth that I'm shaken out of my haze.

"I think my dad is up to something, and I want to help you. For Ava." Her eyes are glassy. Has she been crying?

Or does she want me to think she's been crying?

"Why?" I ask.

Elle tugs on the sleeve of her jade-green sweater. Not a single hair is out of place in her blowout. "I wasn't totally honest with you at lunch the other day. The thing is, Ava and I were friends."

Okay, definitely a trap. "Spare me."

Elle's laser eyes zero in on all my vulnerabilities. "What? You think because of your stupid obsession you knew everything about her? Clearly not."

They say the Antichrist can pull your darkest fears and desires right out of your brain.

I'm not going to let her push me around. "If you're trying to endear yourself to me, try harder."

"We didn't broadcast it to the world or anything, but we *were* friends. Last summer, my dad forced me to do this

314

volunteer project in Whitley, and that's where we met. We had this total *Heathers* feud for about a second, and then we bonded and grew to love each other or whatever."

I force a laugh. "Okay, if you want to sell me on this, regurgitating the plot of every made-for-TV movie about girls at summer camp seems a little lazy, don't you think?"

Elle's heart-shaped face pinches with irritation. She's used to everyone falling at her feet. "The Rosalind Coalition. Look it up if you don't believe me. They teach math and science to girls in underserved communities. My dad made me give up my amazing summer taking business classes at Stanford to teach chemistry to poor people, but Ava was into that shit."

I think back to the way Elle stood up to her dad the other day. How she didn't want to exploit Ava's death.

After everything I've learned, the flicker of irrational jealousy I feel is ridiculous. Still, last summer was the summer of me and Ava. If Elle's telling the truth, Ava came over to my house every day, and I didn't know anything about this.

But then, there are a lot of things I didn't know about her.

Elle is much taller than me. I glare up at her. "Okay, say I believe you were friends. What makes you think your dad had something to do with her death?"

Elle slides the pendant on her necklace back and forth. "He's been taking all these meetings with this guy. I think he's an investor or something? I heard them talking about the Basement, what kind of profits it turns. I had no idea my dad even knew what it was, but I think he might be the one running the place."

My head pounds. This morning, I was certain Dorsey was the boss, too. But then Austin set fire to everything I believed.

Elle continues to fidget with her necklace, not meeting my eyes. Sometimes, when people are uncomfortable, the best thing you can do is shut your mouth and let them talk.

"And he mentioned someone. A girl. He didn't say anything specific, but it was the way he talked about her, you know? It sounded like he killed her."

I remember the way Dorsey called Ava an opportunity. An obstacle. The way Matt Caine talked about Lucy. Never saying enough to incriminate himself, but *I* would know what he did to her.

I know what Elle means.

"Why now?" I ask her. "I asked you about Ava days ago, and you said you didn't know anything."

She twists a strand of hair around her finger, the truest sign of vulnerability a girl like her ever reveals.

"I was trying really hard not to see what was right in front of me. It doesn't make me a terrible person for not wanting to admit my father might be a murderer. Would you? If your precious grandfather had killed one of your friends, how would you feel? Our relationship is complicated, but he's still my dad." She crosses her arms over her chest and sniffs, like she's holding herself in. It's a gesture I know. I've made it before myself.

Fuck. Am I feeling empathy for Elle Dorsey?

"How did your dad even know Ava?" I ask. "Had you ever seen the two of them talking or something?"

Elle gives a tense shrug. "She came over to my house once or twice. The two of them talked about stupid political stuff. I think he mentioned something about a summer internship?" She rolls her eyes. "I didn't think it was that weird. He's like that with everyone."

It's another one of those things that could be something, could be nothing.

I know it's a deal with the devil, but I have no idea how anything fits together anymore, and I need answers wherever I can get them.

"You want me to trust you? Prove it. If you bring me something serious I will consider letting you help."

"I will." Her eyes are bright and earnest. "I'll get something big. I promise."

"Be discreet. I have enough problems as it is."

She looks at my cheek again. "Seriously, what happened to you?"

"Nothing," I say for the thousandth time today.

"Did you go to the Basement last night?" Her well-groomed eyebrows are still furrowed.

How would she know that? I stand a little straighter. "Why?"

She looks over her shoulder, then lowers her voice. "I think maybe my dad got tipped off that you would be there. Last night, I overheard him talking to some other guy, who said he could make sure you were there. In exchange for a package or something. It didn't make sense at the time, but now..." Her eyes drift to my cheek again.

A cold, black dread spreads from my stomach all the way to my fingertips.

So I was right. It was Dorsey who sent those men after me. It's not that I didn't already know, but hearing it out loud just makes it all the more real.

And then there's the other thing. Valentine is the one who convinced me to go to the Basement last night. Promised me something I wanted to get me there. He was so cagey. Nervous.

Those guys were waiting for me, like they knew I'd be there.

Valentine fought at my side. He beat the man who cut me into the ground. And the way he looked at me after, the things he said. The kiss. That couldn't have been an act.

But he was the only one besides Cass who knew I was going to the Basement, and I know for a fact that she would never sell me out.

Elle's been watching me this whole time. I fight to keep my face blank. She could be storing all of this away to use against me later.

All I say is, "Thanks, I'll look into it. But I need something bigger than that if you want to play for real." I turn and walk away before I can break completely.

The bathroom floor is hard and cold. I'm not going to history today. It was a miracle I even made it to the bathroom before I lost it. Now I'm sitting on the floor in the big stall, trying to hold myself together.

With shaking hands, I take out my phone and search for the Rosalind Coalition, the nonprofit where Elle claims she befriended Ava. This I can do. Focus on a task. Ignore my feelings. Cass would tell you: it's what I'm good at.

Thinking about her makes my screen blur in my vision. I breathe in through my nose and swallow. Pull myself back in.

The organization's home page has a slideshow of photos. Three young girls work together on a computer. Another girl measures bright blue liquid in a beaker. The slideshow changes again. A group photo: a dozen middle school girls, all wearing the same teal T-shirts. Some of the volunteers cluster together at the back, and there, dead center, are Ava and Elle. Arms around each other's backs. Elle is midlaugh, like Ava cracked a joke.

She looks like the Ava I thought I knew. Not the sterile, stripped-down version everyone seems to remember, or the more confusing version I've been uncovering in my investigation. This is the Ava who made inappropriate jokes and gave perfect side-eye.

The shakes grow more violent, and I drop my phone.

I pull my knees up tight against my chest. All of the tears I've held back this week come pouring out. Tears for Ava, for all of us, even for me. My stomach aches and clenches with the force of it. My cut stings with salt water. The bruises on my back and arm throb. I hold myself and fall apart.

I paw the floor for my phone. I can barely see to write the text to Cass:

Bathroom by the auditorium please come I need you

I know I don't deserve it. Maybe she won't come. Maybe I finally pushed her over the edge. But I'm bawling on the floor of the bathroom, and I don't know if I can get up without her.

Ages later, the door opens, and Cass's red Vans approach.

She takes one look at my snotty, tear-streaked face and I can see her anger melt away. She slips into the stall and sits on the floor next to me.

I curl up into her side as a fresh wave of sobs breaks over me.

"I'm sorry," I choke out before she can say anything. The dam breaks completely. In an uncontrollable flood, I tell her everything I haven't been able to say. My confusion, and want, and guilt about Valentine. The disappointment on my grandfather's face. All the ways I've let Ava down in this investigation, and all my twisted feelings about the secrets she kept.

And Cass, my best person. How I hurt her every day, without even trying.

I talk and talk, gulping, choking, sobbing the words out. Cass lets me lean against her shoulder, soaking the sleeve of her shirt.

When I finally run myself dry, she lets out a long exhale. "Well, Flora. I reckon you're pretty fucked up in the head."

I start to laugh, but that only gets me crying again.

She wraps her arm around my shoulders. "Oh, you complete idiot. Why have you been carrying all this shit around? Wouldn't it be easier to talk about it before you implode?" She gestures to my wet, puffy face.

I know she's right, but it never feels so easy.

"I really am sorry." My voice is still raspy with tears. "I shouldn't have said any of those things this morning. I know you're in this with me. You wouldn't bail."

For a second, I almost tell her about the surveillance photos. The news clippings on my desk. *YOU'RE NEXT.* I don't know why, but those are the only things I held back.

Cass pulls some toilet paper off the roll and dabs at my face, wiping away the mascara and the mucus. The gentleness of her touch sets my lip quivering again. It feels so good not to be fighting. I don't know if I could take seeing the hurt on her face again when I tell her there are more things I hid from her. At least not right now.

We're quiet for a long time as Cass cleans my face.

"Ava was running the Basement this whole time?" Cass asks eventually.

"I don't know what to even think about it."

Cass tosses the wad of paper in the toilet. "We don't know the full story. She might have had her reasons. It doesn't necessarily make her a bad person."

I nod. I know this, but that doesn't make it any less confusing.

Something else has been bugging me. "The numbers don't add up."

Cass looks at me expectantly.

I open the calculator on my phone, talking through the numbers as I punch them in. "I would guess they had a crowd of about five hundred people the times I've gone, and each one of them is paying twenty dollars at the door. Based on everything Valentine's said about the schedule and his pay, the boss is still walking away with something like five grand a night after paying all the fighters. Even if there was only one fight a week—and we know there's more sometimes—they would have made close to two hundred thousand dollars in ticket profits alone since last summer, not even counting all the gambling and drink sales. Ava's tuition makes up less than half of that."

Cass nods. "So where's the rest of the money?"

"Exactly. She paid for school in cash. She would have needed a safe place to hide it."

"Not in her room," Cass muses. "You searched it. Plus it's too obvious. Her mom might've found it while she was cleaning or something."

"I feel like that's a risk anywhere in her house," I say. "But I can't see how it's safe to hide that much cash anywhere else, either."

"Maybe she had a business partner?" Cass throws out. "The other half of the money would be theirs."

It's so obvious, I could kick myself.

I couldn't figure out how to make the things Austin and

Elle told me fit together. I was so convinced that Dorsey was the one in charge. The whole operation of the Basement is too slick, too well organized. It always felt so unreasonable that the kids I go to school with could pull something like that off. But it doesn't have to be one or the other.

Dorsey and Ava were business partners. They met through Elle last summer. Dorsey could hire people like Boyd, pay off the police, handle all that cash. But he would have needed someone on the ground to recruit fighters. He wouldn't want a bunch of kids knowing about his involvement, and no high school student would trust an adult making that kind of offer. That was Ava's job, and she would have been good at it. She was well liked. People trusted her.

Only something went wrong, and he wanted her out.

I explain my theory to Cass.

She chews her lip while she thinks it over. "I'm not saying I don't believe you, but why? Dorsey's a *congressman*. And he's already rich. He has a whole lot to lose if he gets caught. Would that kind of money even be worth it to him?"

It's a fair point. "I don't know." Something Elle said a few days ago comes back to me, though. "Dorsey ran for Senate once before, but he lost. Elle thinks he'd do anything to win this time, and it's not like you can ever have *too much* campaign money, right?"

Cass raises her eyebrows. "That could make sense. Getting elected to the Senate is way more prestigious than the House, and it would be a good stepping-stone to other stuff, too. Like running for president."

We both lean back against the wall, thinking.

Cass asks, "So, are you going to talk to VT?"

"No."

"Flora."

I shake my head. "How many times does someone have to stab you in the back before you stop handing them the knife?"

I don't want to believe he would do that again, but I can't deny that something was off last night. Every time I've doubted my instincts about him, it's come back to bite me.

"He saved your life," she says quietly. "Why would he do that if he sold you out?"

I remember the gentleness of his fingers as they smoothed the bandage over my cheek. The sweet burn of whiskey as I kissed him. His breath against my neck, unsteady with wanting.

The idea that any of that could have been faked makes me furious.

"I don't know why he does anything, and I don't care."

"Yeah, that's why you're crying your eyes out in a bathroom stall."

I ignore her.

Cass sighs. "At least give him the chance to explain. I mean, since when do we take *Elle Dorsey* at her word? You have trust issues, and Elle feeds on chaos. Maybe you only believe her because it confirms all the toxic bullshit you already thought."

"How else would Dorsey know that I was there last night? It's not like *you* told him. No one else knew." I lean my head against her shoulder.

"True, but there were a bunch of other people from school there, plus you ran into that man Boyd. It was a wig and some makeup, not exactly a CIA-level disguise," she points out. "Or Elle could be lying for her own weird power-bitch reasons."

"I don't know." I think of the glassy, fragile look in Elle's eyes this morning. "You should have seen her earlier. I think she might have layers, as wild as that sounds."

Cass turns her head toward me in slow motion. "Oh, my God, tell me you don't have a crush on Elle Dorsey now."

"Um, what? No! I meant—"

Cass laughs. "Of course you do, she's totally your type."

It's like a pie to the face. "Excuse me?"

"She's all combative but damaged inside. You're a narcissist, Flora. You're attracted to people who remind you of yourself." She blinks at me innocently.

"Are you..." I narrow my eyes. "You're fucking with me. Torturing me because I was such a bitch earlier?"

"Yep. But seriously, give VT the chance to explain himself." She fishes her car keys out of her bag. "Take these. Get the real story."

I stare at the keys dangling from her hand. I want so badly to take them.

If he did betray me again, it's going to hurt a thousand percent more this time.

"No, I'm a mess as it is." I gesture to my red, puffy face. "Any more emotional crap will have to wait."

Cass gives me a wry smile. "I think that's the motto on the Calhoun family crest."

CHAPTER 23

I pound on Valentine's door. It's 6 a.m. on a Saturday, and I don't care if I wake the entire city. My head isn't any more sorted than yesterday, but waiting to talk to him has only converted all my hurt and confusion into fury.

Valentine opens the door. His eyes look drugged with sleep, and his long hair sticks out in different directions. The adorableness of it makes me a thousand times more pissed.

I slam past him, into the apartment. "I want the truth. No more games."

He shuts the door behind me and yawns. "Mornin', Cherry."

I point at him. "Cut it out with the cute nicknames. Tell me. Did you set me up the other night?"

He looks more awake now. His silence is the only answer I need.

Even though I saw it coming, the pain of it nearly levels me to the floor.

"Right." I turn for the door. "I'm done. Stay out of my life."

He reaches for me. "No, wait—"

I slip away. I don't want him to touch me. Don't know what I'll do if he touches me.

"Please. You gotta hear me out."

I grab the door handle. "I really don't."

"I have a lead I think you'll want."

The ability to shoot laser beams out of my eyes would be really useful right about now.

"Funny how your 'leads' are always either nothing or nearly get me killed." I walk out into the hallway.

This is the last time I'll ever see him. I stomp all over the little voice reminding me of that.

Fuck him. Fuck the soft Valentine, and the vicious one. I'm done trying to figure out which one's real. It doesn't matter anymore.

He follows. "I got a stack of documents that belonged to my sister. Think it might have something to do with Dorsey."

I pause.

His wild, desperate eyes search my face, like he was afraid of never seeing me again, too. I don't know how that can be true, though, considering how many times he's lied to me.

"Speak." I brush past him back into the apartment.

"You weren't supposed to get hurt." He shuts the door

behind him. "Boyd approached me the other day. Said he had something I wanted, if I could get you to the club. Something from my sister."

"I guess everyone has a price," I snap.

Just like that, the earnest, pleading look is gone and he's ready for a fight. "I've been searching for my sister's killer for a year. You think I'm going to give up on that because a pretty girl walks by? Would you?"

I guess that answers my questions about the kiss and what it meant. Good. Makes this easier.

"No, but you asked for my help," I remind him. "Side by side, isn't that what you said? Didn't think you'd throw me under the bus first chance you got, but maybe I'm naive."

He shouts back, "You should have been fine! I was going to be with you the whole time. I thought I could get what I needed from Boyd *and* keep you safe. Two birds, one stone."

"But you didn't!"

"You think I don't know that? You're such a goddamn stubborn lone wolf that of course you ran off on your own. Don't know why I didn't see that one coming. If you'd stayed put like I told you, none of this would have happened."

My blood scalds me from the inside out. "So we're back to this being my fault? You set up this insane plot without filling me in, but I'm to blame when everything goes to shit?"

He tugs at his hair. "No! I know I fucked up. You think I felt nothing, watching that piece of trash cut into you like that?"

"I don't know what you think or feel. Every time I think I have you figured out, you tell me some sob story about your past, or stab me in the back, or kiss me, and I don't know what any of it means! And now you've lied to me. Again. I trusted you."

The words take me by surprise. I didn't realize it until now, but in spite of everything I did trust him. I don't think this would hurt so bad if I hadn't.

The cut on my cheek throbs again.

The dreamy way he looked up at me as I drove the getaway car.

The sound of his voice as the three men closed in around me—the blazing relief to know I wasn't alone.

His hands on my face. Goose bumps rising under my touch.

There's a long silence. We've both revealed too much.

He hangs his head. "I'm going to show you that you can trust me, for real this time."

"Why?" I ask before I can stop myself.

"You know why." He gives me a look that could start a forest fire.

We are barely two feet apart. If I touched him now, he wouldn't pull away. I could kiss him. Pull him onto that sad, lumpy couch and work out all our twisted, furious need with my skin pressed to his. My blood rushes hot to my cheeks, and I know my face must be glowing red as my hair.

"So what did you get?" I force myself to ask.

He grabs a manila envelope off one of his barren bookshelves and pulls out a stack of papers. "This is what Boyd gave me." He steps close. Too close, but I don't move. "I haven't looked at them yet."

The words don't make sense. I force myself to stare at the papers in his hands so that I don't have to see the tender, hungry way he's looking at me.

"This stuff is from your sister," I say. "You nearly got me killed to get it, and you didn't look?"

His voice is so low, it's more of a vibration than a sound. "I waited for you."

Don't ask. Whatever you do, don't ask. "Why?"

"I was terrified when I realized you weren't sitting at that table." He reaches up, and seconds turn to hours in the time it takes him to graze his thumb along the edge of my bandage. I squeeze my eyes shut. "This is my fault. I kept trying to open the envelope yesterday, but I felt sick every time I looked at it. If you hadn't broken down my door this morning, I would've come and found you. Swear."

I jerk away from him. "Don't. Don't promise me anything anymore."

He steps back a little. Enough that I can breathe. The pain I glimpsed earlier is back, but this time he doesn't try to hide it.

"What do you have?" I crane my head to read the documents he's holding.

He flips through the pages. Government forms, from the look of it. The title on the first page reads, SCHEDULE A (FEC FORM 3X) ITEMIZED RECEIPTS. A box at the top says NAME OF COMMITTEE. Underneath, someone typed PROGRESS TOGETHER USA. The rest of the page has a long list of similar entries. Some of them have the names of actual people, but most are corporations and businesses. Each one has a dollar amount next to it anywhere from $5,000 to $150,000.

"What's Progress Together USA?" I ask.

"I don't know," he says.

"How do you know this stuff is really from your sister?" It seems awfully convenient, a stack of documents showing up right around the time that Boyd needs something from Valentine.

"Thought about it," he admits, "but it fits. FEC is the Federal Election Commission. That's the sort of thing Annie was working on before she was killed."

That's the thing about people who want to exploit you, though. They figure out what you want to believe, and they give it to you.

We don't need to get into that now.

He keeps flipping through the pages. Most of them are pretty similar to the first, until we find one halfway through the pile that looks different from the others. It's some kind of internal memo on Progress Together letterhead. There's a note about a contribution made by EVAH LLC. The corporation donated $100,000, with the stipulation that the money go toward political ads and policy research for Congressman James Dorsey.

Acid pools in my stomach at the sight of his name. The papers rustle as Valentine's hands shake.

There are a few more memos, all with the same kind of information. Dorsey isn't the only politician listed. Valentine gets to the bottom of the stack, but there's nothing else there. No note. No letter. He stares and stares at the last page, but no message from Annabelle appears.

"Are you okay?" I ask.

He sniffs once. "Yeah." In brisk, economical movements he shuffles the papers back together and hands them to me. "I want you to take these."

"What?" After what he did to get this stuff, he's just going to hand it over?

"The mistake I made wasn't bringing you to the Basement— it was keeping the plan a secret. If I'd told you what Boyd wanted, we could have run the play together."

I stare at the sagging, grimy cushions on his couch. There's a yellowish stain by the seam. He knows I want to believe him, but I can't give in this time.

Valentine continues. "Been alone for a while now. Guess I forgot how the whole team thing works. Take this stuff. Find out what you can. It might be what we need to bring Dorsey down." He presses the papers into my hand. His fingers close over mine. "Flora, I'm going to keep on trusting you until you trust me back again."

Gramps is passing through the front hall when I get home. He freezes when he sees me.

I wish that didn't hurt so much. With Mom, I got used to it eventually. But Gramps has never been afraid of me before.

I can see it in his eyes now. The way they zero in on the papers Valentine gave me. I still have the stack clutched to my chest. His gaze travels up to my face and lands on my bandage.

I could ask him about the documents. I have no doubt he could figure out what this stuff means, or at least point me in the right direction. I could tell him something, open up a little bit, show him that I *do* trust him. That he's one of the people I trust most in this world.

But two nights ago, he demanded I end my investigation.

He hasn't said anything about it since, hasn't spoken to me at all, and I have no idea where we stand.

He walks back into the kitchen.

I bring the papers up to my room.

I don't ask for help.

CHAPTER 24

The Google search on my computer screen goes blurry. My eyes ache as I scroll down the list of hits for EVAH LLC. I let them fall closed. One second of rest, and then I'll keep moving. The clacking of computer keys and Olive's and Cass's slow, focused breaths almost lull me to sleep. I force my eyes open and keep scrolling.

The three of us are sprawled across my bed, armed with laptops and notebooks, trying to make sense of the documents Valentine gave me yesterday.

"So here's what I have," Olive says. "Progress Together is a pretty well-known super PAC. They support moderate Democrats in both the Senate and House."

"And Dorsey is one of them?" I ask.

Olive's hunched over her laptop. Her face is inches from the screen. "As far as I can tell. I know for sure they've paid for a bunch of his ads, which would be pretty expensive, but it's hard to track how much they've spent."

I wait for an explanation, but she keeps typing.

I nudge her ankle with my foot. "What do you mean? Don't campaigns have to disclose this stuff?"

"Oh, honestly," Cass says. "Don't you read the news?"

This is why I hate research. Now that Olive's involved, too, it's doubly annoying.

I throw my pen at Cass. She ducks. "Look, I get it. Both of you are smarter than me. Less condescension, more information, please."

"Super PACs are kind of a loophole in the system." Olive shifts sideways to face me, jostling the plate of half-eaten cookies between us. "They can raise as much money as they want, but they're not allowed to just hand it over to the campaign. They can pay for stuff like ads or research, but they're not supposed to work *with* the campaigns on any of it."

Cass adds, "They all find ways around that, though. Like, a campaign aide suddenly quits and opens a super PAC, so they already know everything the candidate wants. This is kind of a big deal right now." She tosses my pen back at me.

Dear God. Researching campaign finance law has got to be one of the most boring ways to spend a Sunday.

"Why do we care about any of this?"

"We need to trace these donations so we can figure out where Dorsey's money is coming from, but super PACs make

338

that difficult." Olive pulls out one of the papers Valentine gave me. "This is a disclosure form, where they're supposed to report all their donors. So, theoretically you can't pretend to be some super-progressive candidate who's all about taxing the rich and then take donations from Wall Street, because these forms are public. Anyone could look that up. But"—she points to one of the EVAH LLC contributions on the list—"if the donor sets up an LLC with a vague name, then it's way harder to trace where the money actually came from."

"This is how politicians get away with doing illegal financial shit," Cass says. "If Dorsey were laundering money from a teen fight club into his campaign funds, this is how he would do it."

"But isn't the LLC registered somewhere?" I ask. "Doesn't someone have to have their name behind it?"

"We still have to figure that out," Olive agrees.

If Dorsey was tied up in dirty political money, it makes sense that he'd want to kill Valentine's sister to keep it quiet, but I still don't know what that has to do with Ava. What went wrong between her and Dorsey? I thought maybe it was about Molly, but she got hurt months ago. Why would Dorsey wait to kill Ava *now*?

I climb over the tangle of papers and limbs to get off the bed. "My brain hurts. I need coffee. Anyone else?"

"Yes, definitely." Cass doesn't look up from her computer.

"And more cookies!" Olive hands me the crumby plate.

Downstairs, I'm stacking some of my grandfather's salty chocolate chip cookies on a fresh plate when I hear the sound of our mail slot opening in the front hall.

My hands go clammy. One of them is still clutching a cookie. The chocolate turns greasy in my grip.

It's Sunday. This time, I know for sure it's not the mail.

Once again, a manila envelope is waiting for me in the front hall. I peer out the window onto the street but, just like last time, there's no one there. The weeklong migraine I've been nursing rears its spiked head.

This is not worth freaking out over. They're only pictures. Creepy, but it's not like I don't already know I'm in the crosshairs.

I reach inside and pull them out.

My heart stops.

My grandfather baking in the kitchen, framed by the glass French doors. The photographer must have been in our backyard.

Cass at a traffic light. Her mouth is open like she's singing along to the radio.

Olive leaving ballet practice in Mrs. Temple's car pool. She's staring out the window of the van, looking off into space.

Valentine and me leaving campus. Taken last week, when we went to the crime scene. He's laughing, and I'm looking up at the sky like I'm begging the universe for patience.

On autopilot, I walk back to the kitchen. The mug of coffee I poured is sitting on the counter. I take a sip, burn my tongue, and stare at the top photo in the stack. The one of Cass. Another scalding sip, eyes on the photo.

I flip through the pictures again. Gramps. Olive. Valentine. Cass.

It shouldn't come as a surprise. People are getting hurt. *I* got hurt. Whoever's watching me isn't going to stop until I drop the case. It was only a matter of time before they came for the people I love. I should have expected it.

But I didn't.

I shuffle through the stack once more, but I'm not really seeing anything.

Cass and Olive's mingled laughter drifts down the stairs. Moments ago, I sat between the two of them on my bed. My two sisters. I felt almost safe.

What would happen if I stopped? What if I went upstairs right now and told Cass and Olive to stop what they were doing? Would we be safe then? And what about Austin, or Damian, or any of the other kids who have their own sad, desperate reasons for getting involved with the Basement?

I should tell them. Cass and Olive should know that they're in danger. They should be allowed to choose for themselves.

Cass is going to be furious with me, but I have to tell them.

I grab my backpack off the coat hook. The first batch of pictures is still smashed in the bottom somewhere. I slide the new ones in there, too, then bring the bag and our snacks up the stairs.

I pause with my hand on my bedroom door. This is going to scare them, and I hate that.

Cass is on the phone when I enter the room. "Uh-uh. Oh, s-sure." She traces circles on the floor with her toe. Two bright pink spots rise on her cheeks.

I shoot a questioning look at Olive, who grins and stage-whispers, "It's a *boy*."

Of course. Only Elliot can make Cass look like such a fluffy bunny.

Cass ignores us. "Definitely. I, um, actually wrote a song myself. I want to hear what you think." She gnaws her lip as she listens to his reply. "Me, too. Five thirty? I can do that. I'll see you then." She hangs up.

"Date?" Olive asks.

Cass hugs herself. She's still very pink. "No, Elliot wants to meet up to talk about some new songs."

"So the rest of the band will be there, too?" Olive's face is pure innocence.

"No," Cass admits. Olive and I trade looks, and Cass stomps her foot. "Stop it, both of you. Not another word. You"—she points at Olive—"are an infant and know nothing. And you"—she points at me—"have the most problematic love life of anyone I know. You don't get to have opinions on this." A giddy smile tugs at Cass's mouth.

The second I pull those pictures out of my bag, that smile will vanish.

I force myself to play along, pressing a mock-wounded hand to my chest. "Uncalled for! Olive's the one who said the d-word."

"You mean *date*?" Olive singsongs.

Cass covers her face with her hands and screams.

She looks so happy. Seeing her like this makes that ever-present pressure in my chest ease.

Last year, Cass dated Leo Todd for almost seven months before breaking up with him out of the blue in April. She claimed he "got boring" and never wanted to talk about it, but I'm reasonably certain that was just Cass code for *My boyfriend actually wanted to spend time with me, but I was always too busy taking care of Flora, and I got sick of arguing with him about it.*

She and Olive continue to bicker about her not-a-date, and

that transitions into what Cass will wear. Like sisters. This is my family, in this room right now.

I will tell them. Soon. Maybe tonight, once Cass gets home from her date, or tomorrow morning. I take up so much space in her life. Every time she tries to have something good, even for one night, she ends up having to drop everything and rescue me anyway.

I leave the backpack by the door. I can let them be happy a little while longer before I ruin it like I always do.

Cass gives me a funny look as I hand her a mug. "You okay?"

"Peachy."

Cass's concern deepens. "Your face is all weird."

I point to the bandage. "Scar Face. Makes me look way more screwed up."

"Who knew that was possible?" Olive mutters, and Cass laughs. The sound makes the barbed wire around my chest loosen a bit.

Olive says, "While you were downstairs, I found something on the LLC front." She turns her computer screen toward us. It's a Google search: *how to set up an anonymous LLC.*

Cass reads down the page. "Why is Delaware mentioned so many times?"

Olive's face is lit with the same excitement I feel when I

get a new lead. "Because Delaware is the easiest place in the world to set up an LLC. There are entire companies that only exist to register corporations under their name. You own the business, but your name doesn't appear on any public records. They call them ghost companies."

"Okay, but we don't live in Delaware," I point out.

"It doesn't matter. Look." She clicks on one page, InstaLLC. "We can set up a ghost corporation on the internet. It costs about two hundred dollars, and we never need to set foot in the state or talk to anyone on the phone. Wanna do it?" She gives me a mad-scientist smile.

I roll my eyes. "Let's save the sisterly bonding for later. How does this help us?"

Olive's smile fades. "Well, the whole point is to keep the real LLC owner private. It's going to be hard to trace any of them to an actual person." She deflates, and I recognize that, too. The glittering rush of discovery replaced with the flat gray of a dead end.

"So we're stuck." I lean my head back against the wall and close my eyes. Those grainy photos are burned into the back of my eyelids. If we don't solve this case soon, someone's going to get hurt. One of *them* will get hurt.

"Hey." Cass pokes my knee. "It's a good start."

It's not enough. It'll never be enough. Olive's and Cass's

warm, familiar bodies on either side of me were comforting a few minutes ago, but now I'm claustrophobic. I jump off the bed and pace the room. Olive and Cass watch me with matching worry.

"No," I mutter. "Even if we figure it out, there will never be enough proof to arrest him."

"We've only been at it for a little while," Cass reminds me, "and we already have a lot of information. We'll keep digging."

I shake my head, more at myself than at her. We're running out of time.

Cass asks, "Do you want me to skip meeting Elliot? I could stay here and keep working on tracing the LLC."

"You might as well go. We're not going to find anything." The razor wire is constricting around my lungs again, and I can't breathe.

I don't know if it's all this complicated legal bullshit, or those photos, but this very moment it's actually hitting me: we might fail.

Dorsey might get away with this.

"Hey." Cass gets off the bed and grabs me by the shoulders. Her brown eyes are filled with conviction. "We're not giving up. We will make him pay."

I wish I had that kind of faith in us. In me. But the whole world has been built to serve men like Dorsey. Like Matt

Caine. I know exactly what happens when you try to tear a rigged system down.

If I really want to end this, once and for all, I have to make use of every resource I have.

"Hang on." I grab Valentine's papers and head downstairs.

My grandfather is in his office. Now that he's retired, it's basically a library. A place where he can get away from the rest of us now and again.

I take a deep breath outside his door. I can do this. He won't turn away from me. I knock.

"Yes?"

I hold out the papers. "I need help." I can count on one hand the number of times I've said those words.

To the untrained observer, he might seem unsurprised. But I'm not untrained—he's the one who taught me how to read people. There's no widening of the eyes, no raised eyebrows, no fidgeting with his clothes or the objects on his desk. It's the absence of those things that exposes him. I can see the years of CIA training at work, ridding him of all those messy, reflexive movements most people make when they're anxious.

He sets his book down carefully. "What can I do?"

I explain the documents and the LLC situation. "Please tell me you have some black ops buddy who can figure this out?"

He adjusts his reading glasses and takes the papers. I try not to fidget as he reads.

Without lifting his eyes from the documents, he says, "It's not easy, you know. Being your parent."

His tone is mild, but the words sting anyway. There's a cup of pens on his desk. I adjust them one by one so that they'll all lean the same way.

He continues. "You can't understand how terrifying it is to see you hurt."

My shoulders draw tight together.

He flips a page. "I know you do not tell me everything. You go places without my knowledge. Engage in activities you'd rather not discuss. I seldom force you to share the details. I know you will tell me the truth if I ask for it, and that's enough."

After a long pause, he says, "When we spoke before you left the other night, that was the first time I wasn't certain you'd answer me honestly. When you came home injured, I lost control."

Every pen is oriented the right way now.

"I can't promise it won't happen again, but I am always on your side, Flora. If you ask me for help, I will give it to you every time."

I want to believe him. He's looking over those documents

like he didn't just tell me three nights ago to drop the case, but what happens when I get hurt again? Or if I show him those photos? And now Olive's in danger, too.

Gramps shuffles my papers back together and sets them on his desk. "I have a few people I can call."

I could tell him. No matter how scared he is, he's trying. He's not running away like Mom. And it would be a relief to not be the only one who knows exactly how much danger we're all in.

If you ask me for help, I will give it to you every time.

The doorbell rings, and I practically explode out of my skin.

Gramps gives me a curious look. "Are you all right?"

"I'm fine. Tired. Makes me twitchy."

His head is still canted to one side, evaluating me.

"I'll get the door." My knees won't stop locking as I leave the room.

I wipe my sweaty hands on my jeans before opening the door.

Valentine's hands are in his pockets and he's rocking on the balls of his feet like he's nervous.

I go warm all over, then want to smack myself.

"Flora? Who is it?" Gramps says behind me.

Oh, God. Please no.

Gramps takes a long look at Valentine. His eyes sweep him from top to bottom. They pause for emphasis on the black eye, the cut lip.

This is so much worse than I even imagined. My tongue is bone-dry. I have lost the power of speech.

Sensing that I can't save him, Valentine blurts out, "Lab partner. Got a project for the science fair. VT Yates." He holds out his hand, then adds, "Sir."

Could he have come up with a more transparent excuse?

Gramps shakes his hand. He turns to me with one eyebrow raised. "Flora."

Seriously. Someone kill me.

I break down. "Okay, fine. He's an informant."

He doesn't react. "And how do you two know each other, exactly?"

"Well, he was supposed to insert himself into my investigation and then double-cross me, but he's really, really bad at his job."

Valentine's eyes go flinty. "I'm standin' right here."

"It's not anything I haven't said to your face before," I snap back.

Gramps looks back and forth between us. "I see. Mr. Yates, you may wait for her on the porch. Flora, a word?"

Valentine goes outside. Gramps is looking at me like he

knows there's something more than information going on between us.

Finally, he sighs and says, "Be careful, please."

With Valentine, I'm not sure that's possible. Add that to the list of things I definitely cannot tell my grandfather, though. I nod.

"I meant what I said before." His eyes land on my bandaged cheek. "You ask for help, I give it to you. Always." With one last long look, he returns to his study.

I exhale. It could have been a lot worse.

Valentine is leaning against my porch rail. "Your pop seems pretty chill with the whole Nancy Drew routine. Must be nice." He shrugs like it's a casual thing to say, but it reminds me how lonely Valentine must be.

This is what he does, though. He gets that soft look in his eyes, and I go all mushy inside, and then he does something stupid.

I scowl at him. "I can't get through a single day without you showing up to confuse things, can I?"

The hopeful expression vanishes. "You asked me about Molly Sawyer?"

"What about her?"

"Turns out she has a little brother. Visits her every day, around 3:30."

It's 2:45 now.

"You want to go talk to him?" I ask.

"Kid might know something. I was a little brother once. We see more than people think."

He's trying to prove himself to me, like he said yesterday. As usual, I don't know how I feel about that.

Upstairs, I tell Cass and Olive the plan.

"I'm coming," Olive says at the same time that Cass goes, "Okay, let me pee and get my shoes on."

"You're both staying here," I say.

They start to argue, but I talk over them. "Valentine and I have this covered. I need you two on research duty. You're way better at it than me. You be the brains, Valentine and I can be the muscle."

Olive's cheeks go pink with pleasure at the compliment, and I feel like a real shit for manipulating her. Olive *is* better than me at research, but that's not the whole reason.

They're safer here. Someone obviously wants Molly Sawyer to stay buried, and Cass and I were spotted the last time we went to the hospital. After the newspaper clippings in my room, I'm not so sure the house is safe, either, but at least Gramps is here.

"Besides," I add to Cass. "You have a date. I don't want you to miss that."

Cass flushes, but she's still suspicious. "VT's going with you?" She knows that normally I wouldn't go on a mission like this without her.

"Uh. Yeah," I answer.

She raises an eyebrow. "Glad you two made up."

"It's not like that." I protest because she expects me to, but it's easier if she thinks I'm trying to get alone time with a cute boy, and not deliberately lying to her.

Her mouth twitches. "Yeah, and I'm definitely not going on a date tonight. You two go...*muscle*...together. I demand details later."

CHAPTER 25

I pause on the threshold of room 317. Molly looks like she hasn't moved at all since I last visited, which, *duh:* coma. It's still eerie, like time doesn't pass for her the way it does for the rest of us.

She's not alone in the room. A boy, maybe ten or eleven, sits next to her bed. They share the same shape to their lips, the same turned-up nose.

He looks up when we walk in. "Hi?" He inches closer to Molly, like he can protect her.

I give him an awkward wave. "Hi, I'm Flora. I'm a friend of Molly's."

The wariness in his eyes fades, and he scoots back in his chair. "I'm Max." He frowns. "Molls doesn't usually get visitors, besides me."

"You come here by yourself?" I ask.

He nods. "I live a couple blocks away. Dad doesn't mind, usually."

It's a little weird to let a fifth grader walk to the hospital by himself, but I'm not the kid's social worker. "How's Molly?"

Max smiles down at his sister's sleeping face. "Really good. The doctor told me she might wake up soon." He straightens her covers.

A voice from behind me says, "Didn't I tell you last time? It's family only."

The same nurse from the other day is standing in the doorway.

"It's okay, Sophie," Max says. "They're with me. They're Molly's friends."

Sophie the nurse keeps a skeptical eye on Valentine and me—between the two of us we have one black eye, one gashed cheek, and one split lip—but her voice is softer when she speaks to Max. "Come and get me if they bother you, okay?"

Sophie shoots a warning look at the two of us and leaves.

"Sophie seems really strict at first, but she's one of the nice nurses," Max tells us.

I take one of the other visitors' seats next to him. "It's great that you come see your sister so much. Are you guys close?"

Max nods. "Uh-huh. Molls is my best friend. Some people think that's dumb, but it's always been the two of us."

"So, Max," I venture, "do you know how Molly got hurt?"

Max looks between Valentine and me. "The police say she got robbed." He doesn't sound too sure of it.

"We won't get you in trouble," I reassure him.

He looks at his hands in his lap. "She told me it was a secret."

I lean closer. "If we know more about how she got hurt, maybe the doctors can help her get better." It's a dirty trick. I can't wake Molly Sawyer up any more than I can raise Ava from the dead.

He looks back at his sister, torn. "I saw her leave that night. I think she went to the place."

"The place," Valentine repeats.

Max nods. "The place she always went."

"Where was that?" I ask.

"Molls used to go out at night, after Dad fell asleep." Pink spots of embarrassment appear on the tops of his cheeks. "She let me sleep in her room when I had nightmares, but sometimes I'd wake up and she was gone. I promised not to tell."

"What about your parents?" I ask.

Max shakes his head. Looks at his shoes. "No. I never wake him up."

Valentine stiffens beside me, but I keep my focus on Max. "So what's the place?"

He pops his knuckles. "I know I wasn't supposed to, but one time I followed her."

"At night?" I mean, he's obviously independent enough to come here alone, but really?

He nods. "It wasn't very far. She walked to this big empty building and went into the basement." He cracks another knuckle. "I didn't want to go down there."

"Did you tell her?"

"No. She'd be so mad."

"Did Molly ever bring home money?"

He won't meet my eyes.

"It's okay. We won't tell," I promise again.

"She hid it under her bed. In a box of, um, those things girls use." His face glows red.

I resist the urge to laugh. "Tampons?"

"So our dad wouldn't find it." In my peripheral vision, Valentine twitches again.

"Was it a lot of money?"

He nods. "Molly said it was our adventure fund."

"You two were going somewhere?" Valentine's voice is tight and clipped.

Max answers, "She said one day she'd have enough, and we could go away."

"Anywhere in particular?" Valentine asks before I can get another question in.

Max shrugs. "It changed a lot. She used to tell me stories

when I couldn't sleep. Sometimes it was Alaska. We would see moose and the aurora borealis. One time it was Egypt, and we were going to live inside a pyramid. I knew it wasn't real, but she liked to talk about it."

Sounds like Molly wanted to run away from something. But what?

"Just the two of you?" Valentine's arms are crossed over his chest. Every line of his body is pulled tight like he might snap.

His intensity is making Max nervous. "Yeah..."

"Not your dad?"

Max's eyes flick around the room, pausing on the door behind us like he's watching the exit.

"Where'd you get that scar?" Valentine points to a faded white line on Max's chin.

A splinter of ice lodges itself in my chest. I have a sudden, horrible feeling I know where Valentine is going with this.

Max looks at the ground and mumbles, "Busted it. I fell down the stairs."

"You ever break your arm?" Valentine asks. His eyes are locked on Max's face.

The cold feeling spreads. I look at Max more carefully, searching for clues and hoping I don't find them.

There. Peeking out from the neck of his sweatshirt: what looks like the edge of a fresh bruise.

Max cracks the knuckles on his other hand, not meeting Valentine's eyes. "Um, my bike one time. I fell off. And I tripped over a crack in the sidewalk once."

My heart shatters. The scars, the broken bones, the excuses. Someone is hurting him.

He looks so small in his chair. His feet don't quite reach the ground.

That's why she was fighting. Molly was saving money so that they could escape. She got hurt, and now she's stuck here, and Max is all alone at home with a monster.

"Fall down a lot?" Valentine is still pushing him.

Max's shoulders swallow his ears. "I'm really clumsy."

"VT," I warn. Max is obviously terrified. He probably hasn't told anyone about this.

Valentine ignores me. "What about your ribs?" I shoot him a look, but one glance at his face and my heart breaks all over again. He put it together before I did, because he's lived it, too.

"Enough." I put a hand on Valentine's arm. He tries to shake me off, but I'm not going to let him scare this kid to death just because he's falling apart. He looks at me with hollow, unseeing eyes and I tighten my grip. He blinks. Looks at me, then Max, then walks out of the room without another word.

I turn back to Max and attempt a reassuring smile. "This is really helpful. Can I give you my number? You can call me if Molly wakes up, or anything happens."

"Oh, sure." He takes a battered notebook out of his backpack and writes down my number in careful, precise handwriting.

I pause, unsure of what to do. Do I tell someone? But then what happens when Molly wakes up? I've heard stories about siblings separated forever. I don't know anything about this. For all of my problems with my family, I have never truly had to worry about being safe, or loved, or fed.

"Max," I try, "I'm here because I'm trying to help Molly, kind of like a detective. If anything happens to you, if anyone hurts you, or you need help, you can call me, okay?"

It doesn't feel like nearly enough. Max nods, but his expression is blank and distant now, and I know he won't call.

I lean back against the passenger-side window of Valentine's car. The dash clock says it's almost five o'clock. The dying light gilds his profile.

He doesn't look at me. After leaving Max, I found him in the parking lot smoking a cigarette. It didn't look like it was his first.

I'm still angry, but I also feel an aching sadness for him. I spend enough time running from my own emotional baggage. I know how much it sucks to get smacked in the face with it out of nowhere.

His eyes are steady on the road, but his lower lip trembles slightly. He clenches his jaw, and it stops.

I don't need to overthink this right now. His hand rests on the gearshift. I reach across the center console and place mine on top of his.

Valentine looks at me in surprise, but his subsequent smile is so sudden and fragile that I don't immediately pull away. He rubs the back of my wrist twice with his calloused thumb. His skin on mine is a sliding piano scale down my spine.

He turns back to the road but doesn't let go of my hand. "Mind if we make a pit stop? Got something I wanna show you."

"Okay. Why not?"

"Yeah." His voice is soft. "Why not?"

He takes an unfamiliar exit and pulls over in a wooded area.

Outside the car, I pull my jacket tighter around me. The trees block out the last bit of sun. Valentine walks off into the woods, and I follow.

We don't go far. After about twenty paces, the trees open onto a hidden overlook perched above the Hudson River. The parkway runs like a jewel-bright ant trail below. New York and New Jersey reach for each other across the water.

Valentine leans against the railing and lights a cigarette. "I used to come here on the way back to school. My family lived in White Plains, wasn't a long drive, but I didn't go home much. Even when I did, before long I'd start feeling like I was suffocating, and I'd have to leave. On the drive back to school, sometimes I felt like I might wreck the car if I didn't get out and scream or something. Found this place. I've never seen anyone else here."

He squints into the dying red sun. "My whole world at Juilliard was so shiny. Glittering. I'd go home and feel like I was rotting from the inside out. This place was my reset."

For a couple minutes, we stand there and watch the shimmering reflection of the sun setting on the river. I don't fill the silence.

"I knew her a little." Valentine's voice is rough. "Molly. Spoke to her once or twice at the club. Nice girl, I think. I barely remember. I didn't recognize her name when you asked. I'd heard a girl got hurt. Never thought much about it."

I'm not sure where he's going with this.

He exhales smoke. "After Annie died, I was done. Didn't want to need anyone anymore. Wasn't worth the effort. I kept my head down, stuck to my own thing. What that girl and her brother were going through at home—it was right there in front of my face, and I didn't even remember her name."

My heart rattles at the bars of its cage. "It's not your fault," I tell him, even though I know from experience it's a meaningless thing to say. It never makes you feel better to hear.

"Know that." He gives me a bitter smile and stubs out his cigarette on the railing. "Still, makes me think. Been pushing everybody away for so long, but it hasn't made me any better."

That pulling feeling hooks itself around my solar plexus. Like inertia, like physics—undeniable—but I plant my feet against it.

Valentine must feel it, too, because he takes one step toward me, then another. I'm close enough to see the gold flecks in his brown eyes, the way the light catches on his eyelashes.

Valentine curves his hand around my cheek. His fingers span my jaw and graze the skin of my neck, the space behind my ear. My eyes drift shut. I am utterly, perfectly still, every atom in my body vibrating with the strain of not touching him.

He kisses me, and it's different this time. Less desperate. A slow, liquid slide.

His body molds around mine until there is no negative space. I slip my hands under the back hem of his shirt and across the bare skin of his back. I can feel the scrape of his goose bumps under the pads of my fingers.

Valentine groans low in his throat, and my limbs turn to warm honey, lit golden in the fading sun. It is gentle and burning and sweet and ferocious, and maybe this time we don't have to stop.

I pull back slightly but don't let go. Valentine presses his forehead to mine. I can feel the rise and fall of his chest against my own.

"I can't," I say against his cheek. His skin smells like smoke and soap. I want to go back to kissing him. I want to kiss him everywhere.

He steps back, and there's a slight resistance, like two magnets being pulled apart.

The golden afternoon has disappeared, and the whole world has gone the dusty purple-gray of twilight.

The warm, languid feeling is gone, and I'm freezing cold. "I'm sorry, I care about you—"

"Don't." He cuts me off with a sad smile. "The trust thing, I get it."

I *want* to trust him.

After a few seconds, Valentine sighs. "C'mon, Cherry. It's getting dark. Don't want your old man to worry." He turns and walks back up the path, but I don't follow.

At the mention of my grandfather, it hits me all over again. When I get home, Olive will fill me in on her research. Gramps will make dinner. Cass will call later to talk about her date. My mother left me, but I am not alone.

Valentine will go back to his dark apartment with one kitchen chair.

I could invite him home with me. Let him into my life. What I said before was true: I do care about him. But every inch I let him draw closer makes it that much harder to push him away.

Valentine's back disappears into the dark. The distance between us is agonizing once more.

Wanting him has never been the problem. But my trust is such a fragile, brittle thing, and Valentine's been alone for so long his heart has atrophied, and the combination of the two makes it all impossible.

Back home, I shed my stuff in my room. My hand stills on the strap of my backpack. I never did anything with those photos. I pull out both sets now.

Olive, staring out the car window on her way home from ballet.

She's in her room right now. I can hear her presence through the wall we share. Computer keys clacking. A drawer opens and shuts.

I could tell her. I could do it right now.

Footsteps from Olive's room. Her bedroom door opens.

I shove the photos in one of my dresser drawers. I slam it shut as she pops her head in.

"How'd it go?" she asks.

"Good! Fine!" I sound a bit breathless.

"You okay?" She frowns.

I tuck a strand of hair behind my ear. "Um, yeah. Weird emotional stuff. Lot to think about. Did you find anything while I was gone?"

"Nothing important. We'll keep digging, don't worry."

On an impulse, I pull her into a hug. "You know I love you, right?"

She laughs and pushes at my shoulder. "Yeah, but, like, don't be weird about it."

She goes back to her room, leaving me alone again. I stare at my dresser drawer.

I'll tell them. I will. I have to.

Not tonight.

CHAPTER 26

The front entrance to the school looms overhead like a gaping cinder-block mouth. I don't want to be here on pretty much any given day, but that's especially true today. Those photos have me jumpy, looking over my shoulder so often my neck is starting to crick. Last night, after everyone else went to bed, I checked the cameras I installed around the house after I received the newspaper clippings, but there was nothing. The photos must have been taken before I set them up.

As we walk up the steps, Cass continues the recap of her meetup with Elliot last night, down to every facial expression and ambiguous punctuation usage.

I try to focus. "What did he think of the song you wrote?"

"He was so nice. I mean, I barely know what I'm doing, and he's been writing music for ages, so I was really nervous."

"Your writing is good," I insist. "It doesn't matter that it's new."

She smiles. "That's what he said. He was so encouraging and supportive, and he had all these really good suggestions, but it wasn't, like, patronizing or mansplainy or anything, you know? Ugh, he's perfect."

"How annoying is that?"

"Seriously, how dare he?"

I have never seen Cass this hopeful and excited. She's the type of person who forms instant crushes on half the people she meets—the checkout guy at the grocery store, the kid in her math class who sometimes wears a FUTURE IS FEMALE T-shirt, the hot mailman. But I can tell she's really into this guy.

As we push through the front doors to the school, my phone buzzes. It's a number I don't recognize: Bathroom by the auditorium, 3rd stall. Come alone—E

Cass raises her eyebrows. "Wow, Elle's really gotten into this whole covert ops thing, hasn't she?"

I laugh. "Maybe we should get her one of those funny glasses-and-mustache disguises."

"As long as it's made by Dior," Cass agrees. "You want me to come with you?"

"Nah, I think I can handle Elle Dorsey. I don't want to spook her."

"Okay, see you in English." We part ways.

There's an OUT OF ORDER sign pasted to the door of the

bathroom. Cass wasn't kidding. Elle really does fancy herself a baby spy.

She's waiting for me inside. One hand clutches the strap of her oversize cream-colored purse like there's something important inside.

"Took you long enough," she says, even though she texted me less than two minutes ago. It's like she rehearsed how this scene would go after watching too many noir films.

"What do you have?"

She chews her glossy pink lip. "I went through my dad's office last night," she explains. "I didn't know what to look for, but I found this." She reaches into her bag and pulls out a sheaf of papers. She hesitates for a fraction of a second before she hands them over to me.

I flick through them quickly. Bank statements. Lots of them.

"I don't know if it's useful," she says, "but I figured you wouldn't be able to get this kind of stuff from anyone else."

"No, this is good," I tell her without looking up. The transaction amounts are all large, thousands of dollars apiece.

My eyes land on the account holder's name at the top of the page, and the back of my neck tingles. James Dorsey is not the name associated with this account. It's registered to EVAH LLC.

The same company that was on the Progress Together documents.

I point to the weird combination of letters. "Does that name mean anything to you?"

Her mouth tightens. "Yes, unfortunately. They're initials. Mine and my mother's: Elle Victoria and Andrea Helene. That asshole is totally embezzling money or something, and he has the balls to put *my* name on it."

Elle looks away, and I could swear she's blinking back tears.

"I thought there was something wrong with me," she says. She wraps her arms around herself, like she's trying to hold it all in. "I've worked so hard to impress him, and it's never been enough. But apparently, all this time I've been trying to get the approval of a murderer."

She turns back to me, and now there's no doubt about the tears glistening in her dark eyes. "Do you want to know the really fucked up thing, Flora? There's a part of me that *still* wants it. He's my dad, you know? I could take these documents to him and tell him that I figured it out. That I know what he's up to. And wouldn't he think I was so fucking clever? Wouldn't he finally have to respect me then?" She shakes her head with disgust, the sadness in her eyes evaporating until all that's left is fiery rage. "Do me a favor, Flora? Nail him. Make sure he rots in prison. I'm done being his daughter."

I don't like Elle. But her life would be so much easier if she had chosen to stay oblivious. I have to respect her for making this choice.

"Thank you," I tell her sincerely. "This could make a huge difference. Can I be in touch if I have any follow-up questions?"

"Text me. I don't want anyone to see me talking to you."

Just when I was starting to not hate her.

Elle exits the stall. She checks herself once in the mirror before she leaves the bathroom. For a second, I see another tiny glimmer of vulnerability in her expression, but then she runs a finger under her bottom lip, fixing her lip gloss, and she's Ruthless Elle again. Her boots click on the tile as she walks out the bathroom door.

I look at the documents again. Dorsey is using an anonymous LLC to make contributions to his own campaign. That's big. Didn't Cass say something about this? That if he wanted to launder the money from the Basement into his campaign accounts, this is how he would do it? We still have to prove that that's where the money came from, though.

I text pictures of the bank statements to Gramps and Olive: EVAH LLC is Dorsey's. Is there a way to figure out where the money originates?

Olive texts me back within seconds: Computer lab next period, I'll look into it

Gramps follows right after: I will get in touch with my sources.

God, I love them both.

I haven't totally figured it out. I don't want to put anyone in danger, but I also remember what Valentine said about being alone so long he's forgotten how not to be. I don't want that for me.

If this is who I am, if this is going to be my life, I'd rather have them fighting alongside me than do this alone.

In English, I want to tell Cass everything about Elle, but Mr. Kelly keeps doing this annoying thing where he wants to teach us stuff. Every time he turns away, Cass and I lean our heads together.

"You know"—Cass keeps one eye trained on Mr. Kelly as he writes on the board—"here's Molly, with this horrible reason why she needs to fight. I guess I can kind of understand why Austin was so upset. I mean, no one deserves to be in a coma, but Molly's life was so hard already."

Mr. Kelly turns back toward the class. Cass and I separate.

"All right, folks, so what do we think about the repetition of the phrase 'So it goes'?" He calls on Ben Zadeh, on the other side of the room, who spouts off something he almost certainly read on the internet.

Mr. Kelly taps his whiteboard marker against his chin as he listens.

Cass resumes whispering. "You know who we never asked about the threats?"

Ben Zadeh finishes his SparkNotes-fueled ramble, and Mr. Kelly turns to jot down something on the board.

I lean back to Cass. "Who?"

She faces front but whispers out of the side of her mouth. "Paige."

She's right. Oh, my God, she's right. I just assumed Paige couldn't have been behind them, especially after she got hurt, but she obviously wanted Molly to stay a secret, too.

During lunch, Cass and I make it our mission to find Paige, but she's not in the cafeteria. Cass asks some of her friends where she is, but they all shrug and avert their eyes.

I get it. They're not her friends anymore. It may have started with Molly—seems like a lot of people were angry with Paige for that—but her beating last week was a message to the whole school: *This girl is toxic, stay away.*

"I know where she is," I tell Cass.

As I suspected, Paige is sitting at a table by herself in the library. She has a textbook open in front of her and a Tupperware of salad.

It's only in movies that friendless kids eat lunch in bathroom stalls. Those of us who actually have no friends eat in

373

the library, where we can pretend to be too busy with work to bother with trifling concerns like human contact. It's where I go whenever Cass isn't around during lunch.

We sit down across the table from Paige. The swelling in her eye has gone down a bit, but her face is still a ruin.

She barely looks up. "I don't want to talk to you." She turns the page in her textbook and takes a bite of her salad.

Paige has good reason to be afraid, but I can't let her stonewall me anymore. "I already got the full story from Austin. I have enough to go to the police. Once the cops start looking around, there's a lot of angry people who'd love to tell them how you put Molly in a coma."

Never mind that the police wouldn't listen to me. Paige doesn't need to know that.

Her fork pauses. "I don't know what you're talking about." Her posture is completely rigid, except for the tiniest tremor in her chin.

"It's all going to come out," Cass says gently. "You know it can't stay secret forever."

Paige looks at her, then me.

She folds in on herself, face in her hands. Her shoulders shake as she cries, and I know she's fighting to stay as quiet as possible in the empty stillness of the library.

"I don't know what to do," she chokes out. "I didn't mean to hurt her. It was an accident."

"Tell us what happened," Cass urges.

Paige wipes her eyes. "I can't. They'll kill me if they find out I'm talking to you again."

"We're going to get the Basement shut down for good," I promise. "They're not going to be able to hurt you, or Molly, or anyone else."

Paige trembles as she tries to get her tears under control.

"Tell us what happened after Molly fell," Cass says. "Who set it up to look like she'd been mugged?"

Paige picks up her pen and positions it at a perfect right angle to the edge of the table. "This guy, he's kind of like the manager?"

"Boyd?" I prompt.

She nods. "He told me not to worry, he'd make sure Molly got to the hospital. I followed up," she adds defensively. "She got checked in and everything. I didn't see what else I could do. I can't make her wake up. We all signed up to fight. We knew it wasn't safe, and Molly chose it anyway. No one forced her."

I frown. Molly was being exploited. That's not the same thing as a choice.

"Did you know why she was fighting?" I ask.

Paige keeps playing with her pen. "Yeah, I knew her story. Makes it easy for everyone to hate me. Molly was like this wholesome little white girl with a tragic past, and everyone thinks I'm a stuck-up black bitch."

375

A vision of Paige standing in the center of a roiling, hateful crowd. Someone's drink trickling down her broken face. Austin looming over her as she scrambled to get in her locker. He was fighting, too. What happened to Paige could just as easily have happened to him.

All that rage and hatred when they were just as complicit. She's right. It's not fair.

"So why do you put up with it?" I ask. "Why fight?"

"It's hard to explain." She gives a frustrated shake of her head. "My whole life is like this regimented thing. I have perfect grades. I got a 1560 on the SAT. I go to galas with my parents and make pointless conversation with their business associates so that they'll pull my mom aside and tell her she did a wonderful job raising such a charming and 'articulate' daughter." She looks between Cass and me, her expression earnest. "I *know* I'm super-privileged, but sometimes I feel like I'm going to shrivel up and die from trying to be so perfect all the time.

"This girl Ainsley from the country club was the one who first brought me to the Basement. She just wanted to get drunk and party, but I was completely obsessed. The lights, the blood, the crowd...it was about as far away from my regular life as I could get. I went back five more times before Ava approached me and asked if I wanted to fight. I turned out to be pretty good. People bet on me, cheered for me. I *liked* it. I started going to the gym to practice on the weekends. And I thought maybe I could tolerate the other stuff if I at least had one thing of my own, something I was good at that I did just because I liked it, and not because it would look good on my college applications."

Paige and I are different in a lot of ways, but I kind of get it. How it feels to be good at something, to enjoy it, even when everyone else thinks it's fucked up.

She takes a deep breath and straightens the collar on her starched white button-down. "Like I said, it makes me an easy villain. Everyone felt so bad for Molly, and I didn't even need the money."

I lean across the table. "None of them came forward, either. They have no right to judge you. But *you* could tell the truth. Come to the police with us. We can bring that place down."

She leans back, away from me. "No. Even if Boyd doesn't have me killed, don't you see how this would play out?" She does an exaggerated newscaster voice: "Angry black girl beats up white people for sport, leaves one girl in tragic coma." She shakes her head. "It'll be the end of my life. College. Career. All gone. It won't matter that I've been perfect, poised Paige all my life. They'll find the angriest, thuggiest picture of me to put up next to one of Molly hugging a puppy. I know how this goes. I told Ava the same thing."

She's not wrong.

Cass has a thoughtful expression on her face. "You talked to Ava about this?"

Paige shrugs. "Yeah. She felt bad about Molly. She said she'd talk to the police with me. But then it's *two* black girls preying on the innocent white children. No. Molly will get better, or she won't. That's up to her doctors. Coming forward now won't fix anything."

And just like that, I know what happened.

Molly got hurt. Ava felt guilty. When Paige wouldn't come forward, Ava decided to bring the Basement down from the inside. It would explain why there's such a long gap between Molly's fight and Ava's death. She would have needed time to gather evidence of Dorsey's involvement.

Only he found out, and he killed Ava to keep her quiet.

It definitely sounds more like the Ava I knew. The kind of person willing to risk everything to admit she made a mistake.

Or maybe that's what I want to believe. Here I am, trying to assign her some kind of virtuous mission. Is her death any easier to bear if she's a martyr?

No. Ava's murder is wrong, no matter what choices she

made. I'm going to keep digging until I find the truth, whatever that is.

Besides, I need irrefutable proof before I go to the police. Paige is right—if the media finds out that Ava was running some ultraviolent fight club, they'll turn on her like rabid dogs. According to them, victims only deserve justice if they're blameless virgins who have never so much as jaywalked. I saw what happened with Lucy, and she was a rich white girl from a "good family." For Ava, it'll be so much worse.

I turn my attention back to Paige. "You sent us threatening messages. The text, the writing on my locker—that was all you?"

She has the grace to look ashamed. "It's better for everyone if all this stuff stays quiet."

Cass pushes back. "Not Austin. You could have really hurt him."

"Austin nearly got me killed because he couldn't keep his mouth shut." Paige gestures angrily at her broken face. "All I did was remind him that he has just as much to lose as the rest of us."

The bell rings.

Cass turns to me. "I can't be late to French. You good?" I nod.

After she's gone, I turn back to Paige. "One more thing. What about the photos?"

"Photos?" Her expression is blank.

"The surveillance pictures. You left them at my house. And the newspaper clippings in my room."

She shrugs. "Sorry, I don't know anything about that. I doubt I'm the only person who wants things kept quiet, though."

CHAPTER 27

I leave Paige and walk to chem.

Someone falls into step beside me. "Red."

I do a double take. "Okay, you can't keep showing up here. I have an actual education to deal with." I try to keep my tone light, but my eyes fall to his lips.

Valentine's face is very serious. "Something came up. Remember Boyd, the guy who gave me the documents?"

And now kissing is the last thing on my mind. "You probably don't want to remind me about that."

He ignores that and pushes on, insistent. "Boyd approached me last night, said he caught another break for me. A woman upstate, in a psych hospital. He claims she might have been a witness to Annabelle's death, and Boyd has her patient file."

I slow my pace.

Valentine keeps talking. "I ask what I owe him for it, and he says I should consider it thanks for my loyalty, and maybe I wanna skip town a few days to check it out. He'll get someone to fill in for my matches."

My breath comes sharper, faster. Things are getting scarier and scarier, and now Valentine's going to disappear. That's where he's going with this, right? He said it himself the other day: his priorities have been clear from the beginning. If he gets the chance to pursue a lead on his sister, he'll take it, even if it means leaving me behind. It's hard to blame him for that.

I wait for him to say more. We're almost to my classroom.

I can't take it any longer. "So are you going?"

"No."

The bottom falls out of my stomach. "No?"

He stops walking. "Gonna see this through to the end."

I stop, too. I want him to stay. I still have no idea how I feel about him, or I do know but don't want to know.

I want him to stay. I'm sure of that, at least.

Then again, what if it were me? Chasing down a clue about Olive, or Cass? I would have left without saying good-bye.

Maybe. I mean, that's what the normal me would do, right? What everyone would expect?

I wish he would stop looking at me like that. His eyes touch every part of my face.

Maybe I wouldn't be able to leave, either.

He runs a hand through his hair. "I'm staying. I'm making

the right choice this time. If this woman is real, she'll still be there in a few weeks. Not here looking for credit or forgiveness, Flora. Thought it seemed suspicious is all, getting that offer right now. That's what I'm here to tell you: a storm's coming. You're in danger."

I frown. "Why now?"

"What do you mean?"

"Okay, so maybe Dorsey knows you helped me fight off those guys the other night, and he wants you out of the way, but why now?" I ask again. "It's been days since that happened, and he hasn't tried anything to hurt either of us since. Why now?"

Valentine doesn't follow. "Maybe he was biding his time. Getting his murderous ducks in a row."

"Yeah, maybe. Or maybe we did something that got his attention. Spooked him." The second I say the words, I know. I pull out my phone.

It rings forever.

A woman answers, "Park Memorial Hospital, how may I help you?"

I steady my voice. "Yes, can I please be connected to room 317?"

The nurse connects me. Max Sawyer picks up after a couple rings.

"Max? This is Molly's friend. I came to visit yesterday?"

Valentine steps closer to hear Max on the other end.

Max says, "Oh, hi. She's still not awake. Don't worry, I won't forget to call."

"I know, Max, it's okay. Listen, has anyone come by to visit your sister? Asked you any questions?"

"Uh-huh. A man came last night, but he didn't talk to me."

A tendril of dread winds itself into a knot around my intestines. "What did he look like?"

"Um, he was wearing a suit. He was old, I guess. He talked to the doctors a long time."

"What did he say to them?" I ask.

"He asked how Molls was doing, and the doctors told him she's getting a lot better. I don't think they knew I was listening."

Valentine and I make eye contact. It's Dorsey, or one of his lackeys. It has to be. He's the only person involved who's powerful enough to bully doctors into giving up private information.

Now he knows Molly could wake up at any minute, and if he's got the hospital staff in his pocket he probably knows that we talked to Max, too.

Dorsey has already killed at least once to keep this stuff a secret. I don't think he'd mind doing it again. Valentine's right: a storm's coming. Dorsey can't afford a liability like Molly, and with her already in the hospital it would be so easy to eliminate the threat.

"Thanks, Max," I say. "Can you stay there and keep an eye on your sister for me? Call me if anyone else comes by?" Regret hits me the second the words are out. It's such a stupid thing to ask. What's Max going to do to keep her safe? He's a kid, and now he might put himself in danger trying to protect her. Valentine shakes his head.

"I will, I swear," Max says, and the vise of guilt tightens in my chest.

"If the man or anyone else comes back, call me right away," I repeat. Too late to take it back now.

Max picks up on the panic in my voice. "Is everything going to be okay?"

"Yes, I promise," I lie.

"Hi, yes. I'm calling about a patient, Molly Sawyer?" I'm in Cass's car, on the phone with the hospital yet again. "You need to post security around her room. Why? Because someone wants to hurt her! No, this isn't a threat. Please—" The nurse on the other end hangs up. It's about the seventh time that's happened. I've called the hospital and the police multiple times, but no one will take me seriously. Gramps isn't answering his phone. I bang my fist against the car door.

"No luck?" Cass asks.

"No! And they've reported my calls to the cops by now. Fuck!" I slam my head back against the seat.

"Calm down. We'll figure it out."

I'm scaring Cass, but I can't help it. "There's no time to calm down! She's in danger, and she's helpless, and I told her ten-year-old brother to protect her, so now he's in danger, too!"

"Call Richmond? Maybe she can help," Cass suggests.

"I already did. She told me to leave Molly alone and hung up on me." Probably too afraid of pissing off her beloved sergeant again.

Cass bites her lip. She's out of solutions.

No one will listen to me, and every second that passes puts Max's and Molly's lives in more danger.

I can't breathe. It's all happening again. Like Matt Caine. Dorsey killed Ava, and now he might kill Molly, and I can't stop it. People are going to get hurt or *die,* and it's all my fault.

Cass reaches over and puts her hand on top of mine. "Hey. We got this. You and me, right? If the police won't protect Molly, we will."

"We can't." I choke on my own breath.

"We can." Cass's voice is firm. "Let's stop at your house, see if we can catch your grandfather, and then go to the hospital. If the police won't keep watch for Molly, we will."

I wish I felt as strong as Cass right now. "And what are we going to do if someone really does show up to hurt her?"

Cass's expression is hard. "Then we'll have proof, and Richmond will have to listen. We're not going down without a fight."

But Gramps isn't there when we get home. I search the house twice, panic rising with every step, but nothing.

"Gramps? *Gramps!*" I throw open every door on the second floor, even though I've already looked in all these rooms.

I check the hall bathroom for the third time and catch sight of myself in the mirror. My lank hair is falling out of my bun, and sweat shines on my forehead. I look possessed.

"I tried calling him again," Cass says from behind me. "He's still not picking up."

I can barely hear her. The car is in the driveway, but he's not here. There are a thousand possible explanations, but only one gets stuck in my brain.

Someone got to him. Why else would he not be here when I need him?

"It's okay," Cass says. "Let's just go to the hospital, and he can meet us there later."

What if he can't? What if he's tied to a chair somewhere? What if he's dead?

"Hey." Cass grips me by the shoulders. "Look at me, Flora. You're just panicking, but we're so close. We're going to go protect Molly, and Gramps will be fine. He'll come find us."

I try to focus on her, but my eyes dart everywhere, like I'm an animal being led into the slaughterhouse. I cannot make my lungs fill with air.

Cass pulls me tight to her chest. Squeezing me so I'll feel safe.

"You are the bravest person I know," she says. "It's okay to freak out a little bit, but Molly needs us. If anyone can set aside their feelings for a few hours to help someone, it's Flora Calhoun. Right?"

Impossibly, I laugh. It sounds like a drowning person's gasp for air, but it's something.

Only Cass could save me like that.

I breathe in the familiar citrusy scent of her shampoo, and I'm back to myself.

"Let's do this," I tell her.

She beams. "That's my girl."

"I need to wash my face," I say. "Give me a sec to pull myself together?"

She looks at me and grimaces. "Probably a good idea."

I pause in the bathroom doorway. "Thank you," I tell her abruptly.

"For what?"

I don't know how to put it into words. "Being braver than me."

Cass gives me the warmest, kindest smile, and I know I said the right thing, even though it's way too small to fit all the love I have for her.

I don't linger in the bathroom. Don't let myself pause too long on the hunted look that still hasn't quite left my eyes. I splash some water on my face, dry my hands, and leave. It's time to end this.

Cass isn't waiting for me in the hall.

I poke my head into my room. "Hey, are you re—"

I stop short. My palms go cold.

Cass is standing next to my dresser. One of the drawers is open. She's holding a manila envelope in her hands. The surveillance photos. Hers is on top. I shoved them in my dresser yesterday and forgot to hide them properly.

"I needed a sweater," she says faintly, not lifting her eyes from the photo of her, taken by a murderer.

CHAPTER 28

"It's not what you think—" I start, even though that's the dumbest thing I could say.

She stops me. "It's *exactly* what I think. You got these and you didn't tell me?"

I don't say anything.

"Tell me I'm wrong," she says.

I still don't say anything.

"When?" she asks.

"Cass—"

"When?"

It whispers out of me. "It started last Tuesday."

She sucks in a breath through her nose. She blinks. "You've had these for almost a week."

"I was going to tell you, I swear—"

"When? When it was all over with?" She drops the photos on the ground.

"No! I *was* going to tell you, but you had your date, and rehearsal. You were so happy—"

"Bullshit!" Cass has a good four inches on me, but the way she looks down on me right now, it might as well be four feet. "What about five minutes ago? That tender little heart-to-heart we had? Seems like a perfect time to come clean. Or last Friday, in the bathroom? You've had plenty of chances—you just didn't want to."

"I panicked! I wanted to tell you about it, but then things were good between us, and I didn't want to ruin it. I thought I could end the whole thing before you even had to worry about it."

Silence.

"You do ruin everything," Cass says in a deathly quiet voice. "Flora, it *sucks* to be your friend."

I flinch.

She steps closer. "Do you remember when I had the flu last year?"

I nod, not sure where she's going with this.

"I had a hundred-and-two-degree fever, but I lied to my mom and told her I was fine. If I missed any more classes I would lose credit, you know? Because of you. I have no friends, all because of you." She gathers steam, her voice rising. "When I heard about rock ensemble, I almost didn't even audition because I was so afraid to spend one night a week not being there for *you*!"

"I know," I choke out. "I know it's my fault."

"You don't get it!" she yells. "I don't mind doing any of that stuff. I thought we were partners. Equals." Angry tears streak down her face. "But this whole time I've been bending over backward to prove to you that I care just as much as you do, and you still don't trust me."

I'm crying, too. "I do. I trust you more than anyone."

Through her tears, Cass gives me a burning look. "If you really trusted me, you wouldn't treat me like a *sidekick*."

She turns to leave.

No. She can't. I step toward her. "Cass, wait—"

"Drive yourself to the hospital. I'm done." She brushes past me and out the door.

Cass's footsteps echo through the house. The front door opens. I hear voices. A moment later, the sound of her car driving away shatters my heart.

She's gone. Cass is gone. Lots of people have left me before, but I have never truly been alone. Until now.

What was it Elle said last week? *It was only a matter of time before you actually made it to zero friends.*

She was right.

Olive appears in my doorway. "Flora?" She's still wearing her backpack from school.

My voice sounds far away. "I ruined it. It's all my fault."

Olive gives me a sympathetic look but says, "Yeah, pretty much."

That jars me out of my daze a bit. "Are you trying to comfort me?"

She shrugs, unapologetic. "You don't need comforting. You screwed up. Fix it."

"I don't think I can," I tell her. My hands shake. I don't know what to do with them. "She won't come back."

"She will," Olive insists.

I'm not so sure. First Gramps, now Cass. I'm so good at doing the one thing I am most afraid of: pushing the people I love away for good.

The thought makes my whole body shake with grief. I should chase after her. Apologize. *Make* her see how sorry I am, that I can change.

But Max and Molly are still waiting for me. Their lives are in danger, and it's my fault. I don't know where Gramps is. He could be anywhere, hurt or captured or dead.

Those thoughts send my pulse rocketing. "I have to go to the hospital. Molly Sawyer, I have to get to her, but Cass—"

"Stop," Olive says, her voice loud and firm. "I'll go with you."

An icy trickle of fear in my gut. "No. It's too dangerous."

Olive's eyes dart to the photos still puddled on the ground.

"I've always been in danger. You really want to argue with me over lines in the sand right now?"

I open my mouth to say something, maybe apologize.

"Don't bother," she says, but her voice is gentle. "Let's go."

As we drive to the hospital, Olive says, "What do you think she'll say if she wakes up?"

"Molly?" I dart my eyes to her, then back to the road.

"Do you really think she knows anything about Dorsey? None of the people at your school did."

"I don't know," I admit, "but Molly's the only one who might be able to tell me the full story of what happened that night."

I glance at Olive, and she gives me a reassuring smile. Her eyes go wide. They're fixed on something over my shoulder.

I turn in slow motion. We're in the middle of an intersection, waiting to turn.

A large white van barrels straight toward us.

Everything stops for a moment. It's me and the van. Staring each other down.

The whole world zooms back.

I step on the gas. I swerve the wheel. The explosion comes anyway.

A screeching blast of glass and metal and smoke and noise. Louder than anything I've ever heard.

I reach for Olive, but I'm a rag doll flying through the air, taken over by the brutal, awesome power of physics.

A second explosion. Even louder than the first.

A knockout blow shatters into my jaw. The airbag. All the sound is sucked from the car. There's ringing in my ears, and nothing else.

Are we moving? Are we stopped? I can't tell.

White dust from the airbags covers everything. It filters through the air, dancing in the light. It coats my eyelashes, my nostrils, my lungs.

I blink in slow motion. The world goes dark, then light again.

More dust. The smell of burning chemicals.

I blink again. A cinematic slow fade in and out and in again. Can I move? I try. Every part of me hurts.

Blink. Cough a cloud of snowy dust.

It's as though someone else operates my limbs. Forces me to unbuckle my seat belt. Grasp the door handle. The door makes the same smooth, electronic chime as always when I open it. The ordinariness of that sound is absurd enough to cut through the ringing silence in my ears, but the rest of the world is soundless as I stumble from the car. A fog of airbag dust billows out of the open door with me.

The street is a mess of shredded metal and broken glass.

The sun is too bright. Brighter than usual. People rush to help. A man says something. I watch his lips move. It's so bright out here. I try to look left and right, but the muscles in my neck scream and tear in agony.

Where is it? Where is the van? So bright. I can't find it.

The man says something again. No sounds make it through to me. I shake my head. A woman. On her phone. Her lips move pointlessly, too.

The man looks over my shoulder. I turn.

Olive has not gotten out of the car.

The front passenger side of the car is smashed against a telephone pole. That was the second explosion.

All my sound comes rushing back.

Yelling. The woman on the phone asks for an ambulance. Honking horns. Traffic rushes by, as though life goes on.

The next bit is a series of disconnected images.

I scream and pull at Olive's door handle.

Blackness. Silence.

Someone drags me away from the car by my shoulder. It hurts.

The void.

An ambulance. A fire truck. I think I'm still screaming. I should stop. I can't.

Olive, limp and broken in the arms of a firefighter. Her

skin is a color no human skin should be. That insidious white dust streaks through her red hair.

Stillness.

Olive is on a stretcher in the back of an ambulance. I force my way in. The ambulance races to the hospital. Someone tries to tend to the cuts on my fingers. We hit a bump in the road. Olive's head lolls sickeningly on the stretcher.

This is all my fault.

CHAPTER 29

The hospital hallway is doing the Alice in Wonderland thing. It stretches on and on forever, then contracts until I'm about to run into the far wall. Purple-black-green spots float in and out of my vision, like that moment right before you pass out.

As soon as we got here, a swarm of ER doctors descended on Olive's stretcher. They rushed her off without a second glance in my direction. I was left in the care of a nurse, who bandaged me up.

Olive is unconscious, but all I have are scratches. A bad bruise where the airbag hit me in the face. A welt on my shoulder from the seat belt.

I hear myself asking a nurse for Olive Calhoun's room. Hear myself choke out, "She's my sister."

Once my wounds had been tended, I had to talk to the police. A man and a woman. I couldn't remember if I knew them or not. From our conversation, I was able to piece together what happened. I swerved away from the van. It's a rookie mistake. Something teen drivers often do in accidents. Turning the wheel makes it easier for the car to spin off the road. The van hit the back of the car and pushed the tail around. Olive's side smashed into a telephone pole.

The van drove off before anyone could get its plates. I don't bother telling the police that it's him. It's Dorsey. He did this. They wouldn't believe me anyway.

I'm outside a gray door that looks like every other gray door in the building. I push my way in.

My grandfather looks up. He's here. No one took him. He's not dead in an alleyway somewhere.

Before I can say a word, he crosses the room and wraps me in his arms.

"You're here," he says, almost to himself. "You're alive."

All my scrapes and bruises ache in his arms. My tender jaw is smashed into his chest. I don't pull back. I want him to take care of me for one more second.

But Olive's in that bed, and I'm the one still standing. I swallow my tears and step away.

His gaze lingers on my bruised chin. "I came as soon as I got the call. I was having coffee with a friend, I didn't hear my phone." The ragged apology in his voice makes me feel infinitely worse.

Olive's red hair fans across her pillow. Her freckled skin is covered in a delicate, grisly web of yellow, purple, black, blue, red, and green. The crisp white bandages on her arms and jaw and legs are too pristine in the dingy fluorescent light. Looking at them hurts my eyes.

The van aimed for me, but I swerved, so I'm only scratched and Olive is unconscious in that bed.

"Flora?" He brushes a stray hair from my forehead. The tenderness of the gesture hurts. "Are you all right? Please talk to me."

"It's my fault," I whisper. "I did this."

He steps back. "No."

My bones ache like they might burst through my paper skin. "It is. I'm the reason she's hurt."

"No." He turns to face the wall. Away from me.

"Yes." I step back into his field of vision. He needs to look at me while I say this. "I've been getting threats. Dorsey has people watching the house. Watching all of us. I knew about it, and I didn't tell you. It's my fault she's in the hospital."

"No!" he shouts, then reels himself back in. He rubs a hand over his face. "It's mine. It's my responsibility to protect you. Both of you. I let this happen."

"Then we both failed." My voice rises. "If it's your fault, then it's mine, too." An overwhelming emotion bubbles out of me. Anger, or sadness, or some combination.

"Stop." He straightens Olive's bedsheet. Her fingers are curled around the top edge. Even those are bruised.

"No, look at me. Get angry! Blame me!"

My grandfather sits down in the chair beside the bed. He closes his eyes. For the first time in my life, William Calhoun looks truly old. There is something about hospital lighting that illuminates the saddest versions of us all.

I stand there, panting, hurt inside and out, waiting for him to say something.

He does not open his eyes when he speaks. "Every time I look at you, all I see is my failure. You're a child, and I failed you. It's my fault."

"I'm not a child. I haven't been since Lucy MacDonald."

Now he looks at me with ancient, sorrowful eyes. "No. Horrific things have happened to you, but that pain did not turn you into an adult. You've never grown up at all. You are the same child you were when you put your running shoes on that morning. It's my fault that I did not take care of you, then and now." He turns his attention back to Olive.

Of all the cruel words my mother ever said to me, none ever hurt as much as this.

I wait and wait, but he doesn't look at me again.

I pause with my hand on the doorknob, but I can't bring myself to look back at him. At that bed.

"I'm sorry," I whisper. For him. For Cass. For Olive.

"Don't leave the hospital," he says. That's it.

I turn the handle and go.

I wander the hallways. Eventually I'm too weak to keep walking, and I sit. I sit and stare for a long time. I don't know how long.

"Flora?"

I look up. Max Sawyer stands a few feet away, looking confused. Some instinct or muscle memory led me to the third floor.

He inches closer. His eyes run over my various bruises and bandages. "Are you hurt? Why are you crying?"

I didn't realize I was until he pointed it out. I wipe the tears from my face. "It's complicated. Is your sister okay?"

"Yeah." He beams. "She's awake. She's really tired, even though she's been sleeping for a long time."

"That's good. Good she's awake." My voice breaks.

He sits down next to me on the bench. "Are you sure you're okay?"

This is what my life has become. The only person left to comfort me is a ten-year-old.

I don't have the energy to lie to him. "Not really."

"What happened?"

"I messed things up with my family. Now my sister is hurt."

"I'm sorry." Max gives me an understanding look. Despite my best efforts, my tears break free again.

He pats me on the back. "It'll be okay. She'll be all right, even if it takes a long time."

I bury my face in my hands and cry sticky, snotty tears onto my palms. "I want to help her, but everyone else wants me to stop, and I don't know what to do."

Max continues to give me awkward pats on the back. "You should help your sister. Sometimes sisters say they don't want help, but they really do. That's why I talked to you about Molly."

"It's more complicated than that." I sniffle and scoot away from him.

"Okay." He folds his hands in his lap. "Well, can you come talk to Molls? She needs your help, too."

I lift my face from my hands and look at him. I can't say no.

Max leads me to Molly's room. She looks worn, but she's sitting up in her bed. The skin under her eyes is deep violet. The TV is on in the background, but it's muted.

She looks between Max and me, and there's something fierce in her expression, like she would leap out of bed to defend him in a heartbeat, despite the gray bloodlessness of her lips. She twists her hospital bracelet round and round on her bony, frail wrist.

I sit down at her bedside. "Hey, Molly. I'm Flora. I've been making friends with your brother."

"So he says." Molly takes in all my cuts and scrapes with leery exhaustion. "Who are you, exactly?" Max sits sideways on his sister's bed. Molly reaches out and grabs his hand without taking her eyes off me.

Molly's protectiveness, even after waking up from a coma, makes my chest constrict. This is the kind of sister I'm supposed to be, but Olive always ends up taking care of me instead. Now she's in a hospital bed.

"My name is Flora Calhoun," I repeat. "I'm investigating the murder of Ava McQueen. I think you knew her?"

Molly's eyes go big and round, and she looks very young again. "Ava was murdered?"

I nod. "About a week ago."

Molly bites her lip but doesn't cry. After a moment, her face evens out. All emotion gone. I guess she's used to hiding that stuff, too.

I wish Cass were here.

I try again. "Molly, I know about the Basement. I think Ava's death was related to your accident, and I think you're in danger now. You and Max will be safer if we catch the people who did this. Please tell me what you know."

"Why am I in danger?" she fires back. "Max says I've been here for three months. Why now?"

"Because of me," I admit. "When I started asking questions about Ava, I think someone got nervous that I would figure out what happened to you. And then it started looking like you might wake up."

"So this is your fault, and you want me to tell you all the stuff they would kill to keep quiet?" Her hand tightens around her brother's. "No. Not happening."

"Molly, these are bad people. They already killed one girl. Do you think they're going to risk letting you live now that you're awake? You could talk at any time." I hesitate. What I'm about to say is a low blow. "It's no secret why you fought. The person running the fight club will know exactly how to hurt you most. Killing you might be the least of your problems." I look meaningfully at Max.

Molly glares at me like she might kick me out. Then: "What do you know already?"

I run through the basics that Paige shared about their fight.

Molly nods. "That's true, from what I remember. I wasn't totally under, though, not at first. It was like..." She closes her eyes to remember. "The world kept fading in and out. First I was in the ring, but the lights were so bright. I shut my eyes. It felt like I only blinked, but when I opened them again I was somewhere else. A car. Nice one, leather seats and stuff. I heard people arguing, but it was hard to make out. Like, first it sounded really far away, and then loud, and then quiet again."

This is way more than I hoped for. If Molly hadn't been totally unconscious, she might be able to ID Dorsey.

"What were they arguing about?" I ask.

Molly's eyes are still closed. She winces, like she's straining her brain to think. "Even when I could hear them, it was like I only understood pieces. But I recognized one of the voices. Ava. She said they needed to get me to the hospital, and the other person didn't want to do that. They wanted to make it look like an accident, because otherwise they'd get in trouble."

I lean forward. "And you didn't recognize that voice?"

Molly hesitates for a moment, then shakes her head. "No. It was hard to hear them at all. I knew Ava pretty well, so it took me a while, but I figured out it was her."

"Was it a man or a woman? Old or young? Any identifying features at all?"

"No." Molly shakes her head. "I was fighting to stay awake at that point. All the sound was fuzzy. Then I went under, and I woke up here."

I try not to look disappointed, even though I still don't have an ID on Dorsey. Molly can confirm that she got hurt and someone tried to cover it up. If I can get proof that Dorsey was the one in charge, Molly's testimony will still count for a lot.

"Thank you." I put all my sincerity into those words.

"I know you have a lot to lose, and I've already asked for so much, but if it comes down to it, will you say all this stuff to the police?"

Molly hesitates. Looks at her brother. Nods.

"I need more evidence," I tell her. "I want the cops to have no choice but to believe you. For now, stay here, stay together, and call the police and then me if anyone tries to come in this room. I'll be back as soon as I have what I need." I stand and turn for the door.

"Hey, Flora?" Molly calls.

"Yeah?"

Her expression goes fierce again. "You sucked us into this mess. I'm trusting you to keep my brother safe."

CHAPTER 30

I find myself knocking on the one door that will still let me in.

Valentine opens the door. "What happened?"

I happened. "It's Olive," I whisper. "They got to Olive." I walk past him into the apartment. I know Gramps wanted me to stay at the hospital, but I couldn't bear it anymore.

Valentine follows half a step behind me. As I take off my jacket, his eyes skim over the bruises on my jaw, the bandaged cuts on my hands.

"What did they do?"

I bite my lip. My whole existence narrows to the feeling of my front tooth digging into that soft, wet flesh, the sharp pain of it the only thing holding back my tears. How do I have any left at this point?

"Car accident," I tell him, hating the pathetic tremble of my voice. I keep my face turned away. As scared as I am, I know exactly what those words will mean to him.

"A car accident," he repeats, his voice flat.

"A hit-and-run." I pick at the bandage on my left hand. It's clean, no blood leaking through. Just a scratch.

That bloody, beet-colored bruise creeping across the right side of Olive's face like a stain.

Valentine is completely still.

"They were heading right for me," I tell him. "I-I swerved. I'm okay, but Olive..." I suck in a rattling breath. My hands are shaking again. "Olive hit a telephone pole. She's in critical condition, and I—" My voice gives out on me.

I look up at him, finally. Valentine's eyes are closed. One hand makes a fist, and it's shaking, too. Like mine.

"She wasn't supposed to be in the car with me." I can hear the plea for forgiveness in my voice, but I'm talking to the wrong person. "She shouldn't have gotten hurt. It was supposed to be me."

Whatever tether Valentine had on himself snaps as he screams and punches the wall. His fist comes away bloody. He breathes in sharp, harsh pants. He clenches his mangled hand, squeezing his eyes shut tight.

"Please look at me," I say.

He does. I shouldn't have asked. This is why he wears the mask. The pain, the terror—this is what he's been hiding.

I collapse on the couch with my face in my hands. As I stare into the blackness of my palms, it all becomes real. I'm more alone than I've ever been, and I'm nowhere near a resolution.

This is how I felt in the last days of Matt Caine. He was slipping through my fingers, and I knew it, but I couldn't stop. I wrecked everything. Lost Mom. All because I couldn't stop.

Have I learned anything?

"I think," I start, and it physically hurts to say the next words, hurts like I might double over, but I force myself to say them anyway. "I think it's over." I bite my lip again and taste blood. "I can't beat him. Dorsey. I keep thinking I've got him, that I'm one step ahead. Today, it was Olive. Tomorrow it'll be Cass, or you, or me. I-I'm scared of him. And he's not scared of me."

Valentine steps closer. "You're scared?"

"Yes." The trembling is spreading from my hands up my arms to my spine, until all of me is one quivering mess.

"You're scared of him, and you want to stop?" Valentine's breath is still sharp and fast.

"I think I have to." A few tears break free and tumble down my cheeks.

I knew we were in danger before. I knew the cost. I told myself I could be smart enough, quick enough, to bring him down, and everyone would be safer for it.

I was wrong.

"No," Valentine says. "We're not giving in. He's not getting away with this. Not again."

For a moment, the only sound in the room is our shared gasps for breath as we try to control our tears.

Valentine crosses the room and kneels in front of me. "Listen to me." He takes my hands. His grip is painful on my cuts, but I don't care. "Listen. That monster took away the one person I ever cared about in the world. He ruined my life. Today he tried to take you away, too, like it was nothing. Like it was easy. He's not going to stop. We can't run from this. I tried, and it didn't work. It's gonna hurt, it might cost us everything, but we have to take that bastard down."

I can't. I can't do this anymore. Not after the way Cass looked at me. After Olive in the hospital. After the way my grandfather's shoulders shook with his suppressed sobs.

"There's something else." I open my eyes but keep them trained on my lap. Not looking at him. Not looking at our entwined hands. "Something I should have told you."

"I don't care." He squeezes my hands harder. "Do you hear me? I don't care. We're in this together. We're not giving up."

I don't want to tell him, but I've learned that lesson, if nothing else.

"Someone's been watching us," I say. "I received photos.

411

Surveillance pictures. Of me and my family. Of you. I should have told you right away."

I brace myself for him to pull away, but he doesn't. Not yet.

"Well, this is your life, isn't it, Red?"

"What?"

Valentine squints at me. "This is your life, this sort of thing. Bad men chasing you. Getting hurt. This is what you chose for yourself. Things like this will never stop happening."

This is the moment. The moment yet another person realizes I'm not worth it. That I ruin everything I touch.

"It changes nothing," Valentine says heavily. "This means nothing to me."

I pull my hands from his. "What do you mean, nothing? Don't you get it? We're in danger, *you're* in danger, and I lied to you."

"Yeah, that was real stupid of you. So? I've fucked up enough times, it was your turn. You're a dangerous person to know, Flora Calhoun. And I threw in with you anyway." He looks me dead in the eye. "I never thought you were Nancy Drew. You're not some cartoon character, running around with a magnifying glass. I meant it when I told you before— you're the real thing."

Somehow, this is worse. This faith. Trust. I feel ready to fly apart at the seams again. I wrap my arms around myself to stop the loose bits of me shuttling off in all directions. I clamp my teeth down around the little half scream, half sob that threatens to rip out of my throat.

A week ago, I was sure. I was so sure. This time was going to be different. I was going to be better. And I fucked it up again, like before. Someone's going to get away with it. Like Lucy. Like Valentine's sister. No one will pay for Ava's death, and she'll be just another body who was once a living, loved girl.

This is the truth I've known for a long time. There are those with power, and with a flick of their wrists they can will us dead. The repercussions for them are nonexistent. The repercussions for the rest of us are life-and-death. And we all choose to look the other way, pretend this isn't happening, because the real truth is too terrifying: we are—*I* am—ultimately powerless.

"Hey," Valentine says. "Hey. Look at me. Flora, look at me."

I open my eyes. He's still kneeling before me. I meet his gaze full on. His pure, wild fear matches my own.

The tears start again.

"Hey, hey. No. None of that." He grabs me by the arms. His grip isn't gentle. "We're not doing that now. We're not falling apart. You got me? We're not." His voice is low but insistent. "Listen to me, you crazy girl. You pulled me into this. Into the heart of darkness with you. I'm fucking terrified, but I'm seeing it through. Yeah, there are people who want us dead. But we are *not* falling apart. Do you get me? Be scared. Be terrified with me. But you're not going to run. Not going to hide. We're fighters, you and me. Scrappers. We don't lose, not like this."

Valentine looks at me *that way* again. The way I usually shy away from. Too close. Too much. Only now, with everyone else gone, I don't want to push him away.

"I know how you're feeling right now," he says. "I'm not going to tell you it's not your fault. Won't tell you it'll be okay. But I am right here. Right next to you. Ready for the fight. I see you, Flora, and I'm not running from you. You with me?"

"I don't know," I tell him honestly.

He nods. "Yeah. That's okay for now. You will be." He stands. "Go get in the shower."

I stare at him.

He tugs my arm until I get to my feet. "Shower, take a minute to yourself. Turn the water up hot, have a nice cry, get it together. Then we'll come up with a plan."

I can feel it, as though from far away, the familiar impulse to snap back with some punchy retort. Banter. Roll my eyes.

Instead I ask, "Where are your towels?"

I take the longest, hottest shower I can bear. I don't cry. I feel shriveled, dehydrated. The tears have finally run out. As the water warms my skin, that candle flicker of rage comes back to life in my belly, and it's a relief.

I'm ready to hurt, to maim, to kill.

I emerge from the bathroom in a cloud of steam. In the kitchen, Valentine looks up from the pot he's stirring, and his eyes sweep over every inch of me. He swallows. He doesn't resume stirring. I look down and finger the edge of the threadbare over-size shirt he lent me. It smells like him. Soapy and boyish.

"What are you making?" I peer into the pot on the stove, even though I can still feel him looking at me. It's mac and cheese, the fluorescent-orange kind.

"Is this what you usually eat for dinner?" I laugh.

"No"—he looks defensive—"but you need some comfort right now, yeah? Nothing more comforting than Kraft."

"True." Still, it makes me think of something my grandfather said. *You've never grown up at all.*

He continues stirring. I trace the edge of one of his kitchen tiles with my bare toe.

"Shit." Valentine hisses in pain.

I look up. He's sucking on one of his knuckles. The skin is still peeling and bloody from when he punched the wall.

"Stop. Your mouth is a cesspool of bacteria." I take his hand and inspect it.

"It's a scrape."

415

"Please, you're totally mangled." I brush my finger over one knuckle. His skin jumps and tenses beneath my touch. I look up, and he's smiling at me in a goofy, dreamy sort of way.

Here, in his kitchen, over Kraft mac and cheese, all masks are finally stripped away.

For good, I hope.

I hold out my hand for the spoon. "Gimme. I'll stir, you shower. Clean yourself up."

He hesitates. "You sure? You don't mind being alone for a minute?"

"Take care of yourself, then we'll eat."

I man the stove while Valentine showers. It's soothing, in a way, stirring the radioactive orange goop.

My phone buzzes, and my heart does double Dutch when I see Cass's name on the screen.

Heard about Olive. So sorry, I hope you're ok. Found something. Can we meet?

I fumble a little typing my reply but finally get out:

Yes of course. I want to apologize face-to-face. I'll meet you anywhere

Her reply comes back fast:

Where are you? I'll come to you. I think I have proof about Dorsey, and I want to apologize too

I text her the address, and she says she'll be here in a couple minutes. I close my eyes for a moment. Everything is broken right now, but the idea of fixing things with Cass makes me feel like maybe we'll all survive this.

I turn off the stove and put a lid on the food. In Valentine's room, I pull my grimy jeans back on, my mind racing with what I should say to Cass. I owe her a real apology, and this time I'm not going to let myself get swept up in the case and avoid having yet another important conversation. She and I are going to talk this through until I've made her see how much I care about her. And *then* the three of us can check out whatever she found together, as a team. That's how we're going to bring Dorsey down.

The water is still running in the bathroom. I scribble a quick note that I'm just heading downstairs to talk to Cass, and I'll be back up soon.

Outside, I stand on the curb and watch for her car. The street is dark and quiet. What could Cass have found on Dorsey? Whatever it was, it sounded big. Maybe she found a way to prove that the EVAH money came from the Basement.

Someone grabs me from behind so fast I don't have time to scream before the cloth is over my mouth. A sharp, dry smell fills my every sense. Clogs my nose, my eyes, my pores. It's so powerful, I can't help but collapse back into the arms that are wrapped around my chest.

Darkness closes around me, and I realize belatedly that I have not passed out yet. It's simply very dark in the car trunk I've been stuffed into.

My blood is turning to mud, thick and slow in my veins. My eyes are heavy. I try to reach into my coat pocket, but it's as though the air around me has turned to viscous, cloying sap. My fingers are stiff and clumsy. My phone flops onto the floor of the trunk with a hollow thud. It takes all of my concentration and strength to push four buttons and shove the phone back in my pocket.

And then I lose consciousness for real.

CHAPTER 31

I wake to the sound of lapping water.

My brain is muffled in layers of cotton batting. With Herculean effort, I crack one eye open. The world has lurched horribly to one side. Everything is at a nauseating ninety-degree angle. Three sluggish heartbeats later, the picture orients itself. I'm lying in a fetal position on rough, damp cement.

I pry my other eye open. Try to swallow. Something pulls tight against the skin around my mouth. Duct tape.

A pair of brown high-heeled boots walks toward me. Each footstep booms like a battering ram inside my skull.

"She's awake."

That's up for debate.

I try to roll onto my back, but my limbs won't cooperate. I rock and convulse like an overturned beetle. Cold metal kisses the bare skin at my wrists, my waist, my legs. I'm chained.

"Roll her over," the voice attached to the boots says. A girl. A girl I know.

Hands grab me, jerking me into a kneeling position.

My vision shifts again, trying to right itself. Trying to find something stable to lock onto.

The girl comes into view. She looks so much like her father.

"Hi, Flora." Elle Dorsey smiles at me.

All the saliva gushes back into my mouth at once, and I retch against my duct tape gag. Elle takes a neat step back. A man in a suit stands at her side. I recognize him, too. Boyd. The manager of the Basement. In my foggy, half-drugged state, I finally realize where else I've seen him. That day I waited outside for Cass. Elle with the tennis ball. The fancy car, complete with driver.

My vision clears, almost too much, everything in oversharp focus. We're at the Whitley Reservoir. Shadowy pines surround us on all sides. The black water is still lapping away. Waiting.

I can't take in enough air with the duct tape over my mouth, and a panicked roar swells in my ears. Copper coats my throat. My teeth are chattering so hard I must have bitten my tongue. I don't even feel it.

Elle cants her head to the side and evaluates me. Gone is her usual bratty mean-girl act, replaced with something far colder and more calculating.

She glances at Boyd. "Do it."

No hesitation. No buildup. This is it. I'm going to die.

Boyd is already reaching for me. I scream and scream, but against my gag it sounds like nothing more than a muffled whimper. I thrash uselessly. My chains rattle and clank against one other, echoing through the watery quiet.

The vibrating buzz of a phone makes everything pause.

Boyd checks his screen. "It's the bookie."

Elle sighs. "Take it. This can wait." Boyd doesn't move, and her tone goes icy. "I said *go,* and tell him one of the guys working his table has been taking side bets. I want the person found and dealt with tonight."

Boyd walks off into the trees to take the call. Elle turns her attention back to me.

My heart is still pounding, smashing against the front of my chest like it's trying to escape and save itself. Boyd will return any minute, and then they'll kill me.

Elle's still watching me. She doesn't smile, but there's something like pleasure in her expression, like she's enjoying seeing me on my knees.

She takes a step closer and crouches before me in one smooth motion. She grips my chin in her hand. I try to jerk away, but her manicured nails are like the iron jaws of a fox trap. She rips the duct tape from my mouth. The cold air stings my raw skin. The second my mouth breaks free, I let out an unearthly wailing shriek of pure, unadulterated terror.

It echoes across the water. The sound is hollow, empty. It ends. The world is silent. The woods watch and say nothing.

"Feel free to continue"—Elle stands and smooths her dress—"but you only have a few more minutes to live, so freaking out seems like kind of a waste of time."

I fight to catch my breath. She's right. The scream felt good. I needed it. But no one's coming.

"I'm curious," Elle muses, like we're having a chat over coffee, "did you consider even once that it was me?"

"No," I answer. "I didn't think you were smart enough."

Her lips thin with irritation, but she turns it into another beauty contestant smile. "Wow, you are a really bad detective."

I gulp more air. "So the fight club was your idea. You ran the whole thing, and you got Ava to recruit other kids because people trusted her."

Behind my back, I finger the edge of the chains, testing for give.

As a kid, I did love magic. Houdini. Miracle escapes.

Elle purses her sweetheart pink mouth. "I know what you're doing."

I try not to rattle the chains as I feel along their length.

"Molly Sawyer got hurt, and Ava panicked. She wanted to put a stop to the whole thing, so you killed her to shut her up."

There's one lock pressed into my lower back. Another at my wrist.

Elle raises her eyebrows. "What a fascinating theory. Why don't you go talk to the police? Oh, wait." She casts a theatrical glance at the water.

I ignore her. "Was all of this just a ploy to get back at Daddy?" I manage to dip one finger into my back pocket. There's a bobby pin in there. There's always a bobby pin in my back pocket.

A muscle twitches by Elle's eye. "No." She brushes a stray hair out of her lip gloss.

I see through it, though. A flash of that tender, exposed part of her.

"Must be hard"—I can feel the metal edge of the pin—"living with a dad like that, who only sees you as a means to an end."

"Enough." She rolls her eyes, but her jaw is tight.

"I have no use for you," I say. "I paraphrased a bit, but that's what he meant, right? After the memorial?" I try to hook my finger around the pin, but it slips.

Elle bends her face closer to mine. "Do you really think you're going to trick me into a confession? This isn't

Scooby-Doo. You are dying here tonight, Flora. You can give up on whatever scheme you're plotting."

"Do it, then." My mouth is dry around the words. "I'm totally helpless. Why wait for Boyd? Throw me in the water yourself, Elle."

"Well, if you want to speed things along..." Elle straightens and laughs, a tinkling dinner-party kind of sound.

In a way, Elle and I aren't so different. The more scared she is, the more *Elle* she becomes, like a character.

I try again for the pin, my finger bent awkwardly. "It's harder, isn't it? The second kill. Now that you know what it's like."

Elle flinches. "That's enough." She regains her composure quickly, but I saw it.

"You know, it occurs to me"—my tone is casual, but my heart pounds in my throat—"you must have really trusted Ava to let her be your business partner."

Elle watches me with wary-animal eyes.

"You were telling the truth, weren't you?" I say softly. "She was your friend."

She inhales but doesn't release it.

"Do you know what Ava looked like when she died?" I struggle to keep my voice steady. Even saying those words is nearly enough to make me lose it, but if anyone needs to hear this, it's Elle. Ava's killer.

She doesn't say anything. She's perfectly still. But I know she's listening.

"At first I thought she was already dead. She was so pale, and she wasn't moving. But then I saw her eyes...she was afraid."

Elle shivers. Her jaw clenches.

"I tried to call 911, but I already knew it was too late." My breath hitches. "I held her in my arms. I tried so hard to save her, but I knew it wouldn't be enough."

All of the images I've held at bay since that night come flooding back, and this time I don't fight it. I let them drag me under.

"I had my fingers inside her chest. Inside that bullet wound you put in her heart. Trying to stop the life from gushing out of her. Her blood was everywhere, all over me. I felt her pulse getting weaker." The tears flow free down my cheeks, cold in the night air. I don't try to stop them.

Distantly, I'm still aware of the reservoir. The wind lifting Elle's hair. The soft lapping of the water. The scent of pine trees. I can still feel the edge of the pin in my pocket, and I know I should keep trying to fish it out, to escape.

But I'm not really here. I'm crying for help in a dirty alleyway. Ava's chest is warm under my hands, even as the blood drains out of her. Goose bumps rise on my arms. I'm wearing nothing but a T-shirt—my sweatshirt is tied around Ava, trying to stop her bleeding. I can hear the sirens in the distance as I beg Ava to hold on a little longer.

"You should have seen her eyes," I whisper. "She knew she was dying, and she was so scared. And then nothing. She was gone."

It breaks my heart all over again. The Ava I knew was so strong, so brave, so powerful, and even when she was dying afraid in my arms, she was still that girl. Until her heart stopped beating, and her neurons stopped firing, and she was gone.

I open my mouth, but there's nothing more to say, so I scream instead. Not like before, not a cry for help. Agony.

All the pain that has brewed black and noxious inside me pours out as the scream goes on and on. The pain of Ava, gone forever, and Lucy, lost, forgotten, never avenged. Mom leaving. My grandfather on his knees. Cass walking out. Olive nearly dead in the hospital. The force of it threatens to rip me apart, and every bruise, every wound on my body—the airbag blow to my cheek, that man's fingerprints on my arm, the gash under my eye—screams along with me.

Ava is gone. It hurts, and it hurts, and it hurts.

I am so small, hunched here by the water, but my scream fills the whole sky. The pain changes. Still brutal, agonizing, but what was twisted and dark and rotten is now sharp and clear. Like starlight.

My breath gives out, and again I hear the echo of my scream ripple across the water before everything is still once more.

I come back into my body. It aches. My throat is raw.

Elle's eyes are closed. Silent tears track down her face. She trembles. Trying to hold it all in.

My voice is hoarse. "You killed her. Ava was your friend, and you left her on the ground in the cold to die by herself."

She shakes harder. Clenches her fists.

"You had no use for her anymore, right, Elle? Just like your father."

"Stop!" she cries out. Her eyes fly open, and even though I'm chained at her feet, she's the one who looks afraid.

Elle sniffs and tries to get herself back under control, but the tears keep coming. She crosses her arms, hugging her chest tight, but the shaking won't stop. No matter how hard she fights it. I know.

"I didn't want to hurt her," she whispers.

My lungs fill with air.

"I just wanted to talk to her." Elle's voice rises. "I only brought the gun to scare her, but she wouldn't listen! I built the Basement from nothing. It's the one thing in the world that's *mine*, and she was going to ruin everything!" Elle looks at me, and I have never seen her so wrecked. Eyes red and wild, makeup a smudgy mess, her breathing harsh. She says, "I shot her. I shot Ava."

Those words nearly crack me open again. I already knew, but hearing Elle admit it sends grief slicing through me.

"And what was the point?" Tears continue to stream down Elle's face even as she tries to defend herself. "Molly woke up. Was it really worth getting so upset about? Ava made this huge fuss, and it got her killed, but for what? Molly's fine, like I said she would be."

Rage burns the last of my tears away. That she could justify killing Ava this way. Claim that *Ava* was the one who overreacted. My anger focuses me. I hook my finger around the pin again.

Elle hugs herself tighter and looks at the ground. "I was going to call 911. I wanted to. But it was bad, right? I mean, she died anyway, and there was nothing I could have done. You said it yourself. It was too late, and I-I had too much to lose." She draws a deep breath, pulling herself back together. Letting herself believe it's not really her fault. "It would have been easier if it were a mugging. We could all move on with our lives." She sniffs again and wipes at her cheeks, but she only smears the mascara more.

"But *I* couldn't move on." My voice crackles with fury. I finally manage to slip the pin out of my pocket. My finger shakes with the strain of not dropping it. "I wouldn't let it go. So you set your dad up to take the fall. You planted all of those documents and then passed them along to me."

Elle shrugs. "That was always my last-resort plan. My father knows what he wants to know. To him"—she gestures behind her—"Boyd is my driver, and I could never be capable enough to run something as complex as the Basement. It's easier for him to believe that."

There it is: that flash of hurt again. You can tell yourself your parents are crap. You can hate them. But it still hurts.

"Come to the police with me." My wrist feels like it's about to break, I have it bent back so far to reach the first lock. I stab uselessly with the pin, searching for the hole. "Tell them all of this. It'll ruin him."

"What?" She takes a step back from me and stands up straighter. "No. I'm ending this tonight."

"It's too late for that," I insist. "You can kill me, but the truth is going to come out." The pin slips into the lock. "You know politics. You know how this works. If you try to hide it, when the real story comes out, that you killed Ava and tried to set your own father up for it, everyone will think you're a sociopath. They'll feel bad for him." I wiggle the pin, trying to get it to catch. "You want to say a real *fuck you* to your dad? Be the one to come forward. You murdered Ava. You're going to pay for it no matter what, but you can at least tell your story first, before he puts his spin on it."

She looks at me for a long time. Standing there at the edge of the water, with the moon shining in her sad eyes, she looks my age for the first time tonight.

But I don't feel bad for Elle. She killed Ava, not to mention all the other lives she's hurt with the Basement.

She opens her mouth to say something. A twig snaps, and she whirls around.

Boyd has returned. "Your father called while I was on the phone. He wants you home soon. Let's get this over with."

Elle looks back at me. She hesitates.

"I see." Boyd looks at me, too. The feeling of his eyes on me makes my heart start to pound again.

My wrist burns as I scramble with the lock.

Boyd says, "This has gone on long enough. We end this *now*. I'm not taking the fall for you."

Elle looks at Boyd like she's seeing him for the first time. "You don't make these kinds of decisions."

The first lock pops free, and I swallow my cry of relief. There are more locks to go, plus Elle and Boyd to contend with once I'm loose. I'm smaller and faster than them. I can do it.

Boyd shakes his head. "Typical. You know, until now I had almost forgotten you were a teenage girl."

Elle rears back. "What's that supposed to mean?"

"It means I'm not letting your ridiculous emotions get in the way of what has to be done." He strides toward me.

Elle cries out in protest.

I drop my bobby pin on the cement.

I scream again.

Boyd doesn't pause. He hoists me up by the arms. Like I'm nothing. Like I'm weightless.

For one interminable moment, I am airborne. I can only watch and scream as the still, glassy surface rises to meet me.

I crash into the water.

I didn't have the foresight to stop screaming, to shut my mouth up tight. It fills with dark, brackish water. I cough and choke, but there is nothing but water. Always more water, ready to fill me.

Cold, so cold. Like a weight. Dragging at me.

I kick and thrash, a bone-shattering desperation flickering and spasming in me, but there is nowhere to go. Nothing but water.

Dark, so dark. I was never afraid of the dark. But this is black, flat, endless.

Lost, dizzy, so deep. In the void. No up, no down. Nothing but water. Always more water.

It seeps into me, not just my mouth and nose but my ears,

my eyes, my very pores, and I grow heavier and heavier still, until I cannot fight any longer, and I am left a broken body spinning gently in the current.

Something drags at me. I give a weak jerk, but I am too water-logged to fight.

My face is cold right down to the skull. There are sounds, echoing in the deep, but they, like everything else, are formless.

I drift.

Pain. So much pain.

Guess I'm not dead.

My bones shatter. An unbearable thudding pressure on my chest. I scream, but all that comes out is torrents upon torrents of water. An entire reservoir's worth, coughed up onto concrete. I gag and choke, but there is nothing but more water spewing and spewing out of me.

"Flora? Flora, can you hear me?"

A deep, throbbing hum aches in my bones. It's me. I'm shaking so hard I'm hurting myself. I try to stop, but I can only tremble and jerk more spastically.

"Get the blanket. Bring it to me!" someone shouts, their voice knifed through with panic.

432

Hands, brushing lank hair from my face. They're gentle, but the touch feels like sandpaper against my raw, waterlogged skin.

"Flora, I have you. I have you. I found you."

I am lifted, something wrapped tight around me. I think I am warmer. The shaking doesn't stop.

"I found you, I'm here," someone is repeating over and over, like they're trying to convince themselves. I slip away again.

I come to in the back seat of a car.

My grandfather's car.

I'm still shaking, but not so violently. Someone's undressed me, and I'm wrapped in a space blanket.

I feel physically blue.

"She's awake." Cass twists around in the front seat. She watches me without blinking.

I blink enough for the two of us.

"Flora? Are you with us?" A deep voice. My grandfather's. He's driving. He's also soaking wet. Somehow, he still manages to look pulled together. His hair is slicked back from his forehead.

I open my mouth. All that comes out is a hoarse death-rattle wheeze. I seem to be out of water to spew, though, so that's a plus.

My grandfather looks at me in the rearview mirror. I nod. *I'm with you.*

I look at Cass and try to convey all of the many questions I have with the shape of my eyebrows.

She bites her lip. "I put a tracker in your phone the other day, before you went to the Basement with Valentine. I meant to tell you, but I forgot about it with everything else."

The words don't make any sense.

"Wh-hhh..." I cough, and when my voice finally comes out it sounds like it's buried in mountains of sand. "What about your text?"

Cass looks at me blankly. "What text?"

My brain still feels waterlogged. "You found something?" She still doesn't react. "You were coming to meet me."

"I never texted you." Her eyes still hold all the hurt from earlier. "I didn't want to talk to you."

I know I didn't imagine that message. Elle must have figured out how to spoof Cass's number, to lure me out. I'll have to ask Olive about it. My aching throat tightens at the thought of her.

Cass hesitates. "I did find something, though. Dorsey's not the killer. It's Elle."

I can only stare.

"After we fought, I couldn't just go back to school," she

explains. "I figured if Ava were really trying to bring the Basement down, she would have been collecting evidence." Cass pulls something up on her phone and hands it to me.

It's a picture of Elle. She's at the Basement, standing in the shadows near the back exit like she's watching a fight. The picture is grainy and dark, but I can tell she's smiling.

I swipe through. There's a few more. In one, Elle sits at an old steel desk, counting money. I can tell from the cement walls it's in the same tunnels under the hospital, maybe a small utility room she converted to an office.

"How did you get these?" I swipe through them again.

Cass clearly finds my surprise irritating. "I talked to Ava's parents. Told them what we'd found, and what we thought Ava was doing. They helped me figure out her cloud log-in. Amazing what you can do when you're just honest and straightforward with people, right?"

I'm so in awe of her, the jab doesn't even hurt. "So how did you know to come save me?"

Cass gives me an exasperated look. "I'm pissed as hell at you, but I still worry. I wanted to check up on you before I brought the photos to the police. When I saw you were at the reservoir, that didn't seem right."

I start to cry for the billionth time tonight. Cass never bails on me. I should know that by now.

"Stop it," she snaps. "I'm still angry. Don't give me the grateful puppy face and think that's going to make it okay."

I inhale and nod. I deserve that.

The metronome click of the turn signal.

I look out the window and frown again. "Where are you going?"

My grandfather's eyes go steely. He uses a long beat of silence to tell me exactly how stupid he thinks I am.

"The hospital," he says.

I sit up in my seat.

"No." I wheeze like one of those dragon-nail ladies in the antismoking commercials.

"Flora, don't be an imbecile. It's tiresome." He tries to sound disdainful, but his knuckles have gone white on the steering wheel.

"No," I say, and my heartbeat, so timid and exhausted a moment ago, ratchets up again. "Please! We have her. We have her! You can't do this!" I scrabble at the door like I mean to jump out, which I recognize is earth-shatteringly dumb, but I know that if I go to the hospital Elle will get away. Another one is going to get away.

My grandfather presses the child lock. "Are you quite finished?"

I wrap the blanket tighter around my middle. I close my eyes. I take four deep breaths.

436

I stare my grandfather down in the mirror. "Eight hours."

"Come again?"

"I need eight hours," I tell him. "Bring me to the police. Let me close out this case. Then I'll go to the hospital without a fight."

He purses his lips. His eyes flicker back and forth between me and the road.

"They threw me in the water. They threw me in and left me to die. Please."

In the mirror, my grandfather nods once. "Six. Six hours. No more. Then the hospital."

I settle back against the seat. I can close my eyes for a second before we get to the precinct.

A moment later, I bolt up again, electrocuted by panic.

"What? What is it now?" Cass asks.

My phone. When I went into the water, my phone went with me. Cass's phone still in hand, I race to log in to my own cloud account.

My heart climbs the walls of my esophagus as I wait.

The site loads. I take a shuddering breath and hit Play on the new recording saved in my folder.

The sound of a car trunk opening. The metal clank of chains. Muffled voices grow sharper.

Elle speaks, "Tape her mouth, too."

That's the thing movies always get wrong about chloroform.

It takes a few minutes to knock you all the way out. In the trunk of Elle's car, the last thing I did before I blacked out was hit Record on my phone. The app is supposed to automatically upload to the cloud, but did it have time to sync the whole thing before I went under?

I skip forward in the recording.

Elle again. "It was too late, and I-I had too much to lose. It would have been easier if it were a mugging. We could all move on with our lives." I push the Pause button and breathe.

The car is silent for a few seconds before Cass starts yelling, "You absolute dumbass! The next time you put yourself in danger like that to get a confession, I swear to God, Flora, I will kill you myself."

"I'll help," Gramps adds.

I drop Cass's phone on the seat next to me and collapse against the window.

The photos. The recording. On their own, neither one would be enough. Too many ways Elle could lie, make excuses, take back what she said.

But together, we got her.

CHAPTER 32

"You recorded this?" Richmond leans back in her chair. "While Elle Dorsey, the congressman's daughter, had you chained up at the reservoir?"

The three of us are sitting in Richmond's office. For once, I was happy to let Gramps do all my explaining. Without him, I don't think Richmond would have been much inclined to talk, especially considering that I'm wearing a tinfoil blanket, my wet underwear, and nothing else. I wouldn't let him bring me home first. No time. I pull the blanket tighter around me.

I've played the recording for Richmond. Twice. She's seen the photos. Now she watches me from across her desk. Her expression is unreadable.

"Yes." I'm still getting my voice back, but I sound stronger by the second. "I have a witness who can corroborate details about the fight club, as well as Elle's motive to keep Molly Sawyer's injury quiet."

Richmond nods. "I see. Wait here."

"Do you think Elle will try to walk back her confession?" Cass asks after a minute or two of quiet.

I had her. I saw the look on her face as I talked about Ava's final moments. I'd like to think Elle had a change of heart.

But it seems unlikely.

"Probably," I say. "I don't know if Elle has it in her to actually face what she did."

My grandfather straightens his tie. He reknotted it while we waited for Richmond to see us. "I've known girls like Elle Dorsey. She'll toe the party line. Her father will make sure of it."

He's right. We'll deal with that later.

My wooden chair in Richmond's office is making my butt go numb. I'm still so cold.

I lean over and rest my head on Cass's shoulder. She tenses but then leans her head back into mine. My near-death experience has given me a pass for the moment, but I know things are still a mess between us.

Richmond returns. "All right. We have an APB out for Elle Dorsey, and a warrant for her arrest. My sergeant wasn't happy, but with everything you've got here...I have to hand it to you, Calhoun. You have a knack for pissing off powerful men."

She doesn't mean it as a compliment, but I'll take it.

"Thanks." I glance at Cass. "It's a team sport."

Richmond rolls her eyes. "You better have those witnesses you mentioned. This is going to be a tough fight in court." She looks at me. Really takes in the shriveled, wet-rat look I'm rocking, not to mention all the bruises from the crash. "Go home. I'll have more questions for you, but you look like you could use some dry clothes and a week's worth of sleep. We'll be in touch."

Gramps, Cass, and I stand to leave.

As I'm about to walk out the door, Richmond adds, "Try to stay out of trouble, at least for the next twenty-four hours."

"I'll see what I can do," I wheeze.

In the car, I stare out the window. Cass and I sit together in the back seat. I reach for her hand and lace my fingers tight with hers.

"Thank you for saving me."

She doesn't look at me. "You and me, Flora? We're not okay. And I don't know if we ever really will be."

It hurts, but I understand. "I know, but I'm not giving up on you."

She turns back to the front but tightens her grip on my hand.

"Elle's going to have some very expensive lawyers," she says after a bit. "Richmond's right, this fight has just begun."

She's right. Finding Ava's killer was only the first step. The world is built to protect some people and not others. Girls like Ava, like Molly, are left forgotten on the street, and no one ever expects someone like Elle to face any consequences.

I used to think justice meant answers. You figure out the puzzle, and the world is set to rights. But it wasn't that way with Lucy, and it won't be that way for Ava. It's going to be a long road of backbreaking work to make Elle pay.

As tired as I am, the thought doesn't fill me with dread.

I squeeze Cass's hand tighter. "I'm not afraid. We'll do it together."

At first I think she's going to give me some well-deserved skepticism. It's not the first time I've said something like that this week.

Instead, she shrugs. "Well, you only had to die to get it through your thick skull that you need me."

I squeeze close to her. She's warm, and I'm freezing under my blanket. "You're going to be insufferable about the fact that you saved my life, aren't you?"

"Yup."

At the hospital, Cass agrees to sit with Olive while Gramps escorts me through the dizzying chaos of the emergency room. I slip into a kind of lucid dream as nurses and doctors whirl around me. Gramps does all the talking. I mostly stare into space while they make sure I didn't sustain any lasting brain damage in the water.

Hours later, they let me go. We check on Olive before leaving. She's stable, her doctor tells us. She'll wake up soon.

The drive home is quiet for a long time.

Eventually, Gramps speaks. "It is unacceptable that you left the hospital earlier, after I'd asked you to stay."

I sigh. "I know."

He nods slowly. "It is also unacceptable that I was too overcome to properly support you."

It's true, but I can't hold it against him anymore. I've been giving him all these little tests, waiting for him to leave me. To be Mom. But every time he let me down, he only came back and tried harder. That might be the best us two emotionally stunted curmudgeons can manage, for now.

"Don't worry, Gramps," I say. "We'll find new ways to fuck up next time."

His mouth twitches. After a long pause, he adds, "I am proud of you, you know."

"I know." He's said it before, but I don't know if I ever really believed it until now.

"Yes. Well." He coughs. "I should tell you anyway. I'll endeavor to be more open with you. And with Olive."

"Me, too." The words are too small. I don't know how to

tell any of them that it's different this time. I came out of the water *different*.

I remember sitting on my bed a week ago with Olive. She's always been better at this.

I say, "Olive told me that we can't be so scared of each other, the three of us."

Gramps thinks that one over and nods. "She is the most intelligent member of the household. I've always thought so."

I smile. "Let's tell her that."

Back home, I stand in the hot blast of the shower until I start to nod off. I hunt down one of Olive's fuzzy robes to wear. It smells like her, and that makes me feel stronger.

As I towel off my hair, I open my laptop and turn on the news.

Congressman Dorsey is giving a press conference. "I am alarmed and appalled by the accusations against my daughter. As a parent, I love my child unconditionally. But as a citizen and a public servant, it is my duty to support the pursuit of justice no matter the personal cost. That is why I will not be withdrawing my candidacy for Senate, despite the acute pain and suffering my family is experiencing right now. I believe in the future of this state, and more than ever I want to fight for the kinds of policies that will keep girls like Ava McQueen safe—"

444

I slam the computer shut. I'm not surprised, but I am disgusted. How is it that he still manages to exploit both Ava and Elle, even now? I don't feel any pity for Elle, but her father really sucks. It's not hard to imagine where she learned to use people the way she does.

I drop the towel on my bed and find the house phone. I have an important call to make.

It rings and rings, then goes to a generic voicemail message. I chew the inside of my cheek while I wait for the tone.

"Valentine, it's me. Listen, I know you're probably mad. I'm sorry, okay? I shouldn't have left you like that. I didn't mean to, it was unplanned. I was—you know what? It's a long story. Not good for voicemail. Um. It meant a lot. What you did for me last night. And I thought you'd want to know that I'm okay. And I did it. I ended it. So, yeah, my phone is broken, that's part of the long story. Call me on this number. I'm going to the hospital to see Olive later, but I-I wanted you to know. We did it." I hang up before I can ramble any more.

I've been thinking all week that I need to have answers about him. That I need to have my feelings fully sorted, categorized, examined, before I let that go anywhere. We're both such disasters, and I don't think that's getting worked out overnight. But just like Cass, and Gramps, and Olive, he was there with me when it counted. We can start there.

Cass was right. It only took a near-death experience to gain some perspective.

I lie down on top of my comforter and close my eyes. I'll get under the covers in a second.

With my eyes shut, I hear a car pull up in front of the house. The engine turns off. A car door opens, then shuts. Another does the same.

I sit up and look out my window.

A cop car is parked in front of my house. I had kind of hoped I'd get to sleep for, like, a minute before I had to answer more questions.

I lie back on the bed. Maybe Gramps can field this one, and I'll just call Richmond later.

A moment passes. Doorbell. Front door opens. Voices. I roll over, snuggling deeper into my pillow, but my skin prickles with the need to know what's happening.

I trudge down the hall. Take my time on the stairs.

My grandfather stands in the hallway with two cops. Patrol officers. I recognize them but don't know their names right away.

Everyone looks at me, then looks uncomfortable.

There's a Pop Rock's fizzle of fear in my gut. Something terrible has happened.

Correction: something else terrible has happened.

"What is it?" An iron fist clenches around my lungs. Was it Olive? Cass, this time?

My grandfather uses his soft, calm voice. "Why don't we all go into the living room to discuss—"

"Tell me." I have not moved from the foot of the stairs. From here, I can still run.

The cops share a look.

The one by the window steps closer. "Miss Calhoun, we believe you are acquainted with a man named Valentine Yates?"

The fist twists.

I have enough air to whisper, "Yes."

The cops share another look. "What is the nature of your relationship?"

"We're...friends."

"Does he have any family that you know of?"

I shake my head. Terror seeps into my veins like ink in cold water. "His family is gone. He's alone."

The cop by the window nods a couple of times. "Miss Calhoun, I'm afraid there was a fire late last night at 13 South Water Street in Whitley, where Mr. Yates lived. We believe he was trapped inside."

"You believe?" someone asks. It's me. I'm the one who asks. I shake my head again, trying to clear the water from around my brain.

"We uncovered a body in his apartment, but it was too badly burned to identify definitively. We're waiting to hear back on dental records."

My mouth opens and closes, but nothing goes in or comes out. No air. No sounds.

"W-why me?" I finally manage. "Why are you telling me?"

The other cop finally speaks. "We found Mr. Yates's cell phone in his car and looked through the calls. It's something we do when there's no clear next of kin. The last call he made was to you. Actually, your number was just about the only one in there."

That's the detail that breaks me. I turn on my heel and run for the bathroom.

I hear something that might be "sorry for your loss" behind me, but who knows what's real anymore?

I barely make it to the toilet before my stomach empties itself. Mostly spit and bile. I dry heave and retch, desperate to expel something, anything, from inside me, but I can't even remember the last time I ate.

I stay that way for a long time. I might hear voices in the front hall. I might hear my grandfather asking if I'm okay through the door. I might hear him try the knob. Who knows?

A lifetime later, I stand. I wash my hands slowly, step by step. Water. Soap. Lather. Rinse. Repeat.

I wipe my mouth.

Finally, I lift my chin to meet my own gaze in the mirror. This girl is tired. Her skin is sallow. She is wearing her sister's fluffy pink robe, and her eyes are pure rage.

I look at the girl for a long time. Eventually, I see the other parts, too. The parts she's tried to hide under all that fury.

Pain. Fear. Loss.

There's no hiding anymore. Tears well up in my eyes, and I don't try to hold them back. They flow freely over my cheeks. I watch the grief overtake me, and I don't look away.

Another dead body. Another person I care about, gone. My family in pieces.

A wave of hurt rolls over me, and I grip the edge of the sink to keep from collapsing. I might break.

But here's the thing: this time I know that even broken, I can survive.

I think of Cass's words from earlier, in the car.

The fight has just begun.

Acknowledgements

In some ways, writing a book can be a pretty lonely experience. I worked on *You're Next* for nearly four years on my own—just me and Flora, hanging out in the early mornings on my couch. But the truth is, it was only once other people got involved that the magic started to happen.

I want to say a giant thank you first and foremost to the hardworking team at Jimmy Patterson. For the longest time, this book only existed in my head, and to find a whole team of people who immediately understood what *You're Next* and Flora were all about...well, that's nothing short of a miracle. Thank you to Linda Arends, Caitlyn Averett, Liam Donnelly, Tracy Shaw, Virginia Lawther, Dan Denning, Josh Johns, and Diana McElfresh. To Julie Guacci for being a rock star publicist and answering all of my over-anxious debut-author emails with nothing but kindness. Eternal gratitude to Jenny Bak for being the one to see everything this book could be, and to T.S. Ferguson for all of his support in seeing us through to the finish line. And of course, thank you to James Patterson, without whom none of this would be possible.

To my agents Kira Watson and Margaret Sutherland

Brown, as well as the entire team at Emma Sweeney. Kira was one of the first people to really believe in this book, and Margaret, you were one hell of a pinch hitter. Thank you so much to both of you for your support, compassion, and general bad-assery.

To Brenda Drake and the entire Pitch Wars team, most especially my incredible mentor Amy Trueblood: until the fall of 2017, this book had a different title, a different plot, and, largely, a different cast of characters. Amy, you pulled my manuscript out of a pile and saw through all the flaws and weird plot-holes. You didn't just love my story, because that story didn't even really exist yet—you loved Flora. Loved her the way I loved her and helped her to become the larger-than-life character I wanted her to be. Pitch Wars changed my life forever, and none of that would be possible without the gift of your hard work and time.

Not only did Pitch Wars make me the writer I am today, it introduced me to an entire community of beloved writing friends. Thank you to Aty S. Behsam, Layne Fargo, Shelby Mahurin, Lisa Leoni, and especially to Ciannon Smart, Kyrie McCauley, Erica Waters, Margie Fuston, Molly Kasparek, Sarah White, Julie Christensen, and Andrea Contos for reading earlier drafts and providing such invaluable feedback and enthusiasm for Flora and her story.

Shortly after I moved to Portland, I took a writing class hoping to make friends in my new city. I could not have imagined how lucky I would get. Thank you to the Writing Crones—Elena Wiesenthal, Susie Frank, Lori Ubell, Mary Rose, and Dolores Maggiore. You have read every draft, every revision, every complete and total overhaul of the plot. But more than that, thank you for being the dear friends I was looking for. A special shout out to Emily Whitman for bringing us all together. And thank you to all the other critique partners, early readers, and writing friends who have cheered me on along the way—Suzanne Robbins Goddyn, LeeAnn Elwood McLennan, Michelle Janikian, Rachel Kass, Izzy Hardin, Hazel Frew, and Kimberly Keeping.

Saying thank you to my parents seems wildly inadequate, so I'll go with this instead: I love you both. Mom, thank you for teaching me not just how to read, but how to love reading. You told me I was a writer before I ever knew it myself. Dad, thank you for not just reading an early (terrible) draft of this book, but for calling to provide insightful commentary about dialogue and plot twists. Everything I know about being a working artist, collaborating with others, and how to tell when a story isn't perfect, but it is done—I learned all of that from you. No one is as lucky as I am to have parents like you two, and I won't hear otherwise. Also thank you, I guess, to my siblings—Sarah, Janey, and Louis—my creativity was forged in the fires of your mockery, bullying, and withering sarcasm (I love you all).

To Maggie and Lorenza, the two sides of my Libra scales. So much of the beauty, kindness, and magic I try to put into the world is inspired by you. The stars had something right when they brought us into the world in perfect, near-symmetrical order. I am so glad I found you.

Last, and always, to Xander. Thank you for making dinner because I'm too busy writing, helping me brainstorm solutions to impossible plot-holes, and telling me you're proud of me when I'm sobbing hysterically because I think I broke my book... again. You believe that my dreams are important, that my story deserves to exist, and that means everything to me. Thank you for being the most supportive partner in the world, and for not complaining (much) that time in late 2014 when I woke you up at 6 a.m. to read you seventy pages of a brand-new story I'd just started about a snarky girl detective.

About the Author

KYLIE SCHACHTE lived in nine different cities—from Moscow to Los Angeles—before making her home in Portland, Oregon. She studied creative writing and psychology at Sarah Lawrence College, and *You're Next* was a Pitch Wars 2017 selection. When she's not writing, Kylie can be found attending concerts, exploring the Pacific Northwest, and refereeing between her tiny cat and giant dog—the cat always wins.